UNBEARABLE PLEASURE

Jason pulled Gabrielle across his chest, savoring the cool smoothness of her skin against his own far more warm flesh. Her long, shimmering red hair fell about his shoulders as she covered his face with light kisses.

At perfect peace, Gabrielle reclined languidly in Jason's arms, enjoying the heat of his body as greatly as that of the sun. The bond of trust seemed to deepen each time they were together, and certain he would answer her question seriously, she inquired softly, "Jason, is love always like this?"

Jason's smile filled with amusement as he responded. "You mean the feeling of pleasure so intense that you neither laugh nor weep but only crave more no matter if the cost be your very soul?"

Gabrielle slid her fingertips across his chest and he caught them in his hand, drawing her palm to his lips. "Yes, that is precisely how I feel when I am with you. Is it the same for you when you are with other women?"

He considered his answer for only a brief instant before responding. "I have known other women, Gabrielle, been with them, that's true; but never, never was it as complete as it is with you. It was never making love before."

He leaned down to kiss her then and Gabrielle knew that no other man would ever give her the pleasure she found in Jason's embrace. . . .

SAVAGE STORM
PHOEBE CONN

ZEBRA BOOKS
KENSINGTON PUBLISHING CORP.

ZEBRA BOOKS

are published by

Kensington Publishing Corp.
475 Park Avenue South
New York, NY 10016

First printing: November 1985

Printed in the United States of America

Chapter I

   While in his younger days many of the early residents of the
Oregon frontier had regarded Jason Royal as a hellion who'd
meet an early and violent death, he had scoffed at their dire
predictions and had lived to prove them wrong. He'd not deny
that he'd killed a man or two, but in honest fights over
questions of honor, never wantonly or as a hired gun to satisfy
another man's thirst for vengeance. Now at twenty-eight, he
was a respected citizen of the Willamette Valley, an
accomplished scout who'd become a wagon master of
considerable skill, responsible for the lives of dozens of others
as well as his own. Tall and well built with glossy black curls
and gray eyes which were more often than not filled with
amusement, his height and obvious strength made most men
hesitate to cross him, and those few fools who did soon
regretted it. A natural leader, he had a calm, easy manner
which inspired confidence, but his patience had its limit.

   "Let's call it a day, Clayton. I've lost count of how many
young women we've interviewed, but each seemed less
attractive and considerably less intelligent than the previous
one."

   Clayton Horne chuckled to himself as he straightened up the
desk, collecting the applications and placing them in neat
stacks. "Don't be so critical, Jason, you know the men who are

5

paying for their passage to Oregon City are just average in appearance and intelligence. They want wives so badly, I'm certain the young women I've selected will seem like great beauties to them regardless of your opinion. The men will be grateful, and you saw for yourself how eager the women are to go. We're providing a service which is desperately needed, and I'd say appreciated by both the men and women involved."

Jason shook his head, unconvinced still. "How I ever let you talk me into allowing you to escort twenty prospective brides along the Oregon Trail I'll never know, but since you've selected the women you need, let's not stay cooped up in this hotel room. Let's go on down to the bar." Glancing in the mirror above the dresser, Jason stopped to straighten his tie. He felt uncomfortable in the new gray suit Clayton had insisted he wear, but he had to admit a more formal appearance had the desired effect upon the ladies he'd met in Kansas City—and he was not thinking of those who'd agreed to marry men waiting for them at the end of the Oregon Trail. His reflection took on a rakish grin as he thought how little trouble he had impressing women even dressed in his most worn buckskins. Clayton envied his luck with romance, calling it a talent, but whether or not he'd been born with it, didn't concern Jason as long as it continued to bring him the beautiful women he wanted—when he wanted them.

"Well, what do you say?" he asked.

Clayton pulled the gold watch from his vest pocket and flipped open the engraved cover to observe the time. "No. You go on downstairs but I'll wait, if only to tell any others who might come that the interviews are over."

He exhaled slowly, as tired as Jason by the carefully planned routine they'd followed all day. He was a tactful man, and although he'd sent away most of the young women who'd come to apply, none had left in tears. He wanted to be certain none did.

"Oh, what the hell."

Jason sank down into the overstuffed chair near the

windows and slung his right leg over the arm to get more comfortable as he again loosened his tie. He resigned himself to waiting the full time they'd stated in the advertisement they'd placed in every major newspaper in Missouri. Knowing how desperately men in the Oregon country wanted wives, Clayton had seen arranging for the transportation of suitable females as his civic duty and as a fine opportunity to make a considerable profit as well. As the United States had grown, men had frequently been forced to advertise in newspapers in major cities to attract women to new settlements on the frontier. This enterprise was merely a group effort, rather than an individual one. Jason had laughed when the older man had first suggested that they transport a small number of mail-order brides, adding that if the scheme worked as well as he thought it would, each wagon train Jason led would bring more women until every man willing to pay their price had found himself a wife. From the outset Jason had thought the scheme ill-advised because following the Oregon Trail was a long and arduous journey, and certainly not one he'd recommend to young women, but the eagerness with which Clayton's plan had been received by the bachelors they'd approached had finally convinced him to give it at least a fair trial. "Poor bastards." He had muttered softly to himself, for he could not imagine loneliness being so profound as to inspire either a man or woman to marry a stranger.

A hesitant knock at the door startled both men from their thoughts. Clayton, being the one seated nearest the door, rose to answer the summons. As he had expected, another young woman stood before him. Having already decided not to question any more candidates, he began his speech as soon as he opened the door.

"Good afternoon, my dear. I am Clayton Horne and I want to thank you for coming for the interview. However, all twenty places have already been filled. Perhaps you'd care to apply again next spring."

Despite Jason's pessimism, Clayton was certain they would

soon be deluged with requests for brides and this trip would be the first of countless others.

"I have your advertisement in my hand, sir, and it clearly states interviews will be conducted from ten until six today. It is not yet six."

Jason looked up, intrigued by the young woman's slightly husky voice as well as by her insistent manner. Clayton's stocky form blocked his view so he could see nothing but the top of her bonnet and the hem of her skirt, both of which were black, a black as deep as midnight on the plains. Admiring her spunk, he was too curious not to enter the conversation and spoke as he rose to his feet, remembering to adjust his tie as he went to the door.

"Your watch must be incorrectly set, Clayton. By mine it is only five-forty-five and we've plenty of time to speak with Miss? . . ."

"Miss MacLaren, Gabrielle MacLaren," the young woman responded with a bright smile, relieved she'd not been turned away after all.

Jason tried not to stare, but although he knew his glance was far too intense, he could not seem to manage a more discreet gaze. Gabrielle MacLaren was simply the most beautiful young woman he'd ever seen. She was quite tall, yet slender of build, her superb figure scarcely disguised by the confining lines of the somber black suit she wore. She was very fair, with translucent skin so flawless it could only be compared to fine porcelain. Her long hair, which she'd worn loose beneath her velvet bonnet, reached clear past her waist. It was a lustrous, deep red—*auburn* was the word that suddenly came to his mind—but rather than having brown eyes as he would have expected, her long thick eyelashes framed eyes of a bright clear blue—the same vivid sapphire hue that inspired poets to write lyric verse and composers to burst into song. Her delicate features were exquisite. Her pink-tinged lips had a gentle Cupid's-bow shape, her nose had only the slightest upturn, and her chin had a soft point giving her face the shape of a heart.

Her features, therefore, provided the perfect complement to her incredible eyes, and he could not seem to find his voice to speak his own name so entranced was he by her beauty.

Amused by his young partner's captivated stare, Clayton ushered their visitor inside. "May I present my associate, Jason Royal. While I am charged with the responsibility of selecting the young women to become our clients' brides, he will be in command of the journey over the Oregon Trail."

Gabrielle extended her small gloved hand but the tall, dark-haired man was staring so boldly that she was really terribly embarrassed. He was very tan, handsome, and appeared quite fit as if he enjoyed the rigors of the outdoor life, but it was the rapt expression that made her blush.

"How do you do, Mr. Royal." In the late afternoon sunlight which filtered through the lace curtains at the window she could not discern whether his eyes were gray or green, but they held such an admiring glow that she forgave him his apparent lack of manners. When he helped her to her seat an unruly lock of hair fell across his forehead. He combed it back quickly with his fingers as if he were a small boy trying to look his best for an important guest. It was a charming gesture and so, wanting to put him at ease, she attempted to begin a conversation.

"I hope you will overlook the fact that I am dressed in black. I am not a widow, although your advertisement asks for 'marriageable young ladies' and a widow is certainly free to marry."

Clayton gasped in shock, "Good lord, you have an excellent point there. I did not even think that we might attract widowed ladies to our enterprise. Perhaps we should rephrase our advertisement to make that point more clear."

Gabrielle read the neatly folded advertisement carefully, as if she hadn't memorized it during the many times she'd read it and debated with herself whether or not to apply.

"I think you should leave this exactly as it is. There must be men who would be happy to meet a pleasant young woman

9

whether or not she is a widow."

Fascinated by the softness of her voice as well as by her logic, Jason agreed quickly. "You are undoubtedly correct, Miss MacLaren." Bringing another straight-backed chair up close to the desk so he might sit beside her, he continued in an encouraging tone. "You must forgive me if this question appears impertinent, but why has a young woman of your intelligence and charm been attracted to this form of proposal? I am thinking only of ways to improve our advertisements, you understand," he added hastily, knowing he sounded daft and not understanding why.

"That is far too long and complicated a tale to relate in the few minutes we have remaining before six o'clock, Mr. Royal. Let me explain only that I wish to go to the Oregon country because I'm sure the future will be far brighter for me there than in Liberty where I was born."

"Yes, of course," Jason replied impatiently. "The lure of adventure is a compelling one, I understand that well. But in addition to free passage you must agree to taking one of the men who has paid for the journey as your husband when you arrive." Glancing up at his friend, Jason gestured toward the folder which contained small sketches of the twenty men who were anxiously awaiting the arrival of their brides. "Show her the drawings, Clayton."

That was a prearranged signal between the two men; as they'd interviewed each young woman only the final candidates had been given the privilege of viewing the drawings. Some of the women had scarcely looked at the faces. Knowing that the men existed was all that mattered to them. Others, however, had wanted to know more about the men, their interest being in the financial success of their prospective spouses, not in their appearance. But Gabrielle studied each of the twenty pencil drawings with great care before she looked up.

"These sketches are superb, so lifelike. I'm certain I would be able to recognize each and every one of these men the

10

moment they entered the room. Who was the artist?"

Jason could not believe she was praising work he considered barely adequate, but he admitted to having done it himself. "I drew them. I thought women would want to see what their choices were so they would not be disappointed after they'd made such a long trip. I have little talent, but—"

"Surely you do not believe that, Mr. Royal, for these are marvelous sketches. You've captured the very essence of each man's character." Laying the drawings out one at a time she proceeded to show him what she meant. "Look at this first one; you see how bashful his smile is? I'll bet he's quiet, rather shy, but an industrious worker who would make a very dear husband. Am I right?"

Clayton looked at Jason's flabbergasted expression and laughed out loud. "That is Johnny to be sure, Miss MacLaren. What about the others?"

"Well now, let me see." Gabrielle laid the pictures in groups. "A man's expression tells a lot about him. These two seem too stern, either they are rather grim in their outlook on life, or they wanted to appear that way to attract a more serious-minded woman." In a few minutes' time she described all twenty men, placing them in several categories, but all her comments were kind. If a man was not in the least bit good-looking, she would say he appeared to be a hard worker or that he would have a way with animals, or that she could tell he'd love to have a large family. She came up with any number of observations which would have pleased the men pictured; then she sat back and waited for her two companions to respond.

"You are right about them all, every last one, Miss MacLaren, although I'd not have thought it possible you could tell so much from my sketches. We refused to take money from any man we knew to be a heavy drinker or careless with his money. So there are none among the group with faults too great for an understanding wife to forgive."

"That's right, Miss MacLaren." Clayton joined in amicably, "We accepted only men we'd like our sisters to marry, if we

11

had them. We've attempted to do the same with the women, to provide brides these men can be proud of."

Glancing down at the array of drawings, Gabrielle asked shyly, "Am I supposed to choose one of these men now? Is that your plan?"

"No," Jason replied, feeling the relief he saw mirrored in her eyes as well. "No, not at all. We want to provide ample opportunity for the men and the women to be satisfied with their choice. We plan to host a series of parties when we return home, but I doubt the men will want to wait more than a week or two before they propose to their favorite. With luck, it will all work out so everyone will be happy." At least he prayed that it would, despite his many misgivings.

"Unfortunately, Miss MacLaren, as I told you at the beginning of this interview, all twenty places have been filled. We cannot take you this time." Clayton got to his feet, indicating that the interview was over, but Jason reached out to touch Gabrielle's arm, hoping she would stay a moment longer.

"Miss MacLaren, quite frankly, this is the first time we've attempted such a venture and we're by no means certain all the young ladies we've selected will, in fact, return tomorrow to begin the preparations for the trip. If you will tell me where you're staying tonight, I will make every effort to contact you in the morning should we have an opening."

Gabrielle bit her lip nervously, the first gesture she'd made which indicated her true emotional state, and then replied hesitantly. "I buried the aunt who raised me this morning, that is why I arrived at so late an hour. I left my belongings at the front desk downstairs. I was hoping that I would be accepted. I suppose it was foolish of me not to consider what I would do if I weren't, but truly I have nowhere to stay for the night unless I take a small room here at the hotel."

Seeing the concern in Jason's eyes, Clayton kept still, knowing what his partner wanted to do but seeing no way they could take the lovely young woman with them unless one of

12

the others decided not to go. To have twenty-one women who knew there were only twenty men waiting for them would cause strife for the entire length of a journey that would be difficult at best. No, he wouldn't take her unless for some unexpected reason he didn't meet his quota of twenty tomorrow.

"I'm certain we can find you a hotel room, Miss MacLaren, but if you'd expected to travel with us, is there anyone in Liberty who will take you in should you return?" Jason racked his brain to think of some way to help the striking beauty by his side, but he realized from Clayton's worried expression that his friend would not bend the rules he'd already stated. They'd agreed that one or two extra men would make the competition more keen, but having one or two extra women would be disastrous. It would mean endless bickering for the whole trip and then they'd have to find extra men in a hurry, which would mean they might not be able to maintain the standards set. "If only you had been able to arrive this morning," he offered lamely, sorry he could think of nothing better to say.

"You needn't look so pained, Mr. Royal, after all I am not your responsibility." Gabrielle smiled, trying to cheer him up since he seemed so downcast by her predicament.

Responding to her comment, Jason rose to his feet and offered his hand. "Since you have come to Kansas City to answer our advertisement, you are indeed our responsibility while you are here. I know Clayton has other plans for the evening, but I would be very pleased if you'd join me for dinner and then I will see that you are given lodgings for the night, at our expense, of course."

Clayton raised his eyebrows in disbelief. The plans they'd had for the evening included playing several hands of poker and then going to one of Kansas City's better-known establishments where entertainments of a far more exotic nature could be had for those willing to pay the price. Since this would be their last night in the city he'd not thought Jason would want to miss those amusements for any reason, but

13

clearly his partner seemed to think Miss MacLaren worth his time. Clayton decided to play along with the ruse if that was what Jason wanted.

"Yes, indeed, I have several business matters which need my final attention. We will meet in the dining room after the breakfast hour tomorrow morning, Miss MacLaren, if you will join us at ten I can tell you then if we've had any cancellations."

"Thank you. I will be there." Gabrielle turned to look up at Jason Royal. "I would like to have dinner with you if your invitation is a sincere one, but I do not want you to think this is something you must do, like a disagreeable duty which can't be avoided."

Jason broke into the easy grin ladies usually found irresistibly charming as he disagreed. "Miss MacLaren, if I didn't want your company, I would not have extended the invitation."

Offering his right arm, he escorted her from the room and down the stairs to the hotel's elegantly appointed dining room. As soon as he'd placed their order he leaned forward to take her hand—she'd removed her gloves—and turning her palm up, he observed slyly, "Your clothing is very fine, and by the smoothness of your hands I'd say it's plain you've never had to work a day in your life. We have the entire night to talk so tell me the truth as to why you responded to our advertisement because I can't believe all the bachelors in Liberty aren't in love with you. Why would you risk a long and dangerous journey to marry a stranger?"

Gabrielle frowned slightly. "It looks as though I won't be making any trips except for the return to Liberty for the time being, Mr. Royal, so your question is an irrelevant one." She pulled her hand from his and placed it in her lap to avoid any further advance on his part. His glance was still far too direct, and while his interest in her seemed sincere, he made her uncomfortable. She regretted having accepted his dinner invitation.

14

"Why don't you trust me?" Jason asked, surprised that she'd be so reticent about confiding in him.

"It is not a matter of trust, Mr. Royal, for I was ready to place my life in your hands so to speak. It is simply a matter of my own choosing. I do not intend to burden you with my sorrow."

Struck by his own insensitivity, Jason hastened to apologize. "Forgive me, you said you had buried your aunt only this morning, and I did not mean to suggest any disrespect to the woman's memory if she were dear to you."

Gabrielle's eyes filled with tears but she blinked them away. "My aunt knew of my plans and she could not object since I am eighteen and did not require her consent to leave Liberty and go where I chose."

Since she was at least replying to his comments, Jason prompted the lovely young woman to continue. "I wish you could have met a few of the others we spoke with today. Some were impossibly foolish, others so eager to find a husband I think I could have shown them sketches of grizzly bears and they would not have objected. None saw what you did in my drawings, that the men are real, live human beings with flaws as well as virtues who want partners to share their lives. I know them all, and frankly, none seems a fine enough man to win your love."

Puzzled by his comment, Gabrielle didn't realize she had taken his bait as she began to describe her views in more detail. "There was no mention of love in your advertisement, but life is too difficult to maintain on the frontier without a spouse. What you've offered provides men and women with an opportunity to meet and marry to improve their lives. If love should enter into the bargain, then both will be pleased, but even if it doesn't, both will be far better off than they would have been alone."

Astonished that so attractive a creature would scoff at love in such a fashion, Jason asked quickly, "How can it be that you value love so little? Have you yet to feel its spell?" He understood love well enough himself, although he had no illusions that he would ever be so foolish as to succumb to its magic. What he enjoyed was the expression of love, which was magic in itself even if the object of his affections was a woman with whom he'd spend no more than one night.

A wistful smile graced Gabrielle's lips as her eyes filled with sadness. "I have been far more fortunate than most women for I have known a love of such beauty it will fill my heart to the last of my days. I know I will never encounter the same devotion in a man again, nor do I wish to try. My reasons for going to the Oregon country are purely practical ones, Mr. Royal, I am willing to marry an honest man who wishes to have a wife, but I do not expect to find love."

Jason sat back in his chair, unable to comprehend how the amazing young woman before him could come up with two such contradictory statements in so short a span of time. Before he could ask her to explain more fully, their waiter returned to serve steaming bowls of vegetable soup which smelled so delicious they began to eat. When he glanced up, he found his guest was eating with the same hearty appetite he'd shown and he began to laugh.

"I'm sorry, but you're obviously as hungry as I am and the food here is excellent."

Gabrielle returned his smile as she agreed. "I've had no time to eat all day. I was afraid I'd arrive too late to speak with you, which of course I almost did. It didn't occur to me that you would select the women during the day. I thought you'd speak to everyone and then make your choices."

"That was my suggestion, but Clayton felt it would be unfair to make those who'd come a great distance wait all day for our decision. As it turned out, his plan worked fairly well. At least I thought it had until you arrived." Jason watched as Gabrielle brought her silver soup spoon to her lips for a dainty sip. Her manners were as flawless as her appearance, exactly as he had expected them to be. As soon as she had finished he encouraged her to continue her story. "If you've known such a

16

magnificent love as you describe, Miss MacLaren, why are you not planning to marry that man?"

Gabrielle took a small sip of water; she'd declined his offer of wine as an extravagance she could not accept. Stalling for time, she glanced at the others in the room. Most of the hotel's guests seemed to be men, and she suddenly realized several were staring at her most rudely. She looked back at Jason to hide her embarrassment.

"Boys and girls seem to pair off early in Liberty. At least Beau and I knew from the time I was no more than five and he was seven that we would eventually marry. My aunt didn't approve of him for reasons I never understood. She seemed to see only his family's modest means rather than what a fine person he was."

"Well, if the woman has died, what is stopping you from marrying Beau now?" Jason asked abruptly, although he hoped she had a thousand compelling reasons to prevent that from happening.

As she replied, Gabrielle's thoughts turned inward. She could see Beau clearly in her mind. He'd been tall and blond, with rich, warm brown eyes that had always been filled with love when he'd looked at her. He was quite the finest-looking man she'd ever seen, as handsome as a prince. "My aunt did all she could to discourage our romance, all to no avail. We planned to wait until I turned eighteen and then be married whether she'd give us her blessing or not. Our dream was to go to Oregon and build a small farm into an empire. I know it sounds incredibly foolish, but that was our hope."

"It is not in the least bit foolish to have dreams, Miss MacLaren." Jason was mystified now. He wanted her to come to the point, but he did not want to be so rude as to demand that she did. If he pressed her, he felt she'd simply stop speaking and then he'd never learn what had happened between her and Beau. "What happened to that dream?"

Gabrielle found his deep voice and tender tone very soothing. The glance she'd found so unsettling only moments

17

before seemed sympathetic and she was sorry she'd misjudged him, however briefly. "Beau had an opportunity to go on ahead. An uncle of his was moving his family to the Willamette Valley and he invited him to go along. That meant we'd be separated for a time, but if Beau could find land and begin building our home before I arrived, we thought it would make our decision to marry seem less impetuous. They began the trip in early spring when the rivers were the highest, and while fording the Platte his uncle's wagon snagged upon something—a tree branch, a boulder, it's not known what. You must know the route well. Two of the youngest children were swept into the water and Beau dove in to save his cousins."

"Was he successful?" Jason asked in a whisper, suddenly knowing how the story was going to end and dreading the tragedy he knew would come.

"Yes. He got them to the riverbank where others took the children to safety, but he was swept away by the current. They were unable to recover his body. That is what pains me most, that he does not even have a grave I might visit, for we had always thought we'd spend our lives together and be buried side by side." Gabrielle looked down as tears began to roll silently down her cheeks. "I am sorry. I didn't mean to tell that story—not ever—to anyone. I beg you not to repeat it."

Jason pulled his handkerchief from his pocket and handed it to the weeping young woman, thankful he had a freshly laundered one to offer. "I give you my word on it, I will never tell a soul that story. Did your aunt blame herself for Beau's death? Had she allowed you two to marry, then your young man would not have been with his uncle."

Gabrielle looked up; she'd dried her eyes and had forced herself to adopt a calm façade no matter how wretched she felt inside. "It is difficult for me to even begin to describe my aunt's reaction other than to say it was unabashed glee. It would never have occurred to her to accept the responsibility for his death, nor should she have, for surely our fate is in God's hands alone."

"Of course," Jason agreed promptly. Religion of any type was not something he'd contemplated seriously, but he could accept her view as the true one since it seemed to give her comfort. "And you still wish to seek your fate in Oregon, is that it?"

"Yes." Gabrielle paused while the waiter returned with their entrées. She had been given as large a serving of roast beef as Jason and was certain she'd never be able to finish it all despite her earlier hunger. "Everyone in Liberty knows I was Beau's girl, and I can't bear the way people there look at me now. It's as though he died only yesterday rather than a year ago; their pity is so clear in their gaze. If I live there until I am one hundred I will always be that poor Gabrielle MacLaren whose fiancé died so tragically. I have no hope of having a happy life there, and now that my aunt is dead, there is absolutely no reason for me to stay."

Jason chewed the succulent roast beef slowly as he watched her cut a tiny bite from her meat. They would spend the entire night dining if she continued to eat so fastidiously, but suddenly he didn't care. He was content simply to be with her, to share her pain as he'd never shared another woman's grief. "To say I am sorry does not seem to be nearly enough, Miss MacLaren. Since you want to go so badly, I will see if I can't arrange for your passage somehow. I am taking a large number of people this time. If there is no room for you with the young women we interviewed today, then I will simply find space somewhere else."

"Can you really do that?" Gabrielle's tears had made the blue of her eyes even more vivid, and now her gaze was not only rapt but fascinating as well.

Laughing, Jason nodded. "I am the wagon master, Miss MacLaren. The entire wagon train is my responsibility, and what I say goes or people are invited very quickly to take their wagons elsewhere."

Gabrielle smiled in return, for his mood was infectiously pleasant. "Aren't you very young for such a job? I thought the

19

wagon master would be a veteran of many trips along the trail."

"Oh, I am indeed a veteran. I began at a very tender age." Seeing that her interest was sincere, Jason related the tale of his first trek upon the Oregon Trail, being careful never to mention any incident which involved even the slightest peril upon the water. She was so charming a companion he was surprised when he looked down and found not a morsel remaining on his plate. Wanting an excuse to continue their conversation, he ordered apple pie, which he ate as slowly as possible while she sipped her coffee and smiled at all his stories as if they were a delight to hear. When finally he could delay no longer, he folded his napkin and placed it beside his dessert plate.

"I promised to arrange for your lodgings. Let's see what's available." He signed the tab for their dinners and, taking her arm, escorted her to the reception desk.

"Miss MacLaren will need a room for the night, just add the expense to my bill."

The thin, balding night clerk swallowed nervously as he explained why that request must be denied. "I am most dreadfully sorry, Mr. Royal, but the hotel if filled to capacity. We don't even have a closet to let."

"Nor do we want one!" Jason replied crossly for it had not even occurred to him that he might be unable to find Gabrielle a room. There were other hotels, but none in which he'd care to leave any woman alone for the night, most certainly not one as lovely as Gabrielle. "I believe you have her luggage. I'll take it please."

"Where are we going?" Gabrielle whispered anxiously, for like Jason she had lost all track of the time and had not realized the hour was late until she'd glanced at the clock upon the wall behind the desk.

"You'll see." Jason carried her one valise in his left hand while he laced the fingers of his right in hers. With long sure strides he led her out the front door and down the sidewalk to the corner of the two-story building. "Clayton and I have a suite of rooms, the drawing room where we interviewed the young ladies and bedrooms on either side. I'll give you my room, for the rest of the hotels in this town are far too rowdy to serve single ladies."

Gabrielle looked up and down the street. She'd made such infrequent visits to Kansas City that she could not dispute his description of the inns, but she doubted taking his room was a proper solution.

"That is very generous of you, Mr. Royal, but I will be on my own for the rest of my life so I might as well begin tonight. Surely there is one hotel where I'll be safe, even if the other patrons are boisterous."

Displeased that she'd argue, Jason raised his voice to a commanding tone. "Miss MacLaren, I told you I do feel responsible for your welfare. We will go around to the rear entrance and up the back stairs to my room. I will sleep on the couch in the drawing room and that way I'll be certain you are safe. No one will know you slept in my room unless you tell them so, which I trust you have sense enough not to do."

Stung by this rebuke which she regarded as being totally unwarranted, Gabrielle lashed back at him sarcastically. "I've had little need to practice the kind of discretion you're suggesting, Mr. Royal, but I understand why it is to your advantage to protect my reputation."

Jason began to swear, then caught himself before he pronounced a filthy word that he knew would upset Gabrielle even more. He didn't know what had gone wrong between them after they'd spent such a pleasant evening, but something definitely had. Rather than waste time on apologizing, he continued around to the rear of the hotel and then, taking the adjacent stairway, led Gabrielle to the door of his room. He placed her satchel at his feet as he took the key from his pocket, but when he heard someone approaching he hurriedly unlocked his door and nearly shoved the startled young woman inside, grabbing her valise before he followed her into the room. The covers of the high iron bed had been turned down by the maid and the lamp had been lit, these courtesies lent the room a romantic mood which he attempted unsuccessfully to ignore.

"What have you packed in this bag? Surely your clothing is not so heavy!" He carried it to the foot of the bed before turning to face her with a far from friendly glance.

Gabrielle untied her bonnet and removed her gloves, placing both on the marble-topped dresser as she replied. "I imagine it is the books which make it such a burden. I should have packed them separately."

"Books?" Jason was puzzled as to why she'd need more than a Bible which was the only book most people had in their homes. "Do you enjoy reading so much?"

Gabrielle laughed at his confusion. "Why of course, don't you?"

"I know how to read," Jason declared promptly, but seeing that did not satisfy her curiosity, he asked, "What sort of books did you bring?"

"Poetry mostly, a volume of Shakespeare, a novel or two, just my favorites, for I know the winters are long and amusements will be few." That they were standing in his bedroom conversing politely about literature struck her as being ironic since she'd not wanted to take his room in the first place, let alone entertain him there.

"Do you honestly think any of the farmers, one of whom might soon be your husband, will be interested in such a pastime?" Jason asked with a sly grin, but Gabrielle misunderstood his remark.

"Just because a man makes his living from the land does not mean he is stupid, Mr. Royal. I have always planned to be a farmer's bride. Should the man I marry not know how to read I will teach him, and read to him myself while I do."

Thinking he'd be wise to let her think that had been the intent of his question in the first place, Jason agreed. "I am certain he'll appreciate your instruction and be a wonderful pupil, Miss MacLaren." Deciding a strictly professional attitude was the best choice, he gathered up the things he'd need for the morning and started for the door which connected that room to the drawing room. "I will bid you good night now; you'll find this a comfortable room and I'll see you tomorrow at ten."

"Mr. Royal?" Gabrielle followed him to the door, afraid she had offended him by being so reluctant to accept his hospitality. "I want to thank you again for taking me to dinner, and for giving me your room. I didn't mean to appear ungrateful. You have been very considerate, particularly when I'm not even one of those you selected as a prospective bride."

Jason opened the door and tossed his belongings on the nearest chair before he turned back to face her. As she looked up at him, her expression was so sweet it seemed most natural for him to bend down to kiss her good-night. He had meant to do no more than brush her cheek lightly but she lifted her lips to meet his instead. Her lips were soft, opening easily with only slight pressure from his, and she relaxed against his chest with such easy grace that he wound his fingers in her long, flowing tresses. Holding her mouth captive beneath his own, he savored her delicious taste until he could no longer catch his breath. When at last he had to draw away he was stunned by the strength of the desire she had aroused in him, for her kiss had been filled with a promise of passion he'd never felt in any other woman. That it could come from one with such an innocent smile astonished him all the more. His own smile grew wide as he realized she knew far more of the art of love than her very proper appearance had led him to believe.

Gabrielle stared up at the handsome man she'd so recently met and felt her face flood with the bright color of a deep blush. She'd not expected that kiss nor the depth of her own response, and she was horrified by what he must think of her lavish display of affection when they were little more than strangers. Wanting to end the regrettable incident swiftly, she tried to close the door but Jason blocked her way.

"If you need me later, I'll be right here. I meant what I said

23

at dinner; I'll find a way for you to come with us." Jason's admiring glance filled with astonishment as he saw the confusion in Gabrielle's gaze turn to fury. The bright blue of her eyes grew purple with rage as she replied to what he'd meant as reassurance.

"That is not a very subtle hint, Mr. Royal. Is it a bribe you expect? Well, if you think I'll sleep with you tonight, or on the way along the Oregon Trail you're wrong! If there is not a place for me with the other brides tomorrow morning, then I will earn my own passage in a respectable fashion! Good night!"

Jason was so startled by her angry outburst that he had to dodge out of the way to avoid being injured as she slammed the door in his face. He could not understand how the remark he'd meant to be comforting could have been so badly misinterpreted, but as he stood there contemplating the question, he realized the innocence of his comment was not the issue—it was the ardor of his kiss. No, damn it! It was the ardor of her kiss which had inspired him to return it!

"Women!"

He swore loudly and with a swift kick he hit the connecting door between their rooms. In response he heard Gabrielle turn the key in the lock and cursed again. Well she could just find her own way to Oregon now, for he'd be damned if he'd take a vixen like that and wish her upon one of the good-natured farmers who was waiting for a bride. That idea appalled him so greatly he turned his back on the door as if it might respond to his anger, but gradually, as his reason returned, he knew he had to take Gabrielle home with him if for only one purpose, to teach her how wrong she was to think she was through with love. Love was for the living to enjoy, and she was far too desirable a young woman to have only the beauty of a memory to warm her nights. That one kiss had been enough to convince him she would be a delight in his bed. He wanted to make her purr with pleasure, to hear her sob his name as the ecstasy he knew he could bring her poured through every inch of her most splendid female body. He had never wanted any woman as

24

desperately as he now wanted the vibrant beauty in the next room. He had not imagined her to possess such a fiery disposition, and he suddenly felt an unexpected pang of sympathy for her recently deceased aunt. Surely her impetuous niece had driven the woman to an early grave. He vowed not to let Gabrielle get the best of him again and, with a deep chuckle, went to find Clayton. He knew where the man would be enjoying himself. Jason could scarcely wait to sample similar pleasures. Kansas City had many gorgeous women, and if he couldn't have Gabrielle MacLaren that night, he planned to be content with the affection of several others.

Chapter II

Rushing from his bedroom toward Jason's Clayton Horne halted abruptly in the center of the drawing room when he saw his friend seated upon the couch. The young man was dressed in his gray suit, neatly groomed in preparation for the morning's meeting, but he sat with his head in his hands, clearly unready to face anyone as yet.

"You've only yourself to blame for the miserable way you feel, Jason, but that's slight consolation I know."

Although he was fifteen years older than the handsome young man, Clayton regarded Jason as his closest friend. Their travels together had forged a bond of trust which both valued; still, Clayton was fond of giving advice although he knew Jason seldom heeded his words.

Jason looked up with a wicked grin. "It was worth it, Clay, every last minute."

Clayton laughed as he shook his head reproachfully. "At my age, it's a choice between liquor or the ladies, and I can tell you women are one pleasure I will never give up. Besides, I feel better this morning than I have in years which is one boast you certainly can't make."

Jason knew he had not simply gotten drunk; he'd gone way past mere inebriation. He considered himself lucky to have found his way back to the hotel even though it had been after five A.M. when he'd managed to do so.

"You know I never drink a drop on the trail, so I can tolerate a hangover or two when I'm in Kansas City."

Clayton chuckled at that thought for he knew Jason to have remarkable powers of recovery which he'd admired on more than one occasion. Pausing before the mirror, he patted his hair hoping to make the unruly sandy waves follow the shape of his head rather than stick out in all directions as they tended to do despite his lifelong efforts to tame them. His tan skin showed only a few slight wrinkles at the corners of his clear blue eyes and he was quite pleased that he looked so fit that morning when Jason had plainly overindulged himself. Satisfied with his appearance, he turned around.

"That's good to hear, for I need your advice on a problem which has just presented itself. We must make a decision immediately and since you had far more opportunity than I did to speak with Miss MacLaren, I'd value your opinion."

Clayton knew he was the more deliberate of the two. He pondered questions for days while Jason would give a matter no more than a moment's consideration before rendering a decision. That Jason's judgments were nearly always superior caused Clayton considerable chagrin, but he had made no attempt to adopt the younger man's far swifter mode of thinking when he feared he simply lacked the intelligence to do so.

Because of the intense pain which throbbed in his head, Jason doubted he could give a fair opinion on any subject, let alone the volatile Miss MacLaren.

"Why do you ask?"

Clayton pulled up a chair and sat down opposite his friend. "Do you recall meeting a man named Joshua Taylor back home?"

"No. Should I?" Jason asked cautiously. He sat up straight and tried to focus his eyes upon his watch. They still had an hour before the meeting would begin, and he had expected to use that time to rest. He yawned sleepily, then tried to give

28

Clayton his attention; but that was a difficult task.

"Well, I was hoping you knew him because while the name's familiar I can't seem to place the man." Tapping a thick white envelope against his fingertips, he explained. "I found this letter at the desk when I went downstairs for breakfast this morning. Food is something you might consider, by the way. The letter is from Mr. Taylor and he says he's sorry he took so long to make up his mind, but he wants to come in on our venture. He enclosed the amount the others paid plus a little something extra for our trouble. He wants us to bring him a bride too."

"Joshua Taylor is his name?" Jason reached out and took the envelope, hastily scanning the neatly penned letter he found inside. "Well he mentions the names of three of the men we included. Says they're close friends and says he has good land and a sturdy house built. He probably doesn't want to be the only bachelor left among his friends. What do you think?"

Clayton frowned, his worry plain, "We were so careful with the others I was hoping you could vouch for Taylor since I can't. He would make twenty-one and then we could take Miss MacLaren with us. I couldn't help but notice how interested you were in her. Not that I didn't like her immediately too, because I did, but she seems to be too elegant a creature to wed a farmer and be content to work from dawn to dusk. I'll leave it up to you: shall we accept Taylor's money and take her, or not?"

Jason shrugged as if the matter were of little importance to him. "Let's wait and see if all the ladies we asked to return actually do so. If we have less than twenty then Miss MacLaren will be a substitute; if all twenty are there at ten, then we'll accept Taylor's money and take Gabrielle for him."

"You mean tell her this Taylor is to be her husband?" Clayton asked incredulously.

"Why not? They both seem to have cut things pretty close. I'd say they are a perfect match."

"Well, I don't know." Clayton refolded the letter and

replaced it in the envelope. "They'd be the only ones without a choice then and that just doesn't seem fair."

"All right, then don't tell her about Taylor!" Jason replied irritably. "We'll just tell her we've received another bachelor's fee and she'll be among the brides going with us."

After a moment's hesitation, Clayton nodded. "Fine. Were you able to find her a nice room?"

"I gave her mine." Jason nodded toward the door. "I haven't heard a sound from her as yet though. She might just sleep right through our meeting if you don't knock on the door to awaken her." He had no intention of risking such an action himself after the way they had parted.

Startled by that possibility, Clayton got up and walked over to the door. After listening closely for a long moment he knocked several times. "Miss MacLaren? It's Clayton Horne, I don't want you to be late for the meeting, my dear."

Jason waited for what he hoped would be a sweetly worded reply but Clayton's call went unanswered. "She must be a sound sleeper. Try knocking again." When Clayton's insistent pounding again brought no response Jason got to his feet and, after crossing the room quickly, tried the door and found it unlocked.

"Wait a minute, you can't just walk into Miss MacLaren's room!" Clayton cried out in dismay.

"Aren't you forgetting the room is mine?" Jason brushed past him to find the bedroom empty. The bed had been slept in, the towels by the pitcher and wash basin were damp, but the lovely Miss MacLaren was gone and so was her cumbersome valise. Exasperated, Jason threw up his hands in disgust, "Well, that settles it, the lady's gone so whomever Joshua Taylor might be, he's out of luck."

"Damn!" Clayton muttered angrily. "Why couldn't things have worked out as we'd hoped they would? I could have used Taylor's cash for additional provisions!" Disgusted, he jammed the stranger's letter into his pocket and went back to

30

his room. Meanwhile Jason stood, silently enjoying the subtle trace of the young beauty's perfume which still lingered upon the morning air as an erotic reminder of the intimate moment they'd shared and he remembered all too well.

Gabrielle walked briskly along the crowded sidewalk. She couldn't just sit in Jason Royal's room while she waited for the hours to pass so she'd again left her valise at the desk and had struck out on her own to explore the town and to distract herself from the inevitable rejection she was sure would come. Kansas City was only a short distance from Independence where the wagon trains formed before they set out on the Oregon Trail, and the merchants seemed to be doing a good business selling supplies which would be needed for the trip. Gabrielle could feel the excitement in the air as families swept past her, their faces aglow as they made last-minute preparations for their great adventure, and she envied them. She was so close to making the journey, and yet she knew if only ten of the young women Mr. Horne expected to attend the final meeting arrived Jason Royal would insist there was no place for her. The more she thought about their late-night confrontation the more mortified she became. She raised her hand to her lips as though people she passed in her walk could see how wantonly she'd behaved. She had never expected to kiss another man the way she'd kissed Beau, with the slow, sweet passion his love had always inspired. Jason Royal had simply caught her by surprise that was all. He'd taken advantage of her mood, encouraged her to confide in him, and then had pushed the trust he'd inspired to it's limit. Well, perhaps not to its limit since she'd come to her senses so swiftly, but had she not been so shocked, she was certain he would have suggested they share her bed. His bed she supposed it was actually. Furious all over again as she thought of the nerve of the man, she forgot to watch the time and then had to lift her skirt and run from the far end of the

31

town all the way back to the hotel, much to the delight of the gentlemen she passed with no more than a breathless smile.

Clayton Horne was pleased to see all twenty young women had returned as promised and nudged Jason. "It's after ten, why don't you begin."

Jason nodded absently as he looked around the room, silently counting the young ladies who were seated in a semicircle in front of him. Coffee and tea had been served when suddenly it seemed to him that he and Clayton had made a terrible mistake. They had selected young women who could sip tea politely, who had pretty smiles and bright glances; but what they should have sought were strong lasses who could not only face the hardships of the Oregon Trail but survive them. Clearing his throat, he began in what he hoped would be such a convincing tone that the assembled ladies would quickly flee.

"Good morning. Mr. Horne and I would like to take this opportunity to thank each and every one of you for responding to our advertisement. As some of you know, in the early 1840s, countless numbers of single men braved the rigors of the Oregon Trail to establish farms in the fertile valley of the Willamette River. Last year, by treaty with Great Britain, the United States gained exclusive control of the Oregon country and now, in 1847, the route is traveled by families following in the footsteps of the many gallant early pioneers. However, single women being so few, the men who were among the first to arrive have begun to despair of ever finding brides. Mr. Horne, being the sympathetic friend that he is, offered to do his best to bring ladies as charming as you to Oregon City, where you'll find men eagerly waiting to become your husbands." Jason paused for a moment, wanting to be certain he had their rapt attention before he continued. "While that happy prospect is what brought you all here, what lies ahead is beyond imagining. The way is more than difficult; it is tortuous, fraught with perils which will surpass your worst fears. We will have to cross two thousand miles of inhospitable terrain, brave the harshness of the elements and the fury of Indian tribes who see our passage through their lands as an assault by an enemy force. You will be only a small portion of a wagon train consisting of more than fifty families—the wagons are already assembling just outside Independence—and as soon as we join them we will make plans to depart on what for many will be the last journey they will ever take."

Jason hoped they understood the dangers to which he was referring, but their fascinated stares told him little. "I went to Oregon by the ocean route as a child, so when I first crossed the narrow path that was to become the Oregon Trail I traversed it in reverse, going from the coast to Independence. Had I not known, when I served for the first time as a scout for a wagon train in 1843, that the beauty which awaited us was worth our sacrifice, I would have been among the first to turn back. There were few families on that trip that did not lose someone: a precious child, a dearly loved wife, a pretty bride as each of you ladies will be. The trail has killed the strongest of men, but the suffering it inflicts upon women is especially cruel. I want all of you to take a few moments to reflect upon your own lives, to consider in your hearts the warm and safe homes you are leaving behind, the dear relatives you may never see again. I will not fault any of you who wishes to withdraw her application. I will place them upon the table by the door, simply remove yours as you leave. This decision is the most important one you will ever make, and I caution you to weigh your choices carefully; for once the Oregon Trail is begun, you will not be able to turn back."

As Jason carried the neatly printed application forms to the front of the room, he saw Gabrielle MacLaren standing just inside the door. How long she'd been listening he didn't know, but he could tell by her expression that she had counted those present and knew she had no chance of being included in the group unless someone left. He had not thought the mere sight of her sad, sweet smile would stir him so, yet he found her even more lovely than he had the previous afternoon. Walking to her side, he whispered softly, "Please wait a moment longer, some are sure to leave."

Gabrielle disagreed and said so. "After that impassioned plea none will dare admit to having so little courage as to back out. You have your twenty brides, Mr. Royal, I'm certain of it."

Jason was unconvinced, but when, as she had predicted, none of the young women stirred, he turned his back on the room so they might converse with some degree of privacy. "You mean I only strengthened their resolve, my warnings did not discourage them?"

"I am certain their decision was made as mine was, the very moment I chanced to read your advertisement." Gabrielle had been able to observe little other than the young women's proud posture as they sat on the edges of their chairs. "You have a determined group here, but as you can see, there is no place for me."

She lifted her chin proudly, for she was positive he'd not forgotten her refusal to consider some alternative arrangement for her passage. She'd not be going to Oregon with his wagon train. It seemed that her aunt had reached from beyond the grave to ruin her plans for living at least part of the dream she'd had with Beau. She'd not cry again; she'd keep her sorrow to herself as she'd learned to do. She extended her hand to say goodbye.

"I wish you good luck, Mr. Royal. I hope your journey is both a safe and swift one regardless of your fears."

"My fears are well founded in experience, Miss MacLaren, but I insist you remain a moment longer to hear what I have to say. It was no mere chance that you happened to see our advertisement, but fate. Another bachelor has joined our list of clients and we need to provide twenty-one brides instead of twenty. If my speech did not have the desired effect upon the others, did it influence you to return to Liberty or do you still wish to go with us?"

Gabrielle tried to read the expression in Jason's eyes. They

34

were gray—she saw their color clearly now—a deep, piercing gray, and she knew she had to respond with the utmost tact. "I want very much to go to Oregon, to have a home and a husband waiting for me to arrive would make the journey worthwhile no matter what the risk. I only hope that what happened between us last night will not make the trip an impossible one for me."

Jason chuckled at that taunt, for despite Gabrielle's poise and composure, she was very young. He could tell she had given the incident far more consideration than it had deserved. She had probably not kissed any man since her beloved Beau had left Liberty to make his way west, and undoubtedly her anguish over their embrace was tinged with guilt. His anger with her had melted away the moment he'd seen her standing at the door, and he teased her now with a ready grin.

"You mean the horrors you'll have to survive on the trail do not compare to the agony of my affection?"

"Mr. Royal!" The auburn-haired beauty's creamy complexion took on a bright blush as she stammered. "There is nothing wrong with your affection, it was merely so unexpected that I—"

"I will be happy to forget the incident entirely if you will, Miss MacLaren." Jason's eyes took on a teasing sparkle that let her know he forgot little.

"It is the only way I will consent to go, Mr. Royal. As you pointed out, to begin the journey is to accept one of the men waiting at its conclusion as my husband, and I do not want him to regret that I made the trip."

Offering his arm, Jason smiled warmly. "That would be impossible, Miss MacLaren. Now won't you come with me to join the others?"

Gabrielle licked her lips slowly. "I suppose the worst that could happen to me is that I could die." She would then be with Beau again so that prospect scarcely frightened her; it was having to live without him for the rest of her life that was terrifying. At the very least she could live her life in Oregon as they'd planned. "Yes. I still want very much to go with them if I may."

Startled by her comment, Jason offered calm reassurance as he escorted her to a vacant seat. "Believe me, Miss MacLaren, if I leave Independence, Missouri with twenty-one brides, I will arrive in Oregon City with each one in perfect health. You have my word on it." The other young women turned as Gabrielle sat down, some smiling in a friendly fashion, others merely curious, and Jason saw on the faces of the prettiest, a sudden flash of jealousy so thick he knew he never should have let Clayton talk him into arranging to transport other men's brides in the first place.

While the rest of the announcements would be brief, Jason could not shake his earlier feeling of foreboding. Knowing the sooner they began the journey the more swiftly it would come to an end, he began to address the assembled group in the hope that they could soon be on their way.

"We have arranged for carriages to take you to Independence. As Mr. Horne cautioned you yesterday, luggage must be kept to a minimum. We'll need most of the room in the three wagons we've assigned to your use to transport our provisions. We'll separate you ladies into three equal groups, but other than storing your luggage and sleeping in the wagons, I doubt you'll want to spend much time riding in them. I think you'll prefer to spend most of your time on horseback. We have a large selection of gentle mounts so I'm sure even those of you who have little experience with horses will soon become proficient riders. Now are there any questions before I leave to summon the carriages?"

Gabrielle raised her hand quickly, "Mr. Royal, I have my own horse, will I be permitted to bring him?"

Jason had not even considered how Gabrielle had gotten from Liberty to Kansas City by herself, but he responded with a smile. "If the horse can carry your valise I'd say he's brute enough to make the trip, but I warn you, we'll lose many a horse to Indians all along the route. If he's stolen no effort can be made to recover him."

36

"I understand." Gabrielle had no intention of allowing the stallion she'd raised from a colt to be stolen by any man, Indian or white, but if he were, she'd certainly get him back herself. Knowing an open declaration of such a vow would only make the situation between Jason Royal and herself even more difficult than it already was, she simply smiled as if she agreed with his terms. There were several more questions which were concerned with minor details. He answered them quickly and then excused himself to run his errand.

Since the carriages were coming from the same livery stable where Gabrielle had boarded her horse, when Jason left to summon the transportation for the others she hurried to catch up with him. "I didn't realize I'd be the only one to bring my own horse," she commented anxiously, hoping she had not caused the young man a problem he'd not foreseen.

Noting her troubled expression, Jason halted abruptly, but he had to let several people pass them on the sidewalk before he could reply. "One more horse matters little, Miss MacLaren, and I'll be happy to pay the bill for his stay last night. We can simply tie him behind one of the carriages if you'd rather not ride him today."

Gabrielle considered his question thoughtfully before she replied. "If the others will be riding in the carriages I should too, since it will afford us the opportunity to become acquainted."

Surprised she'd have thought of such a good point when he hadn't, Jason promptly agreed, but when the groom brought out her horse he could only gape. Rather than the gentle gelding he'd imagined her to own, the animal was so high spirited a stallion the frightened lad could scarcely hold him. Gabrielle, however, took the reins and by talking softly to the magnificent animal soon stilled his anxiety with no more than abundant affection and a calm, gentle touch. After only a few moments her stallion seemed sufficiently reassured by her return to stand at her side without further complaint.

Embarrassed that the horse had behaved so badly, Gabrielle

quickly apologized for him. "He is unused to being away from home as you can see, Mr. Royal. He is not usually as nervous as this. Unfortunately, there was no way for me to explain to him yesterday afternoon that he had not been abandoned."

Jason found it difficult to believe so slightly built a young woman could possibly handle such an animal, but the stallion was standing quietly now as she stroked his velvety soft nose lightly. A roan, his reddish brown color was only slightly lighter than his mistress' hair. He had four white stockings and a white blaze that gave his glossy coat a handsome accent. In all respects, he was as great a beauty as his mistress.

"What do you call him?"

"MacLaren's Sunrise is his name, but I've always thought that a bit pretentious and prefer to call him Sunny instead," Gabrielle explained with a smile. She was very proud of her horse and could tell by Jason's interest he was favorably impressed.

"Sunny he is then." Jason continued to give the stallion an admiring glance while he waited for the carriages to be brought to the front of the stable. "How did you manage to convince that overprotective aunt of yours to allow you to ride this beast?"

At that question, Gabrielle gave him a disapproving glance from beneath her thick fringe of dark lashes. "Naturally she preferred that I hitch him to our buggy, but he is a fine mount and gives me no trouble." She did not expand upon her aunt's opinions, but it was apparent she felt the woman had been as wrong about Sunny as she had been about everything else.

"I'm glad to hear it. However, if he's too much for you I'll insist you ride a more docile horse and we'll use Sunny to pack provisions." Jason had no intention of wasting the animal's obvious strength when it could be put to a good use.

"You'll do no such thing!" Gabrielle responded indignantly.

With an impatient sigh, Jason responded tersely. "Miss MacLaren, as I believe I told you, I am in charge of the entire wagon train and if you'll not promise to obey my orders you'll be left behind!" Jason put his hands on his hips, determined that he'd damn well end any argument promptly.

Gabrielle took a deep breath before trying to speak in a more responsible tone. "You know how much this trip means to me. You needn't threaten me; I'll be most cooperative since I have no other choice."

"See that you remember that fact, Miss MacLaren, because I'll not remind you of it again!" Grabbing the stallion's reins from her hands, Jason led the horse out to the three carriages which were now lined up in front of the stable and tied him securely to the rear of the last one. When he turned, he saw that Gabrielle had started walking back toward the hotel. The proud line of her back and the length of her stride plainly disclosed her angry mood. He was tempted to go after her and send her home. Clearly she was going to try his patience to the limit every step of the way, but although she had an enchanting beauty, he was uncertain that the delights her charms promised would be worth the aggravation. As if he could read Jason's thoughts, Sunny snorted derisively, defending his mistress with a toss of his finely shaped head.

"Don't worry, Sunrise. I'll ride you myself before I'll make a pack mule of you." Jason slapped the horse's rump playfully as he walked away, intent upon loading his charges into the carriages and beginning the trek to Independence.

When Gabrielle reached the hotel she found Clayton Horne had the others waiting amidst heaps of luggage, and it was obvious that the directions the young women had been given about limiting their belongings had been disregarded. She had bound her books separately that morning to lighten the weight of her suitcase. Then she had asked the desk clerk to send her things out to the steps so she'd be ready to board a carriage.

While Clayton seemed to think that since the carriages had carried their assembled baggage three wagons could also, Jason surveyed the mound of luggage with dismay and explained

39

through clenched teeth, "There has got to be something each of you can leave behind. When you find your wagon has to be unloaded five or six times each day to prevent the wheels from becoming permanently stuck in the mud when we ford streams, then you'll begin throwing away your heaviest items first. Let's start doing it now!" He walked among the young women, offering suggestions for each until he came to Gabrielle.

"I have just this one bag, and I will be responsible for it." Gabrielle was certain Jason Royal would think a woman needed no more than one dress, but she had already sorted her belongings at home and had brought only those she could not do without. All the other young women had come with a relative or two who could take any rejected article back home, but she was alone and so had no one who'd want her castoffs should she have any, which she was certain she hadn't.

Jason paused no more than a moment in front of the auburn-haired beauty. "You have shown such remarkable restraint, Miss MacLaren, I'll not ask you to discard anything unless you'd like to leave a book or two."

Gabrielle thought he might be testing her. However, his glance seemed friendly, not challenging, so she responded confidently. "I prize my books most dearly of all."

"Then keep them," Jason muttered under his breath before he moved on, but he was pleased she'd seemed to be in a compromising mood for a change. He turned back and smiled, a sly teasing grin which made her blush. Laughing at that unexpected reaction he moved on, encouraging the others to lighten their loads so they could depart in time to reach Independence by midafternoon.

More than an hour passed before he was satisfied he'd convinced his charges to leave a significant amount of luggage behind, and so Jason was unprepared for the lengthy leave-taking which followed. Embarrassed fathers hugged their daughters shyly, brothers simply kissed their cheeks, but their mothers and sisters wept openly at seeing their loved ones depart when they knew they'd most likely never see them again. He overheard more than one comment about precious little grandchildren who'd never be seen and had to turn away. It was a heart-wrenching scene yet he saw the determination in the young women's faces and knew each was happy with the choice she'd made regardless of her relatives' pain. Clayton and he had thought twenty a manageable number, and twenty-one no different, but as he looked at the brides they would be escorting he now saw each as an individual with romantic dreams lighting her eyes. He suddenly hoped none of them would become ill or injured on the journey, or become sorry they had decided to make such a perilous trip to wed a stranger. He could not help but feel responsible for their happiness, and as he glanced over at Clayton he could readily see from the man's worried expression that he suddenly had the same misgivings. Gabrielle was standing at his friend's side. With no one to bid her farewell she seemed so alone he felt drawn to her and was tempted to walk over to speak with Clayton on one pretext or another so he could include her in their conversation, but he forced himself to remain aloof. He wanted simply to teach her a lesson, to show her love was meant for the living to enjoy. Unwilling to become as loyal to her as her stallion, he stood alone too, vowing he'd show her no special treatment. Meanwhile he wished he could think of some clever means to inspire the other young women to bid their families a final goodbye.

Clayton was as moved as Jason by the tearful farewells. Finally, able to stand no more, he withdrew from his pocket the list he'd made and announced it was time to load and board the carriages. After the drivers had stowed the luggage aboard the appropriate vehicles, he helped each young woman into her assigned carriage, then climbed up beside the driver of the second while Jason took his place beside the driver of the first. As they started down the road all those left behind waved and blew kisses, calling out last goodbyes in voices choked with tears, while the young women leaned from the carriage

41

windows to reply with far more optimistic farewells. Sunny, his glossy red coat glistening in the sunshine, trotted along behind the third carriage in which his mistress rode. He seemed to be the only traveler untouched by the sadness of their departure and unaware of the great adventure which lay ahead.

Chapter III

As soon as the excitement of Kansas City had been left behind an uneasy silence fell upon the occupants of the carriage. Each looked curiously at her companions, uncertain what was expected of her now, until one young woman leaned forward. She pushed her blond curls off her forehead, and her conversation became so animated she often repeated the gesture.

"I think we should introduce ourselves since we'll be together for the next several months. The sooner we become friends the better it will be for all of us." With an enthusiastic smile she continued. "My name is Barbara Renwick."

Gabrielle was seated on the opposite side, by the far window, so she waited a moment for one of her companions to respond. When none did, she volunteered her name. "I'm Gabrielle MacLaren and I, too, hope we can become good friends and remain so once we reach Oregon City."

"You're not serious!" A brown-eyed beauty with glossy black curls scoffed rudely. She held herself proudly, clearly having a great deal of self-confidence. "Where men are concerned, women cannot possibly remain friends."

"You sound as though you speak from vast experience, Miss? . . ." Gabrielle hesitated, hoping the haughty woman would supply her name.

"Stewart, Iris Stewart. But since you are dressed in black I assume you are a widow and must know something of men yourself. I'm surprised Mr. Horne would accept a widow, or that you would apply. Did your late husband leave you penniless?"

Gabrielle found herself the object of six pairs of curious eyes at that question, but since she and Beau had not been married she'd never thought of herself as his widow. Her grief had been every bit as deep, however, and she hesitated before replying. "It is my aunt who just passed away. As she was the only mother I have known, it seemed to me to be disrespectful to dress in more colorful clothing today but I will put these garments away tomorrow. I have never been married, nor do I believe from Mr. Horne's comments that any of the others have either, Miss Stewart."

After a moment's silence the young woman seated opposite Gabrielle spoke. She was very pretty, with hair the golden shade of ripening wheat and eyes of a vibrant green. "I'm Erica Nelson and I'm curious as to why you think it will be impossible for us to become friends, Miss Stewart."

Clearly bored by having to respond to what she considered so obvious a question, Iris yawned, pausing to cover her mouth before she explained. "It is clear to me from the sketches we were shown, as well as from what Mr. Horne said about the men, that some are far more attractive and successful than others. I plan to marry the man who can provide whatever comforts I desire; I'll settle for no less and you women would be foolish to do otherwise. We will all, therefore, be interested in the same two or three men. Whatever friendship you think we'll develop in our travels will end abruptly then."

Gabrielle glanced over at Erica and saw by her perplexed expression that she also disagreed with Iris' comments. "I for one am more interested in my future husband's character than in whatever wealth he may have accumulated before I arrive. Many of the men are young. They can't be expected to have achieved the goals they will eventually attain. I think one of

44

the joys of marriage is building a life together."

Iris shrugged disdainfully, positive Gabrielle's views were idiotic. "Fine. You marry one of the lads. I will marry a mature gentleman who will be the husband I deserve."

"Oh, I'm confident you'll get what you deserve, Iris," Gabrielle replied sweetly and when Erica began to giggle she knew she'd made a friend. Since the young woman seated beside Erica had not joined in the discussion as yet, Gabrielle encouraged her to introduce herself to the others. "Won't you please tell us your name?"

After a long hesitation during which she glanced nervously at each of her traveling companions, the brown-eyed brunette finally responded shyly. "I am Margaret O'Connor and I hope only to marry a kind man who will provide a nice home. He needn't be rich, just pleasant of disposition and I will be content."

As Iris responded with a scornful glance, Erica complimented Margaret with a sweet smile. "I'm certain there are many such men among those who sent for us, Margaret."

When the two young women remaining did not speak promptly, Barbara tapped the knee of the one seated opposite her, a blonde with pale blue eyes and long dark eyelashes. The girl first responded with a bright blush and then spoke softly, "My name is Marlene Berger and I'm hoping to meet a man who will want to have a large family."

"You'll have to sleep with your husband often to accomplish that feat, my dear," Iris offered sarcastically as if that possibility were most repugnant to her.

Blushing even more brightly, Marlene murmured that she understood that, but clearly she was appalled as were several of the others to think Iris would be so bold as to mention the closeness of the relationship which existed between a husband and wife. Dreadfully embarrassed and afraid the other woman would tease her further, Marlene was thankful when Iris appeared to be more interested in the passing scenery than in her companions and remained silent for the moment.

Knowing she was the only one who had not yet spoken, the young woman beside Marlene leaned forward to introduce herself. "I am Johanna Wayne and I first heard of the Oregon country when the Presbyterian church was raising money to fund its missions there. Bringing the gospel to the savages is a worthy goal, don't you agree?"

Noting the Bible clutched tightly in Johanna's hands, Iris offered slyly, "We'll remember that if we're attacked, Miss Wayne. We'll send you out to sing a few hymns and perhaps the Indians will be so enthralled they'll let us pass by unmolested."

Large tears welled up in Johanna's brown eyes as she looked to the others for support. "It is unkind of you to make fun of my beliefs." Her light brown hair was as curly as Barbara's but she'd tamed it by pulling it atop her head in a firm knot before putting on her bonnet.

"Miss Stewart seems to have several views I don't share, Johanna. I'm certain your faith is your own business and you need not concern yourself with the rudeness of others," Gabrielle said sympathetically.

"Are you calling me rude?" Iris' dark eyes flashed with anger as she challenged Gabrielle to defend herself or withdraw her remark and apologize.

Gabrielle thought the dark-haired Iris a most unusual choice for Clayton Horne to have made as she seemed so different in temperament from the rest of them. Gabrielle had watched all the young women as they'd sorted through their luggage and bid their farewells, she'd had nothing else to occupy her attention. The vast majority of the prospective brides were blondes, and pretty petite ones. While a few, like Iris, had dark hair, she was the lone redhead. For as long as she could remember her aunt had tried unsuccessfully to squelch her continuous defiance and had blamed the vibrant hue of her niece's hair for her failure to do so. Gabrielle had never considered herself to be hot tempered, but being accustomed to arguments she was not in the least put off by Iris' threatening stare.

"To criticize Johanna, as you just have, was unforgivably rude, Miss Stewart, there's simply no other way to describe it."

Seething with rage, Iris looked at the others in the carriage, hoping to find an ally, but seeing the innocence of their expressions she knew she was defeated for the moment so she turned away. However, she vowed she'd pay Gabrielle back for that insult at the first opportunity.

Barbara Renwick waited only a moment to be certain Iris was not going to respond and then she attempted to turn the conversation in a more pleasant direction. "Quite frankly, since so many fine young men have left Missouri for Oregon or California, or have joined the Army to fight in the Mexican War, I despaired of ever finding a suitable mate. I thought Mr. Horne's advertisement too good an opportunity to miss. Did you all think the same thing?"

"No!" Iris replied in a vicious whisper but she refused to expand upon that comment.

"I simply wanted to go to Oregon," Gabrielle said, revealing no clue as to the motivation for her actions. She'd promised herself never to reveal the story of her lost love to another soul. She was desperately sorry she'd confided in Jason Royal when he'd proved to be so unreliable a friend, and she now meant to guard the secrets of her past more carefully.

"I happen to like adventure." Erica joined in brightly and the sparkle in her green eyes revealed her spirit with a merry flash.

Surprisingly, it was Marlene who spoke next. "I was living with my sister and her husband. They have three small children, and while I knew I was a help to them, I wanted a home and family of my own. I'm afraid that I didn't see any other way of meeting a nice man than the one Mr. Horne offered." She looked down at her hands, folding them primly in her lap as she prayed Iris would not taunt her again.

"It was my mother who encouraged me to apply," Margaret explained. "Her parents had arranged for her to marry my father and they fell in love, so she hoped I would be fortunate too. Since I had met no one else, I did not see what I had to lose in making a bargain with Mr. Horne."

When Johanna realized the others were waiting for her to respond she spoke proudly. "I knew a man who would pay for a woman to make such a long journey in order to have a wife would be responsible and I hope devout as well."

Gabrielle had been interested in each of the young women's comments and she smiled as she summarized them aloud, hoping to help herself remember their names as she did. "It seems Barbara and I both want a fine young man of good character. Since Erica longs for adventure, I'd say she wants a man who'll give her an exciting marriage. Margaret hopes for kindness in a man, Marlene for a man who loves children and Johanna for a man who shares her devotion to God. You are the only one who mentioned money, Iris, so I don't think you need worry the rest of us will want the same man you do."

Erica and Barbara flashed Gabrielle saucy smiles while the other three girls being far more reserved let their approval show in their grateful glances. Iris, however, refused to give in. "We'll just have to wait and see, won't we? I think the men with the best land near town, with the real houses built of finished planks and windows made of glass, and with furniture brought from the East will be more in demand than those with crude log cabins filled with Lord knows what, and you'll be the ones to eat your words." She'd known as soon as they'd entered the carriage that Margaret, Marlene, and Johanna would provide no competition for her. They were attractive but too quiet, rather sweet, she supposed, with their childlike views of men and marriage. They lacked the spirit she knew wealthy men admired. Barbara was attractive, but Erica and Gabrielle were true beauties and they'd undoubtedly have their pick of the men for they were witty and confident as well. She wished she'd gotten a better look at the rest of the young women, but she'd had such a terrible time convincing Jason Royal she needed all her luggage she'd had no opportunity to assess her other rivals more closely. "Do you suppose since we're riding together to Independence we'll have to share the same wagon for the next five months?"

"I for one won't be offended if you find one of the other groups more compatible, Iris," Gabrielle replied casually, hoping the obnoxious young woman would, indeed, find company she liked better elsewhere. Unfortunately Clayton Horne gave her no choice for a while. When they reached the outskirts of Independence where the wagon train was forming he assigned each group of seven which had ridden together to a separate wagon.

"The journey is a long one. You may change your wagon assignments a dozen times if you wish, but please consider your temporary placement the best possible for the time being. The drivers are unloading the carriages now so please check to be certain you have all your belongings before they return the vehicles to Kansas City. Then, no matter what has been forgotten, it will have to be left behind."

Gabrielle watched in astonishment as Iris approached the solidly built man with a coquettish step. She batted her eyelashes coyly and spoke in a seductive whisper, charming Horne completely as she told him should anyone be dissatisfied with their assignment she'd be happy to trade places in the interest of achieving harmony for the entire group.

Erica moved close to Gabrielle to whisper. "Did you hear that? How gracious of her!"

"I wondered why so difficult a woman was chosen; now I understand what her interview must have been like. If she manipulates all men as easily as she just did Mr. Horne, she should have no trouble finding a rich husband."

"Rich, Miss MacLaren?" Jason had walked up behind the two young women in time to hear only the last of Gabrielle's remark and he sneered in disgust. "I hate to disappoint you, but none of our clients can be classified in that category.

Perhaps with your inspiration, however, your husband may attain a great deal of wealth which I'm certain you'll be able to tell him how to spend."

Gabrielle wheeled around, angered that he would think her the mercenary sort when she knew she most definitely was not. "You misunderstood me, Mr. Royal, I—"

"It doesn't matter what you said, Miss MacLaren, when your intention obviously is to do the very best that you can for yourself. Now I would appreciate it if you and Miss Nelson would help the driver remove your belongings from his carriage so he can return to Kansas City; then you may gossip to your heart's content," Jason remarked impatiently, clearly having no interest in hearing any explanation Gabrielle might care to give for the comment he'd overheard. "I'll take Sunny off your hands for the night since you'll be busy packing your wagon, but beginning tomorrow morning he will be your responsibility again."

Gabrielle blushed deeply, hurt that he thought so little of her and knowing there was no way for her to explain anything to the man when he took so arrogant a tone. "Thank you, but I'll be happy to see to his care tonight if you'd rather I did."

"I said I'd do it and I will!" Jason responded crossly. "Now I really must dismiss the carriages, and unless you plan to wear that black suit all the way to Oregon City I suggest you make certain your belongings have been removed!"

Startled by the anger in his tone, Gabrielle moved back. "Yes, sir!"

With a fierce scowl, Jason turned to move on but he'd not taken ten paces before Iris overtook him. Taking his right arm and pressing her slender figure so close to his side he could scarcely walk, she smiled sweetly as she repeated the same generous offer she'd made to Clayton, to trade her place and move to another wagon should any young woman be dissatisfied with her assignment.

Gabrielle bit her lip to keep from screaming a most uncomplimentary word, but it was Erica who supplied it in a

50

low whisper.

"Bitch! Let's hope she's able to move before noon tomorrow."

"Sundown tonight would suit me better!" Gabrielle was deeply hurt that Jason had misinterpreted her remark so badly, but seeing the smile he gave Iris brought a sick feeling to her stomach and she knew it was not due to the effects of the carriage ride. He'd been so abrupt with her, curt to the point of being rude, and there he was flashing that disarming grin at Iris as though he liked her immensely. Why couldn't he see through the transparent act this self-centered young woman was performing solely for his benefit? More importantly, why should she care what Jason thought of Iris? There was no reason why his opinion should matter to her, none at all. When she noticed Erica watching her closely Gabrielle attempted to make her think she'd been observing Iris, not her handsome companion. "What do you suppose she's after?"

"Whatever favors he can arrange for her, I suppose. Maybe she's just practicing her technique since the opportunities to do so might be few on the trip. Let's just see to our luggage before Mr. Royal comes back to complain to us again. He certainly seems to take his responsibilities seriously, and I for one don't want to hear him yell at us again."

"Yes, I'm coming."

Gabrielle could carry her valise now that she'd separated the books, but it was not an easy task or one she thought she could manage five or six times a day as Jason had predicted she might have to do. She'd tied the books together in a neat stack with string she'd acquired from the hotel clerk, and now attempting to balance the two loads, she carried her things the short distance to the back of the wagon where the others were trying to decide how best to organize their possessions.

The wagon had already been loaded with provisions: bacon, flour, salt, pepper, coffee, potatoes, carrots, and apples. A heap of bedding and an assortment of pots, pans, tin plates, and other utensils filled most of the remaining inside space, while barrels of drinking water had been lashed to the sides. The sturdy Conestoga wagons were named for the town in Pennsylvania where they were manufactured. All were brand new, their white canvas tops sparkling in the sun, because no wagon ever survived the Oregon Trail in good enough condition to make a return trip.

Barbara sat down upon her suitcase and waited for someone to make a suggestion. Neither Marlene nor Margaret had any ideas, and Johanna began to thumb through her Bible searching for some relevant verse to cover their situation.

When Erica gave Gabrielle an imploring glance, she stepped forward. "If we sort our belongings so the clothing and things we'll need on the trip will be readily accessible that will help us place the articles we'll use later in the luggage we can store on the bottom."

"That makes sense," Erica agreed quickly. She bent down to open her two bags and rearrange her possessions. "Why couldn't Mr. Royal have thought of that when he had us all searching through our luggage for things to discard?"

Gabrielle turned around to be certain Jason couldn't overhear that criticism. "Men have different priorities, that's all. What's important to him is different from what would be our first consideration." Even as she spoke she couldn't understand why she'd be making excuses for the young man, but she was certain what she said was true.

Erica looked up with an impish smile. "I certainly hope there are more like him in Oregon City, but it is difficult to tell from the sketches he showed us whether or not the men are that tall and handsomely built."

Shading her eyes with her hand, Gabrielle turned to watch as Iris and Jason continued on down the line of wagons. "Yes, I suppose he is good-looking now that you mention it."

"As if you hadn't noticed!" Erica laughed out loud at that prospect but when Gabrielle simply appeared embarrassed and didn't respond she didn't persist in her teasing. "Since I have two bags and you have one, do you want to organize our things

52

together so we can use one bag to store the things we'll not need for a while?"

"Why yes, if you don't mind." Erica had almost as many pretty dresses as Gabrielle did, but in addition she'd brought along a quilt which took up a lot of space and an intricately fashioned, crocheted tablecloth. "That tablecloth is lovely, but do you think any of the men will have crystal?"

"If not yet, they soon will have, won't they?" Erica was delighted to have found so nice a friend, and while she helped Gabrielle to arrange her things the two young women teased each other playfully.

When Jason Royal walked past their wagon leading Sunny, he did no more than shake his head for he could not imagine why the young women were working so diligently to store their belongings when they'd have to unload them so frequently. Rather than stop to offer any advice, however, he decided to simply let them find out for themselves how futile their efforts were.

While Jason was a skilled scout, able to find shortcuts through even the most treacherous terrain, it was Clayton's ability to organize which made him a valuable partner to their enterprise. He had hired drivers for each of the brides' wagons. They were mature men who'd be unlikely to distract the young women from the purpose of their trip, for not one of them had been handsome even in his youth. They had been hired to tend the teams of oxen and to take turns preparing the meals so the young women didn't have to assume that tiresome responsibility until they were married. Starting with the first evening, the three men proved their worth by assuming a fatherly attitude toward their charges. The young ladies found this both charming and reassuring. Clayton hoped, with the help of the drivers, he and Jason could provide adequate supervision to secure the young women's comfort and safety. Alarmed by Jason's predictions of peril along the trail, he had introduced himself to all the families making the trip and to his delight had found one with two attractive daughters of marriageable age.

Not that he expected to lose any of the girls he'd chosen, but if he could pick up an extra bachelor or two in Oregon City he'd get the fee for providing the introductions while he'd not had the responsibility or the expense for the two young women's travel. If Joshua Taylor had decided he wanted a bride since all his friends would have one, then Clayton hoped there would be a few other men who'd be similarly inspired.

Paul Slaughter was the driver assigned to Gabrielle's wagon, a gray-bearded man with the diminutive stature and ready wit of an elf. After walking around on the pretext of speaking to his fellow drivers, he'd come to the conclusion that the prettiest girls were in his care. Knowing that voicing such an opinion aloud would create rivalry and unnecessary strife, he kept his thoughts to himself. Still, he was pleased.

While Gabrielle had been busy supervising the packing of her group's wagon, Jason had spoken with the head of each family and had made certain all the wagons were adequately prepared to begin the journey at sunrise. As always there were men who faced what lay ahead with remarkable good humor while others were so taciturn by nature he could not tell what they were thinking. And, unfortunately there were a few chronic complainers. These last he knew would not be satisfied no matter how swift or how easy their journey might be.

Now clad in his comfortable buckskins, he was far more confident that the trip would be a success than he'd been in Kansas City and he was as anxious to leave as any of his fellow travelers. He looked forward to the excitement of the trail for while he recognized its dangers he enjoyed meeting these challenges. He'd unsaddled Sunny soon after they'd arrived at the campsite but had left his bridle on, the reins tied to the rope confining the other mounts. While the stallion had not proved to be difficult, Jason planned to side-tie the horse, placing hobbles on his left legs so the stallion could be turned out to graze during the night without any risk that he would run away. Sunrise, however, saw Jason approaching with the leather thongs in his hands. Letting out a wild cry the horse reared up on his hind legs, ready to strike the young man with his hooves should Jason dare to come any closer.

Jason began to swear as he leaped out of the way; he had more than enough problems to handle without an unmanageable horse. But Gabrielle heard the commotion and came running. She was certain Jason had used a whip on Sunny and she grabbed his arm only to see he held no more than the hobbles.

"Why didn't you call me rather than attempt to do that yourself?" she asked heatedly, her outrage as plain as her stallion's.

Sunrise had yanked loose the rope by which all the horses had been tethered and had sent more than two dozen mounts scattering in all directions. He stood motionless, however, all four hooves firmly planted upon the ground, his ears laid back against his head, his nostrils flaring, and an evil gleam in his dark eyes as he dared Jason to touch him.

"It is not too late to geld that beast, you know!" Jason shoved Gabrielle's hand from his arm, as disgusted with her interference as he was with the mischief her stallion had caused, for although he considered himself to be an expert horseman he had not anticipated the trouble Sunrise would cause.

"Don't be absurd!" Gabrielle responded defiantly. Still dressed in her elegant black suit she pushed past Jason, grabbed her horse's reins, and, lifting her skirt aside, swung herself upon his back. She rode as easily bareback as most men did in the saddle, and using Sunny's speed and agility to every advantage, she began to circle the stray horses, forcing them back toward the wagons where Jason and Clayton caught them easily. By the time the last one had been recovered, both she and Sunny had regained their composure but, unhappily, Jason had not. Seeing his furious expression, Gabrielle slipped down from her stallion's back and led him to the young man's side.

"I should have warned you how greatly he distrusts

strangers, but I thought since you were with me at the stable this morning and saw how badly he behaved you would have realized that. Still, no harm has been done, you have all your horses back."

Jason's piercing gray gaze swept Gabrielle's svelte figure slowly. She'd put on quite a spectacle but seemed to be totally unaware of the stares of the curious crowd which had gathered to watch her. "Where did you learn to ride so well?"

Surprised by that question, Gabrielle hesitated a moment too long. Then she explained, knowing he'd understand who she meant. "A friend taught me; we spent a great deal of time riding together."

Sorry he'd asked since Beau was not a man with whom he could compete, Jason slapped the leather thongs against his hand as he gave her an order, his stern expression a clear warning he expected to be obeyed. "That's not an effort I want to see you repeat, Miss MacLaren, see that Sunny is side-tied so he can graze without straying; then I'll give you the hobbles for all the other mounts too. Since none is as obstreperous as your horse, you should have the job completed within minutes."

"Are you trying to punish me?" Gabrielle asked curiously. "I plan to do my share of the work, and I don't mind helping you care for the animals." Her bright blue eyes regarded him coolly, hoping for some sign he'd become more reasonable, but the muscles of his jaw were tense, his gaze dark, if anything he was growing more angry rather than calmer. When he didn't reply, she gave up her effort to placate him as hopeless and took the leather thongs from his hand. She then led Sunny toward the expanse of lush grass where the horse could spend a restful night with an abundant supply of food. She scratched his ears playfully as she removed his bridle and spoke in a low soothing tone while she attached the side tie and when she was satisfied her pet could walk comfortably if not run, she gave him a tender pat to send him out to graze.

"Did you ever see anything like that?" Clayton whispered softly to his friend. "She has a rare talent, a real gift for

56

working with horses."

Jason had been as entranced as the older man with Gabrielle's ability. He'd seen Indian braves handle their mounts with the same easy grace, but never a white man and most certainly never a white woman. "I have a feeling that is perhaps the least of her talents, Clay, but this was a disruption we didn't need and I'll not permit that stallion to cause such havoc again."

"Oh, certainly not." Clayton agreed readily, but he stayed to watch while Jason turned away. Gabrielle moved down the line of horses, talking to each as if it were an old friend, her touch gentle but firm, and while it took her more than the few minutes Jason had mentioned to accomplish the task he'd assigned her, no one could have pleased the animals more.

Noting that Jason had gone, Gabrielle returned to her wagon where she found Iris complaining because they'd have to eat their dinner either standing up or seated upon the ground. "Did you really expect a dining table and chairs to appear magically each night, Iris?" Gabrielle took the tin plate Paul handed her and thanked him warmly. He'd roasted two chickens and baked biscuits which were as light and feathery as any she'd ever tasted. She took a bite as she went to sit down beside Erica, then called to the man to show her appreciation. "This is delicious, Paul, do you have experience as a cook?"

"Sure, I've been eating my own cooking all my life!" He replied, a twinkle in his eye. "I'm glad you're enjoying the meal, but there will be plenty of times when we'll have to make do with bacon."

"Can't you men hunt along the way so we'll always have fresh meat?" Iris asked as she finally resigned herself to taking a place beside Margaret on the grass.

"I am a mighty fine hunter now that you mention it, miss, but where game is scarce skill doesn't fill the stew pot. Just enjoy each meal as it comes and let me worry about the next one."

Iris looked at her companions and whispered so Paul would

not overhear. "I know we were chosen for our beauty, but none of us will be pretty if we are no more than skin and bones by the time we arrive in Oregon City. I expected Mr. Horne to have made some better arrangement for our food than he has. We are going to become dreadfully tired of bacon and biscuits. I never even liked them in the first place!"

Marlene and Margaret continued to eat in embarrassed silence, not wishing to become involved in any conversation based on Iris' complaints. Johanna sat talking quietly with Barbara. Both ignored the striking brunette while Gabrielle and Erica exchanged knowing glances and simply enjoyed their dinner without bothering to respond to Iris' comments. They had decided that afternoon just to ignore her and hope she would soon move to another wagon, but after they had finished eating and all twenty-one young women moved about and got acquainted, it soon became apparent that Iris alienated everyone with whom she spoke. She monopolized each conversation, criticizing anyone who dared to disagree with her opinions, and she soon found herself standing alone while the others chatted happily, filled with excitement at the adventure they'd undertaken. She knew how to captivate men but she did not use that same charm on women. By the time the cooking fires were all extinguished and the girls were getting ready to go to sleep, Iris had not found anyone she liked, nor had she realized that no one had liked her either.

The bedding was soft, and by trying different positions the young women who shared Gabrielle's wagon soon found they could sleep comfortably. However, they were still too excited to close their eyes. As always, Barbara was in a talkative mood. She described her best friend's reaction to her announcement that she was going to answer Mr. Horne's advertisement.

"She was shocked, absolutely horrified, but for men to seek brides through newspaper advertisements is nothing new and I didn't see it as a scandal. Besides, I didn't want to stay at home and wait years for a man to find me when Oregon seems to be filled with men who want a nice wife. I don't think what we're doing is wrong; it's merely sensible. That's the way I look at it, and thank goodness, so did my mother."

Erica moaned softly. "You should have heard my parents, but I convinced them this is what I want to do, and since I have two older brothers with children who live near them I don't think they'll be too lonely without me. What did your folks say about this, Gabrielle?"

"My parents died when I was a baby. An aunt raised me and she's gone now too. There was no one I needed to ask, but even if there had been, I would have come whether or not I'd received permission."

"I hope you marry a man who does not expect obedience then," Iris offered sarcastically. She'd not shared her thoughts with her wagonmates, merely her usual flippant criticisms.

"I shall make a point of asking each of the bachelors what he thinks on that subject, Iris. Thank you for the wonderful suggestion," Gabrielle replied sweetly but she could not stop her giggle as Erica poked her in the ribs.

"That's a good idea. We should think of some questions to ask so we can get to know the men quickly. Then we won't waste time on those whose views don't suit us," Barbara stated enthusiastically.

"Just ask to see their homes, Barbara; they will tell the whole story," Iris recommended, as if she'd given the matter a great deal of thought. "You'll be able to see exactly how the men live and what sort of life each can offer you."

"Will Mr. Horne permit that?" Marlene whispered. "Will he allow us to visit the men's homes without a chaperon?"

"Certainly not!" Johanna protested sharply. "I'd never go out to a man's farm, why who knows what he might try to do!"

"I will explain it to you if your mother didn't, Johanna," Iris remarked impatiently, thinking her companions impossibly innocent. "I'll even draw pictures if you need them."

Before Johanna could summon the courage to respond, Erica spoke up, "I'm certain none of us needs your lessons, Iris, but speaking of drawings, let's ask to see the sketches of

59

the men again. I didn't really get a chance to study them very closely and I'd like to. We could at least learn each man's name and that would be sure to impress them favorably. Why don't you ask Mr. Royal tomorrow if we can have the sketches, Gabrielle?"

"You want me to be the one to ask him? Why don't you just ask him yourself?" The question had caught Gabrielle off guard and her confusion was apparent in her voice. She didn't want anyone to think she knew Jason Royal better than they did, but clearly Erica suspected something more had happened between them than what she'd observed.

"Oh, no reason." Erica stifled her laugh with her hand, but now the others were curious and waited quietly for Gabrielle to respond.

When the silence became so thick it was nearly suffocating, Gabrielle forced herself to reply nonchalantly. "I don't mind asking him, but I'll wait until he's in a reasonable mood since I've found him to be a bit quick tempered."

"Then I'll ask him," Iris offered brightly, eager for an excuse to talk to the attractive young man. "I think he is the nicest of men, so considerate and polite, not in the least bit moody. He'll not refuse me."

"That settles it then; you ask him, Iris. Now let's go to sleep. Dawn will come unbearably early if we don't." Gabrielle changed the subject quickly, glad the matter of asking Jason for the sketches had been taken off her hands, since he'd apparently taken the same dislike to her that he'd taken to her stallion.

"Surely they don't expect us to rise with the sun!" Iris shrieked in disbelief.

"Good night, Iris," Gabrielle replied in so emphatic a tone the young woman did not speak again, but though they all lay silent, none fell asleep quickly.

Gabrielle wondered why Erica had wanted to tease her about Jason. Perhaps because he'd been so rude to her that afternoon, to say nothing of the incident with Sunny, but she

60

didn't want her new friend to think she was attracted to the man for then she'd just tease her all the more. In truth, she didn't even like Jason Royal now that she knew him better. He was bright and he could be sympathetic and sweet when it suited his purpose, but she'd soon discovered how selfish that purpose had been. She blushed deeply at the memory of his kiss and was thankful the others could not see the color in her cheeks. Well, why shouldn't the man know how to kiss? By the looks of him and the ready way he had responded to Iris' flattery, it was apparent he'd had plenty of practice with women. She vowed he'd never have another opportunity to come close enough to kiss her. She didn't understand why he seemed to delight in tormenting her, but she'd not allow him to upset her again. She would simply follow the directions he gave to all the others and do her best to see that Sunny caused no further trouble, for she didn't want the horse to suffer from the heat of his anger either. Perhaps he was as spoiled as Iris, used to having his own way, but that was really no concern of hers since she knew she should think of herself as engaged even if she didn't know which man she'd marry.

She considered it a stroke of good fortune that another bachelor had joined the group they were going to meet, and unaccustomed to such unexpected good luck, Gabrielle included the man in her prayers. She'd have to ask his name, and perhaps Jason could do a sketch of him from memory to include with the other men's portraits. She wanted to be able to thank him and tell him how much his desire to have a wife had meant to her, for without his generosity she'd have been unable to make the trip to Oregon. With gratitude for the appearance of that additional man filling her thoughts, she finally fell asleep, too tired by the day's excitement to dream. She was on her way to Oregon at last, to live the life she'd planned with Beau, even if he would not be there to share it.

Chapter IV

Gabrielle was one of the first to awaken the next morning. She washed hurriedly and brushed out her long hair but left it flowing free as she had the previous day. It was as shiny and straight as an Indian woman's, and had defied all her aunt's efforts to make it curl prettily as the older woman had insisted a young lady's hair should. Its lustrous red color was beauty enough in Gabrielle's opinion, and she had never concerned herself with the matter of curls since she had not been given them naturally. She put on the soft muslin dress she'd laid out before she'd gone to sleep; then as soon as she had buttoned up her shoes, she left the others and ran down the line of wagons toward the horses. She meant to take care of Sunny herself, before he could create any more mischief which would land them both in serious trouble.

Jason and Clayton Horne shared a tent rather than occupying a wagon, and being an early riser by necessity, the young man had placed a small mirror in the notch of a tree so he could see to shave himself in the dim light of dawn. He usually chose the far easier custom of growing a beard while on the trail, but with so many young ladies to escort he wanted to look his best in hopes his appearance would aid his cause. He wanted to appear the most proper of gentlemen so he would continue to have their respect and, more importantly, their obedience. Respectability was not usually so important a virtue in his estimation, but he knew in this case it should be and was acting accordingly. When he saw a blur of blue rush by he turned, startled to see Gabrielle up and about so early.

"Miss MacLaren!" he called loudly to catch her attention as he laid his razor aside.

Gabrielle had been afraid he'd see her, and feeling as though she'd been caught plotting some evil deed, she came to a halt and turned slowly. Her wide innocent gaze provided no hint of her apprehension, however.

"Yes, Mr. Royal?" she responded sweetly, not daring to hope he would be in a more pleasant mood than when she'd last seen him.

He was clad only in his buckskin britches and moccasins which had leggings attached so they fit like a pair of boots. His bare shoulders and back were deeply tanned as if he seldom wore a shirt outdoors, while his broad chest was covered with a tangle of dark curls which tapered to a thin line as they grew down his flat stomach to disappear beneath his belt. He provided a most appealing sight, muscular yet lean, his unusual height and classical proportions making him as attractive an example of the perfection of the male form as had ever been born. When he made no move to don a shirt Gabrielle tried to focus her attention upon his face, but his bare torso was difficult to ignore and she wondered if he weren't well aware of the effect his striking good looks had upon a young woman. That thought infuriated her so greatly she clenched her fists at her sides and hoped he'd finish whatever he had to say promptly.

Jason wiped the last trace of soap from his face with a hand towel as he walked toward Gabrielle. That he was so handsome a man was something he'd realized with delighted surprise when he'd reached his late teens. Like his height and strength, his more than pleasant good looks had evolved quite naturally as he'd grown to adulthood. Now he was used to them and no longer gave his appearance much thought. Since he meant to say no more than a few words to the auburn-haired beauty, it had not occurred to him to dress fully before he did so. The Oregon Trail was such a long one he knew they would see each other too often to worry over such details as completeness of attire before they spoke. In her pastel blue dress Gabrielle looked as fresh and sweet as the spring morning, and he hoped her manner would be as agreeable as the day promised to be.

"If you can offer some help to your wagonmates so they can manage a horse without mishap, I will be grateful as I have no time to give riding lessons."

Gabrielle relaxed immediately when she realized Jason wished to discuss the other young women's comfort rather than criticize her. "Yes, I'm sure everyone understands you have other duties. We had no opportunity last night to discuss our travel arrangements, but I will give whatever help is necessary to see we are not a burden to you." She was sincere in her promise, for the last thing she wanted was to have her new friends singled out as being unable to take care of themselves. "I will encourage everyone to ride for as long as they wish today, but I don't want anyone to overdo and suffer for it tomorrow."

Jason combed back his dark curls with his fingertips as he gave the matter further consideration. He knew a novice rider could suffer considerable pain as a result of such unaccustomed exercise.

"Yours is the only sidesaddle, will that present a problem?"

"No, for I seldom use it. I prefer to ride Sunny bareback since that's so much more comfortable for the both of us." Now that they were talking so easily Gabrielle began to smile, her earlier fears of a confrontation forgotten. That he was so scantily dressed no longer caused her concern because his manner and appearance blended into such a pleasing personality for a change.

Jason was aware that their conversation was progressing smoothly, but now he had to give an order he wanted obeyed. "I can't allow you to ride without a saddle, Gabrielle. The

65

terrain we'll cross is too difficult. If Sunny stumbled you'd topple over his head, and I can't risk the possibility that you might be seriously injured."

While she thought his command unreasonable since he had complimented her ability to ride, Gabrielle was so surprised by his use of her first name that she did not respond immediately. She could not help but smile, for he seemed unaware that he'd addressed her in so informal a manner. Trying to be just as agreeable she attempted to see his point. If she were going to teach the others to ride, she ought to set the best example possible no matter what her personal preference might be. She supposed his concern for her safety was only natural since he was responsible for them all on the journey, and so she put aside the thought he might have some reason to pay particular attention to her well-being.

"I have no desire to suffer any injuries either, Mr. Royal, and since you know the trail so well, I will have to accept your judgment of what is best. Do you have enough saddles for all of us?"

Enormously relieved that she'd not responded with a fit of temper or begun to argue, Jason broke into a ready grin. "Yes, and one is sure to suit you. It will be easier if the ladies use the same mounts and saddles each day. Paul can see to the horses before he hitches up the oxen."

Taking her added responsibility seriously, Gabrielle responded with sudden enthusiasm, "I think I'll teach those who don't know how to saddle a horse how to do so since that knowledge might come in handy too. I don't want Paul to be overburdened with work when we can do some of it ourselves."

Impressed by her ambition, Jason paid her a sincere compliment. "You are a remarkably independent young woman, Miss MacLaren. I suppose you all are or you would not be embarking on such a perilous journey, and it is my hope you will find one of the men awaiting your arrival worth your efforts." Yet he could still not imagine Gabrielle liking any of his acquaintances well enough to marry him.

"Now that you mention it, I was hoping you could make a sketch of the latest bachelor to go with the others. I am especially grateful for his interest in us, even if it is a bit late, and I'd like to be able to recognize him so I can thank him when first we meet. What is his name?"

"Joshua Taylor, but I'm afraid I won't be able to provide a drawing as I'm not certain we've ever met. At least if we have, I don't recall his face well enough to draw him for you."

Gabrielle tried not to let her disappointment show as she replied, "Well, I shall just have to recall his name and when Joshua Taylor is introduced to me, I'll thank him then."

Jason could think of no other reason to detain the attractive Miss MacLaren; yet he did not want to let her go when she was smiling so prettily. She was a very charming creature and he racked his brain for something else to discuss. He could hear everyone beginning to stir, the aroma of simmering bacon and freshly brewed coffee filled the air, and he reminded himself he could not afford to dally with her any longer.

"If you want to take Sunny back to your wagon now you may, I'll see Paul brings a saddle when he brings the other horses for your group."

"Thank you," Gabrielle called over her shoulder as she began to walk away.

When Jason Royal behaved in a reasonable manner, she thought him very likable, and she hoped he would continue to be as polite once their trip began. As she led Sunny back to her wagon, she found it difficult to suppress a smile and told herself she was being very foolish to daydream about him when she'd already agreed to marry a man waiting in Oregon. For all she knew, Jason Royal had a wife anxiously awaiting his return to Oregon City, but that sudden thought, no matter how unlikely, filled her with dread. "Don't be such a silly fool!" She cautioned herself, and reaching her wagon she turned her thoughts to the task of making ready to depart. Jason Royal was handsome and bright, but while his company was usually enjoyable, she'd no time to give him any further thought that morning.

While Erica had not ridden on horseback since she'd been a small child, she nevertheless felt confident to do so. Barbara's enthusiasm for the trip led her to agree readily and she soon talked Johanna into giving the matter a try. Margaret and Marlene, however, were terrified by the prospect while Iris thought the idea ridiculous.

"Of course I know how to ride, I use a sidesaddle, but I've no intention of riding the entire way. I'll sit beside Paul, and since Margaret and Marlene don't want to ride either, they can sit in the back of the wagon."

Gabrielle tapped her foot impatiently. "I didn't say you had to make the whole journey seated upon a horse, Iris, but since you do know how to ride I think you should consider giving it a try since it will relieve the monotony of the trip."

Paul stood aside waiting for the young women to make up their minds. It had not taken him long to realize Iris was never satisfied with anything. Consequently, he had no desire to have her ride beside him. "Ladies, if I may be permitted to interrupt, it is time to leave. Those of you who can ride should do so while I'll take the two who don't know how with me."

As if on signal, Jason's call of "Turn out!" echoed down the line of wagons. The emigrants had had more than enough time to make ready, and when Jason gave the call to set off, the clear ring of authority in his voice let everyone know he expected all the wagons to roll immediately. Knowing he was being paid to drive the team of oxen which stood waiting placidly in their harness, Paul handed the reins of the mounts he'd brought to Gabrielle, then sprang up to the high seat.

"Well, ladies, let's go!" he shouted.

Erica came forward to mount a lively black mare while Barbara and Johanna chose far more gentle horses. That left Iris no choice but to take the bay gelding who'd been saddled with the sidesaddle. She was livid all the same. Marlene and Margaret scrambled up onto the seat beside Paul and considered themselves lucky to have escaped riding for the morning at least. When Gabrielle saw that the others were as ready as they'd ever be, she put her foot in the stirrup and swung herself up onto Sunny's back. The light of dawn barely lit the sky, but as Jason rode by at a furious gallop he gave her a jaunty salute and she blushed to think she'd finally done something to please him.

Erica watched the young man fly by and shook her head as she yawned sleepily. "He certainly seems to have a lot of energy in the mornings, doesn't he?"

Pretending slight interest, Gabrielle replied nonchalantly. "He'd have to have considerable stamina to take on the job of leading this wagon train and to think he's done it more than once is astonishing."

Jason must spend little time in Oregon City, she realized, what with traveling all spring and into the summer then leaving again the next spring to make his way to Independence to begin the route all over again. It was exhausting just to consider how he'd chosen to spend his life, and she began to dream of the men who were awaiting their arrival. They were all farmers, men tied to the land. She knew she'd like that stability. She wanted a husband who'd be content to remain in one place to live his life and share hers.

"What are you thinking, Gabrielle? You have the most satisfied expression and I'm curious as to why." Erica had brought her mare up alongside Sunny so they could chat as they rode, leaving Barbara, Johanna, and Iris to trail behind.

Laughing, Gabrielle explained. "I was thinking how pleasant it will be to be married to a farmer who wishes to travel no farther than into town to buy provisions or to attend church."

"We have been traveling for no more than five minutes, Gabrielle, and I thought you loved to ride. Are you bored already?" Erica teased her friend playfully.

"I do love to ride." Gabrielle gave Sunny a fond pat on the neck as she spoke. "I like to race, or to explore. Just following this trail is not nearly as exciting as going riding usually is for me, but that doesn't mean that I'm bored."

But as the sun rose and the day grew warm, Gabrielle heard an increasing number of complaints from her companions. She refused to listen, however, until they stopped for the midday meal.

The rest at noon was scheduled from eleven until two each day, and even that first day it was a welcome relief from the tedium of the morning's ride. Hot and tired, those gathered in the shade of their wagons half-dozed while their animals grazed on the lush grass nearby. They would follow the Santa Fe Trail for the first forty miles then proceed north when it turned toward the south. The path was well worn, proving to be no challenge to either man or beast as yet, but Iris had had more than enough exercise.

"I'll not ride again this afternoon, I simply won't. I'll sit beside Paul while Margaret and Marlene ride." Iris feared her delicate skin would burn even though she'd worn a bonnet and she didn't dare risk another hour in the sun.

Margaret and Marlene looked beseechingly at Gabrielle, hoping she would help them, but before she could enter the discussion Jason appeared astride his powerfully built stallion. The horse was a buckskin, his light tan color accented by a jet black mane and tail. Lively and quick, the animal was ready to continue the journey and tossed his head impatiently as Jason drew him to a halt beside the wagon. Seizing what she considered to be too good an opportunity to miss, Iris went to him immediately, placing her hands upon his knee as she spoke in an openly flirtatious manner.

"Mr. Royal, don't you think we should take turns riding? It simply isn't fair that some of us have to ride the whole way while others spend their time seated in the wagon."

Jason glanced toward Gabrielle as if he expected some sort of an explanation for Iris' complaint so she stepped forward to offer her own interpretation of the problem. "I think we can work this out for ourselves without bothering Mr. Royal, Iris. No one insists you spend the entire day on horseback so you needn't complain to him." Gabrielle was embarrassed to have

70

Jason bothered with so trivial a matter, especially one she was certain they could work out amongst themselves.

Jason frowned, uncertain what the problem was, but he agreed with Gabrielle quickly. "That's right, just take turns."

Her eyes bright with triumph, Iris turned toward Margaret and Marlene, "See, he said we have to take turns."

"Iris!" Gabrielle had no patience with this selfish young woman who seemed determined to get her own way and who would go to any lengths to do so no matter how childish. That she had both the experience and ability to ride while the two other young women didn't obviously made no difference to her.

Delighted that Jason had backed up her demand, Iris ignored Gabrielle's rebuke and looked up at the young man as she moved to her next point. "The others asked me to speak to you about the sketches. May we please see them again? I thought we should learn the men's names so we may greet them properly."

Since he and Gabrielle had been discussing the sketches that very morning, Jason wondered why she hadn't asked for them then. Apparently, she had only been interested in learning about Joshua, rather than thinking about impressing the rest of the men. Well, the fact that she had some interest in a man no matter how slight offered encouragement to him. Surrounded by the seven young women and with Iris clinging to his leg, he saw only the sunlight striking Gabrielle's beautiful auburn hair and for a moment he forgot what question he'd been asked since she'd not been the one to ask it.

"Clayton has the sketches. You'll have to ask him to lend them to you, but since the other young women will probably have the same idea sooner or later you'll have to return them to him." As he brushed Iris' hands aside, he decided to make their travel arrangements clear since they'd obviously not understood them. "You may all ride or you may all travel in your wagons or any combination of that plan, but if you have any more complaints, address them to Mr. Horne as he is responsible for you, not I." With that command he went to give the order to resume the march, for he wanted to waste no time getting started when they had to make every minute of daylight count.

"It was my idea to learn the men's names, Iris, not yours," Erica pointed out promptly, clearly livid at the lie the woman had told.

Iris shrugged. She was certain she'd impressed Jason Royal favorably and cared little whose ideas she'd claimed as her own. "What difference does it make? We can have the sketches, that's all that matters. I'll get them from Mr. Horne before dinner." With an agile leap, she climbed up onto the seat of the wagon and waited for Paul to join her. "Well, let's go."

Gabrielle looked at Margaret who was near tears and made her decision quickly. "Why don't you ride next to Iris? I'll help Marlene learn to ride this afternoon." She gave Marlene no time to argue but brought the bay gelding up beside her and helped her up into the sidesaddle. "He's a nice horse, it will be like sitting in a rocking chair, you'll see."

Marlene was still apprehensive, but she whispered, "Don't worry, I'll learn rapidly if only to spite Iris!"

"That's the spirit!" Gabrielle responded with a delighted grin, and Marlene began to giggle. She held on to the reins tightly, obviously still frightened, but she rode between Erica and Gabrielle that afternoon, and by the time they stopped for dinner she had lost all fear of riding for they had kept her so amused with their conversation she'd had no time to be afraid.

Keeping her promise, Iris pranced off while Paul was preparing their supper and returned with the sketches in hand. She laid them out upon the grass but made no attempt to organize them in any fashion as Gabrielle had. "Their names are on the back, Thomas and William, this one is Peter, John." She continued to recite the names as the young women gathered around to study the drawings.

"This man looks rather nice." Erica picked up a sketch and

turned it over to read the name. "Lewis Bradley, he seems like a very likable sort, doesn't he?"

Taking the sketch Gabrielle had to agree. "Why yes, he does. Do you suppose he has an adventuresome spirit too?"

"He must or he'd not want to find a bride in so reckless a fashion as he has," Erica pointed out with logic she thought too obvious to dispute.

"Do you think we're being reckless?" Margaret asked timidly, stricken by such a terrible thought.

"Oh, Margaret, I'm only teasing. Now tell us which man you like," Erica suggested, hoping to distract her from her worries.

By the time Paul called them for supper, each young woman had had an opportunity to select a favorite except Gabrielle who declined to choose one saying she wanted to meet the men first. "Frequently nice-looking men are too conceited. I shouldn't want to pick such a man, dream about him for several months, and then find I disliked him immensely the moment we met. No thank you, I want to learn each man's name, but I'll not choose one now to love."

"That's very sensible of you," Iris agreed. "We need to know so much more than what can be seen in a man's features."

"Like his bank balance, you mean?" Gabrielle responded quickly, sorry to have Iris compliment her on anything, but truly she could not look at the sketches and think of any of the men as a possible husband. After Beau had died she'd not thought she'd ever marry, but when she'd seen the advertisement offering an opportunity to go to Oregon she'd seized the chance. Now, looking at the drawings she felt ashamed of herself. She realized one of the men would be the husband she knew she'd never love. There was still Joshua, of course, but no matter what his appearance might be she knew she would be unable to love him either. That thought was so depressing she said little during dinner. She was glad when everyone was too tired to talk that night and soon fell asleep.

The journey continued to be easy. Taking Marlene's

example, Margaret summoned the courage to ride, although she shook with fright the whole time. She'd lived near town, and her family's one horse had been hitched to a buggy whenever there was someplace to go. She thought the sidesaddle too precarious a perch, while riding astride as men did seemed far too unladylike. She much preferred riding in the wagon, but after a few days she grew resigned to her fate and did not complain for she did not want the others to tease her about her fears or to dislike her for being afraid when they were not.

When Gabrielle found Paul yawning sleepily one morning she wondered if he had slept poorly and inquired as to his health, hoping the journey was not proving to be too great a strain on the man for she found his good humor very appealing.

"Oh, I am fit enough, miss. It is just that having a shift at guard duty makes me a bit weary." With another loud yawn, he went back to preparing breakfast.

"Why must you serve as a guard? Don't you already have more than enough to do without that extra duty as well?" Gabrielle thought it most unfair that Paul would have to assume responsibility for the camp at night when he kept such a close eye upon them all day.

"All the men who own animals take their turns, miss, it is as simple as that. Now I know the oxen and the horses you ladies ride are not truly mine, but they are my responsibility just the same."

"Who sets up the schedule, Paul?"

"Mr. Royal, but don't go telling him I'm falling asleep as I don't want him to come checking on me while I'm on guard or any other time either."

Curious, Gabrielle pursued the questioning. "What would he do if he found you asleep when you were supposed to be guarding the camp?"

Paul gave her a skeptical glance, not really believing she wanted to discuss the subject until he saw her concern was genuine. "No one is whipped, miss, nothing so dire as that, but a man who falls asleep has to walk the next day. I mean all day, and if he has a horse he usually rides, he has to just lead him. That is not an ordeal any man makes the mistake of suffering twice I'll tell you."

"Thank you, Paul. I'll keep that information to myself and you needn't worry about my mentioning your name to Mr. Royal, except to pay you a compliment." Taking her breakfast, she sat with the others and ate, but the more she thought about Paul having to stand guard duty the more irate she became. Finally when she could bear it no more she went to find Jason to ask if she might not take their driver's place.

"You want to do what?" Jason asked in astonishment. He'd been saddling his horse when she'd approached and knew he had little time before giving the order to move out.

"I said since I have my own horse, I think it is only fair that I take a turn watching the camp at night. Isn't that the rule, that those owning animals must take turns standing guard to see they're not stolen?"

"Yes," Jason admitted hesitantly. "But each household has a man in charge, and in the case of you ladies, it's your driver. I'll not ask women to take turns at such a task."

"Why not? I'll bet I can shoot a rifle as well as Paul can. He has more than enough to do taking care of us; I'll be happy to take his place when he is scheduled to stand guard." Gabrielle thought her plan very sensible, but she could tell from Jason's dark gaze that he did not.

"Miss MacLaren, I will not ask women to stand guard duty. That issue is not open to further discussion. Now if you will excuse me, I must be on my way." Jason finished tightening the cinch which held the saddle firmly in place upon his horse's back, then he lowered the stirrup and untied his mount's reins. "You'd better hurry too, it's time we got the wagons rolling." He'd not spoken to Gabrielle in several days, but there was no time to carry on a polite conversation now, much to his regret.

"Do you just naturally assume that all women are incompetent, Mr. Royal?" Gabrielle didn't like the way he'd treated her when she thought her offer was both generous and practical.

Seeking a quick end to what he considered a needless as well as an unexpected argument, Jason simply handed Gabrielle his rifle and pointed to a tree in the distance. "I won't make the mistake of asking who taught you to shoot since I have a good idea it wasn't your aunt. Let me see if you can hit that tree."

"Where would you like me to aim, at the top or the large branch to the left?"

"Whichever you choose, Miss MacLaren." Jason folded his arms across his chest and waited while Gabrielle brought the rifle to her shoulder.

"The branch is a better target." Gabrielle lined up the tree in the sight and carefully squeezed the trigger sending the branch crashing to the earth while the loud report of the rifle still hung in the morning air. "Are you satisfied now, Mr. Royal?" Gabrielle considered herself very lucky indeed for she'd not used his rifle before and had had no idea how true its aim might be. Each weapon was different. She simply knew she'd been lucky to hit the branch with her first shot, but she planned to press that advantage for all it was worth. The fact that her right shoulder was now aching painfully from the recoil of the weapon was something she'd just have to ignore.

Jason continued to stare at the shorn limb, his easy solution to Gabrielle's outrageous offer to stand guard surprisingly ineffective. "Nice shot," he mumbled while he tried to think of something more profound to say.

"Does that mean I can take Paul's turn?" Gabrielle asked hopefully.

"No, it does not, but I'll remember how well you can shoot should the need arise." Jason took back his rifle, leaped upon his buckskin stallion, and was gone in an instant, leaving Gabrielle choking in a cloud of dust.

"Damn you!" Gabrielle swore loudly even though she knew

Jason would not be able to hear her curse.

Clayton Horne had observed the scene she'd just played with Jason, and he came forward swiftly to offer some advice. "Miss MacLaren, I must caution you not to question Mr. Royal's authority. The emigrants in countless wagon trains have needlessly suffered through extremely difficult crossings because they lacked a strong leader. Men get overtired, fall into petty arguments, and when the leadership constantly changes, falling upon successively less capable shoulders, increasingly poor decisions result. Then the factions split up the train into several smaller ones, each with their own leader who thinks he knows what is best. Unfortunately, the result is always the same, disastrous and all too often tragic as well."

Gabrielle tried to hold her temper but failed, since she felt Clayton's lecture was completely beside the point. "I am not trying to cause unnecessary strife, nor to question Mr. Royal's authority. I merely attempted to volunteer to take Paul Slaughter's guard duty and he refused to listen to me."

"As well he should for your idea is absurd!" Clayton responded with a booming laugh, dismissing her request with a sweep of his hand.

Her cheeks burning with the anger she could no longer control, Gabrielle sprinted away for had she remained for another second she would have slapped the grin from Clayton's face and she knew that would have caused her no end of trouble. She took several deep breaths as she neared her wagon, and finding Erica ready to mount the spritely mare she preferred to ride, she leaped upon Sunny's back, dug her heels into his sides, and called to her friend to hurry. They often rode ahead of their wagon to escape the dust even though Paul usually managed to join the beginning of the wagon train where the trail was the cleanest. By the time Erica caught up with her, Gabrielle had already decided she'd keep her confrontations with Jason and Mr. Horne to herself, but Erica could readily see something was wrong and tried to ascertain what it might be.

77

"Where did you go this morning?" The green-eyed beauty asked with a careless toss of her honey-blond curls.

"Nowhere, at least it turned out to be nowhere," Gabrielle replied tersely.

Erica had already learned that while Gabrielle was the most patient of teachers, never tiring until she'd helped Marlene and Margaret, as well as several of the girls from the other two wagons, to become both confident and proficient riders, she was nonetheless maddeningly stubborn when it came to her own privacy. That she seemed to be filled with tantalizing secrets perplexed Erica all the more.

"Forget that I asked then," she replied flippantly. "I know you'll tell only what you wish to reveal and nothing more."

Startled by Erica's insight, Gabrielle drew back on Sunny's reins to pull him to a halt. "What does that remark mean?"

"I meant only that you are a very private person, that's all. It is not an insult and I did not mean you to take it as such." The last thing Erica wanted was to start a fight with Gabrielle since she liked her so much, but the young woman's refusal to confide in her frustrated her greatly.

Gabrielle nodded slightly, then turned Sunny back toward the trail. "I simply don't think my life is all that interesting a topic to discuss. I didn't mean to offend you."

With a bright smile, Erica accepted that apology. "We are friends then, aren't we?"

"Of course," Gabrielle replied promptly, the question seeming a silly one to her for she did not think a friendship already established could be so easily destroyed.

"Good. Now tell me who gave you your first kiss," Erica asked with a saucy grin.

Rather than be angry, Gabrielle replied with a jest of her own. "What makes you think any man has ever kissed me?" She'd never speak Beau's name, but she tried to recall just when he had kissed her for the first time. It had been years ago, at Christmas time. He'd brought her a bright green ribbon for her hair and she'd been so pleased she'd kissed his cheek. He had quickly responded by kissing her upon the lips. Her aunt had come into the parlor then and had been very stern with them, sending Beau away and appearing to be as shocked as if she'd caught them making love upon her velvet love seat. Beau had winked as he'd run from the room, and she had thought him very brave for daring to be so bold in front of her aunt.

"Oh, I'm certain you've been kissed, and probably by more than one man too, but if you'll not admit it, I'll tell you about my first love. His name was Leonard."

"Leonard?" Gabrielle began to laugh for that name seemed so unlikely for any man Erica would love. "Yes, please do tell me about him for he sounds like a most romantic soul!" Marlene joined them then and Barbara too, and laughing happily, they all rode along, the hours and miles passing swiftly as they recalled young men they'd known, parties they'd attended, and stolen kisses they remembered fondly. Gabrielle enjoyed her new friends' tales, but none save Erica noticed that she alone revealed nothing of her past.

That same good humor carried the young women through days when Jason's prediction proved correct and they did indeed have to unload their wagon five or six times when the countless streams which crossed the prairie threatened to keep its wheels permanently lodged in the slimy mud of the stream bed. The sun always rose too early after such days as those, but after the less strenuous ones Gabrielle was often a restless sleeper, waking frequently and unable to find a comfortable pose no matter how many she tried. On one such night as she lay staring up into the darkness, she heard the plaintive strains of a far off melody. Sitting up she tried to identify its source. Someone was playing a harmonica, a slow mournful tune which brought tears to her eyes as she listened. Her curiosity would not allow her to rest until she had found the musician so she slipped quietly out of the wagon and with a stealthy step moved toward the hauntingly beautiful music.

Jason laid the harmonica aside as he reached for his rifle, he felt rather than heard someone approaching but he wanted to take no chances. He was seated just outside the circle of light thrown by the flickering fire so his silhouette would not provide a target for some brave's arrow. Every muscle of his powerful body grew tense as he waited in the darkness for the unseen enemy to appear so he could blast him to kingdom come.

"Please don't stop. I didn't mean to disturb you; I simply wanted to listen to the music," Gabrielle called out softly.

"Gabrielle?" Dropping the rifle, Jason got to his feet, moved swiftly to her side, then led her around the edge of the fire into the shadows where he'd been seated. He pulled her down beside him as he gave her a stern warning. "I'm sorry if I disturbed your rest, but you mustn't wander around the camp in the darkness. A less experienced guard would have shot first and then gone to see who you were."

Gabrielle sighed sadly as she looked away. "I meant only to compliment a musician, not to disappoint you again." She could not even recall how many days it had been since she'd spoken to the man about taking a turn at standing guard. She saw him frequently for his responsibilities took him along the line of wagons several times each day, but he had not given her so much as a wave or nod, nor had she expected such attention.

"Disappoint me? That's an unusual way to describe a near catastrophe! Damn it, I could have killed you just now!" Jason was nearly shaking with rage, for his rebuke seemed to have made no impression upon the lively redhead.

"Well, you didn't, so you needn't be so angry with me." Gabrielle leaned forward, hugging her knees as she smoothed the folds of her soft linen nightgown into place.

Jason opened his mouth to argue, then thought better of it since he knew he'd only be wasting his breath. "No, thank God, I did not, but you must promise me you'll not leave your wagon again at night no matter what you hear. It could be an entire symphony orchestra playing dance melodies—I don't care what it is—I want you to remain in your bed!"

Gabrielle stared into the glowing embers of the fire and tried to imagine how such festive music would sound as it came drifting through the stillness of the prairie air. "I love to dance, do you?" she inquired softly.

"Of course," Jason responded without needing time to think, for he would use any excuse to hold a beautiful woman in his arms. He realized her question was completely irrelevant to their discussion, but suddenly he didn't care. She was so very lovely he did not want to remain angry with her. "Unfortunately, I can't play the harmonica and dance at the same time."

Pleased that his mood seemed to have improved dramatically, Gabrielle asked a question. "Does the piece you were playing have a name? It was so terribly sad and yet beautiful at the same time." She'd been astonished to find Jason was the musician, but truly the man's talents seemed to be limitless from what little she'd learned about him.

"No, I was just making it up as I went along. It wasn't anything special."

"Oh, but it was!" Gabrielle protested instantly. "The tune was simply perfection, just like your sketches."

"If it could have lured you to your death, Gabrielle, it wasn't worth playing," Jason responded sadly. A wolf howled in the distance as if underscoring his words, but truly she had given him a bad fright. That he might have shot such a lovely creature in so senseless an accident appalled him.

"None of us knows when fate will overtake us, Mr. Royal, but since you are so cautious a sentry I doubt you would have fired a shot at anyone you couldn't see. I think I was quite safe despite your remarks to the contrary."

"Safe?" Jason pronounced the word skeptically, his mind suddenly painting a far different picture indeed. He had just begun his turn at watch and would not be relieved before dawn. The wagons were neatly arranged in a circle, the livestock grazing contentedly in the center. The travelers were all asleep, and while there was more than one guard, they did not communicate with each other so he and Gabrielle were quite alone. Perhaps the true danger was one she had yet to recognize. "Please call me Jason." He whispered hoarsely but before she could respond he pulled her into his arms, lowering her gently onto the grass which covered the plain with a soft blanket of green. He found her mouth slightly open as she took a breath to protest the strength of his embrace, but he gave her no time to speak as his tongue slipped between her soft pink lips in a kiss he hoped would finally subdue her defiant spirit.

Gabrielle pressed her palms against his chest, but her attempts to shove Jason away proved futile. He was a strong and agile young man, and she realized instantly how foolish she'd been to assume she was safe seated by his side. Perhaps he meant only to teach her a lesson, she thought suddenly; and knowing two could play that game she ceased to struggle and instead slipped her arms around his neck, her fingertips moving through his thick dark curls as she returned his kiss with an ardor she hoped would shock him to his senses.

Far from having the desired effect, however, Jason greeted Gabrielle's unexpected surrender with a grateful shudder that made his passion all the more intense. Her nightgown seemed to be fashioned of endless yards of fabric, but he at last found the hem and slipped his hand beneath it to trace the elegant curve of her calf and then the line of her slender thigh. Her skin was smooth, with the creamy feel of the finest satin, and when he heard her breath quicken he did not stop but raised his hand higher still, his fingertips seeking the soft triangle of red curls as his touch grew increasingly intimate.

Realizing she'd just made the greatest mistake of her young life, Gabrielle found herself unable to resist Jason's gentle touch while his delicious kiss plunged her ever deeper into the madness of desire. She relaxed in his arms, wanting more of the demanding affection she'd first sought to escape. Smooth and sweet, his mouth and hands created a need she could neither deny nor fight, and she wove her fingers in his tangled curls to hold his mouth to hers while her whole body shook at the splendor of his slow, sensuous touch.

Jason shifted only slightly to unbutton the high ruffled neckline of her gown, and his lips left hers to move down her slender throat in teasing nibbles before lingering at the soft fullness of her breast. Her body delighted him. She responded so readily to his loving caresses he would never tire of holding her in his arms and leading her ever deeper into the mysteries of love. This was what he'd wanted, to make her feel alive, to make her crave his kiss as desperately as he craved hers, but the time and place were so shockingly inappropriate he drew back, wanting only to be certain she was as willing for him to continue as he hoped she would be. She had resisted his affection for no more than an instant; then she'd welcomed his advance with a grace which captivated him. But he wanted to hear her speak the words before he moved to possess her fully for he'd not take her like this, with the wild strength of a stallion rather than with the considerate tenderness of a man. He drew back only slightly as he spoke softly. "Say only that you want me as badly as I want you, for that is all I need to hear."

His voice seemed to float on the warm breeze, caressing her as seductively as his fiery kiss, but drawing a sudden deep breath, Gabrielle tried to clear her mind, forcing herself to remember who she was and what she was doing with such wanton abandon. "No, no!" She scrambled away, tugging her wrinkled gown into place as she leaped to her feet. She swayed slightly, her senses too full of him to provide the guidance she needed to remain upright.

"Gabrielle, what is wrong with you?" Instantly Jason was standing too, but as he reached out to draw her back into his arms, she shoved him away.

Sweeping her long auburn hair from her eyes with a defiant toss of her head, Gabrielle responded in a low whisper, "Everything is wrong! Dreadfully wrong! Is this how you men stand guard? Nearly shooting defenseless members of our party while our animals are left to fend for themselves? Should Sunny be stolen I will hold you personally responsible, Jason

Royal whether or not the guard duty was yours to perform!" With that threat she was gone, a flash of white as she streaked away, her feet barely touching the ground as she vanished with the speed of a ghost.

Jason began to swear in one long string of incredibly vile epithets. Was the woman crazy? So out of her mind with grief for her lost love she'd never permit another man to make love to her? He'd been a stupid fool to stop when her response had been so furious a denial of the passion he knew she'd felt as strongly as he had. "Damn!" He swore again and taking up his rifle he decided to patrol his portion of the camp until his senses cooled enough to allow him to again rest by the fire. "The next time, Gabrielle MacLaren, I won't ask since you tell only lies, I'll simply take the gift you're too proud to admit you want to give!" That vow brought a smile to his lips not even the loneliness of the plain could erase. There would be other nights, and he'd have Gabrielle for his own. It was only a matter of time; he was certain she knew that simple fact as well as he did.

Chapter V

Gabrielle had been unable to get back to sleep after she'd fled Jason's embrace, and she moved so slowly when she began to get dressed the next morning that Erica became concerned.

"Are you ill?" she said, reaching out to touch her friend's forehead lightly. "You don't seem feverish."

Trying to smile though her head ached dreadfully, Gabrielle offered what reassurance she could. "I just didn't sleep well so I'm rather tired, that's all."

"Why don't you ride with Paul today then? You're the only one of us who never has, and I'd say you deserve a turn to rest."

"No, really, I'll be fine."

But she wasn't, she was still horribly angry, and with herself not with Jason Royal for he'd shown her what he was truly like the first night they'd met. No, she was furious only with herself for having so little restraint where the man was concerned. His slightest touch set her blood aflame, and it was torture to recall how close she'd come to giving herself to him and for what? Not for love, for there was no hint of that tender emotion in his words, nor was there even the smallest measure of devotion in his actions. He either issued stern lectures on how he wished her to behave or ignored her completely. Obviously he cared nothing for her feelings, but as always he had simply seized an opportunity to pursue his own lusts with no thought of what the consequences might be to her. Still, she could not erase the memory of his forceful kiss from her mind and her lips burned with a shame she found nearly impossible to endure in silence. But there was no way she could escape the prying eyes of her companions and give in to the torrent of tears which blocked her throat with a painful knot. When breakfast was over she took Erica's advice, and her hands shaking with a tremor she hoped Paul would not notice, she climbed up onto the seat beside him.

"Ah, I've waited a long time for your company, miss, but you look a mite downcast this morning." Paul flapped the reins upon the oxen's backs and the sturdy beasts began to pull the heavily laden wagon at the slow, lumbering pace they would maintain until he drew them to a halt for the noon break.

Gabrielle shook her head. "I'm simply tired; I didn't sleep well. I'm afraid I won't be very good company for you."

"I'll be the judge of that. Crawl into the wagon and go to sleep if you like; I won't be offended," Paul suggested with a ready smile.

"Thank you, but I think I'll ride with you for a while." He was such a pleasant man she didn't want him to have to suffer the foulness of her mood, and while the prospect of sleep was an appealing one, she thought she should try and stay awake for a little while at least.

They had traveled no more than half a mile when Jason Royal appeared upon his nimble stallion and greeted them all with remarkably good humor. His smile was wide, but his glance barely included Gabrielle and Paul as he turned his mount to take up a position beside Iris Stewart. His invitation was spoken in such a low tone that the other young women could not overhear, but with a lilting laugh Iris urged her horse to a brisk canter and rode away with him.

Gabrielle turned away. She'd dreaded having to face the young man for there were simply no words to describe the scandalous nature of her behavior during the hours before dawn, but to have him snub her so rudely after their passion-filled encounter stunned her. She had expected, at the very least, an apology. She felt he owed her one since the whole incident had been his fault, but to be ignored as if nothing had happened was intolerable. She felt even worse then, sick to her stomach to think how casually he'd used her and then tossed her aside without a thought when she'd refused to give in to him.

Paul needed no more than a sidelong glance to perceive Gabrielle's deepening depression and to rightly guess its cause. "He would have asked you to ride with him had you been riding Sunny as you usually do. I've no doubt of it. Don't let the fact that he took his second choice upset you so badly."

"Second choice?" Gabrielle's blue eyes flashed angrily as she turned toward the friendly driver. "I have no idea what you mean. Mr. Royal may choose whomever he pleases for company, and I will never object for it is no business of mine!"

Paul cringed in mock horror, his expression one of deep remorse. "Forgive me for mentioning the man, miss. I didn't mean to offend. Apparently Mr. Royal has."

"He did not offend me!" Gabrielle denied hostilely. "He does not even exist in my opinion!"

"Yes, ma'am, whatever you say," Paul agreed promptly, and giving his full attention to the team, he did not risk looking Gabrielle's way again for clearly she was in no mood for conversation on any subject.

The pain in her head grew increasingly more severe until Gabrielle had no choice but to climb over the back of the seat and lie down in the wagon. When they stopped for the midday meal and rest she didn't awaken, and by suppertime she felt far better physically if no less guilty emotionally. Kissing Beau had been a natural expression of her love for him, but Jason's wild kisses had led her into a far different realm, not one filled with the beauty of love but one tormented by untamed desire, the memory of which made her tremble. She would never forgive him for the spell he'd woven on her emotions, never.

In sharp contrast to Gabrielle, Iris was in a festive mood that evening. She had found Jason Royal to be an entertaining companion and could not seem to stop talking about the young man. Since there was no way she could join in any discussion of Jason's considerable charm, Gabrielle excused herself from the group and went to check upon Sunny's comfort. The stallion had trotted behind the wagon all day, and he now greeted his mistress enthusiastically as she gave him the apple she'd been served with her dinner. She stayed with the stallion for a long while, enjoying his sincere affection, and when she finally returned to her wagon, everyone was preparing for bed. She wished that she had another nightgown to wear so she could throw away the one she'd worn the previous night, but she had only the one. The soft fabric slid over her bare skin with the same sensuous glide as Jason Royal's deeply tanned fingertips, and she shivered as she tried to force that erotic image from her mind. Sleep was a long time coming since she'd rested all day, but Gabrielle kept her eyes closed and her breathing even, not wanting her friends to speak to her. Eventually she fell into a troubled sleep.

The next day Jason took a petite blonde from one of the other wagons with him when he rode ahead to scout the trail. The following day another beauty had caught his eye and rode by his side. Gabrielle could not believe the man could be so low as to play one woman against another, but each seemed enormously pleased by his attentions and deeply disappointed when he invited someone new the following day. When that pattern continued, she decided his need to surround himself with beautiful women was a craving she'd never again satisfy. She gave her full attention to her new friends and the passing scene, and none to Jason Royal and his ceaseless pursuit of every female on the train. Whenever she saw him he seemed to be smiling, always in high spirits, and she wanted to shriek, to tell everyone what a devil he was, but she bit her tongue and swallowed the vile names she knew he deserved to be called.

When one morning he approached her, she drew back, barely civil as she responded to his cheerful greeting. He was not on horseback, but walked up to her carrying a large piece of oilcloth rolled up in his right hand.

"I should have given you this weeks ago, if you'll wrap your books tightly in this water resistant fabric they won't suffer any damage when we must ford a stream."

Surprised by his sudden concern, Gabrielle wondered if by some slim chance the man did have a conscience after all. Perhaps he was too proud to come to her with an apology for his shameless behavior but wanted to make amends and had chosen this useful gift as the method to do so. Still, she hesitated to accept his present, not truly convinced his motive was a sincere one.

"You don't need this yourself, Mr. Royal?"

"Jason," he whispered softly so he'd not be overheard by those standing nearby. "No. I want you to have it since I know you want your books to arrive in Oregon in good condition."

Gabrielle reached out cautiously to accept the roll of fabric, thinking he might at the last minute change his mind and jerk it away but he placed it in her hands. His fingertips crossed her wrist as he stepped back and she was shocked by the heat of his touch, appalled to think nothing she'd learned would shield her from the force of his magnetic appeal. He grinned at her slyly, as if he'd had the very same reaction but had enjoyed it.

"Take care now." He touched his hat brim in a friendly salute and then strode off, seeming to have countless other errands which demanded his immediate attention while Gabrielle stood and watched him move through an opening between two wagons and disappear from view. She tossed the oilcloth into the back of their wagon, choosing to wrap her books later, and swung herself up into Sunny's saddle while the others in her group stared at her with fascinated glances.

As soon as they started to ride, Erica caught up to her, as always bursting with curiosity. "Didn't Mr. Royal ask you to go riding with him today?"

"No," Gabrielle replied honestly. "Why should he want my company?"

"Well, why not yours? He seems to be going down some list to see we all receive his attention, but I can't figure out what his order must be."

"I doubt he has any such plan, Erica, but why don't you invite him to go riding if you're so impatient for him to reach you?" Gabrielle suggested flippantly the matter unworthy of consideration in her view.

Erica's green eyes widened in dismay, "What is there between you two, Gabrielle? Whenever anyone mentions that man's name you find some excuse to change the subject or to leave us. Do you dislike him for some reason?"

"No, I despise him!" Gabrielle responded hoarsely; then she was sorry she'd revealed so much when Erica grew all the more inquisitive.

"But why? He seems like such a nice man to me."

"He is lower than a snake, just believe me he is, and don't ask me to explain my opinion, please," Gabrielle insisted promptly, considering the subject closed. Before Erica could demand she explain the reason for her opinions, Marlene brought her horse up beside theirs.

"What did Mr. Royal say to you this morning, Gabrielle?" She asked shyly.

Exasperated that their brief exchange of words had drawn such notice, Gabrielle nevertheless tried to answer calmly since she knew Marlene to be a sensitive soul who'd be offended by her anger while Erica wasn't. "He had some extra oilcloth he thought I might use, that's all."

"Oh." Marlene bit her lip, her nervousness plain. "I thought maybe he had asked you some questions about me."

"Has he bothered you, Marlene? If he has, he's going to be damn sorry!" Gabrielle vowed instantly. She'd been wise enough to see through the scoundrel's motives, but Marlene had the innocent heart of a child and she'd not remain silent if

Jason had taken advantage of her.

"No!" The pretty blonde's denial was instantaneous. "Not at all, it is only that, well, I put something on my application form that wasn't true and I'm afraid he's going to find out what I did and ask me to leave." As Marlene blurted out her confession, tears filled her eyes. She was terrified by the possibility that she might be sent back to her sister's home where she knew she'd never be able to find a nice husband or have the precious babies she wanted so badly.

"What sort of thing was it, Marlene?" Erica gave Gabrielle an astonished glance as she pursued the matter, for she could not imagine what kind of lie the young woman could have told.

Marlene looked first at Erica then at Gabrielle, "I know you'll never tell, but I would not trust any of the others with my secret."

"Of course we'll not tell!" Erica agreed immediately. "Now whatever did you say that wasn't true?" She leaned forward, eager to hear it.

After taking a deep breath, Marlene spoke softly. "I said I was nineteen, but I'm really twenty-three."

"Oh, is that all?" Gabrielle laughed at Marlene's serious expression. "Your secret is safe with us, and I'm certain no one will ever guess you gave an incorrect age. You don't look a day older than nineteen so cease to worry over the matter. Your future husband will be delighted with you no matter what your age, I'm certain of it."

"Do you really think he will?" Marlene asked hopefully.

"Yes, I am positive he will!" Gabrielle was relieved the matter was no more important than that for she'd truly feared Jason might have gotten Marlene into some serious trouble. Not until several days had passed did she recall that conversation and realize that she had not been shown an application form or been requested to sign one. Perhaps it was no more than a formality, but she went to find Clayton Horne to seek his advice since he was the one charged with the responsibility of their care.

Expecting to find the man near his tent, Gabrielle approached with a confident stride but hesitated to intrude when she saw him talking with Jason. They appeared to be discussing some issue of importance so she turned away, meaning to return at a more convenient time but the men had seen her.

"Miss MacLaren, wait! What is it, my dear?" Clayton rushed to overtake her. Although he had tried upon numerous occasions to win the young woman's confidence, he knew he'd ruined whatever chance he'd had the morning he'd made the mistake of laughing at her request to stand guard duty. That had been most insensitive of him and he regretted his mistake deeply. Since then she'd given him no more than the slightest of greetings accompanied by an icy stare, and he hoped to seize this opportunity to impress her favorably for a change.

Gabrielle turned slowly as the stocky man approached, "It was a small matter, Mr. Horne. I can see you are busy so we can discuss it some other time."

"Nonsense," Clayton replied emphatically. He had learned through the countless opportunities he'd had to observe her that Gabrielle was well respected by the other young women in her party. She was both bright and charming, and except for her desire to help with guard duty she seemed very sensible too. "Now come with me. May I offer you some coffee or perhaps a cup of tea?"

"No, thank you." Gabrielle had meant only to ask a brief question, not to pay a social call, and she felt refreshments were unnecessary.

Jason stood aside, a slow smile curving across his well-shaped lips. "Good evening, Miss MacLaren."

"Good evening." Now that they stood in front of the tent Gabrielle found her inquiry difficult to phrase. Jason was watching her expression attentively, not leering or observing her with the taunting stare she'd come to dread. He appeared to be interested in hearing her problem no matter what it might be, and thus encouraged, she attempted to be concise. "One of the women mentioned the application form you had the others sign and I was never given one."

Startled by that report, Clayton looked up at Jason. "How could we have made such an oversight?" They had taken particular care in the wording of the document since these were not truly marriage contracts but simply informal agreements between the prospective brides and themselves.

"As I recall, you dismissed Miss MacLaren before I had a chance to offer one," Jason explained easily. "You had extras printed, why not give her one now?"

Gabrielle tried to appear calm, but it was difficult when Jason simply stared at her while they waited for Clayton to find his store of the forms. If he had said something she would have replied, but he kept silent and so did she. The tension between them was so intense she could scarcely bear it. He seemed to be waiting for her to speak first and she'd not give him that satisfaction and kept still too. When Clayton returned and handed her the application, she scanned it quickly, finding it straightforward in its message. Still, she hesitated to supply the required information. "The others all filled these out for you?"

"Yes, it asks only for the answers to some basic questions and for your signature." Jason moved behind her and, leaning over her shoulder, pointed out the sections which were to be completed. He stood as close as he dared while he spoke. "Clay, she'll need a pen and ink."

Gabrielle found it difficult to even focus on the printed words with Jason's warm breath upon her cheek. He was being polite, considerate; yet she felt his purpose was probably more devious than it seemed and drew away. "I can see what it is I am to do, merely agree to go to Oregon with you. That's all, isn't it? Since I am obviously making the journey, it seems pointless to have me sign this now."

Clayton pursed his lips thoughtfully, "No. It is not pointless, for when you sign our form it makes our responsibility for your welfare complete. Should you fall ill, we will see you receive the best of care, should you require assistance of any kind, we will render it without question. There is a space for our signatures below yours."

Gabrielle still felt uneasy, but she had no reason not to trust the basic purpose of their endeavor regardless of her opinion of Jason Royal's morals. She took the pen Clayton offered, and using a book he held out as a support, she began to fill out the form. When she came to the question regarding next of kin she looked up. "I have no living relatives, shall I just leave this blank or state that?"

"You have no one, Gabrielle?" Jason asked, his concern too genuine to doubt.

"No, not unless I were to count the man I'll marry as a relative and that seems a bit premature."

"Just write none then; that will have to do," Clayton suggested, as surprised as Jason to think this lovely young woman was alone in the world for each of the others had had someone, no matter how remote a relation, to list. "I am sorry I did not realize sooner that we had no completed application form from you, my dear." He waited patiently for her to finish and sign the document; then he wrote his name with a flourish and handed the pen to Jason for his signature. "I'll go and put this form with the others right now before it can become lost."

As Clayton entered their tent, Jason moved to Gabrielle's side. "I'll walk you back to your wagon."

"That really isn't necessary, Mr. Royal. I know the way."

"Jason," he reminded her with a teasing chuckle. "My name is Jason, why is that so difficult a fact for you to remember?"

Gabrielle turned to face him, hoping to end their conversation quickly. "Jason, then. I'd rather walk by myself if you don't mind."

"But I do mind very much. I have few opportunities to speak with you and I'll not waste this one," Jason responded in a serious tone this time, but his expression was still a teasing one.

He really had a most charming smile. His even white teeth

94

flashed with a bright sparkle against his dark skin, but the fact that he was so attractive a man was beside the point in her estimation.

"I think we've said all we need to say to each other," she replied firmly, hoping he would finally see her point and desist in his efforts to impress her.

"Not at all. We have not really had another chance to talk as we did at dinner that night in Kansas City. Won't you please come with me tomorrow? I can promise you a far more interesting ride than you'll have if you remain with your wagon."

"Mr. Royal, please . . ." Gabrielle protested hoarsely, exasperated by his lack of understanding. "The other women seem to enjoy your company but I don't. Why don't you invite someone else? There are still several you've missed."

"You've kept a count of my guests?" Jason remarked with a sly grin, pleased that she'd noticed for he'd hoped she would be jealous of the attention he'd paid her companions.

"No!" Gabrielle thought the man impossibly conceited and was tempted to say so.

Since their conversation was as always going poorly, Jason attempted a different approach. "I have no other time to get to know you all, Gabrielle. Has any of your friends complained that my behavior is too forward, not that of a gentleman?"

Surprised that he would ask such a question Gabrielle took a moment to consider it thoughtfully before she replied. In truth, each of the young women had found him to be the most proper of escorts, amusing, but always respectful in his behavior. "No, they have all been most favorably impressed, Mr. Royal—Jason. But that does not mean that I would be."

Jason forced himself to hold his temper. He had laid such careful plans. The young women were remarkably sweet and he did think each deserved some portion of his time, but he'd also wanted them to be so certain his motives were purely platonic they'd not question his actions when he at last reached his goal: to be alone again with Gabrielle. "Perhaps you are right.

I've attempted to make each of your companions feel confident about her choice to come with us. But I can see you require no such reassurance. In fact, you seem to take exception to every word I speak. I'll not waste any more of my time or yours, Miss MacLaren. When your dislike for me is so intense it clouds your reason."

As he turned away, his disappointment in her seemed so deep that Gabrielle reached out to touch his soft deerskin sleeve, catching only the long fringe in the seam in her grasp, but that gesture was enough to stop him. "Jason, please, you're being needlessly cruel. I think it is simply unwise for us to be alone together." That was a considerable understatement she knew. For her it was not only unwise but dangerous.

Puzzled by that comment, Jason moved close as he whispered, "Are you ashamed to have kissed me? Is that it?"

Gabrielle's creamy complexion took on a delicate blush of rose as she tried to think of some way to deny the truth of his accusation. She had done far more than simply kiss him, she'd allowed him to cover her whole body with caresses which had left her lying limp in his arms. She was not simply ashamed, but mortified, dreadfully embarrassed by the way he could make her forget everything she'd been taught about how a respectable young lady was supposed to behave. Since she would not admit that truth, she looked away, focusing her gaze on a group of children playing a game of tag through the wheels of their wagons.

"Gabrielle, look at me," Jason commanded sharply, yet when she turned her incredible blue glance upon him he found it difficult to recall what he'd meant to say and had to clear his throat to stall for a moment to collect his thoughts. "If you'll come with me tomorrow we can discuss the way you feel. I'd say you owe me that opportunity, wouldn't you?"

Gabrielle could hear the children still, their happy laughter ringing in the clear air of the evening but Jason's gray eyes glowed with the shine of the finest silver and she could think only of him. Perhaps he was right. What harm could there be in going riding together? He seemed sincere in his request for her company and there had been a few occasions when she had actually enjoyed his. Knowing it was evil to hate anyone, no matter what the reason, she reluctantly agreed.

"All right, I will come with you, but only if you will promise to treat me no differently than you have all the others."

Jason broke into a wide grin. "Of course, until tomorrow then." Before she could refuse his attention he took her elbow and escorted her back to her wagon where he left her with a teasing wink that promised far more excitement than the others had seen.

Never one to ignore an interesting situation, Erica moved close to whisper, "Wasn't that the 'snake' who just bid you such a charming good-night?"

Gabrielle glared at her friend, "Yes, I did call him that and believe me it was deserved. He seems to want to change my opinion of him now though and I am trying to be fair, that's all. Stop smirking!"

Erica's grin grew wider. "Just mention my name to him, will you? I'd still like to go riding with him someday soon."

"I'll try to remember to tell him that," Gabrielle promised flippantly, but she knew Erica Nelson's desires would be the last subject she would ever discuss with Jason.

After Jason had given the order to turn out the next morning and had made sure all the wagons were proceeding at a brisk pace, he went to find Gabrielle. He wasn't at all certain she wouldn't change her mind and refuse to accompany him that day, or possibly invite one of her friends to join them. He had foreseen both possibilities and planned to behave in a charming fashion no matter what she suggested, for clearly she didn't trust him and he wanted to win her respect. If he had to be content to wait until another day or to entertain two young women that morning, he was prepared to do so. However, to his immense relief, Gabrielle returned his wave and rode forward to meet him. The two stallions eyed each other warily, neither pleased by the sight of the other, but they were well-trained animals who responded to their masters' commands without giving serious complaint.

Gabrielle had scarcely closed her eyes the entire night. Still, both frightened and intrigued by the prospect of going riding with Jason, she felt elated rather than tired that morning. His smile was warm, not threatening, and she immediately decided to give him the benefit of the doubt on his promise to behave as a gentleman should.

"What is your mount's name? I think he is almost as handsome as Sunny." She teased him with a playful sweetness, her good mood instantly apparent.

Responding with the same ready wit, Jason agreed. "I told you I thought Sunny a beauty, but Duke is as good a horse any day."

"Duke? That's not a very original name, Mr. Royal." Gabrielle observed the horse closely for both his conformation and light beige color were handsome.

"It is a fine name, strong yet concise, and I like it," Jason responded proudly. Then with mock irritation he inquired, "Will you never remember to use my Christian name?"

"I will try," Gabrielle promised, but truly she thought calling him by his first name would only encourage the closeness she wanted to avoid. The others all called him Mr. Royal, how could she address him in a more familiar fashion and not arouse their suspicions? "Why didn't you ask the rest of the women to call you Jason if it is so important that I do?" She glanced at him through the thick fringe of her dark lashes, as if she were still admiring his horse rather than watching for his reaction to her question.

"You must know why without asking, Gabrielle," Jason commented slyly. Why she refused to admit their relationship was far different from the one he'd had with the others in her group, he still didn't understand. Women could be exasperatingly dense at times, but he was certain that was not her problem. "Must I simply tell you outright that you are my favorite?"

Shocked that he would be so bold, Gabrielle reminded him quickly of his promise. "I wish to be treated as if I were the very least of your favorites, Jason. I thought I'd made that clear when I said I'd come with you today." Before he could respond, she offered a challenge. "Do you see that tree in the distance? I will race you to it!" With a lilting laugh she was gone, Sunny's red hide no more than a blur as she streaked past Jason.

Jason urged Duke to take up the pursuit with a burst of speed which brought them close, but the buckskin stallion did not have the speed to catch the far swifter roan and Jason had to concede the race when he finally drew to a halt beneath the shade of the lone tree. The rolling hills which surrounded them were covered with the bright blossoms of the wild flowers that grew in profusion each spring. The way was easy here as they neared the river known as the Little Blue, and Jason hoped the beauty of their surroundings would lull Gabrielle into a less cautious mood. That she had begun such a wild race had astonished him, as did the fact she'd beaten him so handily. "You might have given me a little more warning, but I will admit you beat me."

The wagon train was no more than a tiny puff of dust in the distance now and Gabrielle wondered for a moment if she'd not just outsmarted herself again, but Jason made no move to dismount and draw near. "Yes, I'll admit that was rather unfair of me, but since Duke had to carry the greater weight I'd say the two horses are probably near equals."

"Shall we trade mounts and try it again? That would be a proper test of your theory," Jason replied with a ready grin, surprised that she'd made such a gracious attempt to save his pride.

"Perhaps later. We should give the horses time to rest, don't you think?"

"Oh, definitely. Let's go as far as the river; I want to see how it has changed since last spring. Rivers are a lot like women in many respects, he stated quite casually. "They are very unpredictable." Instantly he was sorry he'd made such a remark, but Gabrielle did not seem to be insulted by that jest and he relaxed again. "The Little Blue and Big Blue intersect just above Turtle Creek. We'll follow the path of the Little Blue up toward the Platte."

Gabrielle was surprised that Jason wanted to give geography lessons, but she listened with rapt interest for he seemed to know the terrain over which they would pass as well as some people knew the streets of Kansas City.

"Do you never get lost, Jason?" Truly interested in his response, she had used his first name without thinking.

"Never," Jason responded confidently. "You needn't worry that I will be unable to return you to your wagon safely this afternoon."

Blushing, Gabrielle stammered a denial. "No, please don't misunderstand my question. In every direction the land is so lovely, but how do you know where the river lies? I couldn't even guess.

"I use the sun as a guide in the daytime and the stars at night, exactly as a mariner does at sea. It is not really all that difficult," he pointed out, glad to explain since she seemed not to understand.

"Oh, yes. I see what you mean." But as they made their way toward the river, the sky began to darken and dense clouds built up on the horizon. As the wind increased the storm moved toward them, obscuring the light of the sun and casting a deep gray haze over the bright landscape. Worried that they'd be caught in a sudden downpour, Gabrielle turned toward the handsome man at her side. "Shouldn't we turn back before it begins to rain?"

Jason looked up as the first large drops began to fall, hitting the ground around them with audible thumps. "There's no time for that, we'll have to make for the shelter of those trees just ahead. We've no time to switch horses as we planned before we raced again." With that comment he dug his heels into Duke's sides, urging the stallion to a ready gallop which to his chagrin Gabrielle quickly overtook and passed. Sunrise simply moved with a far smoother gait, his hooves seeming to fly over the grass without touching the turf. Jason knew it was not a matter of weight which determined the winner, but the roan horse's greater strength and ability. Gabrielle had already dismounted by the time he drew Duke to a jarring halt beneath the cottonwood trees. He kept a small tent rolled up behind his saddle for use in just such emergencies, and after leaping down from his horse's back, he quickly untied it.

"Do you always carry a tent?" Gabrielle asked suspiciously.

"Always. For the weather is frequently inclement in the spring. We have been lucky so far, that is all; it may rain on us many times before we reach the Platte." In a matter of minutes he had set up the small canvas tent, securing it between two of the trees. Taking Gabrielle's hand, he led her inside. The smooth canvas floor nestled down into the grass to provide a mat for seating as they arranged themselves in comfortable positions, but there was no way they could avoid brushing elbows and knees in the close confines of the small enclosure. Noticing Gabrielle's blush, Jason attempted to reassure her that the rain had been completely unforeseen. "You can't blame this storm on me, Gabrielle, for I can't control the weather any more than I can control your opinion of me."

The raindrops slid off the angular planes of the roof and rolled to the ground, soaking the grass with moisture and at the same time providing the sound of a comforting pitter-patter. The trees shielded them from most of the water while the heavily leafed branches provided shelter for the horses as well. "Do these storms last long?" Gabrielle finally asked, hoping the clouds would pass as swiftly as they had appeared, but Jason shook his head.

"It might rain all day." He could not suppress a smile at that delightful prospect, for he'd never expected the good fortune which had befallen him. To have Gabrielle practically seated in his lap was far more than he could have hoped for.

The auburn-haired beauty swallowed nervously. "All day?"

"Maybe even into the night," Jason remarked with a teasing grin. "The wagon train will have stopped so everyone can escape the downpour in their wagons. We will not be missed so you needn't worry so."

Straightening her shoulders, Gabrielle replied confidently, "Everyone knows I am with you, they all saw us leave together."

"And I'm certain they'll notice when we return together too. Is that your worry, that there will be gossip?" There would be, of course; he knew that without asking.

Since she was certain he knew exactly what was worrying her, Gabrielle shook her head. "It is not what they might say that matters."

"What is important then?" Jason asked softly, fascinated to be able to observe her delicate features so closely. Her lashes were long and thick, but her brows were as gracefully drawn as a china doll's. In every way he thought her the most exquisite beauty he had ever seen. He could not imagine another such woman existing anywhere on the face of the earth.

Gabrielle looked him straight in the eye as she replied breathlessly, "What really does happen between us, not what they might imagine."

Jason extended his hand slowly so as not to frighten her. "Put your hand in mine, Gabrielle."

A thousand warnings flashed in her mind, but Gabrielle did not heed them. After a moment's hesitation she placed her hand gently in his and watched as his slim, tan fingers closed over hers. She was certain he could feel the erratic beat of her pulse, but what could he expect when they sat so near? He had left one of the tent flaps open so they would have fresh air, but that courtesy did not seem to help her breathe more easily and she was certain he could see her trembling if he did not feel the tremor in her hand. "Please, Jason, we must not—"

"Gabrielle, don't be so afraid of your own emotions for they will never betray you." With that tenderly worded advice Jason pulled her across his lap, his mouth finding hers, as before, eager to accept his kiss as his fingertips moved slowly down the tiny buttons of her bodice so he could slip his hand inside to caress the flushed tip of her breast. Her skin was fair, cool beneath his touch, but he held her gently, not wanting to frighten her this time. He wanted her to be ready to accept the generous amount of affection he wished to give. He savored each moment, his kiss deep and slow, his touch tantalizingly smooth and sweet.

Despite his reassurance, Gabrielle knew instantly that her emotions had indeed betrayed her again as his marvelous kiss drove all thought of resistance from her mind. She slipped her hands beneath his shirt, sliding her fingertips through the dark curls which covered his chest, and she felt his breath quicken too. That her effect upon his senses was the same as his upon hers came as something of a shock, but she did not draw her hands away. She let her nails tease the taut skin which covered his ribs, and when he sat up abruptly to pull his shirt over his head, she made no move to escape him. The bright blue of her eyes, veiled now by a soft mist, filled with tenderness as she again placed her hands on his bared chest and returned his smile as he lowered his mouth to hers.

Jason had never faced a more difficult challenge, for he knew Gabrielle to possess the most volatile of temperaments. While he desperately wanted to arouse her passion, he did not want to provoke her anger. He dared not lift his lips from hers until he was certain she'd not object to his affection; then he trailed playful kisses down the slim line of her throat as he moved his hand to the buttons on the soft kid boots she wore for riding. He wanted to remove every single article of clothing she wore, and with expertise he proceeded to do so, while to his amazement he found Gabrielle doing the very same thing to him. He could scarcely keep his mind on his task when her

103

hands moved over him with such delicate precision, peeling away the layers of his deerskin clothing with a determination he found astonishing, and he thought of Beau. The boy would have been only nineteen when he'd died, but he'd obviously taught Gabrielle all there was to know of pleasing a man. When they at last lay nude in each other's arms, he was drunk with the delicious desire she had aroused so easily within him.

He longed now to lead her further still, to delay the moment when their bodies would join in a final burst of pleasure. He covered her face with light kisses, then caressed her throat lightly before his lips found the pale pink tip of her breast. Savoring the texture of her silken skin, his tongue moved down her ribs, then his lips teased the smooth flatness of her stomach with lingering kisses before he lowered his mouth to the waiting triangle of dark red curls. Her hands had moved lightly over the rippling muscles of his back as he'd stretched out beside her, but now she wound her fingers tightly in his curls to hold his mouth near. She made no move to resist the teasing probing of his tongue but relaxed in his embrace, allowing him the easy access to her innermost being which he craved so desperately. All reason fled his agile mind then, as he savored the honey sweet taste of her passion with the abandon of a man drunk upon the most exotic of fine wines. He felt the rapture of his kiss shudder down her spine in mounting waves of ecstasy, and when he was satisfied he had tamed her elegant body as well as her proud spirit, he moved to end his own torment. His mouth again sought hers as with one forceful thrust he drove deep within the slender body it had been such a great joy to conquer. He felt her pain then although no cry escaped her throat. Stunned to find the vibrantly loving creature beneath him a virgin, he lay still within her, not knowing how to beg forgiveness for having made so grave an error about her past.

Gabrielle could scarcely breathe. She could only feel the desire which flooded her loins with a stream of fire, and

104

wrapping her arms around Jason's narrow waist, she drew him down into an embrace that stilled all his apologies before he could speak them.

"Do you demand I say it still? Can you not feel how desperately I want you?" she whispered seductively in his ear.

As his mouth again covered hers with an urgency she readily understood, she moved beneath him with a slow, easy grace, accepting each of his rhythmic thrusts as if they were engaged in an ageless dance whose steps she knew by heart. In his arms she had found a rapture so splendid she wanted only to share it. She felt a delectable excitement flow between them until its power surpassed even the longing for life itself, fusing their proud spirits in the flames of a burning ecstasy that left them both trembling with the greatest of love's many exquisite joys. Their need for each other at last satisfied, they lay contentedly enjoying an embrace neither could bear to end until the last raindrop had rolled down the side of the tent and they were bathed in the warm glow of the returning sun.

For the first time in his life Jason was simply speechless, for he'd found in Gabrielle's arms so loving a response to his dream of affection that he was unable to put into words the newfound devotion which filled his heart. He brought a strand of her silken hair to his lips and kissed it tenderly, not wanting the wonderful intimacy they had shared to end as he knew it must. Stopping to kiss her flavorful lips frequently, he pulled on his trousers and moccasins. Then he brought his canteen from where it had been suspended on Duke's saddle so he could bathe away all traces of their ardor from her slender body, but his hands shook so badly Gabrielle took the damp handkerchief from him.

"For so tender a lover, why are you so clumsy now, my darling?" she asked in a voice still husky with desire. She pulled on her clothing with practiced ease despite the close confines of their quarters; then she knelt before him as she brushed his lips with hers. She had learned not only to trust her own emotions, but to trust him as well, and her smile could not have been more lovely. She did not regret a moment of the pleasure they had shared, but she saw by the confusion in his glance that something was amiss. "Jason, what is wrong? Tell me quickly for surely we must hurry or the wagon train will overtake us and we will look very foolish sitting here in this tiny tent when the sun is shining so brightly."

Jason's gray eyes grew dark as he attempted to explain what was bothering him. "I did not even imagine—well, what I mean is it did not occur to me that I would be the first man to—"

Gabrielle sat back, fear spreading up her spine like a cold chill. "What you mean is you thought I'd done this before and therefore would not mind doing it again with you, is that it?" she asked, her eyes rapidly filling with unshed tears.

"No!" Jason replied crossly. "But all you told me of Beau led me to believe that you and he had been lovers."

"I see," Gabrielle replied calmly, certain she had accurately guessed the cause of his remorse. He'd thought she'd been Beau's woman so she would be his without objection. It was as simple as that. She pushed by him and went to Sunny, brushing the last of the raindrops from his saddle before she leaped upon his back. When Jason rushed to her side to grab her stallion's reins, she turned upon him with a furious gaze. "Beau and I were lovers in the truest sense, for each of us was devoted to the other. You are not even fit to speak his name, and I swear I'll kill you if you ever dare touch me again!"

Stunned by that hate-filled threat, Jason could only leap aside as he watched her magnificent mount streak away. He screamed in frustration, devastated to think she had again misunderstood him so greatly but knowing the fault had been his. He should never have mentioned his mistaken belief about her relationship with Beau. The man's memory was sacred to her. Without realizing it, Jason had violated the trust she'd had in him only moments before. He loosed the lines which held the tent and, rolling it up tightly, tied it behind his saddle. Then instead of returning to the wagon train he rode on to scout the river, for he did not trust himself to face anyone while fury filled his heart. He had won and lost Gabrielle's love in the space of a few brief hours, and the depth of his own folly was not something he would ever forgive.

Chapter VI

While the memories of the night she'd joined Jason by the campfire had filled Gabrielle with a heavy burden of guilt, she had no trace of remorse over the romantic interlude they'd shared during the rainstorm. She felt not the least bit guilty for having made love to this man whose charm had previously caused her so much mental anguish. She had simply ceased to struggle against the attraction which had existed between them from the moment they'd met. When Beau had died she'd been so numbed by the pain of his death she'd thought that would be the way she'd always feel and she had closed her heart to desire, making it a shrine to his memory. Perhaps it was simply her youth, her inexperience with life itself, that had made her lose all hope for the future, but Jason had restored her faith in herself as well as in the richness of love's beauty. She still considered Jason Royal a scoundrel, a devil in the beguiling disguise of a handsome young man who knew how to manipulate a woman's emotions with remarkable ease. However, she had learned a valuable lesson in his arms and it was one she meant to remember. She again had the faith to trust in her own emotions, indeed, to allow herself to feel the very emotions she'd thought her heart no longer capable of holding. If Jason Royal had proved to be unworthy of her love, that did not diminish her joy in the giving of it. Where as before she had been blessed with a haunting loveliness, she now displayed a sparkling beauty, but she gave her new friends no clue as to what had made such a difference in her life. When Jason stopped by their wagon as he frequently did, she left promptly on whatever errand needed her attention, knowing Iris would keep him so entranced with her flattery that he'd not miss her presence. She offered him not the slightest bit of encouragement, and should he be so foolish as to greet her personally she pretended not to hear. While she did not admit her growing interest, when they again viewed their future husbands' portraits she found several increasingly appealing. Their easy grins were a promise of the love she now knew she could again feel. She continued to include Joshua Taylor in her prayers as he was special to her and she hoped he would prove to be tall, fair, and the possessor of a ready wit since that was the kind of man she hoped to marry.

While Gabrielle had dealt fully with their brief romance and then had dismissed it from her mind, Jason could not. The incident had meant far too much to him. He could not forget it as easily as the fickle redhead seemed to have done. Taking care not to change his routine, he continued to invite the brides to go riding, but he could no longer concentrate on their conversation closely enough to make appropriate replies. He wanted desperately to relive the few hours he'd spent with Gabrielle. They were his most precious memory, and her brutal rejection caused him a pain only the sweetness of her embrace could ease. Whereas she seemed to bloom with the glow of health, he grew morose and thin, the strain of trying to maintain the optimistic disposition for which he was known was too much for him. Clayton grew so worried about the sudden change in his friend's appearance and behavior he finally felt compelled to risk Jason's anger by mentioning it.

They had just finished their supper, a meal Clayton had enjoyed greatly but which Jason had merely tasted. "I had hoped to lose a few pounds on this trek, but I have ample girth and you were lean to begin with, Jason. If you don't regain your appetite soon, I fear you'll grow too weak to sit your horse and I could no more lead this wagon train to Oregon than I could fly there."

"What?" Jason looked up, only dimly aware that Clayton had spoken.

Losing his patience entirely then, Clayton responded crossly, "Damn it, man, wake up! You've lost weight and can't follow a conversation of more than two words! What the hell is bothering you so badly?"

Jason tossed the contents of his coffee cup upon the ground and stood up to stretch. "There's not a damn thing bothering me. Just leave me be." He walked off then, his stride far more confident than he felt. He had a mirror. He knew how ghastly he looked and the trip was nowhere near over. They still must count the journey in months, not weeks or days yet, but each step of the way was agony for it took him no closer to Gabrielle and she alone made the trip worthwhile.

As Jason strolled around the perimeter of the camp, Gabrielle sat with the girls from both of the other wagons. The twenty-one young women had had ample opportunity to become well acquainted, and while each was closest to the friends with whom she shared a wagon, they often formed other groups after supper to enjoy a greater variety of conversation. Since she loved to sing, Gabrielle had been delighted to find several others who shared her interest. Fortunately, a young woman named Rebecca had brought along a zither, and this evening they were attempting to learn the words of a song, which they sang in unison, while she played the accompaniment on the stringed instrument. While their voices were appealing, they could not seem to harmonize and remember the words at the same time. As a result they were convulsed by giggles when their fun was interrupted by an ear-piercing shriek. While her companions sat, paralyzed with fright, Gabrielle was on her feet in an instant. She ran down the line of wagons toward the screams which were rapidly growing to a blood-chilling intensity. Men were running from all directions, rifles in their hands, as they came toward what they were certain must be no less than an attempted murder if not a massacre of terrifying proportions.

When they arrived to find no more than one man furiously slugging his wife, they turned away, unwilling to intrude upon someone else's domestic squabble. They seemed to think if a man chose to beat his wife that was his own business, but Gabrielle held an entirely different view. When she realized none of the men were going to come to the hapless woman's aid, she rushed into the midst of the fray. She recognized the couple, but didn't know them by name. The man had caught a fistful of his wife's hair in his left hand to hold her fast while he slapped her with the back of his right. Their three little children, terrified by their father's vicious fit of temper, had scrambled under the wagon to hide, but their high-pitched cries for help had drawn the crowd.

Since no one else was going to help the woman escape a brutal beating, Gabrielle grabbed the man's right arm. Distracted by the fiery redhead's grasp, the man released his wife in order to fling Gabrielle away, but she held on and screamed at the woman to run. Outraged by this interference, he turned the full fury of his anger upon Gabrielle, intending to knock her senseless and teach her to stay out of his affairs.

Jason broke through the circle of onlookers, and although he did not believe the sight which greeted him, he did not hesitate to grab the angry man's shoulder and spin him around. His fist connected smartly with the bully's chin. As the man went limp he released Gabrielle, so suddenly she sprawled in the dirt too and lay there, dazed, as Jason plucked the man from the ground by the scruff of the neck and planted another solid blow on his chin. This time Jason left him where he'd fallen. He then pulled a length of rope from his hip pocket, and as quickly as he would have hogtied a steer, he bound the man's hands firmly behind his back. Rolling him over to his wagon, he lashed the end of the rope to the nearest wheel.

"That ought to take care of you until morning, Sam Duffy," he said.

Then he bent down to pull the frightened little Duffy children from their hiding place; there was a boy of about eight and there were two younger girls. He sent them off with their mother to a sympathetic woman who had come forward to render assistance when she saw Sam was in no condition to object. Jason turned back to the crowd then, dismissing them with a wave of his hand.

"You've all got your own business to mind, now go see to it!"

When Jason looked at Gabrielle he found her sitting up and gazing at him with a look of undisguised admiration. He was so pleased that he could scarcely summon enough anger to reprimand her. He wanted only to pull her into his arms and kiss her soundly before the warm glow of respect left her pretty blue eyes. Instead, he reached down for her arm and jerked her to her feet.

"Well, Miss MacLaren, I am responsible for keeping the peace here and I do not recall making you my deputy!"

Before she could offer any argument he tightened his hold upon her arm and drew her along beside him as he made his way back to his tent. This was as good an excuse as any to talk with her, and he meant to lecture her in order to keep her with him for a while.

Startled by his hostile greeting, Gabrielle nonetheless did not struggle to get away but matched his long stride as best she could. "I know it is your job to see everyone behaves properly, but you weren't there and there was no one to help that poor woman unless I did it myself. I wasn't about to join that group of cowards who just stood there gaping as if that ghastly fight had been staged for their amusement!" She was not angry with Jason, far from it, but she was furious at the men who'd done nothing to help the woman she now knew as Mrs. Duffy.

When they reached his tent Jason called to Clayton to bring

Gabrielle a cup of tea to calm her. He then took her over to a thick patch of grass and, sitting down, pulled her down beside him.

"I should just turn you over my knee and give you the spanking you deserve, Gabrielle," he threatened with what he hoped was convincing sincerity.

"You wouldn't dare!" Gabrielle was ready to spring to her feet should he make a move in that direction, but he reached out to take her arm again so she could not get away.

Relieved to observe that none of Sam's wild blows had hit her, Jason attempted to make Gabrielle see the obvious folly in her action. "Why do you suppose those men you just referred to as cowards didn't do something to help Mrs. Duffy? Think about it for a moment; then give me your best guess." Although Jason's gaze was stern, his touch was gentle, a light caress upon her arm which he slowly slid down to her hand, letting his fingers rest tenderly upon hers. He had missed her so dreadfully that he could barely keep the emotion out of his voice as he spoke.

Without thinking, Gabrielle covered his hand with hers, her gesture made with the gracious ease of one confident of her lover's affection, and when Clayton brought her the cup of tea he nearly dropped it when he saw their intimate pose. Grateful for the soothing refreshment, Gabrielle lifted her hands from Jason's to accept the tin cup, unaware of how greatly she had shocked the older man.

"Thank you." She took a sip and then another before she answered Jason's question. "The obvious reason seems to be they would not interfere in another man's argument with his wife for fear he would then do the same in return."

Pleased that she was so perceptive, Jason began to smile. "Exactly, which is why they are all so content to let me handle the disputes here. Try to remember that."

While she saw his point, Gabrielle continued to explain her motivation. "I'd do it again, Jason, really I would. No man should treat his wife so badly. I don't care what they choose to

114

call me for interfering, I'd do it again to save another woman from such a brutal beating as that man was giving his wife."

Jason took a deep breath. "Gabrielle, I am paid to take the risks. If I get hurt, that's just part of my job. I'll not allow you to risk being injured no matter how noble your purpose might be." Suddenly he thought of Beau, the young man who had lost his life to save two children. He knew Gabrielle regarded Beau as a hero, certainly not as a fool. Not wishing to give her the opportunity to think of Beau, he continued quickly. "Now should such an unfortunate situation happen again, and I am fairly certain it will as tempers always grow short with the passage of the miles, I want you to promise you'll come for me so I can take whatever action necessary. Will you promise me that, please?"

Gabrielle looked down at the cup of tea. "I don't know what might happen, Jason. If I am standing right there and—"

"Gabrielle, I want your word on this!" Jason demanded sharply.

"Or what? You'll tie me to a wagon wheel all night too?" she responded flippantly.

"No. I will just spank you right there in front of everyone, because if you behave like a child that will be what you deserve!" Jason vowed with an intensity he knew she would readily believe.

Ignoring his threat, Gabrielle asked calmly, "If you were not the wagon master, but merely one of the travelers, would you have stood by while Mrs. Duffy suffered that beating?" Even before she heard his reply, Gabrielle was certain what it would be.

Jason frowned slightly and then answered truthfully. "No. I would have done the very same thing that I did, but I am a man and strong enough to force my opinion on another man while you were foolish to make that attempt."

As Gabrielle looked deeper than Jason's hostile stare, she noticed the changes in his appearance were remarkable considering the brief span of time in which they'd occurred.

115

Pleased to think it had been his own integrity rather than merely his job which had led him to help Mrs. Duffy, she considered the subject closed and smiled as she inquired, "Have you been ill? You look as though you've lost weight." She could think of no more subtle way to remark upon how tired he looked, but he appeared not to have slept in weeks.

Surprised that she would notice, or care enough to ask, Jason simply shrugged. "I have a lot on my mind, you needn't concern yourself with my welfare."

"Oh, I see, and it is only your job that makes you responsible for mine?" she asked skeptically. "Really Jason, why won't you tell me the truth?"

The truth, he thought with a painful stab of remorse. Speaking the truth had cost him too dearly; he'd not risk it again. "Speaking of the truth, is there not something you wish to tell me?"

Puzzled by that question, Gabrielle leaned closer to whisper. "What do you mean, Jason? I will tell you whatever it is you want to know." Now that they were talking so quietly together she felt the man's tension and sincerely wanted to know its cause. Just looking at his troubled expression caused her pain and she set her cup aside so she might reach again for his hand, her gesture an irresistibly sweet one. "You have seen for yourself tonight that I will risk a beating to help a woman I don't even know. Tell me what sort of help you need for I will gladly give it." She felt the very same rush of emotion which had filled her heart when last they'd been together and she did not understand how she could have been such a fool as to have threatened him with death should he come near her again. "Please forgive me for what I said to you, I could never harm anyone and I'd never wish to kill a man so fine as you." That he had dispatched Sam Duffy so quickly truly had impressed her as greatly as he'd thought it had and she leaned forward to kiss his cheek softly. "Now what is it?"

Astonished by Gabrielle's tenderness, Jason looked around quickly. Pleased to see no one lurking nearby who might have observed that kiss, he tried to smile then as he teased her. "You don't know how relieved I am to hear that. I've been meaning to make out a will just in case—"

"Jason, you stop it this instant!" Gabrielle insisted with a lilting laugh. "Now just tell me what it is I am supposed to tell you. Stop teasing me."

Taking a deep breath, Jason decided it might be best just to be blunt. "You do understand how a child is conceived, don't you?"

Gabrielle's cheeks flooded with color at that query and she could barely find her voice to respond. "Is that what is worrying you so greatly, that I might have become pregnant and would demand that you marry me? Since my father is dead I suppose I would have to ask Mr. Horne to take his place and come after you with a shotgun!"

Jason watched the bright blue of Gabrielle's eyes take on a purple sheen and knew he'd made another grave mistake. "Will you keep your voice down please!" He ordered in a hoarse whisper. "One thing at a time. That I am concerned about you should not be any cause for anger. All I meant to say was that I hope you will tell me should the possibility of a child prove to be a reality."

Gabrielle shook her head. "It isn't. You've nothing to fear."

She was so embarrassed she wanted only to run away from him as fast as she could but she sat still, waiting for him to say whatever he wished in response.

"Damn it! I am not afraid to accept the consequences of my actions, Gabrielle! Are you?"

Lifting her chin proudly, Gabrielle responded truthfully. "No, I am not. Now if this frightful inquisition is over I'd like to be excused."

Jason knew he'd made a mess of everything as usual. He had been worried about her, desperately worried, but not for the reason she mistakenly believed. He'd no need of a wife, but he would have married her without a moment's hesitation should it have been necessary to give their baby a name. He felt far worse now than he had before they'd begun to talk, knowing she thought so little of him.

"I don't look upon marriage as a trap, Gabrielle, but as the most natural way for a man and woman to live. Go on back to your wagon and forget I ever asked what I did. If it insulted you, I didn't mean to do that." He stood up then and, with a gentle touch, lifted her to her feet before stepping back, their conversation over without their having reached the accord for which he'd hoped.

Gabrielle was depressed too for she sensed his disappointment. However, she did not know how she could have responded any differently since she had expressed what she truly felt. "I am sorry I misunderstood the intent of your question, Mr. Royal, but if there were a child, you would be the last person to whom I would turn for help." With that taunting farewell she was gone, her feet flying over the grass. She left him too stunned by her parting insult to give pursuit.

Clayton had gone for a short walk to give himself the opportunity to think more clearly. That Jason was handsome was a fact he'd always known, and he had been aware that he was something of a rogue where women were concerned. Still, the young women they were escorting were so terribly young he'd not thought it necessary to caution his partner against becoming involved with any of them. By the time he'd returned to their tent, however, he had decided that he and Jason needed to have a serious talk immediately. Finding that Gabrielle had returned to her wagon for the night, he did not mince words.

"Miss MacLaren is a most enchanting creature, Jason."

"Yes, she is that." Jason agreed readily, his attention now focused upon his friend's words.

"You really must be more cautious around her, around all the girls in fact. I was shocked to see Gabrielle seated so comfortably and holding your hand in her lap. It is a stroke of

118

good fortune I was the one to see that shocking breach of etiquette rather than someone else. She is very young and foolish, but you have no such excuse. If she cannot keep her hands off you then you will have to tell her to do so in terms she will understand."

Jason started to laugh for Clayton's understanding of what he'd witnessed was so terribly inaccurate. "Believe me, Miss MacLaren is the very soul of discretion. She was worried about me, that is all. She even remarked on how tired I seem to be, just as you did, and I don't think you consider yourself overly forward. You needn't worry that Gabrielle will cause any scandal, nor I either."

"I have your word on it?" Clayton asked skeptically, still not convinced his message had gotten through.

"Of course." Jason meant that promise too, for the last thing he wanted was to damage Gabrielle's reputation or cause her anguish. She might think damn little of him, but he still considered her the dearest of women, and not one he meant to give up so easily either.

"Good." Clayton hoped he'd made some impression upon Jason, but he was still unconvinced. "Perhaps it is not a good idea for you to take the girls riding, that might cause comment."

"It hasn't so far. There are still a few more I've not invited, and it would cause far more comment if I stop entertaining the young ladies in the only way possible."

"I suppose you are right, but be careful, Jason. I mean it."

"Good night, Clay." Jason had listened to enough of the man's fears so he went out to make certain the first group of guards were at their posts. Then he went to bed, on this night to sleep soundly for a change.

Curious to hear what Mr. Duffy would have to say for himself, Gabrielle made her way to his wagon while the others were eating breakfast the next morning. She hoped he'd be

119

good and sorry for being so mean to his wife, but she found him engaged in a bitter argument with Jason.

"The bitch has her eye on every man in sight and needed to be taught a lesson I tell you!" Sam Duffy was nearly as tall as Jason, but much bulkier. His sandy hair was overlong, and his scraggly beard added no note of distinction to his nondescript features. That his wife might wish to look at other men hardly seemed surprising.

"I care little what prompted your argument, Sam. I'll not allow any man to strike a woman; it's as simple as that. You can give me your promise that it will never happen again, or you may leave the wagon train now. Those are your choices."

"You can't do that!" Sam protested indignantly. "I got every right to be here, same as everybody else!"

Jason stood with his feet apart, poised for another fight if that was necessary to end the man's belligerent mood. "Not if I say you haven't. Now make up your mind, I've no more time to waste this morning."

Although Gabrielle could hear the men's conversation, she moved closer still, afraid she might miss something important if she didn't. Mrs. Duffy was standing nearby, far from eager to rejoin her husband's company. Gabrielle felt sorry for the woman. She appeared to have been pretty once, but now her right eye was black and her lips were so swollen she probably couldn't even sip liquids without suffering considerable pain. Gabrielle wondered if she had loved Sam Duffy when they'd married, for it certainly didn't look as though she did that morning. When Jason spotted her he gave her a warning glance as if he expected her to cause some further disturbance, but she just smiled prettily, as if she had every right to be there.

Knowing he was beaten, Sam Duffy had to agree, but he looked far from pleased about it. "All right. You'll have no more trouble from me, I swear it."

"Mrs. Duffy, will you come here please?" Jason waited for her to approach; then he explained what had been decided. "I'll not tolerate another incident like yesterday's. If you even

120

suspect it might happen again, I want you to come to me immediately. Is that clear?"

The battered woman nodded. "Yes, sir," she finally managed to whisper.

Satisfied that his rules were understood Jason turned away. He headed straight toward Gabrielle, not realizing he had drawn Sam's attention to her. The hostile man's expression darkened and an evil gleam appeared in his eyes, but he knew better than to insult the attractive young woman when Jason could overhear him.

"You should have known better than to come over here this morning, but at least you kept your mouth shut. I'm grateful for that." He was pleased to see she bore no trace of the scuffle she'd entered, and he smiled as he greeted her.

Turning to take her place by his side, Gabrielle responded truthfully. "I wanted to know what would happen to the man, that's all. How could he manage to follow the trail if he were all alone? Wouldn't he be attacked by Indians, or become lost?"

"Definitely, that's why he'll be a model husband for as long as the trip lasts. I hope he learned something from this. His wife told me he is a good man except for an occasional burst of jealousy."

"What?" Gabrielle was astonished by that comment. "How can she consider such a man 'good'?"

"It isn't all that unusual for a man and his wife to argue, Gabrielle, but no man has the right to abuse a woman, no matter what the reason for his anger." Jason pushed his hat back, trying to adjust it more carefully upon his curls. His hair had grown too long—he'd simply had no time to trim it—but that was a slight annoyance. "Did your aunt and uncle never have disagreements?"

They had reached her wagon now and Gabrielle took only a moment to explain. "My aunt was a spinster. I have no experience with families except from what I observed in my friends' homes, and their parents were undoubtedly on their good behavior when they entertained guests."

"Oh, undoubtedly," Jason agreed. "You don't know a damn thing about life, do you Gabrielle?" he asked with a sly grin, her innocence now having an understandable cause. Her aunt must have been shocked when she'd had to assume the responsibility for a child, especially one who'd grown up to be such a lovely young woman. Since she hadn't approved of Beau, he could well imagine what the woman would have thought of him.

With a fiery glance, Gabrielle responded sarcastically. "Only what I've learned from you, Mr. Royal. Now good day." She left him then, since she knew he had to give the command to begin the day's march, but when she turned he was watching her, an amused smile on his face. This made her angrier still for she thought she knew a damn sight more about life than he did.

As they rode along the trail that day, Gabrielle noted the continuing changes in the landscape. The rolling hills had given way to a new flatness. This was a barren terrain devoid of the pretty spring flowers whose fragrance she'd so enjoyed. They soon discovered the Oregon Trail was not a well-worn road, but a route which was two to three miles wide. That was why each wagon train's experience was approximately the same, but in subtle ways each was also different.

When Paul had finished serving lunch he sat down with his charges and joined in the discussion of the morning's ride. "We've left the valley of the Little Blue. That's why you've noticed such a difference in our surroundings. We should reach the Platte River by tomorrow afternoon if Mr. Royal keeps to his usual pace and I have no reason to doubt he won't. That man is as steady as they come. He doesn't waste a moment that could be better spent on the trail."

"The Platte?" Gabrielle remarked with a vacant stare, overcome by a sudden wave of apprehension. She'd known all along that they couldn't avoid the river, but she'd not thought the mere prospect of sighting it would fill her with such terrible dread. She could barely chew and set her plate aside after taking no more than a few bites.

"Yes, we've been making a good fifteen miles a day I'll bet. We'll reach the Platte easily by nightfall tomorrow."

"Is that a fact?" Gabrielle whispered hoarsely, feeling she was expected to make some comment.

"We should be able to hunt some, antelope or buffalo. Have you ever tasted buffalo meat?"

"No, I'll look forward to trying it."

As the others picked up the conversation Gabrielle grew silent. She tried to follow her friends' comments as they teased Paul about his cooking, but she could not escape the feeling of foreboding which swelled within her until she could scarcely draw a breath. Excusing herself, she walked toward the horses, knowing her devotion to Sunny would attract no attention, but even as she stroked Sunny's glossy coat she thought only of Beau.

Jason stood in front of the fire over which he and Clayton had cooked their lunch, and he watched Gabrielle with a fond gaze. She is delightfully graceful, rather like a wood nymph, he thought, with her talent for taming even the most spirited of beasts. He had to chuckle then, for he knew her touch to have a far different effect upon a man. Her stallion nuzzled her shoulder affectionately, and they appeared to be such a contented pair that he did not intrude. However, the following afternoon he made a point of seeking out the young woman he'd come to regard so highly.

"Come with me!" he called, and pushing Duke to a gallop, he wasn't surprised when she responded to that challenge. Sunny overtook Duke with a few long strides, and once they were sufficiently ahead of the first wagon to avoid being observed, he drew his stallion to a halt. "I did not want the river to take you by surprise. We will reach the Platte withing the hour."

Gabrielle nodded thoughtfully, as if she weren't already aware of that fact. "Thank you, it is most considerate of you to think of my feelings." Jason continually surprised her, and as usual she wondered what his true motive was for being so kind.

Jason shrugged nonchalantly. "It's only one of my many

duties, ma'am."

"Of course, but it is appreciated all the same," Gabrielle responded seriously, not knowing how she should react to his teasing sarcasm. If only he were not so damned good looking, she thought, suddenly determined to resist the charming grin he was flashing so easily. She'd lost her head completely with him once—several times actually, although the last had been the most devastating in terms of surrender—and she did not want to repeat that intimacy ever again since it was pointless. Had he been a true gentleman he would have asked for her hand before they'd made love, or immediately thereafter. He most certainly would not have waited to see if he had to marry her just to avoid a scandal. Now just looking at him was painful, for she could imagine no fate worse than having to marry a man who didn't love her.

Seeing her glance grow troubled, Jason spoke of the only topic which came to his mind. "We'll follow the South Platte for nearly sixty miles. Should be about five days with good weather. Then we'll cross over and follow the bank of the North fork of the river."

"That sounds like a complicated path to follow, I'm glad you know the way," Gabrielle replied, relieved he'd not said something more suggestive.

"I'll see you aren't lost for a minute, Gabrielle." Jason knew he was flirting openly with her now, hoping to distract her from her gloomy memories in the most outrageous manner possible. "Let's have that race we didn't have the opportunity to try. You take Duke and I'll ride Sunrise if you're willing."

Gabrielle tried to read the message in his glance and in his words, but she saw nothing that led her to believe he wanted to do more than simply race.

"Why not? It was my idea in the first place as I recall."

Jason slipped from his saddle and held Duke's bridle to make certain he would stand still while Gabrielle leaped upon his back. She was as agile as a deer, mounting the animal with no more effort than she would expend in taking a step upon the

124

ground. Satisfied that she was comfortably seated, he turned to Sunny. He stood by the horse's side for a moment, hoping the spirited stallion would be as cooperative as his mistress.

"Has he ever been ridden by a man?" he asked curiously, for he judged Gabrielle's weight to be little over one hundred pounds while he weighed closer to two.

"Only one," the auburn-haired beauty replied sadly, touched by the pain of that unexpected memory. "I have taught him no secret signals, but if you are afraid to ride him we needn't have the race."

Scoffing at the absurdity of that idea, Jason leaped upon the roan and tipped his hat. "I'll let you set the course, my dear."

After surveying their surroundings for a moment, Gabrielle could find no point of sufficient interest to use as the finish line. "Shall we return to the wagons or go on toward the river?"

"If we race back the way we've come, we'll scare everyone needlessly for they'll think we're trying to escape a pursuit. What do you say to racing to that boulder on the rise just ahead?"

"Yes, that's fine." Gabrielle adjusted her hold upon the reins, making certain she'd be able to control Duke. "Since you claim I didn't give you a fair start, I want you to say when to go."

"We'll both count to three then, how's that?" Jason offered agreeably.

Nodding as her expression grew serious, Gabrielle counted with him, but when they reached three and Sunrise took off with a burst of speed, she held Duke back for a second or two before giving him his head. She then tore off after her horse as if she'd wagered her life savings on the outcome of the race and Jason had no idea what she'd done. Duke's long powerful stride crossed the ground with admirable speed, but even with Jason's additional weight Sunny won handily. Laughing as she drew alongside them, Gabrielle congratulated the winner.

"That was an inspired ride, Mr. Royal, but since it was my

125

horse who won I do not feel as though I have lost."

Jason knew she preferred to ride her own horse so he dismounted quickly. As he passed Sunny's reins back to her he whispered in her ear, "I'd say I deserve a nice prize, but I'll settle for a kiss."

Tossing her flowing red hair, Gabrielle gave his request scant consideration before she agreed. "Fine, but you'll have to catch me first!"

She was too quick for him, however, and was in the saddle and gone before he could lift his foot to the stirrup. He had no choice but to stand where he was and swear loudly, for he knew he could never catch her when Sunny was the more swift stallion.

When the wagon train reached the South Platte late that afternoon, Gabrielle found the sight of the wide, muddy river as unnerving as she'd feared it would be. Beau had not died there, but nearly a week's journey ahead, at the place where they'd ford the river. That thought provided her with no consolation, however, and she felt a nearly uncontrollable rage at the river which had claimed her beloved's life. Rather than join the singers after dinner, she strolled aimlessly around the circle of wagons until she heard a man's voice call her name in a low-pitched snarl. He was standing in the shadows and she could see little more than his silhouette, but she could think of only one heavyset man who would wish to greet her so rudely.

"Yes, Mr. Duffy?"

"I'll not have you spying on us, Miss MacLaren. That is your name, ain't it?" he growled hoarsely.

"Yes."

Aware that the hour was later than she'd realized, Gabrielle lifted the hem of her skirt slightly with her right hand, ready to run should the man come any closer. "But I'm merely taking a walk, not spying upon you and your family."

Sam negated her denial with one short obscenity. "I catch you near our wagon again, you'll be damn sorry, now git before I change my mind and teach you the lesson you deserve!"

126

Since Gabrielle knew exactly how he chose to give instruction, she did not bother to reply but walked swiftly away. The man was offensive in the extreme, but what would happen to poor Mrs. Duffy and their children if Jason forced him to leave? Would the woman go with him or try to continue on her own? That was a matter she wanted to discuss with the woman herself, but she'd have to be certain her husband didn't see them talking since he'd taken such a dislike to her. Lost in thought, she walked swiftly by Jason's tent without stopping to say good-evening, but he leaped to his feet to give chase, catching her by the hand and turning her back to face him when they reached the next patch of deep shadow.

"Oh, Jason, don't ever do that again!" Gabrielle protested breathlessly, her heart pounding wildly for in the darkness she'd thought he was Sam Duffy making good his threat until she'd heard his deep chuckle.

"You said I'd have to catch you, and I have. Now don't be such a poor loser," he whispered softly as he drew her into a close embrace.

Gabrielle made sure they were hidden by the shadows before she lifted her hands to his shoulders, thinking herself lucky he had demanded only a kiss. She felt safe in his arms despite his teasing words, and when his mouth met hers she did not resist his affection but returned it, her tongue playfully teasing his until he lowered his hand to her breast. When he slowly caressed the flushed tip with his fingertips, she drew away, for the sheer muslin of her dress offered no barrier to his touch and she was afraid of what would happen should she not flee immediately.

"I have guard duty again tonight. Come and meet me." Jason's lips caressed her ear as he whispered softly, praying she would agree, but before she could reply, he heard a feminine voice calling his name. "Damn, that's Iris. Wait here. I'll be right back."

Gabrielle tried to catch her breath as he left her, the man was impossible to control she realized. To him a kiss was an invitation to so much more she'd not make the mistake she just had again. Thinking she owed him a reply to his invitation, however, she waited in the shadows while he spoke with Iris, but being curious, she crept up to the back of the tent where she could overhear their conversation.

"Why haven't you asked me to go riding with you again, Mr. Royal? You know how much I enjoy your company." Iris moved closer to him, whispering seductively since Clayton Horne was nowhere in sight. "Didn't you enjoy my company more than that of the others?" she purred as she placed her hands upon his broad chest and leaned against him.

Wanting only to be rid of the troublesome brunette as rapidly as possible Jason put his hands around her waist to push her away. "Miss Stewart, I enjoy the company of all you young ladies, but I'll be especially pleased to take you with me in the morning. Now good night. The hour is late." Jason waited impatiently until the flirtatious young woman started back to her wagon and then he ran back to the secluded spot where he'd left Gabrielle. But he found only the haunting trace of her perfume, nothing more.

Chapter VII

As they began their ride the next morning Gabrielle pretended to be very interested in Barbara's reflections upon the scenery. Taking her place beside the talkative blonde, she did not even look in Jason's direction when he came for Iris. Yet she could feel his hostile glance raking over her. The sensation was as painful as if he'd struck her with the back of his hand. Had the man really expected her to meet him in the middle of the night when he'd already made a date to go riding with Iris at dawn? Did he think she had no pride at all? Last night she'd heard his music floating upon the breeze again, the same wistful tune which had drawn her to him before. She wondered if he thought he had to do no more than play his harmonica and she would come to him. He seemed to enjoy the company of pretty young women greatly. She turned to watch as Iris rode away by his side.

"They deserve each other!" She whispered under her breath, bitter because he had so little sense of honor.

The thinly soiled plain which stretched before them supported no trees to provide wood for fires or shade for rest. They had been reduced to gathering buffalo chips for cooking fuel. Fortunately the beasts were plentiful and the trails the animals followed as they made their way to the river provided an abundant source of the useful waste. Iris regarded the task as so far beneath her that she refused to venture out on such an expedition until Gabrielle asked if she'd like to eat only cold food while the rest of them dined on hot. When all the others agreed that that was only fair since she did no work, she had no choice but to agree with their demands although she complained bitterly the entire time they conducted their search for fuel.

"I'd like to wring her neck!" Erica vowed with an exasperated sigh. "It doesn't matter what has to be done she'll not help us do it!"

"We only have to put up with her tantrums until we reach Oregon City, but just think what a life she'll give the poor man who takes her for a wife," Gabrielle stated. She gave Erica a sympathetic smile.

"I think we should warn the poor soul. Perhaps we can save him from such a gruesome fate!" Erica admired Gabrielle's restraint. Her own dislike for the self-centered Iris was increasing each day.

"Somehow I think the men will see through her charm fairly quickly since it is so insincere."

"The way Mr. Royal does?" Erica asked skeptically.

"What do you mean?" Gabrielle responded sharply; then she coughed quickly as if the dust were bothering her to distract Erica. She realized her feelings had been all too evident in her voice.

"I just mean he truly seems to like her company, and he's had time enough to become wise to her tactics."

"He's not one of the bachelors though, Erica, so his opinion of her isn't going to matter. Now let's hurry back so Paul can begin to cook supper." Gabrielle hustled her friend back toward the wagon, distracting her with talk of food so she'd not mention Jason again. She could not bear to think he might have been fooled by Iris' wiles when he had so many of his own.

As if to reward their labors, Paul prepared prairie chickens spiced with sage for supper. He'd showed them how to powder the dry leaves between their fingertips, giving the lesson as if he were personally responsible for teaching them how to cook. Impressed by his tips, six of the girls watched closely. Only Iris, certain she'd find a husband who could afford to hire a cook, didn't bother to listen.

After her initial disgust, Gabrielle found the sight of the meandering river fascinating. She was drawn to it as a child is captivated by the very thing his parents forbid him to touch. Slipping away from her friends after lunch, she rode alone along the riverbank, so lost in dreams of the past she failed to notice the water seeping through the sandy soil at the river's edge. Sunny tossed his head, displaying his dislike for the slippery footing, but she gave his neck a comforting pat to reassure him and rode on. When suddenly his hooves sank too deeply for him to pull them free, it was too late for Gabrielle to recognize the danger he'd felt. The magnificent stallion was caught fast and his terrified shrieks came too late for her to take any action to direct him to safer ground. She swung her leg over the saddle and jumped down from his back, leaping for what she thought was solid soil but it was quicksand too. It caught her tiny feet and sent her sprawling forward on her hands and knees. The wagons were passing no more than fifty yards in the distance, but she feared the noise the wooden vehicles made as they creaked along and the cloud of dust their passage created would prevent anyone from hearing her desperate calls or seeing her waves for help.

She knew nothing about quicksand except what she'd just discovered, but she realized it had to have a bottom somewhere. If only Sunny would stop struggling so violently he might find a firm footing and be able to rest until help arrived, but there was no way to reason with the hysterical horse. With each lunge he made, he sank deeper into the mire. She held onto the reins as she tried to dig herself free, the coarse grains of sand tore her fingertips to bloody shreds but she knew she was fighting for her life as well as his and a little pain was of no consequence. At last she got one foot to dry ground and then the other. Pulling with all her might, she tried to guide Sunny toward the shore, but her efforts were too feeble to turn him and he sank even further into the slime, clear to his chest while she tried frantically to think of some way to save him. She called to him in as soothing a voice as she could manage, realizing that his efforts to pull free were causing him to sink deeper. However, he was too badly frightened to respond with anything more than a renewed burst of strength which succeeded only in sinking him another few inches into the seemingly bottomless pit of quicksand.

Jason had been riding on the far side of the wagons when Duke suddenly grew so agitated he could scarcely control him. Such behavior was so unlike the usually pleasant nature of the horse, he turned away in a wide arc thinking perhaps his mount had been frightened by a snake, but there was no sign of a serpent upon the ground. Something was obviously wrong. He trusted the horse to sense what he could not. Fearing that whatever danger was present might lie near the river, he raced between a break in the line of wagons and headed toward the water. He heard Sunny's screams himself then, and the last desperate cries of a dying beast. He gave Duke his head, knowing the horse would lead him to the creature in trouble. When he got close enough to see that it was Sunrise who had strayed into the quicksand, he dug his heels into Duke's sides to send him forward at an even greater speed. Reaching the riverbank, he grabbed the rope he carried on his saddle, made a flying loop, threw it over Sunny's head, and then secured his end to the saddle horn. As he leaped from Duke's back, he gave him the command to pull.

Gabrielle's tears blurred her vision, but she continued to pull on Sunny's reins, attempting to give Jason and Duke all the help she could. Although the buckskin horse was strong, Sunrise was his equal in size and he remained stuck fast.

Jason looked back toward the wagon train hoping someone else had taken note of their predicament, but there was no sign of additional help on the way. He dared not leave Gabrielle alone while he ran back to summon assistance, and he knew

132

she'd not leave Sunny to go on such an errand herself so he did not even suggest it. Firing his rifle would bring no help either. People would mistake the shots for those of a hunter and ignore them. No. If anything could be done to save the horse, he knew they'd have to do it themselves. Sunrise was fast becoming exhausted and Jason knew unless they thought of something quickly the stallion would be lost. He needed no more than one glance at Gabrielle's terror-filled expression to know that was something he dared not allow.

"Stop tugging on his reins for a moment," Jason ordered as he ran to Duke's side to lead the horse forward to create some slack in the rope.

"What are you doing?" Gabrielle screamed, terrified to think Jason had abandoned the effort to rescue her horse.

"Just do it!" Jason shouted, having little time to deal with her fear when the situation was so desperate. Coming back to her side he explained quickly. "An Indian once told me that it is possible to swim in quicksand. It must be rather like trying to swim through thick porridge but he swore it could be done. Now just call to Sunny and when he begins to make some progress toward us I'll have Duke try again to pull him free."

Since there was no time to argue, Gabrielle turned back to her stallion, praying the unnamed Indian had been right. In a soft enticing tone, she encouraged Sunny, coaxing him to come toward her. For long agonizing minutes he moved no closer to the shore, although he did seem to regain some of his composure. He was noticeably more calm. Then, afraid to believe what her eyes told her, Gabrielle turned to Jason, her face full with hope.

"He is turning this way, isn't he? If only slightly, he is moving?"

"Yes, that's it, keep calling to him, it's working." Jason was as amazed as Gabrielle, but once the horse stopped struggling against the heavy, damp sand and began to move with a slow, easy swimming motion, he began to make some headway although it was minimal.

Encouraged by the voice of his mistress, as well as by that of the tall man by her side, Sunrise kept trying to move and although his pace was heartbreakingly slow when he was nearly a foot closer to them, Jason began to shout to Duke to back away. Drawing the rope tight again, this time with Jason adding his considerable strength to the effort, they at last drew Sunny onto solid ground where his front hooves held fast. With a mighty lurch the roan pulled his hind legs free. He shook himself then, like a wet dog, flinging mud all over Jason and Gabrielle, but they fell into each other's arms. They were so overcome with joy at having saved the horse's life they cared little that he'd gotten them so dirty.

Jason hugged Gabrielle tightly, lifting her feet clear off the ground as he began to kiss her with a passion she thought quite natural after the fright they'd just suffered. She wrapped her arms around his neck and hung on, the depth of her gratitude impossible to express in any other way than by the ready acceptance of his affection. She adored him in that instant, and her kiss drove him to the brink of madness before he had the sense to draw away.

Looking down at her, Jason took a moment to catch his breath; then he released her with a rude shove. "There, how do you like being left begging for more! If only half the emotion in your kiss were sincere, you would have met me the other night!"

Anger was the last thing Gabrielle had expected from him after the triumph they'd just shared. She knew every bit of the feeling in her kiss had been most sincere. He was the one who was the tease, not her. "Did you really expect me to meet you when you'd already made a date with Iris for the next morning? When you are as fickle as that, do you truly expect me to come to you as though I were your slave?"

"What?" Jason stepped back, astonished by her accusation. "How else was I supposed to get rid of that woman quickly? You didn't think I really wanted to have her ride with me, did you?"

"Don't pretend that you didn't or you wouldn't have asked her!" Gabrielle responded in a fit of fury.

She was a mess. There was no other way to describe her appearance. Her light cotton dress was caked with mud, as was her long hair. Not an inch of her wasn't filthy, but that didn't diminish her appeal in the slightest. Jason thought her beauty as beguiling as always, and with a wicked grin he demanded she pay him for saving her horse in the only way he wanted to be repaid.

"When I have been so quick to come to your aid today, I have every right to expect you to come to mine just as rapidly."

"Isn't this all part of your job, Mr. Royal, no more than taking the risks for which you are being paid?" Gabrielle answered defiantly.

"No. This I did for you alone and I think you know exactly how I expect you to show your gratitude. Tonight we will camp near a spring which flows into the river; tomorrow we'll simply rest. It's a good place to do laundry, and the men can hunt. Tomorrow night everyone will be in a relaxed and friendly mood, and when I tell you to meet me, you will do it."

"I will not!" Gabrielle insisted firmly.

"Oh, yes you will." Jason stepped close. "You will meet me, or I will make your life so difficult you will come begging for me to make love to you simply to end your torment."

"You'll never live so long!" Gabrielle answered proudly, certain his threats were empty ones.

"I'm serious, Gabrielle. For starters I'm taking Sunny. You are obviously so careless with the animal you nearly lost him today and had I not come to his rescue you surely would have. I will take him for safekeeping and should you ever prove to be a responsible owner, which I sincerely doubt, you may have him back again."

"You don't mean it!" the disheveled young woman cried.

"Oh, but I do. I'm taking him with me now. If you walk fast enough you can catch up with your wagon and ride with Paul for the rest of the afternoon; if not, you'll simply have a long and tiring walk." Jason grabbed Sunny's reins and held them firmly as he swung himself up on Duke's back and recoiled his rope. "I'll give you your horse now if you'll give me your word you'll meet me tomorrow night without any more silly arguments."

Gabrielle simply turned her back on him as she started across the plain. She was too tired to run so she knew she'd not catch up to her wagon until it stopped for the night. Then she'd have to offer some explanation for the ghastly state of her appearance, but she didn't care. She'd never give in to Jason Royal when he planned to use her so badly. She would have made love to him again, that very afternoon, right there by the riverbank. She'd been so excited by their success and so delighted with his enthusiastic kiss, but such a display of affection wasn't what he wanted. All he seemed to desire was the power to make her submit to him on command and she'd rather die first.

Jason let her go, certain Gabrielle would come to her senses after she walked off her anger. He led Sunny along behind Duke until he came to a stretch of the river where he knew he could safely bathe the roan stallion. He wanted to remove the mud which streaked Sunny's glossy coat before the sun baked it to the consistency of hardened clay. Sunrise, however, quite naturally wanted no part of the river after his narrow escape from its treacherous shores, and laying his ears flat against his head, he refused to approach it. Not one to be outwitted by a horse, Jason used his hat to throw a sufficient amount of water upon the red stallion to rinse off every trace of his harrowing ordeal.

The young man then pulled off his shirt and scrubbed the mud off himself. It was not until his fingertips moved over the hardened muscles of his own chest that he realized how stupid he'd been not to bring Gabrielle with him. He could imagine nothing more pleasurable than joining her in a bath. She'd come into his arms so readily, but he'd shoved her away wanting only to show her how greatly she had disappointed him. He'd been so damn clever. He really should have ridden here with her in his arms. With the excuse of helping her to wash herself clean, he could have entertained her all afternoon with the most erotic amusements. Instead, he had condemned them both to needless frustration when paradise had been within their grasp. When he turned around Sunrise was eying him suspiciously. "I know what you think, horse, but I'll not be content until your mistress is mine!"

Before Gabrielle had walked too far, a small blond boy riding a mule that appeared to have few miles left in him wandered up to her side. "What happened to you, lady?" he asked curiously.

Since he was no more than a child, and a friendly one, Gabrielle saw no reason not to tell him the truth and she replied honestly, "My horse got caught in some quicksand"—she looked down at her badly soiled dress—"as you can readily see."

Looking out over the vacant plain, the young boy grew excited at the mention of quicksand. "Is he dead?"

"No. Mr. Royal has him."

"That's why you're walking?" The youngster inquired perceptively.

"That's why," Gabrielle admitted, glad he'd asked for no further explanation since she'd not have been able to give it.

After a moment's reflection, the boy broke into a wide grin. "You wanna ride behind me? Comet's plenty strong."

"Comet?" Gabrielle had to laugh for if ever an animal lacked the speed of a comet it was this one. "Are you certain I won't be too much for him?"

"Naw, he's a real brute; that's what my pa always says."

"Then I'd greatly appreciate a ride. Thank you." Gabrielle waited while the boy slipped his foot out of the stirrup so she could use it to boost herself up on his mule's back. When he was certain she was comfortable, he clucked to the old mule and they trotted off to catch up with the line of wagons. "My name is Gabrielle MacLaren, what is yours?"

"Timothy Duffy," the boy answered softly, as if he hoped she wouldn't hear.

Gabrielle gripped his shoulder in a frantic clasp. "I think you'd better let me off right now, Timothy. Your dad wouldn't approve of your helping me."

Timothy shook his head. "I knew who you were when I first saw you, miss. Since you helped my mom, I figure I owe it to you."

"That's very sweet, Timothy, but not if it will land us both in trouble. I can't allow that."

"Don't worry. Dad's in the back of the wagon asleep, he won't wake up until suppertime and Mom won't care even if she does see us, which she probably won't."

"Where is your family's wagon?" Gabrielle asked quickly, looking back to be certain Sam Duffy hadn't spotted them already.

"It's near the front today, no chance of them seeing us way back here."

Gabrielle was more frightened for the boy than she was for herself, but since his family's wagon was traveling so far ahead she decided to risk riding with him. "Don't they mind that you don't stay right with them?"

"Naw. They don't care as long as I am there at suppertime to do my chores."

Convinced they were safe for the time being at least, Gabrielle continued to ride with him, but she wished the little boy had been any other man's son than the despicable Sam Duffy's.

While the other young women were too polite to do more than stare wide-eyed as Gabrielle rode up upon the mule's back, Iris let fly a string of insulting questions. "My goodness, Gabrielle, whatever has happened to you? You look simply dreadful! How could you have come to be in such a state? I hope Mr. Horne doesn't see you or he'll be certain you've been raped. You weren't attacked by Indians were you? Tortured by those wild creatures? Where is your horse, you haven't lost

138

him have you?"

When the inquisitive brunette paused for a breath, Gabrielle thanked Timothy again for his kindness and bid him goodbye. As soon as he had left to rejoin his family, she turned to Iris and replied swiftly, "Oh, shut up. It's none of your damn business where I've been!" They had stopped by the spring Jason had described. It was a lovely spot. In the midst of the river were islands on which cottonwoods grew, and the scene was so charming she could scarcely believe how different the river was here. Searching through her belongings, she found clean clothing and, taking soap and a towel, started off for the water to find a spot where she might bathe before anyone else had an opportunity to remark upon her appearance.

Running along behind her, Erica kept still until they found a secluded spot and Gabrielle began to strip off her clothing. "Give me your dress and I'll do my best to wash it clean, but I'm afraid it's ruined. I know you don't want to confide in Iris, but won't you tell me what happened?"

"As soon as I'm clean, I'll do just that." Gabrielle had already prepared her remarks, going over her story in her mind as she'd ridden along behind Tim. "I rode Sunny too near the shore of the river and he stepped into some quicksand, Mr. Royal helped me to pull him free but since he believed the incident was entirely due to my carelessness he took Sunny with him and left me to walk. Fortunately, I met that little boy who has far more manners than our wagon master does."

"That doesn't sound like Mr. Royal to me, Gabrielle, I thought him a gentleman." Erica looked up no more than a moment and then continued to scrub the mud-soaked dress clean.

"Would any gentleman tell me to walk all afternoon when he was holding the reins of two mounts?" Gabrielle asked pointedly.

"Well, since you didn't have to walk, if he just wanted to punish you, I'd say he failed."

Hoping he'd fail in everything he attempted to force her to

do, Gabrielle pulled on her clean clothing and then knelt down beside her friend. "Here let me do that. It's my dress." But her hands were so sore from digging through the quicksand she had to lean back to rest.

"Gabrielle, look at your hands, they're bleeding!" Erica cried in dismay.

"A few little cuts, it's nothing." Gabrielle protested, but she knew she'd have a difficult time doing her laundry with her hands in such an unfortunate condition.

"Just give me that dress and I'll finish it. You'll be no better off if you rinse out the mud and then cover it with bloodstains!"

Sitting back, Gabrielle began to wonder about Timothy's mother. The woman would most probably come down to the water to do her laundry the next morning. Her husband would never come with her so perhaps she could speak with her then to ascertain how the man was behaving. She'd not wanted to question Timothy about him. It seemed unfair to ask the boy about his father, but she still thought someone should be checking up on the family and she doubted Jason had the time to do it.

When she was satisfied she'd done her best, Erica wrung out the dress and stood up. "I'll carry this back for you. Are you certain you're all right?"

"Of course, I'm fine," Gabrielle insisted. "Never better, let's hurry back, Paul might need some help with supper." She pulled on her boots and brushed off the mud, but they needed to be shined. She hoped one of the girls had thought to bring polish with her since she hadn't.

"How long is Mr. Royal going to keep Sunny?"

Gabrielle could not bear to think what she'd have to do to get her dear horse back, but that was not a secret she'd share with Erica. "He didn't say. I'll just have to wait and see I guess."

As they prepared to eat their supper, Erica passed the word softly among her companions, explaining what had happened to Gabrielle since she seemed so reluctant to relate the story herself. Only Iris seemed disappointed that the truth was not closer to her suspicions. She would have liked nothing better than to have heard the redhead had been raped by dozens of merciless Indian savages.

Gabrielle wrapped her fingers tightly with rags the next morning, and with that protection, she was able to wash all her clothes until they were sparkling clean. She had several muslin dresses, two bright cotton prints which she wore for everyday, her lace-trimmed lingerie, and slips. Everything was hung out to dry on lines strung between the wagons. They had seldom had the time or opportunity to wash all their garments at one time and the scene at the river's edge took on the flavor of a party despite the fact the women were all engaged in strenuous work. The prospect of having their clothing again fresh and clean was too pleasant a one to darken anyone's mood. Never one to do any work she could avoid, Iris solved her problem by paying the daughter of a family whose wagon was parked nearby to launder her things. The girl was happy with the money, and Iris was pleased she didn't have to do her own laundry. She joined the others at the water's edge, however, not wanting to miss any of the delicious gossip she was certain would make all the conversations worth hearing.

When she'd finished her own chores, Gabrielle strolled down the line of women still at work, hoping she would be able to find Mrs. Duffy without too much delay. When she saw Timothy minding his two younger sisters, she peered closely at the women working nearby and noticed his mother. She knelt by her side.

"Mrs. Duffy?"

The woman leaned back, her eyes filling with fright as she recognized Gabrielle. "Go away, I mustn't be seen talking to you!" she whispered hoarsely.

"Why not? I only want to introduce myself."

"I asked your name, Miss MacLaren, and while I think you were a fool to interfere in my argument with my husband, I do appreciate what you tried to do."

141

"You call that an argument?" Gabrielle asked in dismay. "I thought he meant to kill you!"

The nervous woman went back to her laundry, scrubbing the collar of a worn shirt. "Leave me be, Miss MacLaren. I didn't ask for your help and I don't need it either."

Distressed that the woman was so ungrateful, Gabrielle hesitated only a moment before getting up to leave. "Just get word to Mr. Royal if you need help, he won't fail you even if you don't trust me."

Mrs. Duffy's lips were set in a firm line. She was too proud to ask for help, that much was plain.

Turning away, Gabrielle stopped to speak to Timothy for a moment. She thanked him again for giving her a ride, and the little boy blushed with pleasure as if his efforts were seldom rewarded with praise. Encouraged, Gabrielle whispered softly so his mother wouldn't overhear. "Please think of me as your friend, Timothy. If I can ever do anything to help you or your little sisters just let me know."

The little girls looked up at the friendly young woman and smiled shyly; then they hid behind their brother's back. "We're all right, miss," Timothy finally mumbled. "Thanks anyway."

Gabrielle bid him goodbye and returned to her friends to enjoy the warmth of the sun. They were all chattering happily about the feast of buffalo meat the men had promised to provide, but she thought only of the confrontation that must come with the hateful Jason Royal.

The men who'd gone hunting for buffalo did not return to the camp until midafternoon for Jason had insisted that any man who shot one of the woolly beasts must skin it and bring back the hide. The hides were to be used to waterproof the wagons when they forded the Platte. While the ribs were delicious barbequed, he demanded that every single morsel of edible meat be carried back to the wagon train to be sliced into thin strips which would be dried into jerky. The hunters left behind on the plains little more than the bones, skulls, and hooves of the dead buffalo since Jason had told them quite forcefully that it was a hunter's duty to make optimum use of each kill. Half the men had remained behind to guard the camp, but it had been agreed at the outset that their families would share equally in the fruits of the hunt.

Paul was delighted with the side of ribs Jason brought him to prepare, but Gabrielle saw only that the man had had the audacity to ride her stallion. She would not forgive him for that. The horse needed a good rest after what he'd suffered the previous afternoon, but from the sweat which poured down his flanks it was obvious Jason had pushed him to the limit of his endurance. She approached Jason to lodge a strongly worded complaint. "You should not have ridden my horse so hard, Mr. Royal. That was not only stupid but foolhardy as well. He is too fine an animal to exhaust chasing buffalo."

Jason tried to suppress a sly smile; then he let it slide across his lips in a taunting grin. "Nonsense, he enjoyed it. He lacks Duke's skill as a mount for hunting; still, he'll learn quickly enough. He has the speed and agility required, but he shies at the sound of gunfire. Perhaps you've not had an opportunity to notice that."

"You bastard." Gabrielle mouthed that insult silently so only Jason could tell what she'd said.

"Why, Miss MacLaren, if you are truly so concerned about how I might treat Sunny why don't you come to my tent as soon as you have finished your supper tonight? We can discuss the matter of his care more fully then." Touching his hat brim lightly, Jason turned the roan stallion away before she could voice any of the stinging insults which rapidly filled her mind.

Gabrielle was furious, but as she turned back toward the others she saw Iris' petulant frown and could not resist commenting sweetly, "He is such a charming man, don't you think, and so kind to help me train my horse." She smiled then, as if she adored him, and when Iris' face filled with rage Gabrielle went to see if Paul needed any help preparing the ribs. She wished she had put the brunette in her place, but she

143

was afraid it would be Sunny who suffered if she did.

The buffalo ribs were as delicious as Paul had promised they'd be, and as they dined the air was filled with the savory aroma of the roasting meat. The travelers relaxed. Full of laughter and good fellowship, they were pleased to share even the brief rest they'd been given. As her friends began to coax Rebecca to play her zither, Gabrielle slipped away, intent upon meeting Jason as he'd demanded but determined to give him not so much as a kind word.

He was expecting her to come. Seated by himself, he played his harmonica softly while he waited. When he glanced up and saw her, he slipped the slender instrument into his hip pocket and stood to greet her. He'd gone to the trouble of bathing and trimming his hair since last she'd seen him. Indeed, he'd shaved for the second time that day, and while he looked devilishly handsome he seemed so genuinely pleased to see her she began to blush deeply. For an instant she forgot why he'd demanded that she meet him. His eyes shone with an admiration she was flattered to think was sincere, and her smile was as delighted as his as she bid him good evening.

"Let's go for a walk," Jason suggested, and gesturing toward the river, he strolled along by her side not reaching for her hand until he was certain they could no longer be observed. "We were lucky this morning, we found a sizeable herd of buffalo just after dawn. They were on their way down to the river and we just picked them off. You probably don't know it but when the Indians kill a buffalo they like to bring their children the liver as a treat. They consider it a delicacy which should be eaten while it is still warm."

Astonished, Gabrielle stopped abruptly to ask, "Raw? You mean raw?" She could barely hide her revulsion at that possibility and hoped she'd misunderstood him.

"Of course raw. They think it is superb. I should have brought one to you so you could have tried it yourself."

"I am grateful that you did not." Gabrielle shuddered slightly, appalled by the thought of little Indian children happily gulping down raw buffalo liver.

"Are you cold?" Jason asked softly, moving his hand to her waist to draw her near.

"No. That was just a rather gruesome picture you painted. If you know of other such quaint Indian customs, please do not relate them to me."

Jason chuckled at her request, his mood far more mellow than hers. "I have great respect for the tribes which inhabit these lands, Gabrielle. It is a terrible tragedy that their customs clash so violently with those of the white man. The Indians have a reverence for all of God's creations which far surpasses ours."

Intrigued by his words Gabrielle gave them careful consideration as she watched his expression from beneath her long lashes. He had seldom appeared so relaxed with her, and as always, she could not help but respond to his charm. That he was so bright and introspective an individual impressed her most favorably as well. "They have every right to try to stop us from crossing their land, don't they?"

Jason wished to go no farther and turned to pull her into his arms as he whispered, "And this is my right, Gabrielle." He kissed her then, very gently, his lips barely touching hers before he drew away. He didn't care what had inspired her to meet him, she had; and he wanted only to make love to her as tenderly as he had the first time. He kissed her cheek then let his lips slowly trace the curve of her throat. She relaxed against him, her arms encircling his slim waist to hold him close. He raised his hands to her temples, sifting the silken strands of her glorious auburn hair as his mouth returned to hers. She was so lovely, so very young and dear. He enfolded her in a tender embrace, pressing every inch of her splendid body against his lean frame and longing to enjoy the same closeness of spirit. As before, she slipped her hands beneath his soft deerskin shirt to caress his bare skin, and he wished there were some way to make her understand what he could not seem to speak in words. He wanted only to hold her in his arms, to cherish her sweetness and savor her beauty, but his mind filled with far more erotic images and he could no longer hide his growing desire.

Gabrielle responded readily to Jason's deep, sensuous kiss. She leaned against him, drinking in his intoxicating taste with such pleasure she made not the slightest objection when he drew her down upon the soft grass at the river's edge. She was aware only of the joy of his touch as his fingertips stripped her garments away and then slid over her bare skin. As before the magic of his loving was so compelling she was lost in its spell, so completely his she no longer heard the sound of the water rushing over the rocky river bed but felt only the pounding beat of her own heart as its frantic rhythm called to his.

The twilight was deepening to darkness, and no one else would be likely to stray so far from camp. Still, Jason knew the beautiful creature in his arms deserved far more consideration than he was able to provide. He longed to make love to Gabrielle in an oversize feather bed where he would have no fear for their comfort or privacy. He held her in a fond embrace, wanting her to feel the joy of the moment as fully as he did, but soon her enchanting smile enticed him to put aside all caution and plunge deeply into the mysteries of love. Needing no more than the invitation in her sultry glance, he followed the instincts he could no longer bear to ignore. Her lissome body welcomed his far more easily this time, with a smooth, sweet rush of heat which enveloped him in a magic all her own. He was enchanted by the graceful beauty in his arms, his heart hers for the asking, but he was too lost in pleasure to speak in any language except that of love.

Gabrielle dug her fingertips into the taut muscles of Jason's shoulders as the rapture which throbbed within her slender body swelled to a shuddering peak. She called his name in a breathless moan, her passion as primitive as his. Wild and savage, it bound them together in an ecstasy which seared their souls with the blazing heat of the same brilliant fire which fused their bodies into one. The star-filled heavens seemed to swirl about them, carrying them aloft on a cloud of pleasure so rich its memory would fill her heart forever. Gabrielle prayed the night would never end for she thought she would surely die when the light of morning burst upon them and forced them to be two polite strangers once more.

Awash upon the same turbulent tide of exquisite sensation, it was a long while before Jason could again think clearly. He was still filled with a contentment so profound he dreaded spoiling its peace by speaking. Finally, he knew he had no other option.

"I must get you back to your wagon, we've been gone far too long as it is," he whispered softly, his lips pausing to caress the smooth swell of her breast before he sat up.

Gabrielle reached for his hand, pulling him back down beside her. "Jason, please wait. Let's not go back." Not now she longed to say, not ever.

Jason hesitated only long enough to kiss her once again before he denied her request. "I am thinking only of you, Gabrielle. I care little what gossip circulates about me but there can be none attached to your name." He brought her palm to his lips, kissing it gently. "Now do not argue. This is only the first of many such nights, I promise you. Just come with me now, for the pain of parting will be no less sharp if we delay it."

Gabrielle slipped from his arms, unwilling to argue, but the risk of gossip was the least of her concerns. She could think only of the love he gave so generously, of the tenderness of his touch, the devotion in his kiss. She did not want to have to deny what she felt in her heart. Their passion had been real, an emotion so strong she could not suppress its expression any more than she could deny its existence. She went quickly to the fresh, sparkling water, splashing it generously upon herself to wash away the fragrance that was more his than hers. She remained silent as she got dressed, neither wanting or needing his assistance this time.

As the moon rose higher in the sky, Jason could see Gabrielle's expression more clearly and his heart fell for he knew she had not accepted his plea for prudent caution. When she was ready to go back, he laced his fingers in hers, holding her hand tightly as they walked back toward the circle of wagons. The sounds of music and laughter still floated upon the breeze. Pleased that he had not kept her away as long as it had seemed, Jason bent down to give her one last kiss, but she pulled away quickly and was gone, leaving him filled with a loneliness so overwhelming he did not even notice Clayton standing nearby until his friend spoke in a low, threatening tone.

"You should not have disregarded my warning, Jason." He stood in the shadows at the back of the tent where he'd positioned himself to await Jason's return. "I make it a point to see the young ladies several times each day. I especially like to make certain they are accounted for at night, but tonight I noticed immediately that Gabrielle was missing from the group. I'm most assuredly not the only one who made that observation."

Jason raked his fingers through his curls. Were it any other man challenging his right to be with Gabrielle he would have settled the matter with his fists, but that tactic was inappropriate now. "Stay out of this, Clay, I mean her no harm."

"No harm!" The older man exploded angrily. "We are responsible for the welfare of these young women, for their health and safety to say nothing of their chastity! How far have you gone with Gabrielle, are you simply taking her for walks in the moonlight while you tell her amusing stories or have you seduced her as well?"

His expression hardening into a furious mask, Jason responded hoarsely. "That is not a question I'll answer. Now excuse me, I've got things that need to be done."

Clayton stepped forward to block his way. "Damn it, you owe me the truth and I demand you tell it right now!"

Jason took a deep breath and his gray eyes gleamed fiercely like Toledo steel. "The truth is a long and complicated tale, one

I have given my word to Gabrielle never to repeat. She regards me as gentleman enough to honor that promise even if you do not. Now stand aside or I'll walk right over you."

Jason's voice was low, his threat so convincing Clayton moved out of his way without giving him any further argument, but both men knew the issue had not been settled between them.

Chapter VIII

Gabrielle rejoined her friends with the same ease she'd left them. Her appearance was flawless still, and when Clayton Horne stopped by to remind them all how swiftly dawn would come, she returned his inquiring glance with a gaze so steady and free of guilt that he turned away without drawing her aside as he'd meant to do. He was certain if he could not make Jason see reason he would have no better luck with a young woman as confident as she.

As soon as he'd given the order to turn out, Jason rode down the line of wagons, wanting only to see Gabrielle. When he waved to her she smiled prettily, but he wanted to make certain she noticed he was alone. He'd invited each of the brides to go riding at least once, and since the practice bothered Gabrielle he would cease to do it. He did not recall that he had ridden with the others to prevent undue comment on the time he spent with Gabrielle. However, Clayton's hostile stare did not lessen, and the two men did little more than nod as they passed each other in their travels about the camp.

With only one more day's ride ahead of them until they came to the spot where they'd ford the Platte, Jason wanted to make certain Gabrielle's every thought was focused solely upon him and not upon the young man who had died there. When the wagon train began the afternoon journey, he deftly cut her horse from the others and remarked with a wicked grin, "This is a fine afternoon for a race, Miss MacLaren."

"Superb!" Gabrielle replied and needing no further encouragement she sent Sunny into a long easy stride, his gallop so graceful the yards melted away beneath his flying hooves.

Jason hoped just once to beat the gorgeous pair, but although Duke gave his best, he could not overtake the spirited red horse. Fortunately, Gabrielle had no wish to defeat either Duke or his master by too humiliating a margin so she pulled her stallion to a halt as soon as they'd left the wagon train far enough behind to insure their privacy and waited for Jason to reach her side.

Weaving his fingers in her long flowing hair, Jason leaned over to kiss the lively young woman he found impossible to resist. His gesture was filled with affection despite the brevity his position in the saddle demanded.

"I have missed you," he exclaimed with a delighted smile. "I wasn't certain you would come with me today since I've had so little opportunity to speak with you in the last two days. I hope you did not perceive my desire for discretion as neglect."

"Do you think I would be here if I had?" Gabrielle asked coyly, her glance a mischievous one.

"No!" Jason cried out in mock anguish. "But you are here and let's not waste a moment of the time we have to share." He led her only a half mile farther along the trail, to a spot upon a rise where they could overlook the river but at the same time be shielded from view. Letting their mounts graze, Jason untied the blanket he'd rolled up behind his saddle. Having had no need for a tent for several days, he'd made the switch in gear, knowing no one would question the use he planned for the soft woolen spread.

Placing the blanket upon the grass he patted the spot next to him as he sat down. "Come here, my pet."

Gabrielle raised a hand to shield her eyes, surveying the deserted landscape which surrounded them. "I keep thinking of those Indians you admire so greatly. What would they say if they discovered us making love?"

Jason chuckled at the absurdity of that prospect. "I really don't know, they might be discreet enough to wait until we finished before they made their presence known. Then again, if they wanted to attack us, that would certainly be a marvelous opportunity to do so. You needn't worry, however, for I have seen no sign of their presence for several days."

Alarmed, Gabrielle turned to face him. "Before then you had?" she asked in dismay.

"Yes. The Pawnee have winter villages on the South Platte, but in the summer they follow the buffalo since it is their primary source of food and hides. I've seen small hunting parties several times when I've gone ahead to scout the trail, but they have had no great interest in us. You should have a good opportunity to observe some Indians firsthand when we reach Fort Laramie. Now stop worrying so about them and please come and sit down here beside me."

He'd tossed his hat aside, and pulled his shirt off over his head, not wanting to stop later to peel off layers of clothing Gabrielle would find in her way. Just looking at her made his breath quicken, but he did not want to appear too eager for her kiss so he lay back upon the blanket to get comfortable as if he had the entire afternoon to spend with her.

Gabrielle stood where she was, but she began to disrobe with the slow, graceful gestures which were so much a part of her charm. She let her dress fall to the grass, then her slips, then as she bent down to unbutton her shoes she spoke softly. "Is it the danger which you enjoy so greatly, Jason, the risk of discovery which makes my kisses so sweet?"

Jason could barely speak. He'd seen women who'd earned a fortune by pleasing men attempt the same artful seduction with far less success than this auburn-haired beauty was demonstrating now. This was a strip tease so erotic but so subtle he could only stare, hoping she would finish before he was driven by the force of his desire to simply leap up and throw her down upon the blanket. She'd spoken, but he'd scarcely heard her words. He realized she was hesitating, her fingertips at the bows which held her camisole in place, and he answered quickly, wanting her to slip the lace-trimmed garment from her shoulders to expose more of her marvelous figure to his view. His voice was hoarse with desire as he spoke. "No. It is you alone, Gabrielle, simply your charm and beauty that I want so badly." She cast the last of her garments aside then and came to him. Her kiss as desperate as his, she pressed her now-nude body along the length of his.

Jason pulled the lithe beauty across his chest, savoring the cool smoothness of her skin against his own far more warm flesh. Her long, shimmering red hair fell about his shoulders, veiling the sunlight from his view, but he saw only her enchanting smile. He hugged her tiny waist tightly as if he feared she might still slip away. Never had he thought any woman could do what she'd done to him. How could he have thought she was the one who needed to be taught the lessons of love when she knew how to give it in such abundance? Her fingertips slid down his sides, then to his belt, and he was sorry he did not know how to disrobe as enticingly as she did. But he did not stop her and she swiftly stripped away the last barrier which remained between them.

Gabrielle covered his face with light kisses. Enjoying the taste of his deeply bronzed skin, she let her tongue slide down his throat to the dark curls which covered his chest. He had the most splendid of male bodies, firm and strong, and she wondered if she could give him the same gift of rapture he had given her with no more than lavish kisses the first time they'd been together. The muscles of his flat stomach grew taut beneath her lips, and when he wove his fingers in her hair to hold her close, she understood what he wanted without being told. He was so easy to love, and love him she did, her devotion growing ever more bold with each beat of her heart. Her mouth was warm, soft, and teasing as her tongue caressed his flesh, and knowing how greatly she was pleasing him, she did not stop until he could stand no more. He was completely incoherent, calling her name in a slurred moan as he drew her into his arms and forced her down upon the folds of the soft blanket to dominate her body with the considerable strength still left in his. He did not want to rest alone on the bed of ecstasy she'd created, so with a tenderness born of awakening love, he caressed her body with a slow, knowing touch until he felt her shudder with pleasure. Then he abandoned himself to the madness of possessing her, confident of how deeply his joy would be shared.

Again at perfect peace, Gabrielle reclined languidly in Jason's arms, enjoying the heat of his body as greatly as that of the sun. Were she to become tan all over, she would have no way to explain such exposure, but she cared little for that small problem. Some clever idea would come to her mind should she ever need an excuse for the golden color of her fair skin. She swept that trivial concern from her mind as she continued to savor the closeness which had grown between them. That bond of trust seemed to deepen each time they were together, and certain he would answer her question seriously, she said softly, "Jason, my aunt told me nothing of the beauty a man and woman can share and truly I do not think she even suspected it. I know you must have considerable experience, but is it always like this?"

Jason propped his head on his hand to look down at his bewitching companion, his smile filled with amusement as he responded. "You mean the feeling of pleasure so intense you can neither laugh nor weep but only crave more no matter if the cost be your very soul?"

Gabrielle slid her fingertips across his chest, and he caught them in his hand, drawing her palm to his lips. "Yes, that is precisely the way to describe how I feel in your arms, but is it the same for you when you make love to other women?"

Jason had to consider her question for no more than an instant. He had kept no count of his sexual encounters, for truly, other than seeking momentary pleasure, there had been no meaning in them. "I have never made love to another woman, Gabrielle, only to you." The coarsest of verbs came to his mind but he would not speak the word to her. "I have known other women, been with them that is true, but never, never was it as superb as it is with you. It was never making love, but only fulfilling the most primitive of man's needs." He leaned down to kiss her then, his passion so tender he wanted never to have to return to the noisy confusion of the wagon train and the seemingly endless weeks of travel which still lay ahead.

Gabrielle knew then without doubt that no man would ever give her the pleasure she had found in his arms, but she could not understand why Jason did not speak of love, of staying together, of being husband and wife instead of lovers stealing precious moments to spend together. She waited quietly in his embrace, gazing up into his clear gray eyes, seeing the reflection of the blue of her own as she prayed he would be moved to finally speak of love.

Instead, Jason sighed sadly. "The hours pass too swiftly when I am with you and we must be on our way without another moment's delay. Now hurry and dress and then there is something more I must tell you."

Puzzled, Gabrielle hoped it would be exactly what she wanted to hear, but sadly it was not. As Jason rolled up the blanket and secured it behind his saddle he began to explain. "Clayton saw us together the other night. He saw nothing more than that goodnight kiss, but he is the suspicious sort and, knowing me, fears the worst."

Gabrielle swung herself onto Sunny's back, sorry Clayton had chosen that particular word to describe their relationship. "He would considerate it 'the worst' if he knew we were lovers?"

"I am being paid to escort you to Oregon City, Gabrielle, not to seduce you along the way," Jason pointed out with a grin. "But I told him nothing, and if he makes the mistake of discussing the subject with you, which I think he has the good sense not to do, you must admit nothing either."

"I see," Gabrielle replied as she combed her fingers through her tangled hair, but her features were set in a determined frown which clearly showed her mood. "What would happen if I told him the truth, Jason?"

"That is not a consequence upon which I care to speculate, my dear. We must be more careful, that is all . . . perhaps meet only when I am on guard duty. You can slip away to meet me."

"You would be satisfied with that?" she asked pointedly, not understanding why deception was so important to him when she longed to tell everyone who would listen how dearly she'd come to love him.

Jason climbed into his saddle and jammed his hat down upon his newly trimmed curls as he replied. "No, of course not, but it is the way it will have to be."

Gabrielle turned Sunny toward the path they'd taken. "Perhaps it would be best if we avoided each other entirely then, Jason."

"You can't mean that!" Jason argued as he drew alongside her.

Gabrielle was silent for several moments then she turned to face him squarely. "Yes. I do mean it. I think we should end this now, Jason, if the risk of a scandal scares you so greatly."

"Damn it! I am not afraid! It is you I must consider, your reputation, your future. Don't you understand that?" He angrily pointed out what seemed obvious to him.

Lifting her chin proudly, Gabrielle made up her mind. "Well, if you are saying the choice is mine, then our brief affair is over, for I'll not live the blatant lie you are offering."

"What else would you have me do, Gabrielle?" Jason demanded harshly. "Tell me what other choice we have and I will gladly seize it!"

"If the answer is not obvious to you, I will never speak it. Now good day, Mr. Royal, and goodbye." Knowing he could never catch her, Gabrielle turned Sunny toward the approaching wagon train and dug her heels sharply into his sides. The red stallion responded with an energetic leap forward, leaving Jason swearing angrily in a cloud of dust as thick as his confusion over Gabrielle's behavior.

Jason screamed every obscenity he'd ever heard and then came up with a few original terms to describe the torment Gabrielle continually caused him. What in heaven's name did the woman want from him that he hadn't promised in the most definite way a man can? He had found her slender body so easy to tame, but her spirit defied him still. The emotions which he'd thought he'd transmitted so forcefully apparently had left her untouched, still he was even more determined to make her understand she was his woman alone.

"You are mine, Gabrielle MacLaren, mine!" he shouted angrily, although he knew she could not possibly hear that desperate vow.

But by the time he returned to the wagon train late that afternoon, he had adopted a far more logical attitude. He would not beg, or plead. He'd not even speak to the woman who'd simply plucked his heart from his chest and trampled it beneath her tiny feet. He'd wait until she asked him to take her back into his arms. He had plenty of time. He could wait, perhaps not patiently, but—damn it!—he could wait.

The weather had become close and sultry, oppressively warm, and Gabrielle's mood was no better than Jason's when they reached the point at which he wished to ford the Platte. The wagons first had to be unloaded so their beds could be waterproofed with the green buffalo hides to prevent them from being flooded, their contents ruined, and the vehicle sunk under the incoming water's weight. When reloaded, the oxen were double-teamed to draw the first wagon to the river's edge. Jason then rode across to gauge the depth of the water and the condition of the river bed before he returned to give the order for the first wagon to roll. On the sandy soil of the riverbank, the water barely lapped over the oxen's hooves, but as they moved out into the Platte the water deepened, the swiftness of the current swelling up around the beasts' flanks and carrying them along until they slipped repeatedly. Losing their footing, they seemed to float in the middle of the wide river, but the drivers and men on horseback urged the teams on until the waters grew shallow again and the oxen could pull the wagon onto the far shore. A joyous shout of triumph went up as each wagon forded the perilous river safely. Slowly, the line of wagons approached the river, as the travelers, who had crossed, wet and weary, gradually reassembled on the other side to await those who still had to ford the waters.

Jason lost count of how many times he'd traversed the swiftly rushing waters of the river, but whenever a man appeared hesitant to begin the crossing he was there to offer encouragement. Likewise, if the animals slipped in the slimy mud and grew panic-stricken, he and Duke were there to haul them to their feet and send them on their way. He was a tireless leader, but when Clayton came to his side he had little time to offer advice for their twenty-one charming charges.

"The women are safer on horseback, Clay, just let them ride across and they will be fine. I have no time to hold their hands while they do it!" He returned to the water then, because another team was moving too slowly and needed his help.

The first of the brides' wagons made the crossing without incident, two of the seven young women choosing to ride with their driver while the others rode upon their usual mounts. The second wagon was not so fortunate. In midstream the wheels caught, the mud providing too slippery a footing for the oxen to pull it free.

Gabrielle stood on the riverbank, her apprehension growing rapidly as she watched the drama unfold upon the water. Along the shores of the river were scattered the half-buried remains of countless pieces of furniture, family heirlooms which had been sacrificed to lighten other wagons that had encountered similiar disastrous crossings. But this wagon contained only the trunks of clothing and the provisions for its seven female passengers. No heavy pieces of furniture could now be cast aside to lessen the load upon the wheels. At least one of the young women had chosen to ride across with the driver, but Gabrielle did not recall who she had been. She now hoped the woman in the wagon was a calm soul who would not become so frightened by the wagon's plight that she might topple into the fast flowing water and be swept away. Clayton rode out into the river to help Jason, both men encouraging the oxen and helping to pull the wagon free. At last they succeeded in encouraging the oxen to exert themselves. The wagon wheels began to turn again, and slowly the wooden vehicle drew closer to the far shore, another successful crossing assured.

Dripping wet, Jason was still standing on the opposite bank when Gabrielle's wagon reached the water. He considered Paul to be the best of the three drivers, and he had no doubt the diminutive man could make the crossing safely. His gaze was not focused upon Paul but on the women following in their wagon's wake. Gabrielle was on the riverbank, obviously offering the encouragement the other women needed to begin riding their horses across. He could not hear her helpful comments, but her friendly advice seemed to be gratefully taken as one woman after another urged her mount into the water and with a firm hand on the reins forced the animal to carry her across.

When Gabrielle alone remained behind, Jason realized he'd been a fool not to consider how reticent Sunrise would be to enter the water after his terrifying brush with death. Horses have a long memory, and once the stallion had associated the river with the danger of quicksand he was sure to balk at entering it again. As Jason should have been able to predict, the horse planted all four of his feet firmly in the sand and refused to take the first step into the swirling waters of the Platte. When Gabrielle began to strike his rump with the ends of the reins, the outraged horse reared up on his hind legs, his forelegs pawing the air. For a moment he seemed suspended in air, frozen in time. A shout of alarm escaped Jason's throat. He was certain the terrified animal was going to throw Gabrielle or crush her beneath him when he lost his balance and fell backward upon her, yet from where he stood, the conscientious wagon master could do nothing to save her.

Gabrielle threw herself forward, and though her weight was slight compared to that of her magnificent mount, the shift in balance was enough to bring the stallion down upon his feet once again. She slipped from his back then, shaking her fist in his face as she tossed the reins over his head and started walking into the river. If Sunny would not carry her across willingly, then she would shame him into making the ford by leading him across, for she could see no other alternative and she'd not leave him behind.

Jason could not believe his eyes. His joy that Gabrielle had escaped being badly injured or crushed to death turned swiftly to horror as he saw her step into the water. An ox could walk through the swiftly flowing river, as could a horse or mule, but no man could possibly make the journey on foot. Most definitely a slightly built woman like Gabrielle could not. She knew how dangerous the river was, yet she was moving right out into it as if she were leading Sunny into a barn for a tasty meal of oats. Furious, Jason got back up into his saddle and, digging his heels into Duke's sides, forced his mount back into the water, but he feared their progress would be far too slow for him to reach Gabrielle in time. He waved and shouted to her to turn back, but she did not hear him or did not understand his frantic call. She kept right on walking out into the river, the water now at her knees and rising rapidly.

"If you won't walk, then you can swim; but—damn it—you are coming across with me!" Gabrielle yelled at Sunny, her hold firm on the stallion's bridle as she yanked his head sharply to gain his attention. "You are no coward. Now come!" She waded out into the water, coaxing the horse along and never once glancing up to see the commotion her action was causing on the opposite shore. Sunrise folded his ears tightly back against his head to show his displeasure, but he loved his mistress too dearly to disobey, even a command which frightened him as greatly as this one did. He took one step into the river, and finding it possible to again lift his foot, he took another tentative step, slowly following Gabrielle's lead.

Clayton's heart leaped to his throat as he realized why Jason had dashed back into the turbulent river. He'd given the young women what he'd thought were clear instructions, but obviously he had overlooked the most important point: that it was impossible for them to swim across the wide river. Now there was Gabrielle MacLaren clearly attempting such a ridiculous feat and he knew exactly what would happen to her. She'd drown. That was all that could possibly happen to her. She'd be swept away when she neared the center of the river and the treacherous current caught her in its grasp. Powerless to avert the tragedy he watched Jason plunge ahead, but time was against him. Not wanting to see such a lovely creature meet such a senseless death, Clayton turned away as his eyes filled with the hot sting of tears.

Gabrielle pulled herself onto Sunny's back as soon as she'd managed to restore his confidence in his ability to navigate the river. She had no fear that he couldn't manage to cross it when beasts as large and plodding as oxen could do it successfully, to say nothing of the smaller horses the other girls had ridden across. Sunny snorted derisively, tossing his long wet mane in his mistress' face, but she ignored his ill humor and forced him with a few well-placed kicks to continue his halting effort toward the opposite shore.

By the time he reached Gabrielle, Jason could scarcely see through the red filter of rage which had descended before his eyes. He yanked Sunny's reins from her hands and then turned Duke around so the buckskin horse could lead the roan stallion through the river. When they finally made it across the wide expanse of the perilous river, he leaped from Duke's back and, plucking the startled beauty from Sunny's saddle, carried her over to a large boulder where he sat down. Turning her across his knee he began to spank her, releasing the fury he could no

162

longer contain.

"That was the single most needless risk I have ever seen anyone take and I told you what would happen the next time you behaved like a child!"

Gabrielle's clothing was soaked with water and provided such adequate padding she felt not a twinge of the pain Jason was trying so mightily to inflict on her. She did not even understand why he was mad, let alone why he felt this public whipping was appropriate punishment. All around them curious onlookers had gathered to stare and laugh, greatly amused by the unexpected spectacle. A few went so far as to call encouragement to the young man, but none came forward to demand he stop. When Jason's fit of temper was at last spent, he released Gabrielle and stood up to place her gently upon her feet. She turned on him then with a fiery burst of anger. Rather than shout so those still chuckling at her could overhear, she whispered, making her words all the more threatening. "Why you would wish to humiliate me so rudely I will never understand, but you've humiliated only yourself with that shocking display of brutality! I would have expected as much from the likes of Sam Duffy, never from you!"

Jason grabbed her elbow as she turned away, not about to let Gabrielle have the last word. "Damn it! You could have drowned trying to lead Sunny across the river, and you knew it!" he shouted, livid to think she was pretending such innocence when she'd known exactly what she was risking.

Gabrielle's eyes glowed with the purple fire Jason recognized instantly. "And you were so devastated by that prospect, so concerned for my welfare that you came after me so you could treat me as badly as this?" Her voice dripped with sarcasm. "That is the way a man treats a woman he despises, Mr. Royal, not one he wishes to protect."

"It would take an army to protect you adequately!" he declared. Then, realizing by the snickers his outburst evoked that they were merely providing entertainment rather than settling the issue, he walked over to Sunny and, grabbing his

163

reins, climbed wearily into the saddle. "I will teach this horse how to cross this damn river, and when I return him to you he will be a most obedient mount!" With that promise he jabbed his heels into the stallion's red hide and rode him back out into the river. For the rest of the afternoon he used Sunny's strength to guide others across, but Gabrielle did not remain to watch for she was certain the arrogant Jason Royal had no more lessons either she or her horse wished to learn.

Once the Platte had been crossed, the next major goal was Fort Laramie which the wagon train could be expected to reach in approximately three weeks' time. Deep ravines marred the barren landscape as the wagons followed the bank of the Northern branch of the Platte River, and only an occasional violent rainstorm brought any change in the monotony of the travelers' days. Prairie dog burrows were so numerous Gabrielle dared not allow Sunny to risk a gait faster than a walk for fear he'd stumble and be seriously injured. The horse was her most prized possession, a link to both the past and the future, and now that Jason had failed her so greatly, the horse was the only living creature she could trust.

There seemed to be few among the emigrants who'd not seen the wagon master spank her as if she were a naughty child. Gabrielle thought his motive less one of fear for her safety than a desire for revenge and she did not intend to forgive him for it. Her true friends had been as appalled as she by Jason's insensitivity while Iris had simply gloated, certain Gabrielle had deserved that beating for a long time.

The strain of the tiresome journey had made tempers short, and Gabrielle found herself unable to watch Jason pass by without a wave of despair overtaking her and filling her throat with a scream of protest she was doomed never to utter. He'd begun to grow a beard, but while that altered his appearance slightly, it did nothing to detract from his finely chiseled features. She knew she was fooling only herself for she loved him still. She wondered if she'd been no more than an amusing diversion to him, a pretty young woman who'd provided the

164

affection he'd craved while he'd given her nothing of himself in return. She had no sweet love letters, no rosebud to preserve in one of her books of poetry, no gifts of any kind to keep as souvenirs of the splendor they'd shared. His glance was cold now when they chanced to meet, with no hint of the tenderness she knew him to possess. No. He'd given her nothing but a new layer of pain to wrap around a broken heart. Yet, one night when Iris began to talk about Jason, she found herself unable to walk away.

"Have you seen the way Christina talks to Mr. Royal? She nearly drools all over him, her flirtation is so obvious."

Confused, Margaret inquired shyly, "Which girl is she? I can't seem to keep the others' names straight in my mind for some reason."

"She's that little blonde with the high squeaky voice. 'Oh, Mr. Royal, you're so big and strong, won't you please lift my trunk for me?'" Iris imitated the young woman with surprising accuracy. "I'll just bet she's lifting her skirt for him!"

"Iris!" Johanna protested sharply. "Must you be so common?" As usual she'd been reading her Bible while the light was still good, but unable to help overhearing what had been said, she felt it was her duty to remind Iris to be more ladylike in her conversation.

"Don't you call me common!" Iris snapped right back. "She's the one who plans to catch that man with the oldest ploy a woman has ever used on a man."

"What's that?" Margaret whispered anxiously, her brown eyes alight with curiosity for she found Iris' sophisticated comments fascinating as did several of the others seated nearby. They had little enough excitement to fill their days and the possibility of a scandal was enormously appealing.

"She'll tell him she's pregnant, of course," Iris explained sarcastically, as if that point were too obvious to merit discussion.

"Oh," Margaret replied with a nervous swallow, "Do you really think she'd stoop that low?"

"I'm sure of it, unless someone else beats her to it."

Gabrielle had heard enough. "Iris, let's talk about something else, any other topic but your imaginative gossip. You're being most unfair to both Jason and Christina by repeating your unfounded suspicions."

Taking up the challenge, Iris walked up to Gabrielle with a defiant laugh. "And why do you care so much about his reputation when he was more interested in that stallion of yours than he ever was in you? I'll bet you're just sorry you didn't think of forcing him to marry you when you had the chance!"

Gabrielle struck the hostile brunette in the mouth so quickly Iris never even saw her lift her hand. She went sprawling in the dirt, blood gushing from a cut on her lip. Immediately she began to scream loud protests as if she had done nothing to provoke such an attack. Disgusted, Gabrielle turned to go but found Jason blocking her way.

Having no idea what had happened, Jason had run toward the wagon when he'd heard Iris' screams. He usually stayed away from all the young women unless some compelling piece of business forced him to speak with them, but he could not ignore shrieks for help. Now, interested in finding out just what had caused all the uproar, he grabbed Gabrielle by the shoulders and turned her around to face the others. Iris had gotten to her feet and was holding a handkerchief to her bruised mouth as she continued to complain.

"She hit me! Look what Gabrielle did to me and for no reason at all!" Iris waved the bloody handkerchief as if it provided solid evidence of the truth of her words. "Why don't you give her another whipping? She deserves one for doing this to me!" Iris began to sob then, huge pathetic tears which were the result of many years of careful practice in getting her own way. "Well, aren't you going to punish her?" she demanded.

Jason had never regretted any action so greatly as he had that unfortunate spanking. It had been such a foolish move he could imagine no crime dire enough to inspire him to raise a hand to her in anger again. However, he was expected to keep the peace so he had to know exactly what had happened between the two young women. "I assume you have some ready explanation for this, Miss MacLaren?" he inquired with what he hoped would pass for admirable restraint.

Lifting her chin proudly, Gabrielle replied, speaking to him for the first time in more than a week. "She made a remark to which I objected, there is nothing more to it."

"What?" Jason was dumfounded. He'd thought Gabrielle would certainly have something more to say than just admitting she'd hit Iris. "I don't suppose you'd care to repeat that remark?"

"Of course not, but I'm sure Iris will." Gabrielle hoped Iris would have the nerve to repeat what she had said, for she knew Jason's reaction would be every bit as negative as hers had been.

"Well?" Jason turned back toward Iris, certain he was fast losing control of the situation.

"It doesn't matter what I said; she had no right to hit me!" Iris shrieked as she began to weep an even larger flood of tears.

Sorry he'd even attempted to straighten out the mess which was so rapidly deteriorating, Jason took Gabrielle by the arm and spoke loudly as he led her away. "We will let Mr. Horne settle this, since that is more his job than mine."

"I don't care what he wants to do to me, the bitch deserved it," Gabrielle whispered.

Shocked by her language, Jason remained silent until they reached his tent where they found Clayton nowhere in sight. "All right now, before Clay comes back, tell me what really happened." He folded his arms across his chest and glared down at her, not letting any of his delight at this unexpected excuse to be with her again show in his expression.

Gabrielle turned away, pacing slowly in front of him as she tried to choose her words with care. "Iris is a difficult person, very critical of others and when she began some rather nasty gossip tonight I asked her to stop."

"I see. You just said something like, 'Stop it, Iris,' and then punched her in the mouth?" He knew he had aroused Gabrielle's temper rather easily, but he'd not thought she would behave that way with her traveling companions.

"No," Gabrielle replied truthfully. "When I objected to her gossip she then made me the target of one of her vicious attacks. It was then I hit her."

Bone-weary, Jason sat down in front of his tent and propped his elbows across his knees. "How could she possibly have insulted you, Gabrielle?"

"I'll not repeat it. You must insist she tell you if you have to know." Gabrielle continued to pace, her mood still a most agitated one. "I don't care what you do to me; it was worth it to finally shut her mouth."

"Look, everybody's nerves are frazzled, but don't you see what you did was no different from Sam Duffy's hitting his wife? You were glad I went to her defense; do you think I should take Iris' side now?"

Gabrielle found it difficult to look at Jason without remembering how comfortable she'd been in his arms. That had been paradise, yet here they were arguing like strangers who could not seem to agree on anything. "I think there is a great difference between his attempting to beat his wife senseless and the fact that I slapped Iris for insulting me."

"Oh, of course. One is needless violence and the other a defense of honor; is that it?" Jason scoffed at her reasoning.

"Precisely."

"Well I'll be damned if I know what to do with you, Gabrielle. You're the best of the lot, by far the brightest and most perceptive. If you start using your fists instead of logic to get your way where will it end?"

Before Gabrielle could reply, Erica rushed up to speak in her behalf. "Mr. Royal, I know whatever Gabrielle told you is the truth. Iris insults everybody and tonight when she mentioned you—"

"What?" The young man leaped to his feet, astonished to

think he had been the subject of the fight between the two women.

Gabrielle sprang forward too. "Erica please, you needn't repeat any of it!"

Not one to back down, Erica continued. "Iris mentioned something about one of the other girls and you, Mr. Royal. Gabrielle said that was most unfair and asked her to change the subject, but then Iris just got more abusive."

Jason had not expected this shocking turn of events, and he hoped Clay wouldn't appear until he'd settled it. "Thank you, Miss Nelson. If I need you to be a witness I'll call you later. Good night."

Surprised to be dismissed so abruptly, Erica nevertheless offered her friend an encouraging smile and turned to go. She sincerely hoped she'd helped her since she knew Gabrielle would never tell Jason Royal what Iris had said.

Facing her squarely, Jason jammed his hands in his hip pockets to keep from wrapping them around Gabrielle's lovely neck. "Shall we begin once again? Now tell me exactly what happened, I think you owe me that much."

"No. I do not. Iris simply has an evil imagination and I'll not repeat her lies."

Jason closed his eyes and counted to five before he looked down again at Gabrielle and attempted to speak calmly. "Thank you for that vote of confidence, for I have given no one any reason to link my name with one of the brides."

Gabrielle stared up at him for a long moment, longing to reach up and kiss the pulse which throbbed so steadily in his throat but she knew she'd lost the right to be so bold.

"Except for me?" she whispered softly, scarcely believing she'd had the nerve to say that to him.

Jason straightened to his full height, his expression growing as dark as his mood. "I have no idea what you are talking about, Miss MacLaren, for nothing ever happened between us, absolutely nothing. We will consider this matter settled, but I want your word you will never strike Iris again no matter what the provocation."

Gabrielle was so hurt by his curt rebuff that she began to back away, uncertain as to what it was he wanted her to promise. "No, it's not wrong to defend myself, and I'll not swear not to do it!" With that fiery outburst she turned and ran, her tiny feet carrying her off into the gathering dusk before he realized he'd said none of the things he'd truly wanted to say.

Chapter IX

When she had first heard the name Fort Laramie, Gabrielle had assumed it would be a fortified stockade staffed by Army personnel in dusty blue uniforms. However, the American Fur Company actually owned the fort and there was not a single soldier in residence. The Black Hills provided an imposing backdrop to the landmark. Built of sun-dried bricks, the outpost was rectangular in shape but blockhouses projected from the two front corners to form bastions. The blockhouses expanded the wall behind which defenders could fire their weapons. The walls themselves were fifteen feet high and were topped with sharpened stakes as an additional measure of security to discourage invaders. Since the main gate was open all day and Indians coming to trade were allowed free access, Gabrielle wondered what enemy might possibly attack the establishment. It was a question she knew Jason would be able to answer, but the indifference he'd shown her during their last conversation discouraged her from seeking him out to inquire. She had decided to simply observe instead so she might learn all she could about Fort Laramie on her own.

Inside the high wall, the fort was separated into two distinct areas. One half was used as a corral to shelter horses and mules during the night, while the other contained the offices, storerooms, and apartments of the residents. The atmosphere was a lively one. Canadian and American trappers came and went during the day, conducting their business, and Indians also were seen about the stockade. For the young women accustomed to no more excitement than they had experienced along the trail, it was a fascinating place. Although their needs for provisions were few, they strolled through the gates of the fort at their first opportunity, wanting only to absorb its stimulating environment if not to contribute to its prosperity.

As Jason had promised, Gabrielle had ample opportunity to observe Indians here. While they inspired her curiosity, Erica clung to her arm, certain their scalps would end up dangling from some brave's lance if they weren't careful.

"Let's go back to the wagons now, please!" she begged.

"You may go back if you wish, but I want to stay awhile longer. I'm so tired of riding it is simply a joy to walk about as though this were a real town instead of no more than a trading post."

Erica was not about to return to the wagon alone, but as she continued to watch the fort's many colorful visitors her apprehension did not lessen. "Do you suppose Oregon City is no larger than this outpost?"

"We've been told very little about the place, but the answer is no. I'm certain it is a thriving town with shops of all kinds. At least I certainly hope it is." As Gabrielle turned she saw Jason crossing the courtyard, his long sure stride a sudden reminder of the easy grace with which his lean body had always conquered hers. She blushed deeply at the memory and her senses were flooded with a desperate longing for him. Looking away quickly to distract herself with a less imaginative subject, she noticed a group of Indian men lounging near the corral. One had apparently dared another to try to ride an unbroken pony, and his friends were laughing heartily as they teased the young brave when he refused to do it.

172

"Have you ever spoken with an Indian, Erica, ever met one?" Gabrielle asked.

"Good Lord no!" The pretty young woman shuddered at the very thought. "Why would I even want to speak with one?"

"I'll bet they have many things to say worth hearing," Gabrielle mused aloud as she continued to watch the group by the corral. They reminded her of the young men she'd known in Liberty, for they seemed to enjoy games just as much. She had not realized Indians had such playful natures or that their young men were so attractive. The braves' bodies were as sleek as panthers, and although they were young their actions had such a timeless quality that Gabrielle felt she was watching a scene which could have taken place hundreds of years earlier.

The young braves, finished with that particular bit of sport, started off toward the trading post, but the one who had begun the joke remained behind for a moment as if tempted to ride the spirited pony himself. When he turned to follow his friends he saw Gabrielle observing him with a curious stare that he found most intriguing. He had seen white women—all the wagon trains stopped at the fort—but this was no farmer's wife with several children clinging to her skirt. This was a pretty young woman no older than himself. A slow smile spread across his face as he thought how striking the color of her hair was, a shimmering red he longed to reach out and touch. Not a man to laugh in fortune's face when it presented him with so fine an opportunity he started toward her, hoping the curiosity which filled her sky-blue gaze would turn to admiration rather than fear.

"Gabrielle, let's go!" Erica cried as she saw the brave walking toward them. He looked extremely fierce to her and she didn't want to stay and find out if her impression was correct.

Gabrielle ignored her friend's pleas and stood still, for she thought the young Indian's ready smile most appealing. He wore only buckskin leggings, a breechclout, and moccasins

173

which muffled the sound of his steps as he seemed to glide across the short distance which separated them. His long hair was glossy black and hung loose over his shoulders. His dark eyes sparkled with the brilliance of obsidian in the morning sun. He was tall and well built, as handsome an example of his tribe as had entered the fort that day, and when he stopped in front of her he simply stared, slowly looking her up and down as if he wished to memorize each minute detail of her face and dress.

The auburn-haired beauty returned his smile shyly, hoping such an open glance was not considered rude by his people. "Do you speak English?" she finally thought to ask, hoping to distract him from his close inspection of her appearance with conversation.

The brave laughed at her question, revealing even white teeth which contrasted handsomely with his dark skin. He asked her a question too then, his language as strange sounding to her ears as hers had been to his.

While Erica nearly fainted with fright, Gabrielle began to laugh too because the young man was so friendly, yet they could make no sense of each other's remarks. When Jason suddenly gripped her arm and sent the brave on his way with a sharply worded command, she was astonished by the hostility in his voice. "Really, Mr. Royal, there can be no excuse for such rudeness!"

"No excuse?" he asked in dismay. "What are you two doing wandering around in here? Didn't Clay tell you not to come to the fort alone?" He looked around quickly then, making sure no more of the girls were strolling about the courtyard. He'd found managing fifty wagons and all their owners' problems a slight chore compared to escorting twenty-one pretty young ladies across the country. But none of the girls had gotten into mischief as often as Gabrielle. He was clearly out of patience with her, and his angry frown deepened by the minute.

Gabrielle blushed with sudden insight. "Oh, I am sorry, but

I didn't realize he meant we weren't to come inside without an escort, I thought he meant we couldn't come alone."

Jason looked over at Erica and saw by her frantic nod that the young women had made a most natural mistake. He released his firm grip on Gabrielle's arm and stepped back. "All right, you did come together and that's at least partly reassuring. But you must not come back unless Paul, or Clay, or some other suitable escort accompanies you. That Indian was one of the Dakota tribe who are camped nearby. Their name means 'friendly ones' and I think you'd agree they are aptly named. What you had hoped to accomplish by talking with that brave I can't imagine, but I'll not allow you to be so foolish again. I am walking you back to your wagon where I hope you'll avoid causing any more problems for the rest of the afternoon at least."

"Must you be so mean?" Gabrielle replied defiantly. "Erica and I came here only to look around and that's all we've done. We've caused no disturbance and were nearly ready to leave without having to be told to go. That an Indian would be as curious about us as we are about him should not be any cause to criticize us. We've done nothing wrong!"

Jason stepped between the young women and took each firmly by the arm as he started walking for the gate. "Since the obvious seems to have escaped you, Miss MacLaren, Indian men flirt with pretty young women for the very same reason white men do. Just use your imagination and I think you'll understand what I mean."

Gabrielle was too embarrassed by that rebuke to respond. Since he knew how easily he'd seduced her, he apparently thought any man would have the same success and she was mortified by that totally erroneous conclusion. She hadn't been flirting with the young Indian, not at all. She'd only been curious as to what it would be like to speak with him. She offered no apology, but as they neared the circle of wagons she made a request. "We can find our way from here, Mr. Royal.

175

You needn't drag us back to our wagon like naughty children."

"Well, since that is what you are, I had thought you needed to be walked all the way to your wagon, but if you'll promise to behave in a more circumspect manner while we're here I'll trust you to make your own way safely." He was only half teasing them, for no matter what order Clayton seemed to give, Gabrielle conveniently found a way to misinterpret it. When neither young woman responded he saw by their expressions that they had not been amused and quickly changed the subject. "Have you had the blacksmith check Sunny's shoes? If he needs to be reshod this is the time to do it."

"It's already been done, Mr. Royal," Gabrielle answered tersely, happy that she had done something right. They were camped beside the fort to make any necessary repairs to the wagons, to reshoe the horses, and purchase provisions. Everyone needed a good rest, but they had so much to do to make ready for the remainder of their journey that no one was idle.

"I'm pleased to hear it, would you check with the others to make certain they have made similar arrangements for their mounts?" Jason always relied upon Gabrielle to assume the responsibility for her companions since she was usually so level-headed and conscientious. "I want to get rolling again as soon as possible. The Dakota are sure to pay us at least one visit and I don't want to provide them with an opportunity to make any more calls."

Erica grew pale at that thought. "What do you mean they will visit us? Must we entertain savages as if they'd been invited?"

Jason chuckled at her innocence. "This is their homeland, Miss Nelson. They expect the courtesy of being offered one good meal and I'll not disappoint them."

Gabrielle's bright glance swept over Jason's features with far more interest than she had shown in the inquisitive Indian. His gray eyes were fringed with lashes as long and thick as her own,

176

and his expression was kind as he spoke to Erica. However, his warmth vanished when once again he turned to look down at her. "The Dakotas camped near the river will probably arrive just before sundown tonight. Men, women, and children will be followed by a multitude of dogs. We need provide no more than fresh biscuits and meat; that will satisfy them. We needn't prepare the delicacy they would serve to their own guests." Jason waited then, a teasing grin playing at the corners of his mouth for he knew Gabrielle would want to know exactly what that might be.

"Since you said they save the buffalo liver for the children, I can scarcely imagine what they think an appropriate treat for their guests," she responded. As he had expected she was too curious not to inquire.

"As I said they have many dogs. They use them to carry bundles of their possessions when they move about, but they consider the fat pups a real delicacy. They usually grab one, just bash in its skull to kill it, hold the carcass over the fire to singe off the fur, and then toss the little critter into the stew pot."

Erica let out a strangled scream as she ran off. She raised both hands to cover her mouth, wanting only to escape her companions before she embarrassed herself by becoming ill right in front of them. Gabrielle was just as sickened by that tale, but she forced herself to swallow the wave of nausea which swept over her and asked, "Well, how does a puppy stew taste? Would you recommend such a dish yourself?"

Jason laughed at her question. As always he was delighted with her courage. "I have eaten it, I'll admit, but I swear I didn't taste a bite since it was all I could do not to run off just as Erica did just now."

Pleased that he would tell her such a thing rather than boast that he frequently ate puppies for breakfast, Gabrielle recalled his earlier comments about his admiration for the Indian tribes. "As you said, their customs do clash with ours, but perhaps if we both try, we can find some way to live together in peace."

Jason's expression revealed his pain as he admitted, "God help me, Gabrielle, I want only to live in peace with you." He turned back toward the fort then and sprinted away as if he'd forgotten the most urgent of appointments. She stared after him, wondering why he still believed she was the one who made that desire impossible.

When Jason returned later to tell the other emigrants that he'd invited a Dakota chief and his entourage to join them for a light supper, his announcement met with considerable alarm. He reassured everyone quickly that it was no more than a formality he observed on each of his trips and that they need have no fear. However, not until the Indians actually arrived, shy smiles lighting their dark faces, did the travelers begin to relax. They kept the Indians together, however, and watched their wagons closely to be certain the savages did not use the noise of the party to cover thievery. When at last the Dakotas returned to their own camp, the relief which swept the wagon train was evident. First a man appeared with a concertina, then another with a fiddle, and before long several couples had begun to dance to their spirited music. The mood became as light and happy as it had been the night they'd celebrated after the buffalo hunt. Soon the festivities began to attract men from the fort, and the party grew in both size and volume. The men of Fort Laramie joined in the fun and invited the women from the wagon train to dance.

As Gabrielle clapped her hands in rhythm with the music, she thought about the Indian who'd laughed with her at the fort. He'd come to the wagon train with the others, but he'd done no more than smile again and had made no attempt to approach her. Surrounded by his friends, he had eaten his portion of the food they'd served and then had left, apparently preferring the comfort of his tipi to remaining to try to speak with her. She knew friendship between them was not possible since they could not even converse in the same language; still she was disappointed that she'd been unable to tell him at least one white woman was not afraid of him.

"Do you like to dance?" Marlene whispered softly. "I have never had an opportunity to learn."

Surprised by that admission, Gabrielle assured the shy blonde it was an easy skill to acquire. "I am certain we can teach you before we arrive in Oregon City, for I know the men there will want to dance with us."

"Oh, no. I had not even thought of that, whatever shall I do?" Marlene turned to watch as a tall, thin man in buckskins came out of the crowd to invite Iris to dance and the brunette followed his moves with a quick, light step. "I shall never be able to learn in time!"

"Marlene!" Gabrielle teased with a sparkling smile, "we will not reach Oregon City for months yet, you will be able to dance beautifully by then." She wondered about the others. Erica would surely know how to dance, and Barbara too. Iris obviously could, but perhaps Johanna would think dancing too frivolous since she was such a serious sort. Margaret was as shy as Marlene. Gabrielle reached out to tap her on the shoulder. "Do you like to dance, Margaret?"

"I love to listen to the music, but I know none of the steps," she admitted apologetically. However, her brown eyes were filled with admiration for the dancers moving so energetically nearby.

"You two just come with me for a moment." Gabrielle took their hands, leading them around behind the nearest wagon. "In no more than five minutes' time I can teach you enough to be any man's partner tonight, now just watch closely." She showed them how to do the simple skipping step that was the basis for most of the dances. "All you need do is follow your partner. The man has to lead and he'll show you what to do. Just smile and pretend you know exactly what you're doing and before long you will." She showed them once again exactly

179

how to move; then she had each of them give it a try. Soon her two pupils were laughing happily as they danced upon the grass, their steps in perfect time to the music.

Jason leaned against one of the wagons. He preferred to remain in the shadows and watch since he felt so little like dancing. He realized the amusement was good for the travelers—there was little fun on the long journey—but he could not dance with one of the brides without dancing with every one of them. Knowing that would take the entire night, he did not want to ask any of them. Clay was dancing with the young women, as were two of the drivers; and the employees of the American Fur Company had taken most of the other girls on their arms. Jason was satisfied that he'd not be missed, but then he noticed Gabrielle was no longer standing on the sidelines. He looked quickly through the assembled dancers, and seeing no sign of her long red hair, he dashed around the perimeter of the enthusiastic group to see where she might have gone. He'd seen the friendly Indian brave that night too and had kept a careful watch on the young man. But had he left quietly with his tribe only to return later alone? Jason pushed his way through the crowd, desperate to find Gabrielle before she came to some terrible harm, and when he found her happily giving dancing lessons he lost all control of his temper.

"You must not wander off by yourselves like this, ladies, the risk is simply too great. Now I'll have to tell the musicians to put away their instruments and send everyone to bed if you three can't remember to stay where you belong!"

While Gabrielle was exasperated at finding herself again the object of Jason's wrath, and for the second time in one day, Marlene and Margaret were so devastated by his stinging lecture that their eyes filled with tears and they began to sob pathetically. The pair behaved like rambunctious children being scolded for breaking a piece of their grandmother's highly prized crystal. Coming swiftly to their defense, Gabrielle explained that they had not gone far and were only

180

practicing a few dance steps so Margaret and Marlene could join in the fun.

It was Jason who was embarrassed then, for he'd not meant to yell at the young women so rudely. "Forgive me if I frightened you; I am overzealous at times, I know. Just go back to the party and enjoy yourselves, and I will want to dance with you myself in a moment." He waited while they turned to go, but Gabrielle pushed her two pupils on in front of her and then returned to speak with Jason in terms so blunt she was sure he'd understand.

"I'm the one you're mad at, Jason, only me. I can take your temperamental outbursts, but most of the other girls can't. They shouldn't be subjected to your constant stern lectures when they don't deserve them. It was Erica this morning. Now it is Marlene and Margaret, who are so sweet they didn't even understand what risks you were talking about. Can't you just take me aside instead of punishing everyone else too?"

"I told them I was sorry. What more do you want?" Jason asked with a weary sigh. He'd not explain again that he was responsible for their welfare when she knew how lightly he'd taken those responsibilities in her case.

"We're not sheep, ewes you're herding across the plains to please some waiting rams! Damn it! We're women and deserve far more consideration than you ever show!"

Jason folded his arms across his chest, barely able to contain his anger as he replied. "Apparently you think I'm the one who deserves the stern lecture now. Well go ahead and give it; I'm listening." But he wasn't, he was listening to the dance tunes the two musicians were playing with such carefree abandon. He wished he could pull Gabrielle into his arms and dance the night away.

"Jason?" Gabrielle called his name softly as she walked to his side, for she much preferred his charming smile to the frown he now wore. "I am not angry with you, and I can't bear the fact you're always so angry with me."

181

Bathed in the soft light of the moon, her expression was so sincere and at the same time so inviting that Jason drew her into his arms and kissed her with a passion so brutally demanding that her lips were bruised by the force of his affection. Yet when he finally released her she did not draw away. She laid her cheek upon his chest and hugged him tightly, wanting all that he could give. "I have missed you so terribly, Jason." She was close to tears herself then, clinging to him and not daring to hope he'd missed being with her as well.

Jason held the slender beauty, sifting her flowing tresses with a tender touch as the memory of her splendid loving filled his loins with a painful ache. He had never needed another woman as desperately as he needed Gabrielle; yet each word he spoke, each gesture he made seemed to be the wrong one. He enfolded her in a warm embrace, praying she would stay with him for as long as they could escape the others' notice, until dawn if only she would agree. "Let us find a place where we can be alone, for whatever torment you have felt is slight compared to mine." He kissed the top of her head lightly and waited patiently for her to agree, but when she drew away the sadness in her expression broke his heart.

"You know that is impossible, every bit as impossible now as it was before. I must go!" With that breathless goodbye she left him, returning to the outer ring of spectators to watch the others while they danced. She wiped the tears from her eyes before they could be seen, but she was so depressed she did not think she would ever again be able to find the simple happiness which made dancing such a joy. It was then she recalled that she had not danced since the last night she'd been with Beau. There had been a party to send his uncle's family upon their way to Oregon, and she and Beau had danced until their feet were numb, not wanting the night to ever end for they knew how many months they would be parted. They would never have said goodbye had they known it was to be forever.

Jason returned to the impromptu party, and as he'd

promised, he danced first with Margaret and then with Marlene. He held the shy young women lightly in his arms, complimented them upon their grace, and was pleased when they blushed with pleasure. It had not occurred to him that any of the brides would not know how to dance, and he wondered what else he and Clayton had failed to consider. He was afraid Gabrielle had been close to the truth. While he'd certainly never regarded the young women as sheep, he'd not thought of them often or gotten to know them. It had all been a business proposition. Men they knew wanted wives and he and Clayton had decided to provide them. How he wished he'd listened to his conscience, for he'd thought the scheme would prove increasingly difficult as the journey progressed. He'd been worried then that the women would suffer, but now he knew it was his own heart that could not take much more.

The Indians appeared at dawn, lances in their hands, their bows and quivers filled with arrows slung upon their backs. They did no more than sit silently upon their ponies, but the mere sight of them was enough to frighten the emigrants into heeding Jason's order to turn out with astonishing speed. Although they were not followed, the wagons continued to roll at a brisk clip and few wanted to stop for the customary noon break. Knowing the animals could not be driven at so relentless a pace, Jason ordered a halt. He'd gone out to scout the trail and had seen no evidence that large numbers of Indians were roaming about, but he was uneasy. The Dakota had not ridden out to bid them farewell for no reason. He posted a double guard that night, and although no one sounded an alarm during the night, at dawn the silhouettes of the Indian braves could be seen atop the nearby hills. They were following the wagon train, silently stalking it, and that second night no one slept.

Clayton paced nervously in front of the tent as he attempted to make Jason see reason. "I think you should give the order to turn back."

Jason rejected that idea as preposterous. "If they want to

183

attack us they will, Clay. It won't matter to them if we're heading east or west. They aren't trying to make us turn back; it's something else they're after."

Startled by that possibility, Clayton asked abruptly, "What could it be?"

"I'm not certain yet," Jason admitted slowly. "But we'll keep right on moving as if we enjoyed their company." He'd cleaned his rifle three times that night, but now he laid the weapon aside. "Try to get some rest, you may need it."

"How can any of us rest with those savages drawing closer by the hour? This is insanity I tell you, we've got to return to Fort Laramie!"

"Why? We can't camp there all summer. No, Clay. And keep your fears to yourself, I'll not have you spreading hysteria about the camp." Jason had been born with the perfect temperament for stress. The worse a situation grew, the more calmly logical his thoughts became. Picking up his rifle again, he got to his feet as he announced, "I'm going for a walk. Now do us both a favor and get some sleep."

He moved slowly around the ring of wagons, walking on the inside tonight so as not to provide a tempting target. He offered the same advice to all who seemed to need it: if the Indians attacked, the wagon train was well prepared to defeat them. When he came to Sam Duffy's wagon he waited a moment, wanting to speak with his wife. She seemed even more nervous than the other women he'd seen that night. Her bony fingers kept wrinkling her apron as she responded to his greeting.

He'd kept a close eye on the woman and her three children, feeling certain she'd not complain no matter how badly her husband behaved, but there was no sign Sam had repeated the brutal assault he'd interrupted.

"How are you tonight, Mrs. Duffy?" he inquired politely.

"I am just fine, sir, thank you."

The woman smiled shyly as she replied, seemingly embarrassed by his interest. Although her once-blonde hair was now lightly touched with gray, she was still remarkably pretty when she smiled.

"I want to hear about it if you're not," Jason reminded her softly, but when her apprehension seemed to increase at that remark, he moved on. She was a proud woman, he hoped not too proud to ask for help if she needed it.

When he reached the brides' wagons, he found all the young women huddled together, their usually animated conversation being conducted in hoarse whispers. The eyes they turned upon him were filled with fright, and he could think of little to say to reassure them. More imaginative than many of the others, Iris' mind was filled with the prospect of gruesome tortures and she leaped to her feet the moment she saw Jason approaching.

"Can't you post more guards to protect us, Mr. Royal? We have no way to defend ourselves against the bloodthirsty savages who could be surrounding us at this very moment!"

Prying her fingers loose from his arm, Jason smiled as if her request were completely unnecessary. "Miss Stewart, you mustn't worry so. The camp is adequately guarded."

"But how can it be?" she persisted. "We have no more than our drivers and they can't stay awake all night!" Iris was terrified, shaking with fright, and this time grabbed his left arm with both hands but he again pushed her away.

"They won't have to, Miss Stewart, there are other guards as well. Now if you'll excuse me, I must be on my way. Good night, ladies." He tried to include them all in his glance, but Gabrielle raised her hand to catch his attention as she leaped to her feet.

"I'll be happy to stand guard, you know I can shoot well enough to do it." She was tired of listening to the frightened whispers of the others and wanted to do something far more active than merely complain as Iris had.

Not wishing to alarm the other young women, Jason kept on walking. He knew Gabrielle would pursue him until she made

185

her point. As she drew near, he whispered so only she could hear, "Come with me and we'll discuss it."

Running along beside him, Gabrielle again extended her offer. "I mean it, Jason. Please let me help you."

Certain her traveling companions could no longer observe them, Jason turned to face her. "You do understand what you're volunteering to do, don't you? You might be able to shoot branches on a tree but do you honestly think you could kill an Indian?"

Appalled by that grisly prospect, Gabrielle nevertheless responded confidently. "Yes. If I had to I could do it."

Jason sighed, sorry she was so naïve. "Not just any Indian, Gabrielle. Let's say a young one, a handsome fellow with a grin which could melt snowflakes before they hit the ground. Ponder that possibility a moment and then give me your answer."

Gabrielle paused to observe Jason's expression closely. He wasn't teasing her now; he was dead serious. "The odds are slim that that particular Indian would appear in my sights."

"It's never easy to kill a man. Don't fool yourself into thinking it's any easier if he's a stranger."

Undaunted by his condescending attitude, Gabrielle refused to give in. "If we are attacked, there will be no time for me to search the Indians' faces for one I recognize. I can think of nothing worse than having to shoot that charming young man, but if he were trying to kill one of the girls, or you, I could certainly do it."

Her vow to protect him so loyally touched Jason, but he refused to accept such devotion. "Let's hope none of us needs your protection, now go on back to your wagon and convince Iris with whatever means are required to keep her mouth shut. She's frightening the other women and you all need your sleep."

"The only sure way to silence Iris is with a well placed fist," Gabrielle declared, a mischievous sparkle lighting her bright

186

blue eyes. She was not at all pleased by her inability to secure guard duty.

"You'll think of something else, Gabrielle. Good night." Jason shook his head as he walked away, he'd been too stern with her he knew, but he'd not allow her to defend the wagon train when that was the surest way for her to be killed.

Before the first ray of sunlight appeared in the eastern sky, every member of the wagon train was wide awake. All eyes swept the hills for some sign that they were being observed, but the landscape remained vacant. Somehow the Indians' absence was more disconcerting than their presence would have been. Everyone suspected this was only a tactic chosen to flay their already tautly stretched nerves. Only the children had any appetite for breakfast that morning so with another swift start they were on their way.

The Indians did not appear until noon, not until the wagons had been turned into their customary circle and the cooking fires had been lit. Then they came. Jason stood, rifle in hand, and watched their column advance. It looked like no war party he'd ever seen so he quickly sent the command around that no one was to fire. Finally one brave left the others and came forward. He rode to a spot halfway between the wagon train and his brothers and then drew his horse to a halt and waited.

"What do you make of that?" Clayton asked anxiously, suspecting a trick.

"I can think of only one way to find out," Jason replied slyly, and with a gentle nudge of his heels, he rode Duke out to meet the brave.

Gabrielle stood upon the wagon seat where she could have the best view, but she had no idea what Jason and the Indian could be discussing. Perhaps they want some sort of ransom she thought suddenly, payment to allow us to cross their lands. That made more sense than merely attacking the wagon train and stealing whatever was left when the battle was over. She tried to count the long line of braves and realized quickly that the Indians outnumbered the men with the wagon train. The emigrants had rifles, of course, but perhaps some of the Indians did as well. When Jason turned his horse around and rode slowly back toward the train she ran to join the group waiting to meet him.

Jason removed his hat and wiped his forehead on his sleeve. He hardly knew where to begin when he saw all the anxious faces staring up at him. "We are in no danger of being attacked for the present so I suggest everyone go and eat lunch." He swung himself down from his horse then and called to Gabrielle. "Will you come here for a moment, Miss MacLaren?"

Gabrielle ran to his side, but when the crowd did not disperse as he'd told them to, Jason took her arm and led her aside. "I am certain you remember my cautioning you against flirting with Indian braves, Gabrielle, but—"

Interrupting him quickly, the redhead nearly screamed in frustration, "What has that got to do with anything, Jason? Now tell me what that brave said!"

Jason led her to a spot between two wagons where they could see the Indians who had not left the position they'd taken. "The one who came forward is your friend. He is the chief's son it seems, and a young man greatly admired for his courage. This show of force is simply to impress you, my pet, for he wants you to become his wife."

Gabrielle's golden tan paled noticeably at that announcement. "No," was all she could manage to whisper.

"Oh, yes," Jason assured her. "I told him since his proposal has come as something of a surprise you would need a few minutes to consider it fully and make up your mind."

The Indians were too distant for Gabrielle to make out their faces clearly, but she remembered the young man well. "Are Indians usually as impulsive as this?"

"No. They are really very romantic creatures who like to court the young women they admire, but in this case there is

188

no time for such a traditional approach. My grasp of the Dakota language is barely adequate for such delicate negotiations as these, but I think I understood him well enough. The Indians have what we would call fanciful names. They do not translate at all well, but this young man is called Scream of Lightning from what I could understand."

Confused, Gabrielle tore her glance from the Indians to look up at him. "Lightning does not scream, Jason. You cannot possibly have gotten his name right."

"Damn it! That is a minor problem here!" the tall man snapped angrily. "How would you describe the sound of lightning—as a crash or a chilling rip? Why not a scream?"

"I am sorry, forgive me." Gabrielle laid her hand upon his sleeve, knowing he was right and her criticism had been inane under the circumstances. "Whatever his name I cannot marry the man but I cannot allow you to carry that message out to him alone. I will go and tell him myself if you will translate for me."

"Gabrielle"—Jason's glance grew dark as he issued a stern warning—"pride is extremely important to an Indian. You cannot simply say 'No, thank you' and expect him to go away."

Her mind was every bit as quick as his and she saw what his real concern was instantly. Although it filled her with a horrible dread, she had to ask. "Do you think if I refuse he may attack the wagon train and take me by force? Could that be his plan?"

Jason continued in the same forceful tone. "If you are thinking you'll offer to go to him to save the rest of our lives, forget it. That's a trade I won't even consider."

Gabrielle looked again toward the long line of braves. "You may have no choice but to consider it if Scream of Lightning won't take no for an answer. Do you think we should rehearse first or just try to make the best of it as we go along?"

Jason was confused by her calm acceptance of a possibility he thought most repugnant. "You would not really consider

189

such a marriage would you? Because if you are going to go out there and say yes, then I'm leaving you right here!"

Gabrielle shook her head emphatically. "No. I don't think we should rule that out as a last resort, but first I would like to try to refuse his proposal as diplomatically as possible. Shall we go? The longer he has to wait the more obstinate he may become."

Jason hesitated, then realizing that no matter what she wished to tell the handsome brave, he would have to translate, he nodded his consent. They rode out a short distance from the circle of wagons and Scream of Lightning again rode out to meet them, his smile wide when he saw that Jason had brought the young woman he'd asked to see.

Gabrielle attempted to smile with what she hoped was the proper reticence, but the prospect of being forced to marry such a friendly soul did not frighten her nearly as much as Jason seemed to think it should. "Please thank him for his proposal and tell him how honored I am that he would want me for his wife."

"I did not mention that he offered to give me forty ponies for you. That is an extravagant sum that not many braves could match," Jason explained before he began.

"Then please tell him how impressed I am that he considers me worth so much." It was only then that Gabrielle realized what a truly bizarre scene they were playing. Here was a man who was little more than a stranger, asking her to be his wife, while Jason, whom she adored, seemed to consider marriage an alternative to be considered only should she need a man to support a child. Which one is the savage? she thought bitterly.

Jason spoke slowly, trying to give the proper inflection to the Dakota tongue. When he paused to ask the young man if he was being understood, the brave replied that he was, so he continued. He made Gabrielle's compliments even more effusive, her praise for the Indian's gesture generous, and her refusal of his proposal as tactful as possible, but when Scream

190

of Lightning's dark eyes narrowed to vicious slits, he knew they were in deep trouble.

Seeing that the young brave was obviously insulted, Gabrielle suggested a new approach. "Jason, I want you to tell him what happened to Beau. Will you do that, please? I think if he understands that the man I loved and hoped to marry is dead, he will see there is a valid reason why I could never love him. He will realize that our marriage would bring both of us only pain."

"You made me promise never to repeat that story. Now you've changed your mind?" Jason was appalled by her request, yet he thought the Indian just might buy the tale if he were able to make it sufficiently convincing. It was pathetic enough to make a stone weep, and since Indians had what he knew to be a highly developed spiritual nature, he was willing to give it a try. "If you can conjure up a few tears it would help me set the scene," he advised Gabrielle in a whisper. To his amazement her eyes immediately filled with huge tears which rolled down her flushed cheeks in a most convincing profusion.

Gabrielle had to do no more than think of Beau's death to weep, but that sorrow had become such a part of her now the tears brought not the slightest feeling of relief. There were several other stories Jason could have told the Indian brave, the most obvious being that she was his woman and so was not about to listen to proposals from other men, but apparently that simple truth had not even occurred to him. Gabrielle looked up at the Indian shyly. She could tell by his rapt expression that he believed every word Jason spoke.

Certain he had the brave's full attention, Jason drew the story out, providing as much detail as possible for he knew the young man would be sure to repeat it. It had been a painfully poignant story when Gabrielle had told it, but when Jason finished with it that day it had become a masterpiece of romantic tragedy. Scream of Lightning was thoroughly convinced that Gabrielle would never again allow any man to win her heart and he sadly gave up his efforts to win her as his bride. He tore an eagle feather from his hair and handed it to her, a reminder of his love he hoped she would accept even if she would not become his wife.

Gabrielle smiled sweetly and she attempted to wipe away the last of her tears before reaching out to accept the token he offered. "Please thank him for this, and tell him I shall treasure it always." Her eyes widened in alarm then as the young brave drew his knife and gestured toward her.

"He wants a lock of your hair. You need not be so frightened; he did not ask for all of it." Jason was so relieved that the Indian had believed his story he thought this a small request to honor.

Gabrielle nodded her approval and Scream of Lightning drew his pony alongside Sunny and reached over to grasp a handful of her hair. She saw by the sorrow in his eyes that he had been hurt, but at least he had been given an excuse which saved his pride. After cutting off what she thought was a too generous amount of her auburn tresses, he smiled before he turned his pony and swiftly returned to his friends, leading them away at a full gallop.

Jason reached over to pat her hand, glad their ordeal was over. "I imagine he'll carry that lock of your hair with him for the rest of his days. It will be the proof of a major event in his life."

Gabrielle held the feather tightly. The brave had ripped out several strands of his own hair with it, and she wound them around the tip, intending to save them. "As I shall keep this also, Jason, for I meant what I said. I do consider his proposal a great honor even if I could not accept."

"For the reason you gave him?" Jason asked softly, hoping in his heart that her feeling for him would have prevented an acceptance.

"What other reason could I possibly have had?" Gabrielle turned Sunny back toward the wagon train, proud to think a handsome young Indian had wanted her to be his bride, even if the man she loved didn't.

Bitterly disappointed by that cool rebuff, Jason rode off to give the order to roll. He cursed himself for hoping, even for an instant, that Gabrielle still had some small piece of her heart to give to him.

Chapter X

Rather than allow imaginative speculation free rein, which he knew would swiftly lead to rumors of dangerous proportions, Jason gathered everyone together before they broke camp that afternoon. Inspired by his success with Scream of Lightning he stated simply that the Indians had been extremely curious about the young women they were escorting, but when he had informed them they were all engaged to men awaiting them in Oregon, the braves had given up their hope of bargaining for white brides and had gone home. The story was just preposterous enough, and just close enough to the truth to be believed. Gabrielle was grateful that she did not have to describe what had happened. She told anyone who asked that Jason had conducted the exchange in the Dakota tongue and she had not understood a word of it. Satisfied that she could provide no more information, the others had ceased to mention the incident. Although it took several days for everyone's apprehension to subside, the Dakota were not seen again in the vicinity and the wagon train continued to proceed along the trail at the steady pace Jason Royal could be depended upon to maintain.

Once the threat of an attack by Indians seemed unlikely, the days became placidly calm. Gabrielle felt as though they had been traveling forever and would continue their journey into eternity. The tiresome monotony of their routine made time seem to stand still, for each day was an exact replica of the last, a preview of the next. Finally the trail left the North Platte to follow the Sweetwater River which flowed by a huge granite formation known as Independence Rock. There the wagon train stopped briefly to make repairs and to rest.

Jason looked forward to the stop at the landmark as much as the emigrants did, for he shared their restless mood in full measure. At this point at least a few men usually seriously considered turning back; yet on this trip none had approached him to discuss leaving the group. He'd kept no record of past journeys, but it seemed to him as though he'd broken up less than the usual number of fights and he'd been called to only one scuffle between husband and wife, for which he was truly thankful. In many respects this was the best trip he'd ever made, but that provided him scant comfort when he saw Gabrielle walk by without giving him more than a slight wave. He longed to caress the soft curve of her cheek or to bring her palm to his lips for a gentle kiss, but he thought himself a fool for dreaming of so little when they had been the most passionate of lovers. He felt no differently toward her now. The pain of his desire made his nights sleepless, but it brought the lithe redhead no closer to him. That she had such great restraint amazed him, for upon more than one occasion he had caught her looking at him with a hunger every bit as strong as the aching need which gave him no peace. She had always turned away quickly, a deep blush coloring her cheeks, but he'd not attempted to force her to speak aloud what she was clearly loath to admit even to herself.

When the wagon train made camp near Independence Rock, Barbara wanted to read all the names painted upon the granite before they added their own. Paul mixed up a concoction of grease and gunpowder to be used as paint and the vivacious blonde quickly volunteered to supervise the project.

"They say everyone who has come along the Oregon Trail has added a name. This rock is a giant register of those moving

196

west. Isn't it exciting to think our grandchildren might pass this way someday and read our names and know what an adventure we've had?" Barbara chattered happily as they walked toward the enormous rock.

"What will our grandchildren be doing traversing this accursed trail? I hope mine will remain in Oregon after what I've suffered to reach it." Iris punctuated her complaint with a toss of her raven-hued curls. "Besides, how long could this sort of homemade paint possibly last?"

Knowing how impossible grease spots were to remove from any surface they stained, Gabrielle was confident their names would remain on view for many years. "I like your idea, Barbara. I hope some descendant of mine sees my name here and appreciates what I've done. That's a very romantic thought."

Iris again disagreed, thinking the project impossibly silly. As usual she did not want to be left out, however, and went along with the others who scampered over the granite to find a place for their names to be written.

Jason had stationed himself midway up the jagged rock to turn back any souls foolhardy enough to want to climb any higher. When he saw that Gabrielle's group planned to read all the names before inscribing their own he called down to them. "There must be five thousand names on this rock, ladies. You've barely got enough time to print your own initials let alone read all the other signatures."

When her friends disregarded his teasing rebuke and continued to read the names aloud to each other, Gabrielle left them and climbed up to sit beside Jason. She knew the only traveler's name she wanted to read had perished long before that point in the trail. "Where is your name, Mr. Royal? Is it way up at the top?"

"Yes, it is," Jason admitted with a sly grin. "Don't tell me you want to see it either because I won't allow you to climb up that far."

"I used to be a very skilled climber, better than most boys at

197

climbing trees, but I've had little experience with boulders of this size." Gabrielle looked up toward the summit, certain if he could reach that she could, but she had no wish to argue with him when they were chatting so pleasantly.

"I didn't picture you as the tomboy type." Jason's voice was low, barely carrying over the happy chatter of those moving on the rock below.

After some reluctance, Gabrielle confessed. "I was one of the best of them, or the worst, depending upon whether you shared my view or my aunt's."

"I'm certain you are ever so much more interesting for having been the child you wished to be regardless of what your aunt wanted." The sunlight sparkled in her auburn hair, making it radiant, and he was more than content simply to sit and talk with her because they'd had no such opportunity since the day he'd sent Scream of Lightning on his way.

Gabrielle found the warm softness of his gray eyes most disconcerting. They were the color of smoke that day, dark and yet inviting. She never knew how any of her comments would strike him, but she, too, wanted simply to be with him while they had this unexpected chance. "How do you manage to live the life you do, Jason? This trip is every bit as difficult as you warned us it would be, how can you bear taking it again and again?"

Surprised by the serious turn of her thoughts, Jason shrugged. "I've been out on my own since I was fourteen, traveling most of that time although I always seem to return to the Willamette Valley. What little excuse I have for a home is there, I guess."

"You have no family living there?" Gabrielle inquired softly her curiosity too sincere to give offense.

"No, my parents are both dead. Their other children died during infancy." Seeing the concern in her azure gaze he hastened to reject any words of sympathy she might offer. "I prefer to live this way, Gabrielle. It is very pleasant to drift with the wind and have no tedious responsibilities which draw me back to any place where I don't wish to go."

Shocked by the coldness of his words when his expression was so inviting, Gabrielle could not help but disagree. "You cannot honestly regard a home and family as a tedious responsibility, Mr. Royal, for the carefree life you describe is a meaningless one, without any goal or anyone to share it."

"Is it?" Jason looked long at her as if her pretty features were the most fascinating of sights; then his glance grew cold and he turned away. "It matters little what you think. It is my life to live as I see fit, not yours."

Hurt by his curt rebuff, Gabrielle did not respond. She sat by his side and watched her friends as they called to one another. They were still reading the many names painted upon the immense rock. "Still, you painted your name here too, didn't you? As if the fact you'd passed this way would mean something to someone, as if it mattered."

Jason laughed out loud at that comment, his mood again a light one as he admitted the truth of her words. "All right, Miss MacLaren. I am as vain as everyone else, I want to be remembered too."

As Gabrielle stood up to go, she whispered softly, "I for one will never forget you, never." She rejoined her wagonmates and when they had at last found what they considered the perfect spot she printed her name neatly in block letters with the sharpened stick Paul had provided. She did not once look up at Jason, but all the while she felt his glance upon her, making the emptiness in her heart all the more painful.

Their rest a brief one, the wagon train continued upon its way the next morning at first light. The incline of the trail grew steep, the journey tortuous and Gabrielle was far too tired at the end of each day to think the hours monotonous. She had already lost weight, but now she became even more slim, her beauty bordering on the ethereal, and when they at last crossed the South Pass through the Rocky Mountains, making their way over the Continental Divide, she could not bear to think they had come but halfway on their journey.

It was Jason's responsibility to see to everyone's welfare so he had noted the changes in Gabrielle's figure. However, all the young women had lost weight. They had been fortunate not to have lost anyone yet, but there were few small children among the families. The little ones were always the first to succumb to the rigors of the trail. The wagon train was making good time. Indeed, it was ahead of schedule so, knowing the emigrants deserved and needed a few days' rest, Jason was making plans to give it to them. They traveled at night to avoid the sun's scorching rays, then followed the Big Sandy River through the Green River Valley, and when they arrived at Bear Lake, Jason called a halt. Here the grass reached a tall man's knees and the trout leaped from the water, just waiting to be caught. It was one of Jason's favorite places along the trail, and when he announced they would remain there for several days, he was greeted with loud cheers of gratitude.

Gabrielle was delighted to have an opportunity to relax for she had never been so tired. There were still animals to look after and chores to perform, but now there was no need to rush. She could launder all her clothing rather than washing it piecemeal in the evening when she hardly had any energy left after a hard day's ride. It was no accident that the trail followed the path of one river and then another whenever possible; the emigrants' need for fresh water was great. With one of the worst stretches of the trail behind them, Gabrielle was happy to simply lie down upon the soft grass and watch the clouds traverse the sky. The valley was so beautiful, she wondered why anyone had ever gone farther.

The rest also did wonders for Jason's outlook. He'd had more than enough of Gabrielle's sultry glances and whispered promises when he needed far more tangible proof of her feeling for him. She was a woman of extraordinary passion, and as he frequently reminded himself, he meant her to be his alone. Why he'd wasted so much time waiting for her to come to that conclusion herself, he did not know. But he put aside that strategy now. Perhaps it was the lush beauty of the valley that made it impossible for him to maintain his former resolve to remain aloof, or perhaps the sudden sense of urgency which gripped him was a premonition he would be a fool to ignore. They had traversed some of the roughest parts of the trail, but the dangers which lay ahead were impossible to overestimate. He could no longer wait to claim the prize he considered rightfully his. Clay had ceased to question his motives where Gabrielle was concerned since he'd maintained a respectable distance for so long, and he hoped his partner would be too busy hunting or fishing to observe that he and the lovely redhead had again disappeared together. Morning was the ideal time, he decided. It was a remarkably innocent time of day when no one would suspect his purpose. That night he could scarcely close his eyes because he was so delighted with his own cleverness. He had only a few more hours to wait, and then Gabrielle would be his for the taking once more.

Gabrielle was down at the lake's edge, rinsing out the last of her stockings, when Timothy Duffy came skipping lightly over the sand. He stopped only long enough to whisper a secret in her ear, and then he was gone, the day too full of promise to be wasted on the intrigues of adults. Startled, Gabrielle watched him go, then she returned to her wagon to hang her wash upon the line. She was too curious to ignore Timothy's message so she walked back to the river which fed the lake and followed it upstream. She climbed over the rocks in her path as easily as if she were sprinting through an obstacle course designed to amuse children. She was agile, the way not difficult. Everyone else had gone to the lake to fish so she met no one along the way. At last she came to a deep pool and found Jason silently sitting upon the bank, fishing very earnestly for trout as if he expected that his catch must feed the entire wagon train.

"Timothy said you had found a climb which would interest me. Whatever did you mean?" She went to his side to see what success he'd had and found more than a dozen good-sized fish, a line through their gills keeping them captive at the edge of the pond while he fished for more.

Jason could not suppress a teasing grin. "You've already covered most of it since the way up here is an incline, but I want you to go just a bit farther with me."

Not in the least bit suspicious, Gabrielle looked around them. "It is a very good day for climbing, but I should think you're doing too well here with the trout to want to leave."

"These fish will be delicious for supper, Gabrielle, but they are no more than an alibi." He pulled his line out of the water and laid it upon the rocks. Removing the worm he'd used for bait, he tossed it back into the pond. "I've known Indians to use mouse ribs for fishhooks, how's that for ingenious?"

"Is that what you're using?" Moving closer to inspect his hook, Gabrielle found it was made of gleaming metal.

"No, I had no time to catch any mice prior to coming up here this morning." He found it difficult not to laugh out loud; he was so pleased she had come to meet him without even understanding why he was so eager to see her. "The fish will wait for our return. Let's go just a little bit higher."

Gabrielle went first, glad she had worn one of her oldest garments that day because she'd thought she'd be doing little more than laundry. The green print on the cotton fabric had once clearly been ivy growing upon a trellis, but she had washed the dress so frequently on the trip it was now a soft, pastel green, the intricate design only faintly visible upon the white background.

They made their way through low-hanging branches, then up a steep cliff to another pool that was slightly larger than the one where Jason had been fishing. Taking her hand, he led her across the smooth stones which formed a bridge at the narrow end of the pond. Then, moving past a cluster of pine trees, they arrived at a small clearing where a blanket and a picnic basket lay awaiting them, and he motioned for her to sit down beside him. "I discovered this place two years ago. I have to get away from the people in the train once in a while or I'd be a poor wagon master, as tired and irritable as any of my charges. I hoped you would not mind if I spirited you away for an hour or two to keep me company."

Gabrielle laughed at his remark. "You're making no sense, Jason. How can you want to get away from everyone and at the same time want my company?" She thought the grassy glade delightful and she certainly had no objection to passing the time with him; yet she could not resist teasing him.

"Does that seem like such a contradiction to you?" he asked softly. "There is a great difference between being surrounded by a noisy crowd and being alone with a beautiful woman. Isn't that obvious or must I explain it to you?"

Instantly Gabrielle's sweet smile was replaced by a look of considerable apprehension. They were most certainly alone, some distance from the others, and while she knew he would not press for an advantage she would not gladly give him, she felt betrayed by her own weakness where he was concerned. "If you want only to speak with me, I will be happy to stay, but if it is much more that you want, then—"

"Must you be so melodramatic?" Jason turned her question aside without answering it. "I have a bottle of wine here, and some cheese I have been saving as well as a few fresh biscuits. I even picked some berries while I was waiting for you. Does that sound like the act of a man with evil intentions?" he inquired with a devilish wink. He poured the rich, red wine into two tin cups and handed her one. "I do hope you will forgive my lack of suitable crystal, but I have yet to find any that travels well."

Relieved to find him in so playful a mood, Gabrielle took a sip of the wine and, with only a little urging, a piece of cheese and a biscuit. The berries were sweet yet tangy, and she thought the meal a most delicious one. Complimenting him frequently on the repast, she soon lost track of how many times he'd refilled her cup so she set it aside, determined to accept no more of the flavorful wine. Enjoying the enchanting mood of the secluded spot, she saw only the warmth of Jason's smile and she thought him even more handsome than when they'd first met.

"I rather like your beard, I don't believe I've ever had an

opportunity to say so, but I think it is quite handsome." She had spoken very deliberately, but the words sounded slightly slurred in her ears and she wondered if he had understood her.

"Thank you, but I will shave it off tonight if you are merely being polite and truly do not like it." Jason set his cup aside and moved closer, his warm breath now brushing her cheek as he spoke.

"Jason . . ." Gabrielle whispered softly, bringing her hand up to caress the curls at his nape when he drew closer still. He leaned across her then, forcing her down upon the woolen blanket which had once before served as their bed. She could not recall what it was she had wanted to say, and when his mouth covered hers she gave up the effort to speak. His lips were soft as he kissed her, barely lingering upon her slightly open mouth before he began to lavish light kisses upon the long sweep of her lashes and then along the curve of her flushed cheek. All the while his hands were undoing the buttons of her dress, then slipping her lingerie from her shoulders, not stopping until her splendid body was exposed to his view. She was far more slender, but her subtle contours were none the less perfect and the tenderness of his mood changed abruptly, bursting into the fire of passion too long denied. His kisses were hot now, searing her fair skin with a tongue of flame as he slipped from her embrace. Intent upon savoring the beauty of her delicate body to the fullest, he traced the swell of her smooth cool breast then spread slow sweet nibbles across her flat stomach. His hunger for her drove him to seek still more, the ultimate intimacy, for he would allow her to keep nothing hidden. He wanted her very soul, his deep, probing kiss eagerly consuming all she could give of her very essence until her surrender was so complete he could not demand more. Waves of ecstasy poured through her loins and flooded her slender thighs with tremors; still he did lift his mouth from her until she lay perfectly still, her breath coming in hoarse gasps as she whispered his name so softly he was not even certain she had spoken. This was all he had wanted, this splendid pleasure he had never sought to give any other woman, and he drew her into his arms, content to hold her in a fond embrace until she drew a deep breath and pulled away, the blue of her eyes brighter than that of the summer sky as she gazed down at him. It was not pleasure which lit her glance now but as furious an anger as he had ever seen her display.

Gabrielle made no attempt to contain the fires of her temper as she lashed out at him. "That was totally unfair, unprincipled, and unethical, to say nothing of unkind. Did you think me too naïve to understand your purpose in inviting me here, or merely too stupid to leave once I had come?"

Jason made no reply to that insulting question. He simply got to his feet, and lifting the startled beauty into his arms, he carried her back through the trees to the pond. Walking to the edge, he tossed her into the chill waters. That bit of horseplay did not cool her mood, however; it only enraged her all the more. She scooped up a handful of water and threw it at him as she screamed exactly what she thought of him in words he had not even imagined she knew.

The whole scene struck Jason as highly amusing, and he tore off his clothing and dove in, laughing at the anger which made Gabrielle impossible to hold. She twisted away from his grasp, as graceful in the water as she was upon the land, but each time she struggled to climb out of the pond he pulled her right back into the depths, dunking her for good measure because he was in such high spirits.

"First you tried to get me drunk, and now you want to drown me?" she screamed as she tried to slap the grin from his face. But he caught her wrist and pulled her slippery form against his chest as he wrapped his other arm around her narrow waist.

"Oh, no. I have something entirely different in mind." With one backward step he moved out into the pond so she would have to swim to keep her head above the water while he could stand quite comfortably upon the moss-covered rocks. He watched the light in her eyes change from confusion to surprise as she realized exactly what he meant to do, what he was doing, and quite easily too since she had no way to escape his embrace. His expression was a taunting one as he drew her hips to his but he did not trust himself to speak and so lowered his mouth to hers, cutting off her last chance for resistance.

Even with the cool water surrounding her, Gabrielle felt only the heat of Jason's forceful embrace. It was useless to fight him when she did not truly want to and when she could not have summoned the strength required had she earnestly desired to elude him. He was far too clever a man when it came to making love. The range of his experience made it impossible to avoid his advances since she could never anticipate his next move, let alone successfully escape it. He had betrayed her trust, yet her own heart was the true villain. She placed her arms about his neck as she wrapped herself around him, lost again in the magic of his passionate embrace.

Jason could only marvel at the sweetness of Gabrielle's touch. What she must think of him he could not even imagine, but he felt this enchanting creature had been created solely to give pleasure to him. Her vibrant body began to melt into his, setting his blood aflame despite the chill of the water in which they floated so languidly. He thought for no more than a split second that they just might drown; then he ceased to worry. To die while making love was too pleasant a way to meet death to cause alarm. His body shook with the rapture she gave, but he held back until the madness of ecstasy swept away his will and in that final thrill he again belonged more to her than himself.

Leaving the pond, they wrapped themselves in the blanket, their bodies entwined as the warmth of the sun filled them with still another kind of peace. There was just no way to refuse this man, Gabrielle realized, for even when she said no very loudly his affection too swiftly turned her response to yes.

"Is this what you mean by drifting in the wind while you seize each opportunity which presents itself and take it to the limit?"

The sun was high overhead, they had no time to discuss anything now; so Jason chuckled at her question as he got up to pull on his clothes. She had never been the least bit shy with him, nor did he feel any need to turn away as he dressed. Each knew every line of the other's body too well for such a pretense. He knew he was handsome and she was a beauty, so modesty was an unnecessary virtue in his view. "You are the one who makes me grab what opportunities I can, Gabrielle. I would prefer that our relationship were a much more regular one."

He was quite serious now, logical, practical, not the ardent lover she found it impossible to resist. Gabrielle tried to strike the same tone. "You want me to meet you more often, but still in secret? With your assurance, of course, that I will not have to bear the consequences of such an illicit affair alone?"

Jason tossed her dress to her as he replied angrily, "You still don't trust me, do you?"

"How can I when I know I will soon be regarded as a 'tiresome responsibility'?" Gabrielle shook out her lace-trimmed lingerie and pulled it on slowly, wondering why the fact she was nude did not bother her. She decided it was ridiculous to consider such a silly thing after the delicious intimacy they'd shared that morning. Although she did not wish to be treated so casually, she had only herself to blame. Jason was a man after all, and a young, virile one who could be expected to want exactly what he'd taken from her. She was the fool to give love so eagerly when he gave nothing in return.

Jason's gaze darkened as he watched the young woman he adored slip back into her clothes. She adjusted her garments with a few smooth touches and then combed out her long auburn hair with her fingertips. When she paused to glance up at him she looked as though she had been doing nothing more than fishing, but he'd not forget what had truly happened between them. He could think of no way to give her the reassurance she seemed to crave and so he did not try. When she could not feel the depth of his devotion in his caress, how could mere words convey his regard for her? "I'll come back for the blanket and the other things later. We'll just go back to the wagon train and say half the fish are yours. No one will suspect a thing at this hour of the day."

"That is why you chose it?" Gabrielle asked curiously, wondering if he would admit how devious his plan had been.

"Precisely. Now let's go."

Jason was as lost in thought as Gabrielle when they started down the rocky hill. He was thinking of the many women he had known and he found he could compare none to her. He was the only man she had known, which he certainly could not say about any of the others. He had been with women he hadn't paid, but he'd not been the first to sample their favors, nor by any stretch of the imagination had he thought he'd be the last. She'd been dangerously close to the truth with her question. He did seize whatever opportunity he had to enjoy being with a woman but—damn it!—none of them had meant anything to him. None had ignited his passion the way she did with no more than the promise of pleasure in her glance. He could not even recall the names of most of the women he'd slept with, hadn't even thought that feat necessary until now. Those encounters had been playful, spur of the moment and brief, and not once filled with the rapture Gabrielle gave in such great abundance. How she had managed to bewitch him so completely he did not know, for the world was filled with beautiful women, and many that could be had for a very reasonable price. He'd had plenty of them, yet their affection had been so empty. He watched her move over the rocks beside the stream in smooth, agile leaps; the path no challenge for one with such easy grace. He longed to be able to read her thoughts. Perhaps she had spoken the truth when she'd said she'd always love Beau. Maybe his cause was truly a hopeless one and her heart would never open to him. He was disgusted with himself then, for in the beginning he had taken this beautiful creature, wishing only to teach her what he thought was one of the most useful of life's lessons. He had treated her as casually as if she were to be his mistress for the trip and nothing more. Indeed, wasn't that what he'd made of her? He'd given her the greatest of pleasure, and taken his own, but he'd not won her trust, let alone her love. The morning had gone exactly as he'd planned it, so why did he feel nothing but guilt rather than the warm glow of satisfaction he had craved?

Moving ahead along the trail, Gabrielle reached the pond where Jason had been fishing and stopped abruptly, for Sam Duffy was seated in the shade with a fishing line in his hand. Gabrielle could tell by his lopsided grin that he had been waiting for them to appear. She cared little what he might think, but Jason's reaction to Sam's greeting was far more hostile.

"Well if it ain't the righteous Mr. Royal and one of his little brides." Sam nearly drooled, his evil leer had grown so wide. "You picked the wrong boy to carry your messages this time, not that Timothy told me nothing you understand. I just like to keep my eyes open and when I seen you speak with him and then he made a quick dash for Miss MacLaren I put two and two together pretty fast. Now I don't intend to tell nobody about this. I'll stay out of your business as long as you promise to stay out of mine. I don't want neither of you comin' 'round my wife and kids again, or the things you want kept secret is gonna be common knowledge. You understand what I mean? You'll have a bride on your hands no man will be fool enough to take."

"I don't make idle threats, Sam, and I'd advise you not to either. You make the mistake of touching one hair on your wife's head, or of saying one unkind word about Miss MacLaren and you're a dead man." Jason spoke in a soft, low tone that made his words all the more terrifying, for it was obvious he meant exactly what he said.

Sam got to his feet, yanking his line from the water and tossing it aside. "Don't you go and threaten me. I know what you been doin', you hear? I seen you in the water and you two sure weren't swimmin' neither!"

"That's it, Sam. You just made your wife a widow." Jason crossed the short distance between them with a flying leap, his

209

first punch catching the obnoxious man full in the mouth and knocking him clear off his feet. Sam never had a chance to run or to defend himself. Each time he fell down Jason yanked him to his feet and struck him again, delivering each blow with more power until the man's face was completely unrecognizable, a mask of blood covering his badly swollen features.

Gabrielle had seen plenty of fist fights, but they had been scuffles between boys. Never had she seen a man so intent on murder as Jason was now. He was methodically beating Sam Duffy to death and for what? Because he was ashamed that the man knew they were lovers? That was hardly a capital offense. She tried to grab his arm, to stop him while there was still some spark of life left in poor Sam Duffy, but Jason shoved her aside and, picking up the unconscious man, tossed him into the middle of the pond. Then he calmly bent down to retrieve the fish he'd left tethered to the line at the water's edge.

"Come on, let's go."

"You're not going to leave him to drown!" Gabrielle cried out in disbelief, appalled by the brutality she'd just witnessed.

"He deserves no better. I warned him and he asked for it. That was his mistake, not mine," Jason explained matter-of-factly as he turned to go.

"You coward!" Gabrielle shouted at his back. But there was no time to argue with Jason when Sam lay floating face down in the pond. She bent down on her knees and leaning out as far as she could, caught hold of Sam's trousers and pulled his limp body to shore. He was heavy, but Jason gave her no help as she struggled to pull him onto dry ground. When she rolled him over on his stomach and pressed down on his back, water poured from his mouth and then he began to retch as he came fully awake. As she moved away from Duffy she was surprised to see that Jason had not left. He stood by, watching her with an expression she could only describe as amazement.

"Why would you want to save him?" he asked angrily. "He'll only repay your kindness by spreading ugly rumors about us we won't be able to stop."

210

"So what?" Gabrielle replied instantly. "My reputation is not worth any man's life. Take your blasted fish and go on back to the wagon train. No one will ever suspect we were together since you'd rather kill than admit it. Mr. Duffy here just happened to slip while he was climbing and fell into the pond, isn't that right, Sam?" She nudged his shoulder with a forceful shove and he nodded since he was coughing so badly he could not reply in words.

Jason knew he had no choice but to go. Gabrielle had so little sense at times he knew he'd just be wasting his breath to try to make her see reason. Her reputation was worth the lives of more than a dozen men like Duffy, and he'd not allow her to suffer when he was the one who could not control his desire for her. "Get him back down into camp as soon as you can. I'll send Paul up to help if you aren't back in ten minutes."

"Don't bother!" Gabrielle called after him, thoroughly disgusted with his ruthless tactics. Turning to Sam, she shook him again, "Well, you heard him. As soon as you think you can stand I'll help you back down the trail."

Sam tried to get up on his hands and knees, but fell back down, too badly hurt to attempt to crawl. He tried to catch his breath, but he'd never been so frightened or in such terrible pain. He began to sob like a homeless puppy.

As disgusted with Sam as she was with Jason, Gabrielle stood up and began to pace by his side. "You brought this all on yourself, Sam. Mr. Royal is a proud man and he'll not allow you to slander his name or mine." Of course it wasn't slander, she knew, merely the truth. "Now I'll wait here for as long as it takes you to pull yourself together because I don't want you to fall back into the water and drown after I went to the trouble of pulling you out."

Sam continued to weep pathetically, his voice hoarse as he begged her to forgive him. "I won't never breathe a word of none of it, miss. I swear I won't." He knew Jason Royal had meant to kill him, that he had not succeeded was due only to this slip of a girl. Duffy was so terrified he could not stop shaking.

Gabrielle tapped her foot impatiently as she waited for the man to rise. She didn't give a damn what he said about her, wouldn't have cared if the whole camp had seen her making love to Jason as though she were a mermaid accustomed to such erotic play underwater, but Jason clearly had another view. A chill of fear shot up her spine as she realized he'd promised to marry her should she become pregnant. Did she truly want to give birth to a child fathered by a murderer, or to call such a man husband? Sam moaned loudly then, reminding her that Jason was not really a murderer, at least not yet. But they still had a long way to go before they reached Oregon and she could not bear to consider what might happen along the way.

Chapter XI

Rather than being the ungrateful troublemaker Jason had predicted he'd be, Sam Duffy became an inspiring example of loyalty. When they had returned to camp he'd told everyone that Gabrielle had happened along the trail just in time to save his life. Because of his cuts and bruises and his obviously shaken state, his tale was readily believed. He then began to follow the young woman about whenever the wagon train camped, offering to perform whatever service she might require from saddling Sunny to unhitching the team of oxen which pulled her wagon. If he were not present himself, he sent Timothy to be certain there was nothing which needed to be done. At first Gabrielle had tried to politely discourage the man's devotion, but he did not seem to hear her refusals and persisted in being so enormously helpful that her friends began to tease her, saying Sam Duffy had been smitten by her charms. She did no more than smile and ask them to be kind to the man. Consequently they did not tease him as unmercifully as they did her.

Jason missed little that happened among the emigrants and he thought Sam's transformation a most remarkable event. The man had shaved off his beard, and had begun to wear clean clothing. If he was not following Gabrielle around and trying to be of service to her, he could be found playing with his children

213

or sitting by his wagon talking quietly with his wife. Far from being jealous, Mrs. Duffy seemed grateful that her husband had become so attentive and she made no complaints whatsoever.

Using Sam as a convenient excuse to speak with Gabrielle, Jason wandered by her wagon one evening and drew her aside. "I would not have left your pet to drown. Had you not pulled Sam out of the pond that day I would have."

Astonished by that revelation, Gabrielle asked impatiently, "Do you really expect me to believe that fairy tale, Mr. Royal? I was there and you had already turned to go when I went to Sam's rescue. It is far too late now to tell me you did not intend to let him drown."

Jason took off his hat and thumped it against his knee several times to brush off the dust before he jammed it back on his head.

"You think damn little of me, don't you?"

His bright glance was as accusing as his question. He had hoped she'd believe him, but she had scarcely listened to his explanation of his intention. He knew, however, no matter what she thought, that he'd have pulled Sam out of the water. He'd only tossed him in to give him a good scare, not to kill him.

"With good reason!" Gabrielle's long, dark lashes nearly swept her brows she was so surprised. "You have given me ample opportunity to observe your true colors, Mr. Royal."

Jason had paid absolutely no attention to her and had not given her one kind word, let alone a compliment, in the many days that had passed since they'd left Bear Lake. He'd been a lover of extraordinary sensitivity that day and then he had retreated behind a wall of silence. He'd become a stranger who valued her reputation above all things. Or perhaps it is his own reputation he values so highly, she thought bitterly. Either way, the result had been the same. He had simply ignored her and his neglect had hurt her badly.

Jason's dark brows came together in a savage frown, his

214

disappointment profound at finding her in such an argumentative mood. "Sam does not bother you, does he? Just let me know if you find his attentions offensive and I'll—"

"You'll what?" Gabrielle stepped close to whisper her question. "Just shoot him this time?"

"Damn it, Gabrielle, you're not being fair!"

She turned her back on him then, leaving him swearing angrily with only the wind to hear. She could not understand his moods. It was not a question of forgiving him for the fury of his passions, certainly not. When she could not even control her own thoughts or behavior, it was ludicrous to attempt to make him admit his lack of judgment had nearly cost Sam his life. What a hopeless mess everything had become, but she could not change the way she felt about Jason nor did she even wish to try. He had raised the barrier which existed between them, and she felt as though she were pounding her fists upon a stone wall each time she tried to break it down. He is like the wind he admires, she thought suddenly, warm, sensuous but maddeningly invisible when what I crave is love of the most devoted and enduring kind.

When they reached the effervescent waters of Soda Springs, the children as well as the adults were delighted by the bubbles that tickled their noses as they tried to drink, making them burst into laughter no matter how serious an expression they attempted to maintain. Gabrielle joined her friends but found it difficult to enjoy their playful antics when Jason was standing nearby. He was, as always, her consuming interest, and she much preferred to watch him rather than concentrate upon the conversation of the young women with whom she spent so much time. He appeared to be as amused as the children. In fact, she'd seldom seen him in so jovial a mood, as if the spring were his own private discovery which he'd been too generous to keep secret. Attempting to be more objective, she thought of the many ways in which he'd helped them all. She was certain he was as fine a wagon master as any man could hope to to be, for despite his strictness, he had infused each

215

step of the journey with a sense of wonder at the beauty of nature. When they broke camp each morning, he insisted they leave the land unscarred by their stay. Too many wagon trains left the terrain littered with garbage, and he considered that an affront not only to the land but to those who would follow in their path. He had an Indian's respect for the prairie, and since it supplied all of their needs he had taught them it should be cared for in return. There was so much about the man to admire, but she found it difficult to watch him that day without tears coming to her eyes for she longed for the tender affection he'd made it impossible for her to accept.

Erica watched Gabrielle drift away from their group as if the sparkling spring held little interest for her and as this was not the first time she'd seen her good friend become so withdrawn, she followed her.

"Would you like to go back to the wagon and talk? Something is bothering you and I don't mind giving you the benefit of my advice even though I know you'll probably disregard it." Erica gave Gabrielle an engaging smile.

Gabrielle shook her head, sending her auburn tresses flying in emphatic refusal. "I always enjoy your company, Erica, but I've no more worries than you or any of the rest of us. I am sorry to disappoint you and I don't mean to be unsociable, but I have no problems to discuss. She smiled with what she hoped would be convincing innocence, meanwhile thinking she could not possibly describe her dilemma. She could not admit she had fallen in love with Jason Royal, had even made love with him several times, but had refused to become his mistress since she could not bear the indifference with which he treated her. That was too shocking a secret to reveal, and she was not even remotely tempted to share it with Erica.

Frowning, Erica did not give up on her efforts. "Is it the men, is that it?"

"What men?" Gabrielle asked, confused by what appeared to be so irrelevant a question.

"The bachelors, of course. What other men could there be!"

Erica replied, as if the matter were too obvious to explain. "Marlene is still frantic about the fact that she lied about her age. Have you never heard her crying in the night? She is certain none of the men will want her and she wants so desperately to have a home and family she can't bear the thought that her dreams won't come true."

Gabrielle looked back toward the spring. Marlene was talking with Iris, or rather listening to Iris as that was the only way any of them could pretend to converse with the difficult young woman. "I'm sorry to hear that. Marlene is so sweet, she's very pretty too; but apparently she's had little attention from men and does not believe she deserves the happiness she craves."

"I can think of no way to help her, can you?" Erica asked hopefully. She'd found Gabrielle to be a very sensible young woman who could be counted on in any sort of emergency, and she regarded Marlene's state of mind as an emergency which needed immediate attention.

"No, if there were several young men about, we could ask them to notice her, or at least talk with her occasionally so she would gain some confidence, but that's not possible here," Gabrielle mused thoughtfully.

After a moment's thought, Erica gave a delighted squeal. "Let's ask Mr. Royal to give her some extra attention! He'd do it, don't you think? He is such a charming man I'm sure if you asked him he'd do it for us."

Gabrielle found it difficult to respond in a tone below a furious shriek, but after taking a deep breath she gave it her best try. "That is the worst idea I have ever heard, Erica. For one thing, it's unfair to treat the man as though he were a gigolo. For another, were Marlene ever to find out he was being sweet to her only as a favor to us she would be devastated. No. The whole idea is absurd, completely out of the question."

Erica stared wide-eyed at her friend, "What's a gigolo?" She asked innocently.

"That is the French word for a man who is paid to be a

217

woman's escort. It is not a complimentary term for they are considered little better than prostitutes," Gabrielle explained in a hushed tone.

Clearly astounded that such an occupation existed, Erica nonetheless believed if there were such men they would definitely be plying their trade in France. Deciding it would be better not to pursue that topic, she asked, "Can you speak French, Gabrielle?"

"Some. My aunt attempted to instruct me in the language, but I was an indifferent pupil I'm afraid. Gabrielle is a French name, so she insisted I know a few words at least."

"Your aunt told you about gigolos?" Erica inquired skeptically, wondering what sort of guardian would reveal such a scandalous thing.

"No, of course not. She gave me French novels to read in the hope of improving my grammar and one referred to such a man. But we are getting off the subject. Do you understand why your idea is such a foolish one?"

"No. We wouldn't be paying Mr. Royal to do it, so no one could call him a gigolo. And how would Marlene ever find out? I still think it's a good idea."

"It's dreadful!" Gabrielle insisted. "You can't manipulate people like that. They both have feelings and it would be disastrous. That sounds more like something Iris would suggest rather than you, Erica, and I don't want any part of it."

Undaunted, Erica refused to give up. "There's Mr. Horne then. Have you noticed how much younger he looks now than when he first spoke with us in Kansas City? I'll bet he's lost twenty or thirty pounds, and if I were to cut his hair the way Mr. Royal wears his, so the curls followed the shape of his head instead of sticking out all over, I'd bet he'd be quite handsome too."

Gabrielle simply stared at her friend dumfounded by her lack of logic. She'd paid little attention to how Clayton Horne looked, but as she glanced through the crowd and saw him talking with Barbara, she had to agree that he did look far more

218

fit than when their journey had begun. Still, no matter how he
wore his hair she thought the idea a poor one.

"By all means offer to cut Mr. Horne's hair if that's what
you want to do, but leave him out of this scheme too. He is
supposed to be escorting all of us to Oregon and he can't have
any favorites. Were he to begin paying special attention to
Marlene, someone would be sure to notice and be hurt because
she did not receive the same courtesy. Just forget it, Erica, and
when we arrive in Oregon City we'll do our best to make
Marlene feel better about herself regardless of what her age
might be."

With so much on her mind, Gabrielle gave the matter of
building Marlene's self-confidence no further thought until
she noticed Clayton Horne sporting a new and very flattering
haircut. The change in the man was really quite remarkable.
He did look much younger, and with his trimmer waistline he
now seemed to have a muscular rather than a stocky build.
Erica only laughed when she asked her about it, but when she
did not see Marlene in Clayton's company she ceased to worry
over what mischief might be afoot because the trail had again
grown difficult.

After the wagon train had left Soda Springs, they had angled
north, crossing a hot, dry plain with little but sagebrush to
improve the view. Their next opportunity to stop for a few
days would be at Fort Hall. There they would rest before
continuing the trail as it followed the Snake River west.

Gabrielle had just finished her breakfast one morning when
Timothy Duffy came running to find her. Breathlessly he
explained that his father needed her help that day. "My ma's
awful sick. She can barely take care of herself let alone my
sisters. Can you ride with us today and help me watch 'em?"

"Why of course I will, Tim. When did your mother fall ill?"
Gabrielle was concerned about the woman, and although they
were not friends she was happy to help her after the many
chores Sam had done for her.

"Mrs. Duffy is ill?" Johanna asked solicitously. "I'd better

219

come along too, just in case." She considered herself a most proficient nurse and at the same time thought it her Christian duty to help anyone in need.

Seeing her worried glance, Gabrielle did not refuse her help. So leaving their horses tied behind the wagon, the two young women rode to the Duffys' rig. Sam Duffy had hitched up his team, but was waiting for them to arrive.

"Amanda took sick during the night and I can't see to her and drive the oxen as well with three kids to watch." He looked far from well himself, having had little sleep due to his wife's illness.

"Johanna and I will be happy to help you, Sam. Do you have any idea what could be wrong with your wife?" Gabrielle thought it would be helpful to have at least some idea what sort of illness she was tending.

Blushing deeply, Sam tried to describe her symptoms, "She can't seem to keep nothing down, she was that way before each of the kids was born so it might be that again, or if it ain't that perhaps something she ate was spoiled."

"It has been hot and food spoils easily in this weather," Johanna agreed, promptly taking charge. "Have you some tea? We'll need to give her plenty to drink regardless of the cause of her sickness."

Sam stared down at the prim little woman, certain he shouldn't have mentioned his wife's condition might be such a delicate one. "Sure, we got a tin of tea. I'll just brew some while the fire's still hot."

"Good." Johanna climbed over the tailgate of the wagon and made herself comfortable beside Mrs. Duffy as she called out. "You wait for the tea, Gabrielle, and then we'll be all set until noon."

Gabrielle smiled at Sam when she saw how embarrassed he was. She had rightly guessed the cause. "You and Amanda are married, aren't you, Sam? It's no disgrace if she is pregnant, is it?"

"Oh, we are married all right. It's only that this ain't the time for another babe is all." He looked around then to be certain Timothy wasn't listening and saw that the boy was playing nearby with his sisters. "We got all we can handle now, miss. Not that I don't love the kids, but they are a handful."

"Well let's just make the tea and let the future take care of itself for the time being, Sam." Gabrielle knew that wasn't an especially reassuring thought, but she could offer little more in the way of advice. The Duffys had few material possessions and so she and the little girls moved to the back of the wagon where they had plenty of room. The girls played with rag dolls while Timothy rode Comet, the mule. Johanna kept up a steady stream of conversation with Amanda, offering her a sip of tea whenever she thought she could swallow it. Sam tried to keep his attention focused on his oxen, but he turned around frequently to thank the two young women for their help.

Jason noticed Sunny trotting behind Gabrielle's wagon but he had no time to inquire where she might be until the wagon train stopped at noon. He tried to make his interest sound only casual when he asked Paul for her whereabouts, but after learning that Mrs. Duffy had fallen ill, he headed straight down the line of wagons, looking for Sam's. He found Gabrielle preparing lunch for the children while Sam and Johanna sat inside the wagon with Amanda who was still too weak to leave her bed.

When no suitable greeting came to his mind, Jason got right to the point. He asked Gabrielle when Amanda had fallen ill. He hadn't meant to direct his anger at her but his reprimand sounded sharp nonetheless. "I should have been told immediately. If it is something contagious then their wagon will have to be isolated from the others before the disease spreads."

Gabrielle asked Timothy and his sisters to sit down and eat before she took Jason aside to explain in a hushed whisper. "There's no need to frighten the children. Sam thinks his wife is pregnant, which I am certain you know is not contagious."

"Well let's hope not," Jason responded with a sly grin, but

221

he had to laugh when Gabrielle's cheeks flooded with color. He wanted to pull her into his arms and cover her face with kisses, but he shoved his hands into his back pockets instead and asked the only question which came to his mind. "If it's just morning sickness, isn't it hanging on a bit long?"

"Frankly, I know nothing about such matters. Johanna kept giving her tea all morning, but I don't think it did much good. Morning sickness is never fatal though, so I imagine she'll be feeling better before too much longer."

"Johanna is here too?" Jason looked toward the wagon, he'd not noticed the young woman had not been with the others. He didn't count heads each morning, but he always found some excuse to ride by and wave to Gabrielle so he'd noted her disappearance.

"Yes, she enjoys being helpful. She volunteered right away when Timothy came to ask for my help this morning."

"I better look at Mrs. Duffy for a moment, just to make certain she's all right." Jason sincerely hoped she was for they were still several days from Fort Hall. He didn't want to have to stop in the middle of nowhere if her mysterious illness were to spread.

"Well . . ." Gabrielle hesitated to say what was on her mind, but since he seemed truly concerned about the woman she whispered softly. "Have you ever spoken with Sam since we were at Bear Lake?"

Jason straightened up to his full height, his gesture a threatening one even if she had not meant to give offense. "No. But I'll not use that as an excuse to avoid speaking with him now. Tell him I want to see his wife and it's not because I'm suspicious about how he's treating her, but because I'm concerned that she's ill. Will you do that for me, please?"

"I will be happy to. Give me just a minute to speak with him and I'm sure he won't refuse."

As Gabrielle turned to go, Jason reached out to catch her arm.

"I won't allow him to refuse. My request is merely a

222

courtesy because I am going to speak with his wife right now, no matter what he says. Is that clear?"

"Yes," Gabrielle responded softly, sorry he would think that threat needed to be spoken. "We are all your responsibility, I know your speech by heart, and I'll see that Sam understands your interest is for the general welfare, not a malicious one."

Jason swallowed the invectives which came to his lips as Gabrielle walked around to the back of the wagon. Why did she insist upon twisting every damn word he spoke until it sounded ugly? He was tempted to just turn his back on the Duffys and let them handle their own problems, but as Gabrielle had said, they were his responsibility and one he'd not shirk.

Gabrielle returned swiftly, her expression filled with anxiety. "I had not realized how desperately ill the woman truly is, Jason. I think you'd better look at her at once." She followed him around to the back of the wagon but waited outside until he climbed down. He'd spent no more than three minutes with Amanda but his face was ashen. "What's wrong? What do you think it is?"

The tall man took a deep breath and then another before he looked down at her and whispered. "I think it's cholera and we'll be damn lucky if we don't lose half the camp."

"Oh, no!" Gabrielle's golden tan faded to a ghostly pallor as she reached out to grab his arm, afraid she might faint at the thought that the plague had overtaken them so far from a settlement where they might receive medical attention. Knowing hysteria would do none of them any good, she forced herself to be calm. "Did you say that to Sam?"

"Not yet." Jason covered her hand with his as he whispered. "You and Johanna have been with her all morning so I can't allow you to go back to your own wagon. You'll have to remain here and do what you can for the children should they become sick. The disease spreads so quickly if they are infected it will soon become apparent."

Shocked by the calm manner in which he was handling what could easily be a death sentence, Gabrielle nodded numbly.

"Yes, of course. I understand. My own parents died of cholera within hours of each other. Since I did not catch the disease then, perhaps I will be lucky this time too."

No longer able to appear detached when he could not bear to consider what might happen to Gabrielle, Jason drew her into his arms, hugging her trembling body against his chest as he stroked her silken hair. "I talked with Dr. Whitman about the disease once. He is a Presbyterian missionary who swore he'd successfully treated cholera with no more than a great sufficiency of fluids and warm blankets. I do not know what else to try."

Gabrielle rested in his arms for no more than a minute; then she stepped back, lifting her chin proudly as she agreed. "Johanna and I will do what we can for the Duffys. Now hadn't you better see about everyone else?"

Jason brought her hand to his lips, kissing her palm tenderly as he'd often longed to do, but there seemed to be no words to express the emotion which flooded his heart. He knew cholera to be a killer, and a swift one. By the time he had scrubbed himself clean and had gone to check on each of the other families she might already have fallen ill. The horror of that possibility terrified him. Unable to think of something to say that would give her hope, he gave her practical advice. "Give the children a good bath. Scrub them clean and then burn their clothes. Find some clothing their mother hasn't touched in the last few days. Boil the water before they drink it and keep everything clean. Make the kids sleep on the ground—I'll provide fresh blankets—and don't let them get back into that wagon. Keep them away from their mother no matter how they beg to see her."

Gabrielle nodded, her mind racing ahead to the necessary tasks. "We'll be all right, Jason. Don't worry about us."

She seemed so distracted he did not try to make her understand how futile her advice was. He knew he would think of little else but the great danger she was in. She was a lovely young woman, but a fragile one; and he hoped that whatever miracle had saved her life when her parents had been lost would save her again. Giving her hands a last affectionate squeeze, he called Sam down from the wagon and talked frankly with him. Jason could read the man's fear in his eyes and he knew Sam had already suspected the truth. Johanna proved to be as courageous as Gabrielle and she offered to stay by Amanda's side to do all she could to improve the woman's chances for survival while her friend tended the children.

Clayton thought Jason had lost his mind when the young man began tossing his clothing into their fire. "My God, man, what are you doing?"

"I've got other clothes, bring me some along with soap and a towel. Unless I miss my guess, Amanda Duffy has come down with cholera, and I don't want to spread it around while I warn the others."

Clayton ran to their pack mules for the items Jason required, his fingers shaking as he searched through their baggage. Then, realizing hysteria was as great an enemy as the disease, he made a valiant attempt to conquer his fear by the time he returned to the wagon master's side.

"We can't leave their wagon behind, of course, but what shall we do?"

"I'm going to take the rest of the wagons on down the trail a hundred yards or so, just to give us some space before I announce what's happened. We'll do our best to see Mrs. Duffy survives. Then if no one else comes down with the disease, we'll go on. But the odds are against this being one isolated case."

"I realize that, but what can we do to protect our girls?" Clayton asked anxiously.

Filling a bucket from a barrel of drinking water, Jason picked up the soap and began to wash every speck of dust from his deeply tanned body. "Gabrielle and Johanna spent the morning with the Duffys so I had to leave them there."

"Dear God." Clayton sank to the ground in a weary heap. "Not everyone dies when they get cholera, Jason. Some always survive, a scant few perhaps, but some always do manage to recover."

"Yes, and some don't come down with the disease no matter how frequently they are exposed to it. Let us pray we have many such fortunate souls among us."

Clayton looked up, startled by Jason's comment. "I did not think you were a religious man."

"I am ready to beg for help from any quarter, Clay. Now hand me my clothes."

Once dressed and mounted upon Duke, Jason gave the order to roll but he soon called a halt. Then he rode down the line of wagons, giving each the news that Amanda Duffy was seriously ill and they would make camp rather than travel any farther that day. He said it was too soon to give the disease a name, but by the time he'd reached the last wagon rumors of cholera had already begun to spread. In 1832 an epidemic had spread from Asia to Europe. Carried across the sea to New Orleans it had swiftly moved up the Mississippi River leaving thousands dead in its wake, Gabrielle's parents among them. Now, in 1847, the disease had broken out again, following the Ohio and Mississippi Rivers. Those moving west in the hope of escaping its deadly grasp now realized they might not be so fortunate. The wagons formed a large circle and the emigrants herded the livestock inside to graze. But rather than mingling with their neighbors as they usually did, each family sat alone, wondering who would be the next to fall ill and praying it would not be one of those they loved.

The Duffys' younger daughter, Suzanna, was four, the elder, Mary Beth, was six. Gabrielle made a game of bathing them and dressing them in the pretty calico dresses she'd found in their trunk. Timothy, however, wasn't about to be fooled. While the other wagons hadn't left them far behind, they had been left all the same, and being a clever child, he had swiftly guessed the reason. His eyes filled with tears as he drew Gabrielle aside.

"Is my ma gonna die? Is that why they left us?"

Hugging his thin little body tightly, Gabrielle told him the truth. "Mr. Royal thinks your mother may have a disease which is extremely contagious. That's why he wanted to separate us from the others before they got sick too. He won't leave us though, and we'll do our best to see that your mother gets well. Now you must bathe and change your clothes too, because being clean will help you stay well."

Timothy wasn't convinced. "I'm not all that dirty." He looked down at his dusty overalls which smelled more like a mule than he knew they should. "Am I?"

"No. But I insist you take a bath. I know you don't need my help but you must do it right now or I will strip off your clothes and scrub you from one end to the other myself. Now which will it be?"

"I'll do it!" Timothy agreed quickly. Wiping away the last of his tears and filling a bucket with water, he ducked around the end of the wagon where she couldn't see him wash. She sent him back twice, but at last, satisfied that he was clean, she gave him new clothes to wear.

While the little girls were also worried about their mother, they did not understand that her situation was so grave and played happily with their dolls or listened attentively while Gabrielle told them stories. She made some soup for their supper and Johanna tried to give some to Amanda, but it made her sick again so they went back to the weak tea. Sam climbed down from the wagon to try to eat some supper, but he was too frightened even to taste the soup Gabrielle had prepared. Apologetically, he tried to explain his real worry. "I know I ain't been much of a husband. I know that. But I've been trying real hard to make it up to Amanda. If I was to lose her now . . ." He broke off then, his voice choked with tears, and Gabrielle put her arms around his shoulders to ease his pain.

"You must not make yourself ill with regret, Sam. The past can't be changed. We will simply have to do the best we can to see that Amanda survives and then it will be up to you to make the best of your opportunities." That word nearly stuck in her throat because she was suddenly overwhelmed by thoughts of Jason. Were she to fall ill and die he would never know that she had loved him, but perhaps that would be best. Then her loss would not hurt him so deeply and he'd have none of the regrets which plagued Sam now.

When he'd eaten what little he could of his own supper, Jason gathered up the blankets he'd collected and walked out to the Duffys wagon. Gabrielle saw him coming and called out, advising him to stay away, but he walked right up to her anyway to hand over the blankets he'd promised to bring.

"How is she?" He glanced toward the wagon.

"No better, I'm afraid. Sam's still with her, but I'll try to encourage Johanna to sleep out here with us tonight."

Jason had never felt so helpless. Unlike Indian braves, this enemy was invisible and had no respect for the courage of its victims. He'd had the worst afternoon of his life trying to reason with people who wanted to flee, not realizing they could be the next to fall ill. No wagon master worth his pay would agree to dropping off wagons so capriciously. He'd told them repeatedly that cholera could be defeated, but not by abandoning those who were ill and letting them fend for themselves. He'd said he'd use his rifle if he had to, but no one was going to leave the wagon train while he had any means to prevent his departure. "I'll come back in the morning, and again at noon. If Amanda has survived this long, she just may make it."

"Oh, I hope so." Gabrielle seized the note of hope in his voice as reason enough to be encouraged. "Sam seems to be overburdened as it is. I don't think he could face raising his children alone."

Jason was not tempted to comment on the man's abilities as a father or otherwise. "Just try to get a good night's rest and I'll talk with you in the morning. I won't leave you all behind; they can't make me do that."

His glance was so serious Gabrielle asked softly, "But that has been suggested?"

"Are you surprised that it has?"

"No, I suppose not. But I know you'll do what's right." Gabrielle had every confidence in him for he'd shown himself to be the best of leaders in all manner of trying situations.

"Now you have decided to believe in me? At the worst of times?" Jason could not understand her sudden expression of trust after the many bitter rejections he'd received. Dismayed, he started back toward the circle of wagons, wondering who'd be waiting to see him when he returned to his tent.

Gabrielle watched him go with no more than a faint smile, for she'd always believed in him, in the kind of man she longed for him to be. "Good night, Jason, and God bless you," she whispered.

Then she turned back to the three children who were watching her with rapt attention. "Let's find a good spot for these blankets, we're going to sleep upon the ground tonight instead of inside the wagon so your mother will be able to rest more comfortably."

She got them ready for bed and then told them a story until all were yawning and she knew she could bring the tale to an end. She'd had little experience with small children but things seemed to be going along all right. The fires of the other wagons appeared to be very distant, and once the sun had set she felt very much alone. The journey was turning out to be very different from the one she had anticipated, but she'd have no complaints as long as they all survived.

Johanna climbed out of the wagon and walked about to exercise her cramped muscles. She spoke quietly to Gabrielle. "If Mr. Royal recommends fluids and warmth then we've been doing all that could be done all day. I had hoped to be useful here, but I had not expected something so severe."

"Would you not have come had you known?" Gabrielle asked in a hushed whisper.

"Oh, I would have come. It is just that I would have liked to have known what the situation really was. I know some of the others, Iris in particular, think me a bit peculiar, but I hope you do not think I am the sort who does no more than read her Bible when the chance to be of some real service presents itself."

"Frankly, I am enjoying the chance to avoid Iris' company for a few days, and I never once thought that you were not sincere in your beliefs. We'll have more time to talk tomorrow. I think you should try to sleep for a while, don't you?" Gabrielle was tired and she knew Johanna had to be as well.

"Yes, I should. I'll do no good if I am falling asleep when my patient needs me. She seems to be resting more comfortably and since Sam is sitting with her I think I will lie down."

"Good night then." Gabrielle lay down upon the blanket she'd placed near the children and despite the hardness of the ground she was sound asleep within minutes. But long before dawn she was awakened by Sam calling her name.

"Miss MacLaren," he whispered, his voice choked with tears. "It's got me too, miss, I feel like my insides are on fire. What are we gonna do?"

Rising quickly, Gabrielle took the man's arm and led him over to a spot close to the remains of their fire. She spread out her blanket and patted it lightly. "Lie down right here. You'll be warm and I'll brew some more tea for you to drink. I'm sorry you've fallen ill, and I know you're going to feel dreadful but we'll see you pull through." She had no idea why she was so optimistic, but her words seemed to help the man. She busied herself with building up the fire and heating the kettle. Then she climbed into the wagon. Satisfied that Amanda was still breathing, she returned to Sam and tried to convince him to drink all he could.

"I don't want anything to drink, my stomach hurts I tell you, it hurts something awful," he complained through a fresh torrent of tears.

"I know it must hurt, but if I must hold your head back and pour this tea down your throat I'll do it!" Gabrielle meant the threat too, for it was obvious to her that people couldn't survive an illness so severe if they refused all liquids.

No sooner had she gotten Sam to cooperate than Mary Beth began to cry and Gabrielle hurried to the little girl's side. She seemed to be burning with fever one moment and then shaking with a chill the next. Soon Johanna was awake and they hurriedly devised a plan for treating their rapidly growing number of patients. With little discussion they agreed the children would be Gabrielle's responsibility while Johanna would continue to care for Amanda and now Sam as well. In less than an hour Suzanna awoke and began complaining of a stomach ache, but Timothy slept through his sisters high-pitched cries and when he awoke at dawn he still felt well.

"I am so happy to have your help, Timothy." Gabrielle looked at his two sisters who were wrapped snugly in their blankets, for the time being resting between bouts of nausea. "I know this will be a difficult time for you, but I want you to find what firewood you can as your sisters and parents will need plenty to drink and I want to boil all their water first."

"Sure I know how to look for wood. I'll find something," he promised. But other than the sagebrush there was little in sight.

"Good. Now how about some breakfast?" Gabrielle had fried some bacon and she insisted he eat some before he went out on his errand. "If you feel dizzy or the least bit ill, you come right back, Timothy. Don't sit down and think you can wait a minute until you feel better. You come right back immediately, do you understand?"

"Yes, ma'am." He started off then, eager to be of some use when their situation seemed such a desperate one.

When Jason arrived that morning, he listened quietly to Gabrielle's report and then told her the disease had broken out among three more families. "I'm moving their wagons out here but I want you to stay with the Duffys. Don't think you can nurse everyone who has fallen ill or you'll become exhausted and none of your patients will survive."

"What wonderful encouragement!" she responded quickly. Then she apologized because she knew she was already overtired. "I'm sorry, none of this is your fault but the girls are dreadfully ill and there is so little I can do."

"Do you recall telling me our fate is in God's hands?" Jason offered philosophically.

Gabrielle remembered that conversation all too well. "Yes, I said that and I believe it too, but that doesn't mean I'll just sit here and watch those sweet little girls die!"

"That's not what I meant, Gabrielle," Jason replied impatiently. "We can all do only so much. You mustn't think you have failed if their fate is not the one you would have chosen. We can expect no more than half to survive and that's if we're lucky, damn lucky."

"Well, fortunately, I seem to thrive on adversity, Mr. Royal, and I intend to see all the Duffys live to see Oregon City no matter what you think their chances might be." She could not help but think he wanted her to choose between them somehow. With four of the Duffys ill and only she and Johanna to tend them, it was obvious they could not provide optimum care for everyone. Who deserved to live, the babies who had all their lives ahead of them or their parents who had just recently rediscovered the love they'd once had for each other? It was not a choice she could, or would make.

Jason had to agree with Gabrielle's assessment of herself. She was an orphan who had lost her childhood sweetheart in a tragic accident, still she had more courage than any woman he'd ever known. He was tired too, but he tried to smile. "Just do the best you can. Keep everyone clean and warm, and force them to drink all they'll hold. I'll bring over another barrel of water when I come back at noon."

He reached up to touch the brim of his hat as he often did, his jaunty salute strangely comforting, and Gabrielle called his name, drawing him back for one moment more. "Jason, I . . . well, that is . . ." The sun was already high in the sky, the day was going to be another hot one, and she could not bring herself to say she loved him at such an inappropriate time. Although she wanted him to know before it was too late, she

232

could not force herself to speak the words.

"Yes? Is there something else?" he asked curiously.

"Could we borrow that small tent of yours? I was thinking of using it as an awning to provide additional shade." The idea had come to her suddenly when she realized she'd have to say something or appear a complete fool.

"I'll bring it. You and Johanna will need a change of clothing too. Anything else I might have forgotten?"

"I'll let you know if I think of something more."

Gabrielle watched him walk away, her sorrow as deep as if they'd parted forever. The words *I love you*, had come so easily to her lips with Beau, why were they impossible to speak to Jason? She knew the answer without a second's pause: Beau had said them first to her. He had made her feel loved in so many ways that Jason did not even seem to suspect existed. Thinking herself foolish for daydreaming at such an inopportune time, she returned to the little girls, soothing their fevered cries as best she could with a thoughtful word and a warm hug.

The disease continued to spread until at least one person was ill in fifteen of the fifty wagons. Inspired by Gabrielle's and Johanna's example, Erica went to help the stricken families and she was soon followed by Barbara, Margaret, and Marlene. Not impressed by their unselfish example, however, Iris did not even consider offering to help those who had fallen ill. Instead, she used her time to get to know Jason Royal better, but he was so distracted by the emergency she often found herself sitting alone with Clayton Horne. Fortunately for her, he proved to be a most charming companion and she did not complain when Jason was unable to join them.

Gabrielle had no such amusement since all her days were exhausting. But each morning when she and Johanna awoke to find their patients still breathing, no matter how weakly, they considered their efforts a success. Timothy had remained healthy, and his parents and sisters, although pale and weak, had survived the worst ravages of the disease. However, more than two weeks passed before they could sit up and tolerate eating something more solid than clear soup and weak tea. While they had no idea how many had fallen ill or how many had died, Sam and Amanda Duffy were convinced they owed their own lives and those of their children to Gabrielle and Johanna, and they missed no opportunity to say so.

When there had been no new cases of cholera in five days, Jason began making plans to move on to Fort Hall. They had fallen way behind schedule, but he considered that concern a trivial one when so many of the emigrants had lost members of their families. When Gabrielle asked him for a final count, there were tears in his eyes as he replied.

"Sixty-one were stricken and of those twenty-four died. We didn't lose half after all, but I think that was more due to the efforts of you and your friends than to luck. Sam Duffy was devoted to you before, but I imagine he will be impossibly loyal now."

"Speaking of shadows, I feel no stronger than one. I have not even thought about Sunny, and I doubt I'll have the energy to ride for several days. Is he all right?"

"He complained bitterly each time I brushed him, so I'd say he's missed you quite a bit." Jason scuffed the top of his moccasin in the dust. "Don't try to ride him until you're sure you can handle him easily. I'd hate to see you escape catching cholera only to die of a broken neck."

"What a touching sentiment, Jason." Gabrielle brushed her hair back from her eyes, sorry he would not admit he'd missed her himself. Of course he had come to check on her patients each day, but he'd gone to each wagon where someone was ill so she knew she'd gotten no more attention than anyone else. Too often she'd seen him with a shovel in his hand and had known he'd been out to bury someone less fortunate than the Duffys. Chilled by that thought, she shivered slightly and he looked up in alarm.

"Are you all right?"

"Yes. This has been difficult for all of us, but I think you've had the worst of it. Will you tell me the truth, does anyone blame the Duffys for this tragedy?"

"Because Amanda fell ill first? No. That was mere chance. I don't think anyone would accuse her of bringing the sickness to us, and should anyone be so damn stupid I'd put a fast stop to it. It's pointless to blame someone for another's death; it won't bring any of them back."

"I know that." Gabrielle looked out over the plain, her thoughts on another time and place, on a young man so full of life she'd thought he'd never grow old. Well, he hadn't gotten the chance to age, no matter how gracefully he might have done it. "A lot of people have died on this trail haven't they, Jason, of one thing or another?"

Jason was already so depressed he could scarcely stand it. He didn't need Gabrielle to start reminiscing about Beau. "Yes. Too damn many have died and I've buried more than my share of them in the last two weeks." He was ashamed of himself then, for that had sounded as though he were complaining about the work involved rather than the tragedy. "I'm sorry, I shouldn't have said that."

Gabrielle laid her fingertips gently upon his arm. "I know what you meant, Jason. I've stayed mostly with the girls from my wagon and the other brides, but you know each person in every single wagon by name, don't you? Don't tell me it's your responsibility to know them either, because you do so much more than what your job requires. I'm sure we'd all say too many have died, but many more have survived and I think that's due in large measure to your guidance. You certainly convinced me we could save the Duffys with no more than boiled water and blankets, and I'm sure you did the same for everyone else."

Jason just shook his head, dismayed that she would wish to compliment him when his contribution had been so slight compared to hers. She had worked tirelessly when her only reward might well have been death. "I had no idea you thought me worthy of any praise. Are you sure the fever hasn't touched you?" He reached out to caress her cheek as if he meant to do no more than check her temperature.

"Since you do not appreciate my compliments, I will cease to pay them." Gabrielle turned away, thinking herself a fool for having tried once again to reach him. "Good night."

"Good night," he answered softly, but a sly smile lit his handsome features. Maybe it wasn't as impossible to impress Gabrielle as he'd thought. Walking on to the next wagon, he began whistling to himself, his mood suddenly a surprisingly optimistic one.

Chapter XII

It was not until they arrived at Fort Hall and Clayton mentioned how pretty Iris Stewart was and how beautifully she had survived the rigors of their travel that Jason took a good long look at her and the other brides. Of the twenty-one young women, six in Gabrielle's wagon had nursed the victims of the cholera outbreak and five from the other two wagons had also volunteered. It was easy to pick those eleven out from the others for they still showed obvious signs of their exhausting labor. While their companions were slender, they were now painfully thin. They still had dark circles beneath their eyes, and they moved so slowly when they walked about the camp to pay calls on their former patients he was afraid their weariness might be causing them real pain. He'd written down their names, meaning to commend them somehow, but Clayton's remark was so insensitive he was outraged.

"It is no wonder Iris is attractive, she's done nothing more strenuous than lift her fork to her mouth since this trip began. I know how some of the girls look; they look as though they've sacrificed a great deal of themselves in an attempt to save the lives of near strangers. I think they're the best of the lot and I'll damn well tell our friends that too!"

Shocked by the ferocity of Jason's anger, Clayton needed a moment in which to find his voice to respond. "I did not realize you would take my compliment for Iris so adversely."

Jason was nowhere near finished with the tirade he'd begun and he continued in the same harsh tone. "I warned you how difficult this trip would be for the girls when you first approached me with the plan to bring mail-order brides over the Oregon Trail. I should never, never have consented to so dangerous a scheme! We're going to remain camped here at Fort Hall until every one of these young women is the beauty she was when we left Independence. I'll put some weight back on them if I have to make them drink cream, but by God, I'll not have anyone tell me Iris looks good when she's no more than the image of pampered self-indulgence and those who look like walking death are some of the most courageous young women I've ever known!"

Clayton still had no idea why his remark had angered Jason so greatly. "You're taking yourself rather seriously, aren't you? A few days' rest will help your mood too. That Iris didn't choose to risk her life needlessly was merely prudent, not selfish. I mean no disrespect to those young women who did put in so many long days to nurse the sick. Of course their efforts are commendable."

Disgusted that Clayton would still ignore the truth, Jason turned away, but he decided right then to make sure that the young women he thought were the most beautiful became the prettiest as well. Rummaging through his belongings, he found his sketch pad and, taking pen and ink, went to find a few girls who wouldn't mind being his models for an hour or so.

Gabrielle was the only one who had known Jason had made the sketches of the bachelors until he asked Erica to pose for him that day. Soon he was surrounded by curious young women who were all amazed to find the wagon master so accomplished an artist. With a careful glance and a few deft strokes he created such a stunning portrait of Erica the others were all eager to have him draw them as well.

"I plan to do a sketch of each one of you, ladies," Jason explained with a smile. "I know the first few days we're in

Oregon City you'll need time to rest and to see to your wardrobes, so my drawings will have to keep the bachelors satisfied until you're ready to see them yourselves. I am certain the men are as curious about you as you are about them, but it won't hurt to keep them waiting if they have at least some idea of how lovely you all are."

Gabrielle watched from the sidelines. She had seldom seen Jason in so charming a mood, and her companions positively glowed with the warmth of his many compliments as he drew their portraits. While at first she thought he was selecting his subjects at random she soon noticed there was a pattern to his choices. He was taking those among them who had served as nurses and she knew how dearly that selfless service had cost them. None of them had come down with the disease, but they all looked as though they had been ill. They were pale and thin and their hair was as brittle as straw while those who had done no more than sit in the shade of their wagons and chat while the cholera epidemic swept the camp were the picture of health. Yet Gabrielle had heard not a single complaint from the women who had done the most, not one word spoken in regret. She was proud to think that none of them thought their looks too high a price to have paid for the lives they'd saved. That Jason clearly thought so too was so dear of him. She loved him all the more for it. He was such a complex individual, passionate, but caring deeply about others. She knew better than to mention how much she admired his purpose, however, and pretended to be surprised when he asked her to come and sit down with him so he could make a sketch of her.

Jason tried to suppress his smile; he knew his expression would give away the depth of his regard for Gabrielle should anyone look closely. He still thought her the prettiest of them all, but her beauty was difficult to separate from her vivid coloring and he swiftly grew discouraged. "I am sorry, Miss MacLaren, but I simply can't do you justice with pen and ink and I have no paints with me."

"Do you enjoy painting too, Mr. Royal?" Gabrielle asked

239

curiously, wondering why he continued to deny his talent was an extraordinary gift.

"I have had little opportunity to do any painting, but I like it well enough." Jason stopped to look up at her again, he had the planes of her face correctly positioned, the delicate curves accurately drawn but without being able to provide the glorious red for her hair or the bright clear blue for her eyes he felt totally frustrated. When two men from their group approached him, he was glad for the excuse to take a break and lay his pen aside. "Is there something you need, gentlemen?"

Jesse Martin cleared his throat nervously before he spoke. He had not expected to find Jason surrounded by pretty young women, but it did not occur to him to ask to speak with the wagon master in private. "Me and Elmer was up at the fort just now, and we heard some men talking about taking the trail to California."

When he paused Jason guessed the question Jesse was about to ask and he rose to his feet to respond. "Yes. There's a trail which leads south. It cuts above the Great Salt Lake, then heads west. I wouldn't recommend that you take it now though. You'll reach the Sierra Nevada range too late in the fall and you might end up like the Donner party did last year. I know you don't want to risk that."

Elmer Radford frowned, clearly confused by that reference. "I heard the name, but I don't recall what happened to them. Was it bad?"

Jason glanced over at the young women who were listening with such rapt interest. He'd thought they would have heard of the tragedy, but apparently several had not for they looked only curious rather than ill.

"It was as bad as possible," he replied softly. "In late October the Donner party was trapped by snow storms so fierce that passage through the mountains was impossible. The men were too weak to raise cabins so their families had to survive as best they could with no more than tents half-buried in snowdrifts for shelter. Their livestock froze to death, and finally they had no choice but to consume human flesh rather than starve. Help didn't reach them until March, and by then only forty-five of the eighty-seven who'd been in the Donner party were still alive, and barely alive at that. I imagine all of them will have nightmares for the rest of their days. Now if you want to try to reach California, by all means go. But don't say you weren't warned of what to expect if you do."

"Well now, I heard Oregon was right pretty," Jasse mumbled to his friend.

Elmer nodded his head up and down rapidly. "Since we started out for Oregon I'd say that's where we should go."

"I'll be happy to answer your questions should you have any others," Jason offered politely, certain his gruesome tale had ended their plans of leaving the wagon train.

"No, sir. Thank you, but we got no other questions, none at all." The two men nearly broke into a run as they left, their fright plain in their terrified gaze.

Jason smiled as he turned back to the brides. "I'm sorry you had to hear that. It's a sad story and if you'd not heard it before, it's a most shocking one. But you needn't worry for I'll not allow anything so desperate to happen to you. Now if you'll excuse me, I'm out of the mood to draw and I'll have to do the rest of your portraits tomorrow."

Easily understanding his request, the girls drifted away in twos and threes whispering amongst themselves of the horrors of the Donner party's fate. They had endured considerable hardships themselves, but nothing to compare with the unspeakable suffering that group had faced.

Gabrielle waited a moment as Jason gathered up his things and then came forward. "May I see the sketch you made of me?"

Embarrassed, Jason handed it to her. "It's not nearly good enough, Gabrielle, not half good enough. You are so much prettier than that poor drawing makes you appear."

"Why thank you." Gabrielle was pleased by his compliment but she thought the sketch quite good. "I look exactly like this,

Jason, or at least I did. That's what you're doing isn't it? Trying to make all of us look as pretty as you possibly can, as pretty as we used to be?"

"Are my motives as transparent as that?" he inquired softly. "With a few days rest and some good food, you'll all be the beauties you were. I hope none of you are worried about your appearance because I'm certainly not."

"Tell me the truth, Jason, I look frightful. I know I do." Yet Gabrielle was laughing, as if the matter were of slight concern.

"I'll not tell you what I think if you don't already know. Now give me that sketch. I promise to do a better one next time."

"Next time? You needn't make another one, Jason. This one is fine." Gabrielle saw no reason for him to draw her portrait a second time.

Jason realized if he made only one sketch he'd have none to save for himself, but that was too sad a point to ponder so he placed the drawing of her with the others. "I am the artist here, and if I'm not satisfied with my first sketch I always make another, I might make fifty before I get it right but I'll expect you to humor me and pose as often as I need you to model."

"Whatever you like, Jason. I only wanted to make things easy for you," Gabrielle stated sincerely.

"Easy?" Jason's temper exploded at that comment. To him it was totally erroneous. "You have never made one damn thing easy for me, lady, and I doubt you ever will!" He walked back to his tent then, half the sketches completed but his mood no better than when he'd started them.

The next afternoon Jason again drew the brides' portraits, teasing them so they'd smile prettily as they posed. Gabrielle was too intrigued by his talent to stay away so she sat behind him to watch him work. She was as fascinated as before by the ease with which he captured the young women's expressions. When he turned to ask her to sit for him again, she was flattered, but tried to refuse.

242

"Have you finished all the others?"

"Every last one," Jason boasted proudly. "But I still want to do yours again."

Gabrielle knew if she argued she'd draw more attention to herself than if she complied with his request so she moved to where his models had been sitting without further comment. She attempted to get comfortably seated, but he wasn't satisfied and came forward to tilt her chin slightly with his fingertips.

"There. Now stop wiggling. This is difficult enough to accomplish without trying to focus upon a moving target. Now just relax, fill your mind with pleasant thoughts and hold still for a few minutes."

Gabrielle took a deep breath and, suitably composed, tried to let her mind go blank. But she was too restless, her thoughts of him far too compelling to ignore. He was so different from her. Sit still and be quiet so he can draw, she told herself. Why does he never say come and sit beside me and tell me what is on your mind? What is he afraid I will say? she wondered.

The darkness of Gabrielle's mood was readily apparent to an artist's keen eye. The line of her brow, the set of her chin were all wrong; but Jason found himself drawing her the way she looked when she smiled with delight. She had very expressive features, and as he completed his sketch he considered giving her the smoldering glance passion infused into her gaze. But he decided to attempt that when he had a few minutes alone to draw her portrait from memory. He could draw a full-length nude he realized with a chuckle. It would be superb but he'd never dare show her such a sketch for she'd insist he destroy it. Nevertheless, he promised himself to draw it at his first opportunity and keep it for his own enjoyment. Pleased with himself for having such an intriguing idea Jason offered Gabrielle a suggestion. "Try concentrating upon no more than the blue of the sky for I want you to look your best. Think how eagerly the men have been awaiting your arrival. These

243

drawings are supposed to whet their appetites not cool their ardor."

Gabrielle sighed impatiently. "Must you have two drawings of me? There's none of Joshua."

"That's beside the point." Jason didn't want to argue. He knew Gabrielle could be a most difficult woman when she decided to oppose him, but the sketch he'd made was quite striking despite the downcast expression she wore. "You make an interesting subject. I'd like to do a profile, but if you're not willing to pose graciously, we'd both be wasting our time."

Gabrielle glanced over at the girls who were still sitting nearby. They were watching him work and listening attentively. However, she knew the real message in Jason's words was not the obvious one. It was ridiculous to sit there seeming to be exchanging polite conversation when the emotions which flowed between them were such volatile ones.

"You've never wasted a second of my time, Mr. Royal. I'm sorry to hear you think I would waste yours." She stood up then, intent upon leaving his presence as swiftly as possible but a sudden wave of dizziness obscured her vision and plunged her into darkness.

"Gabrielle!"

Jason flew across the distance which separated them, catching her limp body in his arms just before she collapsed on the ground. She had fainted so suddenly he was terrified she might never again awaken, and he carried her to his tent rather than to her wagon. He placed her gently upon his blankets and rubbed her wrists as he called her name in a frantic plea. She was too pale, her fair skin as white as ivory, and he turned away for a moment, searching for the bottle of brandy Clayton kept for just such emergencies. Healthy young women did not faint for no reason, but Gabrielle clearly had not regained her strength since she'd left the Duffy family who were again able to care for themselves. When at last her long lashes fluttered slightly, he lifted her head and gave her a sip of the fiery brandy. He set the cup aside when she struggled to sit up by herself. "Just a minute, Gabrielle. You must be more careful. I don't want to see you faint again. It was too great a scare."

Gabrielle frowned slightly as she lifted her fingertips to her aching forehead. She was so surprised to find herself in his tent that for a moment she could not recall how she'd come to be there.

"I must have stood up too rapidly, that's all. I'll be fine now."

"Excuse me just a moment."

Jason went out to tell the young women who'd followed them that Gabrielle was fine but he wanted her to rest awhile before she returned to her wagon. Their curiosity satisfied, the girls began to disperse. Erica had gathered up his art materials and she now handed them to him before she hurried away with the others. Glad they would be alone, Jason returned to Gabrielle and knelt by her side.

"I want you to rest for an hour or two before you try to stand up. Just go to sleep and I'll call you when supper is ready."

"I'm not a baby, Jason. I don't require a nap each afternoon," Gabrielle protested immediately, not wanting his sympathy since she didn't feel she deserved it.

"Believe me I know full well that you are not a baby, but I want you to rest all the same." The color was slowly returning to her cheeks. She looked so pretty that he leaned over to kiss her lips lightly, but when his mouth touched hers he could not bear to draw away. He slipped his hand gently behind her head to hold her fast, his mouth slowly plundering hers until he had at last drunk deeply of the delicious sweetness he had longed to savor.

Breathless, Gabrielle had to ask, "Have you become so reckless of late you will now seduce women in your own tent rather than insisting upon discretion?"

Reacting instantly to her sarcasm, Jason's expression grew stern. "Since that is not a question you should even have to

245

ask, I will offer no answer. Now just go to sleep and I will awaken you later as I promised." But he didn't. She was sleeping so deeply he decided to let her rest until her body's need for food caused her to awaken naturally.

Clayton was as shaken as Jason when he heard what had happened. "Of course you were correct in bringing her here to rest. Her wagon is too busy a place to allow her the proper quiet. It is damned awkward though. She'll have to go back there before dark, I'm sure you must know that."

Jason gave his friend a long, slow glance while he wondered if Clayton truly thought men and women only found each other irresistible at night. Or perhaps actions which were considered respectable in the light of day apparently took on an alarming sense of impropriety under the moon. But he didn't bother to argue with Clayton since the man's misconceptions worked to his advantage.

"I intend to let her sleep right where she is, Clay. The nights are warm and we'll be comfortable under the stars. I'll not awaken Gabrielle when it could be detrimental to her health. I've made no secret of the fact she's here, nor will I try to hide her presence if she stays. If there's any gossip, then I'll take the blame for it, not that lovely woman who's obviously exhausted."

Clayton took a deep breath, ready to argue the matter further until he saw the look in Jason's deep gray eyes. It was too confident for him to risk a challenge. "The young women are my responsibility, Jason. If she sleeps in our tent tonight, I will stay awake to see that her dreams are not disturbed. I will then be able to squelch all gossip before it begins."

"From whom do you think you will be protecting her, just from me?" Jason chuckled at that thought. "I've already said I won't wake her. Do you imagine I enjoy making love to unconscious women or that I have so smooth an approach she'd not awaken were I to join her in our tent? Just what sort of man do you believe me to be, Clay?"

"A damned clever one, that's what!" Clayton knew when he was beaten. He didn't persist in his arguments, but he'd meant what he'd said about staying awake. Leaving Gabrielle in Jason's care was like asking a fox to guard the hen house.

While Jason's smile was a rakish one, he was far more worried about Gabrielle than he'd let anyone see. Pregnant women were prone to fainting spells; he knew that for a fact but he'd not make the mistake of asking if that were Gabrielle's problem. He knew she'd just deny it whether or not it were true. That she'd not give him so much as the satisfaction of raising his own child suddenly angered him so greatly he gave Clayton the first excuse which came to his mind.

"I want to check with everyone, see how the repairs are coming. I know you can guard Gabrielle adequately until I return."

"You can depend upon it!" Clayton called out, wanting for once to have the last word with Jason.

By the time Jason returned to his tent later that evening, he had his temper well in control. He knew it was ridiculous to be angry with Gabrielle for not telling him about a child that might not even exist, but he was deeply concerned about her frail health no matter what the cause. He would have to caution her not to overtax herself again; she was always busy doing something for her friends. He thought back over a few such instances and he realized there were many. She'd taught several to ride, given impromptu dancing lessons, even come to his defense when Iris had made some insulting innuendos. He had to laugh as he recalled that scene. Gabrielle could always be counted upon to be in the thick of things. She'd pulled Sam Duffy out of the pond without a moment's hesitation, and he knew had the Duffys not already asked for her help when Amanda fell ill, she would have been the first to volunteer to go. She seems to have time and love aplenty—for everyone but me, he thought sadly. Seeing Clayton coming out of their tent, he pushed his own jealous thoughts aside and hurried his pace.

247

"Is Gabrielle awake yet?"

"Oh, yes. Wide awake and gone back to her wagon. She seemed fit enough to me. I think a nap was all she needed. There was no cause for you to be so worried about her health," the blond man replied confidently.

"You walked her back to her wagon yourself to make certain she arrived there safely?" Jason asked accusingly, not about to accept Clayton's assessment of Gabrielle's health.

Clayton shrugged. "No. I offered to escort her but she said it wasn't necessary."

"Then you don't know if she ever got to her wagon or not, do you?"

Without wasting the time to tell Clayton what he thought of him for being so careless, Jason dashed through the gathering darkness toward Gabrielle's wagon, half expecting to find her lying in a crumpled heap along the way. He slid to a self-conscious halt when he found her seated alone with Paul, talking quietly while she ate the supper he'd saved for her. She looked up as he entered the circle of light thrown by their fire, her smile a sad, sweet one.

"Are you truly all right?" he finally had the presence of mind to inquire.

"Why yes. Didn't Mr. Horne tell you I was?" Gabrielle was surprised by his question.

Jason nodded, feeling like a fool for having been so frightened when there had been no reason. "Yes, but I wanted to speak with you myself just to make certain."

"As you can see, I am feeling well enough to enjoy Paul's delicious stew."

"Have you had your supper, sir? I made plenty." Paul gestured toward the savory dish which still simmered in the iron kettle suspended over the fire.

Jason was hungry. From the looks of it Clayton hadn't bothered to cook anything and he had no talent for preparing food himself.

"Are you positive there is enough?"

"Oh, yes. The others have all eaten. My girls never eat all that I prepare and it's a shame to see this fine stew go to waste." Without waiting for Jason to agree Paul ladled up another portion, filling a tin plate until it nearly overflowed. Placing a large piece of cornbread and a clean fork on the plate, he moved out of the way to make room for the wagon master to sit down beside Gabrielle.

"Thank you. I've been too busy to eat this evening so I know I'll enjoy this." Taking the warm plate, Jason sat down and after one bite he remarked sincerely. "This is delicious, Paul, but where did you get the meat?"

"Beef can be had at the fort. For a price, of course, but I think my girls deserve a treat now and then." Paul beamed from ear to ear he was so pleased by Jason's praise.

"We all do," Jason agreed amicably, sorry that he'd left the matter of provisions up to Clayton if his partner hadn't supplied fresh meat for the brides. Gabrielle had been eating alone, but he could hear the other young women practicing a song he'd heard often, and curious, he asked about it between mouthfuls. "That song gets better each time I hear you sing it."

Laying her half-eaten supper aside, Gabrielle listened for a brief moment and then agreed. "At least now everyone seems to have memorized the lyrics. We want to learn a few songs to perform for the bachelors. I hope they won't think us foolish for wanting to entertain them as best we can."

"They will be enchanted, I can guarantee it." Jason found it easier to concentrate upon his meal rather than to listen to the words of the song. It was a ballad, a very tender love story, but he'd paid little attention to it until that night. Now the thought of Gabrielle singing the romantic tune to another man filled him with so deep a dread he hoped his expression did not reveal the anguish of his jealousy. Knowing he should say something, he asked the most obvious question. "Do you like to sing?"

249

"Yes, I truly do but my voice is not as good as most of the others. It is too low and so many songs require a clear soprano to sound as they should." That was another of her aunt's many criticisms she remembered. "I think I was the only young woman in Liberty who wasn't asked to sing in the church choir."

That remark brought a smile to Jason's lips. "Your speaking voice is unusual, but I happen to think it is very soothing to the ear. Besides, wouldn't you be disappointed if when you sang your voice could not be distinguished from all the others?"

"You're just trying to make me feel good, Jason, but I know I sound a bit like a very young bull frog no matter how much I enjoy singing. I understand your question though, for I've never heard anyone play the harmonica the way you do. Your tunes are so melancholy, while most people use the instrument to play light-hearted melodies."

Finished with his supper, Jason looked around for Paul to pay him a last compliment, but the man had apparently stepped away and he was quite alone with Gabrielle. "I only play when I'm by myself and then my mood is never a light-hearted one."

"I thought you enjoyed being alone," Gabrielle remarked casually, but she held her breath as she waited for his reply.

"No. What I said was I like being alone with you." It was a ridiculous game they were playing. He felt like a schoolboy hoping to get his first kiss when what he wanted from Gabrielle was as always the most passionate of encounters.

His expression was so wistful that Gabrielle could not help but respond truthfully. "I enjoy your company very much too, Jason."

"Well, then why—"

Gabrielle raised her fingertips to his lips. "Don't say it, please don't. It is far too difficult for me to live the pretense you insist we must. Clayton saw us kiss, Sam saw much more. The risks we've taken to be together have been worth it to me, but I cannot pretend that we are no more than acquaintances while the truth is too shocking to reveal."

Jason got to his feet and then extended his hand to help Gabrielle rise. "Why don't you join your friends where you can sing love songs until your heart is content with no risk at all? I need a woman, not some romantic child whose head is so full of dreams there's no room for a single thought of me. Tell Paul I enjoyed his supper, will you? I don't want him to avoid my company too."

"Jason!" Gabrielle whispered his name in a menacing hiss. "I think you're the one who's never grown up, not me!"

Rather than speak the vile word which sprang to his lips, Jason turned away and walked off. He would have been better off if he'd found her still asleep in his tent, or sprawled in a faint in the dirt. Awake, she was impossible to control, but he knew he was nowhere near ready to give up the fight to try.

The whitewashed walls of Fort Hall glowed in the moonlight, while the rushing waters of the Snake River provided a soothing lullaby, but Gabrielle was inspired neither to join the singers nor to get ready for bed. She wished she had one good friend, someone she could trust who would give her the advice she needed now. Unfortunately, Erica knew far less of life than she did, and none of the other girls were closer friends than she. Johanna would simply quote the verses from her Bible which condemned the kind of relationship she and Jason had. Barbara would be so astonished she'd never be able to keep such a secret to herself. Marlene was no expert on men and neither was Margaret. That left Iris, but Gabrielle knew she'd never confide in that shrew. Beau had been the best friend she'd ever had, but quite naturally, he'd given her no advice for dealing with other men. Her situation seemed so hopeless she was near tears when Paul returned and found her sitting alone by the remains of the fire.

"Mr. Royal wanted me to tell you how much he enjoyed the supper." She spoke softly without looking up from the glowing coals.

"I knew he would." While Paul busied himself cleaning up the campsite he observed Gabrielle's solemn mood. "He is a most interesting man, that Jason Royal is. I thought you two might like a little time to talk. I hope neither you nor he thought it was rude of me to leave."

"No, of course not. We don't need a chaperone." Perhaps that was just what they should have had though, she thought.

"Now wait just a minute here, if I thought a chaperone was required I sure wouldn't have left you two alone together. I figure if you're old enough to get married you are a responsible woman, and I sure think Royal is old enough to look out for himself."

Gabrielle watched the friendly man work. He was a mature gentleman, but what would he say if she asked his advice? If she revealed that she'd fallen in love with a man who took every advantage of that fact without offering any hope of marriage, unless he could not avoid it, she thought Paul would probably be outraged.

"Just what exactly is a fallen woman, Paul? Can you tell me?"

Paul straightened up to look at her squarely, thinking she must be teasing him. But her expression was quite serious. "Well that's not something I'd ever call a lady. I suppose it refers to a woman who's suffered some terrible disgrace."

"Like being a man's mistress perhaps, or having his baby when they aren't married?"

"Gabrielle, if one of the girls is carrying a child, it would be obvious by now. Why none of them is so foolish she could possibly think she'd be able to take a five-month trip to Oregon and then convince her new husband the babe she had four months later was his. So whatever are you talking about?"

Gabrielle knew she wasn't pregnant, but were she to conceive Jason's child she'd never consider marrying another man and trying to fool him into thinking her baby was his. That really would be immoral as well as dishonest. "I wasn't speaking about anyone in particular, Paul. I just wondered what sort of transgressions qualified a woman to be classified as 'fallen.' I was merely curious."

"That's a mighty odd topic to inspire your curiosity, miss. I don't think it's proper for a nice young woman like you to be worrying about such matters."

Gabrielle shrugged nonchalantly. "I think about all sorts of things, Paul. Doesn't it strike you as strange that there is no similar term to describe a man who keeps a mistress or fathers children out of wedlock? Why is there no such thing as a 'fallen man'?"

"Well now, that don't strike me as strange at all since there is such a great difference in the way men and women live. Men like to roam all over the world, search for adventure; but ladies just naturally stay put so once gossip starts it's difficult for them to shake it. That's why they have to be so much more careful. Makes perfect sense to me."

Realizing Paul was not going to come up with anything she'd find useful, Gabrielle excused herself and went to listen to the singers. She covered a yawn, too tired to want to sing herself, and when they all got ready for bed she was the first one to fall asleep.

Making good on a promise to himself, Jason saw that the brides had double the provisions Clayton seemed to think necessary, and when he knew their stay at Fort Hall could no longer be prolonged, he again gave the order to move on. The fort was six hundred and fifty miles from the Columbia River, a journey of perhaps two months' duration which he knew would tax every ounce of the emigrants' remaining strength. Not being a man to dwell upon possible misfortune, however, he thought only that the trail was nearing its end, and was eager to defeat its coming dangers.

The trail followed the Snake River now, first crossing a

253

swampland infested with dense swarms of mosquitoes which tormented the travelers with numerous stinging bites. The landscape then turned barren, the soil parched, the three-foot high sagebrush so tenacious it could upset a wagon if the driver were not wise enough to avoid it. The rocky soil provided so poor a surface axletrees shattered frequently causing long delays while they were replaced. The jagged path ripped the feet of the weary oxen to bloody shreds until Jason convinced everyone to wrap the beasts feet in hides. The Indians bound their ponies' feet in this way when they had to cross such treacherous terrain.

Fort Boise, another outpost of the fur trade, supplied a brief respite, but Jason hurried everyone on, giving neither man nor beast more than the minimum time to rest in his rush to complete their journey. He rode up and down the wagon train each day, offering encouragement, taking a turn at driving the teams of oxen himslf if he saw a man who needed a chance to rest. Whenever he had a spare moment he went hunting for whatever game could be found, always giving the meat to the brides' drivers to prepare and saving little for Clayton and himself. He had guided more emigrants on previous trips, but never had he taken so much responsibility for others upon himself. What he was trying to prove he could not have explained to anyone, but he knew driving himself to the limit each day was the only way he could escape nights filled with longing for the beautiful Gabrielle MacLaren who offered him nothing more than an occasional wistful smile.

Once the trail reached the foothills of the Blue Mountains despair filled the hearts of many, but Jason encouraged them by relating the difficulties of the first emigrants who had taken wagons across the mountains in 1843. It had been necessary then for forty men with axes to labor for four days to blaze the trail which lay ahead. Shamed by the realization of how easy their passage would be compared to that heroic effort, the travelers moved on without uttering another complaint.

Congratulating them, Jason pointed out that the trip was nearly over and to prove unequal to the challenge of the Oregon Trail at this late date was unworthy of them after they'd conquered so many other far more difficult trials along the way.

Several of the mountain passes were so steep wagons had to be lowered by ropes to keep them from careening down the inclines and crashing into a thousand fragments on the boulders below. Jason was so skilled a supervisor he organized crews to man the ropes in short shifts, calling directions in a calm easy tone which inspired confidence rather than fear. No unfortunate mishaps occurred despite the dangers inherent in their task. All the wagons were moved safely down the most treacherous of slopes, and spirits soared when the Whitman Mission at Waiilatpu came into view. Fort Walla Walla lay only a short distance ahead. There the wagons, their wheels removed, would be placed on rafts which would carry the emigrants down the Columbia River for the final lap of their journey.

Dr. Marcus Whitman and his pretty wife, Narcissa, had been at Waiilatpu for eleven years, struggling the entire time against the whims of nature and the shortage of funds available from congregations in the east which supported their venture. A tireless physician, Dr. Whitman found himself caring far more for the Indians' physical ailments than their spiritual needs, but knowing how greatly he was needed, he thought the purpose of his mission was being fulfilled. In the fall of 1847, the mission consisted of a mill, a guesthouse, a blacksmith's forge, and a building which housed a school as well as the Whitman's home. A robust soul, Marcus Whitman greeted the wagon train enthusiastically while Narcissa, a vivacious blonde, was as gracious a hostess to them as she'd been to the countless numbers of other emigrants who had come her way. She had been one of the first women to traverse the Oregon Trail, and she could provide understanding and compassion to all. Delighted when she heard there were twenty-one young women on their way to marry men in Oregon City, she insisted upon meeting each one of them personally.

Gabrielle liked the charming woman instantly. That Narcissa had joined her husband in establishing a mission on the remote edge of civilization made Gabrielle admire her courage. The Whitmans lived a life so close to the exciting one she and Beau had hoped to have, sharing the challenges of carving a home out of the wilderness, that she could not help but envy Narcissa and her husband their good fortune.

Jason slept for fourteen hours straight once they'd made camp near the Whitman Mission and he knew everyone would be reasonably safe for a few days. He had the advantage of youth to make his body resilient, but even he had his limits and he'd exceeded them far too frequently of late. He liked Marcus Whitman and meant to talk with him as soon as he'd cleaned up, but inspired by the near completion of the trail, he unpacked his razor and took the time to shave off his beard too. He didn't realize until he looked in the mirror how thin his face had become, and for a moment he was sorry he was again clean shaven. But he decided he looked no worse than anyone else. The Oregon Trail had taken its toll from them all.

As always, Dr. Whitman was pleased to see Jason, and seeking privacy, the two men went into his study to sit and talk. "How have you been since last we met?" The good-natured physician inquired politely.

"Fine. But I'm growing weary of making this trek. We lost too many good people this time, cholera was the main culprit, then we lost several more in the last weeks due to exhaustion."

Marcus nodded sympathetically. "I know how you must feel, but you've a lively group camped out there. Survivors, every one. I'd say Oregon will be all the better for their arrival, no matter how difficult their journey. Being a bit of a romantic, Narcissa went to meet the brides. You aren't thinking of taking one of those pretty ladies for your own wife, are you?" He was

256

merely making conversation, trying to brighten Jason's mood, and he did not expect the reply he received.

As Jason glanced out the window toward their camp, his expression was a most dejected one. Marcus was a close friend, more like a father since his own parents were dead, and he didn't hesitate to tell him the truth. "I wouldn't even know what to do with a wife, wouldn't make much of a husband when I couldn't tell a woman if I'd be home for dinner from one day to the next. That's no life to offer any woman, especially not one as fine as the brides we've promised to other men."

Sitting forward, Marcus grew serious too, for he saw more in his young friend's dark gaze than he'd heard in his words. "Narcissa is my best friend, Jason. I cannot even recall how I lived before she became my wife. There's nowhere I'd rather be than home when I know she'll be here waiting for me. It sounds as though you've been giving the prospect of marriage a great deal of thought, but it's unfair to make your decision without consulting the young woman involved. Maybe she has some thoughts on the subject."

"That's not the problem, I've already heard her ideas," Jason admitted sadly. "It's too long a story to relate, but there's no point in marrying a woman who's in love with a dead man."

"She is a widow?" Marcus asked curiously.

"No, but she might as well be." Embarrassed to have revealed so much, Jason got to his feet and offered his hand. "I didn't mean to bore you with my complaints, but thanks for listening. It's always good to see you."

Knowing he'd not made his point, Marcus tried again. "I'll give you some advice, son, love is for the living to enjoy. I'm sure you'll find a way to convince your young woman of that."

Jason laughed ruefully, "Oh, no I won't. That's how I made my first mistake way back in Kansas City and it's been my undoing. I'll come by to see Narcissa before we go. Tell her hello for me." He let himself out of the doctor's house and forced himself to think again of practical matters. He knew everyone would be anxious to leave in a day or so and there were last-minute repairs which could not be forgotten. He'd keep busy helping those who needed it and once again push the pain of his own unanswered needs aside.

"Was that Jason Royal I just saw leave?" Narcissa gave her husband a warm hug as she entered his study.

"Yes. I think the young man's in love but unfortunately he seems to believe his cause is hopeless."

Narcissa thought such a prospect unlikely. "I doubt there's a woman alive whose heart Jason couldn't win. He is far too handsome and much too clever to let another man steal the woman he loves."

"Now why didn't I think to tell him that?" Marcus asked his wife, a merry twinkle in his eye.

"Because you're a man, of course, and much too logical to see the obvious. Is the young woman in question among those in the wagon train?"

"I think she's one of the brides, my dear, a woman he's promised to someone else. That was only my impression, but I think it's accurate."

The pretty blonde grew thoughtful as she tried to decide which of the young women she'd met could be the one Jason wanted.

"I know who she is, Marcus, at least I think I do. You'll have to meet her. Better yet, you come and meet them all, and then tell me who you think it is. We'll see if our choices match."

"Is this to be a contest?" Marcus thought the idea rather appealing. "Well, why not. But we must never tell Jason if he writes to tell us he has gotten married that the girl isn't the one we would have chosen for him."

"You have my word on it; you know how good I am at keeping secrets."

Laughing, Marcus gave her a quick kiss. "That is only because a wagon train does not stop here every day and you have so few people to tell!"

Used to her husband's teasing, Narcissa wasn't insulted. She introduced him to the brides, and when they returned to his study each wrote down a name. When they compared them, they were so close a couple it was not surprising that they had both written the same name: Gabrielle MacLaren. They kept their game to themselves, but they looked forward to hearing from Jason soon to see if their choice was also his.

Chapter XIII

An ecstatic mood of elation poured through the emigrants as they reached Fort Walla Walla for they regarded the forthcoming trip down the Columbia River as a slight hazard compared with all the difficulties they'd faced coming overland. The sound of laughter and music again filled the night air, and the brides could scarcely wait to unpack their trunks and try on the dresses they'd saved to wear for their first meeting with their future husbands.

"Husband, isn't that a marvelous word?" Erica let it roll off her tongue several times deciding she liked the sound of it immensely. "Do you realize that after all these months of looking at Mr. Royal's sketches and dreaming about the men we'll be meeting them shortly? Do you suppose Lewis Bradley will be all I want him to be?"

Gabrielle could not help but be amused by her enthusiastic friend. "How can he possibly be that perfect? I am sure being human he must have some faults, but what if you are not the woman he hopes you will be?"

"Well, why shouldn't he like me?" Erica demanded indignantly for she'd not even considered such an unlikely possibility.

"Compose yourself, please. I do not mean to ruin your plans, but you must realize Lewis has a say about whom he'll marry. You can't simply greet him with, 'How do you do, Lewis. Would you like to get married this afternoon?' The poor man would run for the nearest door!" Gabrielle pointed out logically, but Erica was not feeling in the least bit logical at that moment and her expression became an unhappy pout.

"I suppose you're right. Perhaps you have been the smart one not to allow yourself to dream of a man who might not even like you once you are introduced." Erica's unusual green eyes were suddenly veiled by a mist of unshed tears. "It is only that I am not the most patient of women, and whatever shall I do if Lewis is too shy to approach me?"

"I doubt any of the men will be so shy as that, Erica." Gabrielle gave her friend a comforting hug. "Why don't we just take one thing at a time? First we'll go to Oregon City and rest a few days. Then we can attend the first of Mr. Horne's parties and let the men try to impress us favorably. I think after we have gone to all the trouble to make such a difficult journey to meet them, we deserve to be courted with courtesy. We don't have to fall into the arms of the first man who comes to the door."

Encouraged by that thought, Erica had to agree. "You make it sound so easy, Gabrielle, but if you are so clever at charming men why did you have to come all this way to find a husband?"

That was not something Gabrielle had revealed in the many discussions the women had had about the reasons they'd become mail-order brides. Her motivation was going to remain a secret, and she turned that question aside as if it no longer mattered, telling only part of the truth.

"It was the lure of Oregon, Erica. I told you that when first we met. I wanted to live my life there, and I'm certain the men waiting for us will make our trip worthwhile. All we need do is wait and give them a chance to impress us."

"You have far more patience than I do, Gabrielle. I think I'd better stand next to you all the time. Then if I sound too eager you can poke me in the ribs and I'll know I should be quiet."

"You'll need no such help. All I'm suggesting is that you let the men take the initiative," Gabrielle explained confidently.

"That's the best advice I've ever heard a woman give, Miss MacLaren." As Jason walked up behind them he could not help but overhear her comment. "Do you plan to follow such a sensible course yourself?"

A bright blush filling her cheeks, Gabrielle turned to look up at the only man she wanted to impress. He was smiling, teasing her again, and she knew it would be foolish of her to take offense. "I do not want to appear too forward, Mr. Royal, for truly I am not that type of woman. I hope there will be plenty of time for us to become well acquainted with the bachelors before any decides he wants to propose. I don't want to encourage haste in a man when we'll have a lifetime to be married."

Nodding thoughtfully, Jason could not offer much encouragement. "The men have waited a long time, years in fact. Do you honestly think they will be content to take you for buggy rides after church on Sunday or to come calling in the evenings for no more than an hour? I doubt any of you will still be single at the end of two weeks' time."

While Erica thought that a marvelous prospect, Gabrielle did not. She had pushed the thought of marriage as far into the future as possible. "Marry in haste, repent at leisure is still good advice, Mr. Royal. Two weeks can't possibly be enough time for anyone to make so important a decision as the choice of a mate."

"Then by all means, take your time, Miss MacLaren. We want all our brides to be content with their husbands. I just don't advise you to take too much time or you might find the choice has already been made for you."

Smiling prettily, Erica thanked him for his suggestion since it suited her temperament far more closely than it did Gabrielle's, but then she asked a teasing question. "Have you no plans to marry, Mr. Royal? Didn't it occur to you and Mr. Horne to find brides for yourselves if you were going to find wives for so many of your friends?"

Rather than being insulted by so personal a question, Jason laughed. "I think Clay might consider marriage if the mood struck him, but I certainly never will. Business men and farmers need wives, of course, but as a wagon master I'd be home so seldom when I turned up my wife would probably mistake me for a robber and shoot me before she realized who I was. I wouldn't want to risk so needless an injury since it might well prove fatal. Now if you'll excuse me, I'll bid you a good day." With a sly wink Jason strolled off, not remembering where he had been going in the first place. He knew he had only been teasing Erica rather than responding truthfully to her question, but while she had been amused, Gabrielle had stared coldly at him as if she found his jest impossible to appreciate. Yet it was extremely difficult for him to even consider marriage, let alone answer a question about it in a straightforward manner. He knew he had created the impossible situation in which he found himself, but it sickened him to consider how swiftly Gabrielle would be another man's wife. He still had several options open to him, none of them honorable, but with each passing hour they grew more attractive. He was shocked to think to what lengths he would go to keep the lively redhead for himself. A marriage to her, however, would be agony when her heart would never truly be his. He was unwilling to share his wife with any man, even a dead one.

Erica watched the attractive young man walk away and then declared with a saucy smile, "I think two weeks is exactly the right amount of time for a courtship. I want a home of my own, with a real bed to lie down in at night, and I don't want to sleep alone. I want a husband who'll be generous with his affection as well as his money. Do you think that's a scandalous thing to say?"

Gabrielle barely heard her friend's comments she was so lost in her own thoughts. At least Jason had not been angered by Erica's impertinent question but he'd evaded the issue rather than giving any answer she wanted to hear. Apparently he had believed his casual advice would be helpful. Perhaps it was to Erica, who was so eager to marry, but it certainly wasn't to her. Gabrielle truly considered marriage far too critical a partnership to be entered into blindly. She watched the handsome man saunter off and then stop at another wagon to offer some jest which was met with a loud burst of laughter. He had spoken to her frequently of late, but always when she was in the company of one of the other brides and never for more than a minute or two. His manners could not be faulted, but each encounter left her feeling more dissatisfied for he seemed to be trying to make her forget they had ever shared more than idle conversation. She wanted to speak with him alone. What she'd say she didn't know, but she knew it was important that they have at least one more opportunity to talk before they parted company. He owed her at least that much, and she vowed to herself not to let him refuse her request for one last conversation.

When Gabrielle approached him later that day, Jason was so astonished that he did not at first understand her request.

"I beg your pardon?" he inquired incredulously.

"I've had enough of your jokes, Jason," Gabrielle replied impatiently. "I want to speak with you. I said please. Do you expect me to beg for a few minutes of your time?"

Sorry that he had upset her when he'd not meant to, Jason attempted to apologize. "No, of course not. You just startled me, that's all." He frowned then, perplexed that after the many weeks she'd failed to give him more than a word or two in passing she had chosen to converse when he was occupied with the construction of the rafts.

"You don't want to speak with me right now but in private; is that it?"

"If it is possible." Gabrielle hoped no one would think her coming to see Jason out of the ordinary but their conversation was already attracting curious stares from the men working nearby. "I know you are very busy, if you have no time—"

"I will make the time." Jason looked around them to be certain his comments could not be overheard. "Why don't you

265

take Sunny out for a ride in the morning? He must be getting restless. Just slip away from the others without giving them any reason to be suspicious, and I'll meet you about a hundred yards down the trail which brought us here. There's a large oak tree that juts out into the roadway, you'll find it readily enough. Will that suit you?"

Gabrielle hesitated to agree. After all, each time she'd been alone with the man the same thing had happened. Did she want it to happen again? She clenched her fists at her sides, trying to convince herself nothing need happen between them if she didn't want it to. Of course, that would depend more on how Jason replied to her questions than on anything else. Let the man take the initiative, she'd advised Erica, but could she follow that plan herself? Especially if Jason did not choose to take the initiative. . . .

"Well?" Jason asked irritably, not understanding why Gabrielle was taking so long to reply. "I can get away tomorrow morning after breakfast. Do you want to meet me then or not?"

"Yes, I'll be there." As Gabrielle turned away and walked back toward the wagons, she feared she'd only worsened her situation rather than improved it. Clearly the man thought any conversation between them unnecessary or he'd have suggested it himself. Her heart fell at that thought, but she'd meet him in the morning and hope for the best. "It is ridiculous to expect the best from that man!" she whispered to herself. However, if Jason truly cared nothing for her, she wanted to hear it from him. Otherwise, for the rest of her life she might believe that she should have married him rather than one of the bachelors who'd paid him to find them wives.

As luck would have it, Jason was late. Gabrielle became quite depressed as she sat by the side of the trail waiting for a man who apparently had far more important things to do than come to meet her. Having let Sunny graze, she sat beneath the oak tree which provided shade as well as an unobstructed view of

266

you, then forget it. The closeness of our relationship is not something I'd share with anyone." He was angry now. As always she had seemed to see his actions in the worst possible light. He wanted far more than her respect, but he had not even earned that.

Jason was not making it easy for Gabrielle. On the contrary, she blamed herself for not having anticipated that he would prove to be so difficult. It wasn't silence she wanted from him but devotion—some hope that they could have a life together. "In a few days the journey will end. There are twenty-one bachelors expecting their brides to arrive in Oregon City, but I now have mixed feelings about being among them. In many ways I am not the same woman who left Kansas City, and I do not want to enter into a marriage I may regret for the rest of my life. I thought perhaps you would have something you wished to say to me, but I see I was foolish to expect such a courtesy."

As Gabrielle made the first move to rise, Jason reached out to stop her. "Wait a minute. I don't want you to worry about what you'll find in Oregon City until you get there. That's simply borrowing trouble. I think you're fretting needlessly. There are undoubtedly many things I should say to you, but I'll say only this: because what we had was a fleeting alliance doesn't mean my feelings for you aren't deep or that I'll forget you, ever. I would never presume to call a woman as fine as you my mistress and I suggest you don't think of yourself in that way either. It just demeans us both."

Gabrielle took a deep breath then let it out slowly. She had wanted to provide him with the opportunity to propose, but it was obvious he was never going to do so. Their brief affair was over as far as he was concerned, but she didn't want it ever to end. Her future was no less uncertain for having spoken with him, yet she wanted to seize this last opportunity to share the beauty they could create together. Rather than moving away she leaned closer, her lips nearly brushing his as she whispered, "Would you please kiss me goodbye?"

Her request was such a simple one, but to tell her goodbye

was unthinkable, not a prospect Jason could even bear to consider. He gathered her into his arms, his hunger for her too great to be satisfied with a single kiss. He pressed her supple body to his as he stretched out upon the grass, holding her tightly as though he feared she might elude his grasp. Now, after having grabbed for the sweet surrender she'd offered, he wanted to savor it for as long as she would willingly remain in his arms. He moved his fingertips slowly down her spine, cradling her tenderly as he deepened his kiss. She showed not the slightest reluctance to accept his affection, and as her hands moved slowly down the contours of his muscular body, her touch was so tantalizing he could think of nothing but the lavish affection she'd always given him. Her fingertips moved deftly over his belt buckle, freeing that constraint so she could slip her hand beneath his buckskin trousers. Her caress was honey smooth yet demanding. It drove all thought of caution from his mind. He knew he had only to wait for her passion to match his, but restraint did not come easily with so teasing a companion. When he sat up to pull off his shirt, she yanked it from his hands and, tossing it upon the grass, spread eager kisses across his bare chest.

Wanting the same privilege, he whispered hoarsely, "Your dress is in my way, take it off quickly!" He had enjoyed undressing her with a slow sensuous touch, but he wanted her too badly now to indulge in such lazy play. Fearing he would simply rip her clothing to shreds in his haste, he insisted she disrobe by herself.

Gabrielle's slender fingers trembled as she tried to slip off the layers of garments which separated them: buttons, hooks, ribbons. There seemed to be far too much to do and all the while Jason's hands were moving over her. His touch was light, teasing the firm flesh of her thighs, but she could not concentrate on her task when he provided such a compelling distraction. Finally she cast aside the last of her lingerie and he drew her back into an eager embrace his mouth covering hers in a savage kiss which left her gasping for breath when at last he drew away. She had known him as a tender lover whose caress gave the most splendid of pleasures, but he showed no such patience with her now. His fiery kiss burned her flesh as his mouth moved to the fullness of her breast with a haste which seemed borne of desperation, and she drew his mouth back to hers, weaving her fingers in his jet black curls to draw him down upon her. She wanted to set him free from the torment which consumed him but rather than satisfying his desires her graceful invitation inflamed them both. His powerful body conquered hers swiftly then, dominating her gentle sweetness with a strength which left her trembling in his embrace. She could do no more than cling to him as the force of his ecstasy swept through her in a torrent of unleashed passion. Drenched in sunlight, she felt as though she were drowning in the ocean's depths, all life drained from her by a lover who had chosen to tell her goodbye with such intensity. She was too weak to do more than look up at him when at last, his demons subdued, his kiss grew tender once again.

Jason did not draw away, but shifted his weight to spare Gabrielle the burden of it as he gazed fondly at her delicate features. He still thought her the loveliest creature ever born. Her fair skin was lightly tanned by the many weeks she'd spent in the sun, but no less beautiful for its golden color. The blue of her eyes was bright, sparklingly clear, and the thick fringe of dark lashes which framed them seemed too long to be natural. He thought the deep glossy red of her hair marvelous and now preferred that unique shade to all others. She was an exquisite beauty, and while he would never tire of the enchanting sight of her loveliness he was saddened to think he'd given her no pleasure this time but had only taken his own. He lay quite still within her, meaning the joy to be mutual when he took her again. He kissed her cheeks playfully, nibbling her earlobes before he risked asking a question.

"I have never been closer to any woman than I am to you; are we not friends after all?"

Gabrielle raised her fingertips to his cheek. She felt that

question was too dangerous to answer truthfully for she knew were he truly her friend he would not now abandon her to the whim of fortune but would make her his wife. "You are such a handsome man, but I think even more so without a beard." She purred softly, her husky voice a most seductive one.

"Yet when I grew one you said you liked it," Jason pointed out quickly. "Is it just that you like me no matter whether I choose to be clean shaven or bearded?"

"This is true," Gabrielle whispered and she lifted her arms to encircle his neck, to draw his mouth again to hers. She did not want the warmth which filled her to end, ever, for to think they would never again share this same sweet intimacy was too sad a prospect to accept. The tip of her tongue traced the outline of his smiling lips before invading his mouth and his response was immediate. This time, however, he moved with a deliberate slowness, gently arousing her passions to a fevered peak before he satisfied his own undiminished craving for her. Despite the wonder of their pleasure there was a bittersweet sadness to their embrace, that of a longing shared but still not fulfilled. Neither wanted to let go, for each knew what they'd found together would never again be recaptured once they parted. A long while passed before they left the sunlit clearing that morning, and neither had spoken the word *goodbye*.

The rafts were completed rapidly, for the emigrants were so anxious to reach the Willamette Valley they wasted no time in constructing the sturdy vessels. Then wagon wheels were removed to provide flat surfaces so the heavily laden Conestogas would survive the voyage down the swiftly rushing waters of the Columbia without rolling off the floating log platforms. Controlling the rafts by long poles was arduous work—they were cumbersome craft—but since they had provided safe transport for thousands of emigrants the members of Jason's wagon train were willing to rely on them. They faced a wild ride through swiftly moving currents and dangerous rapids, but none appeared afraid as the first raft left the riverbank and moved out into the turbulent waters.

There were Indians about, many hoping to be hired to paddle travelers down the river in their canoes, but Gabrielle was careful not to attract the attention of any braves, handsome or otherwise. She thought the journey down the river would provide more excitement than several of the brides could bear, but the prospect of making the trip in a canoe was terrifying. She stood on the riverbank and watched as Jason supervised the launching of the rafts, giving each a headstart before the next was ordered to shove off. He did not want the rafts themselves to pose an additional hazard along the way. As always he had such confidence that no one questioned his advice, and with a warm handshake and a cheerful promise to see the travelers in Oregon City, he waved them all a hearty farewell.

Turning away when she was overcome by the sadness of the departures after so many months of shared joy and pain, Gabrielle went to find the Duffys so she might bid them a more thoughtful goodbye. The little girls danced around her happily, while Timothy came forward shyly to give her a kiss upon the cheek. There were tears in Amanda's eyes as she tried to say thank you one last time.

"I cried when Johanna came to say goodbye earlier this morning and I'm going to do it again. It's silly, I know, when we might find ourselves neighbors once we all reach the Willamette Valley, but I will never forget what you girls did for our family," she said.

"It was nothing more than you would have done for us," Gabrielle responded with a warm smile. She gave the slender woman a fond embrace, then turned to her husband. "Well, Sam, I do hope Amanda is right for I would love to see all of you frequently. Mr. Horne has a home right in Oregon City, and he'll know where all of us have gone so we can keep in touch."

"You'll not be with Mr. Royal?" Sam was so astonished he did not realize how his question had sounded until Gabrielle turned pale. "I mean, well, I just thought . . ." He grew silent then, knowing he'd already said far too much, but his wife and son were giving him such curious glances that he knew he was in real trouble.

"I'm certain Mr. Royal will know my whereabouts too," Gabrielle responded, as though she'd misunderstood his question. With a light kiss, she left Sam staring after her, as dumfounded as he'd been the morning he'd seen her and Jason cavorting playfully in the nude in the pond above Bear Lake.

Jason had determined the order for launching the rafts and had purposely made Gabrielle's the last since he planned to ride with it. She had shown none of the signs of uneasiness she'd displayed when they were approaching the Platte, but he wanted to take no chance that she might be badly frightened or come to harm. She had not argued with his decision to send Sunrise down the river with Duke on one of the rafts constructed specifically to transport livestock, but he knew she hadn't been pleased that he would not allow her to travel with her beloved horse. He had expected her to fight him on that issue. However, she had seemed satisfied, knowing that such an arrangement was practical for Duke and would be equally satisfactory for her horse. That he could still not accurately predict her reactions pained him, and while he knew no man would ever know the sensual side of her nature as well as he did, he longed to know what secrets she hid behind those haunting blue eyes which always seemed to see to the very bottom of his soul without providing him with the slightest glimpse of hers.

Paul escorted his charges upon the raft when their turn finally came. He was as eager as they to see the lengthy journey end, but he felt a deep pang of sorrow because the pretty young women he had grown to love would soon be going their separate ways.

"We'll all get mighty wet, but this part of the trip is like no other. Now we'll nearly fly compared to the way we crept across the desert."

Grabbing the other long pole, Jason was quick to agree.

"That's true, ladies, think of this as a magic carpet ride." With that teasing remark, he dug the end of the pole into the mud and, with Paul's help, guided the raft out into the current. Damp spray filled their hair and soaked their clothing, but to Jason's delight Gabrielle's eyes glowed only with excitement and not a trace of fear. That she loved the wild thrill of the rapids as greatly as he came as no surprise. She is still the best of the lot, he thought to himself, the very finest woman I ever hoped to meet. And he kept a close eye on her until their journey upon the river finally came to an end.

Chapter XIV

When the weary contingent of brides arrived at Clayton Horne's Oregon City home, they went straight to bed, and it was long past noon the following day before the first one stirred. The house was a large two-story frame structure, and the second-floor bedrooms had been furnished with all manner of borrowed beds and cots. Still, each young woman had a comfortable place to sleep if not much space in which to move around. Not even Iris complained about the cramped quarters, because the house seemed like a palace compared with the Conestoga wagons they'd shared for nearly five months. The young women were so excited over staying in a real house at last that they thought the accommodations more than satisfactory and thanked Clayton profusely for his hospitality.

Their luggage littered the hall upstairs, but it was soon sorted into clothing to be kept and garments which had seen such hard use during the trip they were unfit to be more than cleaning rags. The pretty new dress each prospective bride had brought had to be aired or laundered to restore its freshness, and Clayton summoned Jason to help him string more than a dozen clotheslines through his back yard to provide enough line on which to dry the gowns and the young ladies' frilly lingerie. The colorful apparel attracted considerable notice, and within minutes the bachelors who'd waited impatiently throughout the long spring and summer began to appear at the front door to inquire if they could be of any assistance to the brides. Their motive in being so helpful was obvious to the young women who peeked through the upstairs windows for glimpses of the men who would soon be their husbands. They were delighted to find they could name each one as he came up the walk, and the boldest girls even called out greetings to their favorites.

Gabrielle sat on the edge of the double bed she'd shared with Erica and tried to get the vivacious young woman to hold still. She was trying to alter the waistline on Erica's green silk gown for a better fit. Taking another pin, she cautioned her to stop wriggling. "I am going to poke you, and if you bleed all over this beautiful dress, you'll never forgive yourself. Now stop jumping up and down!"

"I am not jumping! It is just that I am so excited I simply cannot hold still."

"Well, you must. If you don't I'll make a poor job of this and then you'll be sorry when you must attend tomorrow night's party looking like you're wearing a borrowed dress." Gabrielle placed the last pin in the luxurious fabric, then patted Erica on the hip. "There. Now you may take it off, but be careful not to loosen the pins or we'll not know how much to take in at the waist."

"I'll be extremely careful," Erica promised with exaggerated sincerity, and she slipped the shimmering green gown off over her head without disturbing the pins Gabrielle had placed in the garment with such care. "Who's next? We might as well do a fitting for everyone. Then we can all sit down and sew together. It will be fun, just like a quilting bee."

Marlene came forward with a pale blue dress which made her fair hair all the more lovely. "Will you help me too, Gabrielle? I tried to do it myself but I couldn't reach the darts in the back."

"Of course I'll help you. Just turn around and I'll have the

278

darts taken in in a minute." Gabrielle had often helped her aunt make dresses, so it was a simple matter to do no more than adjust the fit of these gowns. "We're all quite a bit thinner but a few well-placed tucks should set everything right once again. We'll be the best-dressed women in Oregon City."

"That's only because there are so few women in Oregon City!" Erica responded with a giggle. She was so delighted to actually be there that she had kept her companions laughing all afternoon with her teasing.

Finally Margaret spoke up hesitantly. "Aren't any of you as nervous as I am about meeting the men tomorrow night? I can't think of a single thing to say, and I'm afraid no one will even notice me."

"They will all notice you," Barbara reassured her confidently. "They'll be certain to meet each one of us to be sure they find precisely the woman they want. You can count on it. Or look at it this way, there are exactly the same number of bachelors as there are women so how can any of us be left standing alone?"

"That's not realistic," Iris pointed out maliciously. "Some of us will undoubtedly attract more than one man and that will leave others without escorts from time to time. But since that situation is unavoidable, you might as well cease to worry over it, Margaret." The conceited young woman offered her advice as if it were proven fact rather than opinion.

"I thought we had convinced you none of us was interested in the same type of man you are, Iris," Gabrielle remarked casually as she placed the last pin in Marlene's dress. "Mr. Horne is hosting parties so we can become acquainted with the men, he's not staging a competition."

"Well, it is that. You know it is," Iris insisted.

"You make it sound as though you wished it were a foot race," Johanna scoffed accusingly.

"Beauty is what will matter tomorrow night, Johanna, not speed," Iris responded sarcastically.

279

Gabrielle saw Johanna's bright blush and came to her defense. "How do you plan to wear your hair tomorrow night, Johanna? If you wear it down like Barbara's I'll bet your curls will be very pretty."

"Do you really think so?" Johanna had not even considered such a carefree style, but since she greatly respected Gabrielle's opinion, she reached up to unwind the tight bun which kept her curls under firm control. As she shook her head, ringlets flew about and then settled in attractive waves which gave her pleasant features a less severe appearance. She suddenly looked very appealing, pretty rather than serious and prim. "Well, is it any better this way?" she asked hesitantly, for the others in the room were simply staring at her with their mouths agape.

"Oh, yes!" Margaret blurted out; then she realized that had been a very tactless remark. "What I mean is, it is a far prettier style. Come over to the mirror and you'll see for yourself."

Johanna moved cautiously through the maze of beds and the heaps of clothing to approach the dresser which had a large mirror suspended above it. She fluffed the ends of her hair and, after a long moment's consideration, seemed pleased with what she saw. "This is fine for parties, I guess."

"Of course it is!" Erica reassured her enthusiastically. "I have a curling iron, not that you would ever need it, but I'll bet I can curl Gabrielle's hair."

Iris shot Erica an evil glance. "Maybe she likes to wear her hair straight; did that not occur to you?" That Johanna now looked so attractive didn't please her in the least. She was confident she could get whichever man she wanted, but she didn't want to face more competition than she'd expected. Gabrielle was already a threat, far too pretty. Iris wasn't eager to see her look even more stunning, as she was sure she would with all that eye-catching red hair softly curled.

Simply to spite Iris, Gabrielle decided curls were exactly what she wanted. "My hair is very difficult to curl, but I'd like to borrow your curling iron tomorrow afternoon if I may."

Erica reached out to touch her friend's long silken tresses. "I think we'd better start in the morning or we'll never finish on time."

Gabrielle laughed with the others, but she knew giving her hair curls might prove to be more of a challenge than Erica had anticipated. She washed her hair after breakfast the next morning and then trimmed the ends a couple of inches to make them even. Then Erica unpacked her pearl-handled curling iron and the stand which held it over a small container of oil. When lit the oil heated the device so it would make curls.

The pretty blonde combed a section of Gabrielle's hair then wrapped it tightly around the hot iron. In less than a minute's time, she produced exactly the curl she'd hoped to make. "You see, I knew this would work. We'll be able to curl only the ends of your hair since it is so long but if you wear it up it will look spectacular."

"Spectacular may be a bit too strong a description, Erica. Let's just try for attractive; I'll be more than pleased with that." Gabrielle tried to sit still while her friend kept up a constant stream of conversation. Erica had grown very talkative since they'd arrived at Clayton's, but understanding her nervousness, Gabrielle did not complain. It took almost two hours to complete Gabrielle's hair and then she helped Erica do hers. By the time all of them had pressed their dresses, bathed, and styled their hair, the party was about to begin.

Jason straightened his tie with a vicious yank, uncomfortable in the confining gray suit after so many months of wearing his loose-fitting buckskins. He and Clayton had always planned to attend the parties for the brides as they knew they'd be unlikely to run smoothly without their direction. Now that the first party was actually to take place, however, Jason hoped to be able to leave as soon as the party got under way. He knew the men would all be pleased with the women he and Clayton had selected, for they were exceptionally pretty and sweet.

However, he had no wish to stand on the sidelines and watch Gabrielle dance with such an eager group of bachelors. She'd attract considerable notice, he was certain. Still, he knew for a fact that she was damned difficult to impress so he didn't think she'd select a man that night and not remain open to the attentions of all the others. No, indeed. Any man who set his heart on winning that beauty was in for a long and trying courtship, but let the bachelors find that out for themselves.

Clayton Horne walked up to Jason as the bachelors began to arrive. "I just talked to one of the men Joshua Taylor mentioned in his letter and he swore he'd never even heard of the man! What do you make of that?"

Jason looked down at his agitated friend. "So? Maybe they met only once and he's just forgotten him. Let's wait until Joshua arrives and we can judge him on his own merits. There's no sense in looking for problems, Clay. We're trying to help the men relax and have a good time tonight. Just concentrate on being a good host."

"Yes, I am," Clayton responded bruskly. "Still, the numbers have to come out even or we're in serious trouble."

"Look, you and I are here. We can dance with the girls. Once everyone arrives it will be so crowded they'll never notice if there are equal numbers of men and women or not. There's the doorbell again. You'd better go answer it and I'll see what's keeping our ladies."

"Why don't you get the door?" Clayton asked slyly.

Jason just laughed and started up the stairs. He didn't intend to go into the bedrooms but simply to stand on the landing until one of the brides appeared so he could send her for the others. To his amazement, he found the hall nearly filled with young women who were trying desperately not to giggle and give away their presence. With a wide smile, he whispered, "The men have started to arrive. It would be very nice if you were all downstairs in the parlor to greet them." Offering his arm to the nearest young woman, he led the group down the stairs, but as he stepped aside to let them file into the parlor, he saw that Gabrielle was not among them.

"She's still doing her hair," Erica whispered for she saw his anxious glance and rightly guessed its cause. "She'll be down in a minute."

Jason nodded, accepting her explanation. However, when Gabrielle had not appeared in five minutes' time, he went up to get her. The door of her room was closed, but as he lifted his hand to knock Gabrielle opened it, ready to step out. With her hair pinned up in a bright cascade of lustrous curls, she was so stunning he could not think what to say and only stared, unable to come up with any lucid comment let alone the extravagant compliment he knew she deserved.

Gabrielle stepped forward to take his arm. "If you have come to escort me to the party, I am ready, Mr. Royal. May I take your shocked silence to mean you approve of my appearance?"

"I have always thought you very beautiful," Jason finally managed to mumble. Then, becoming angry with himself for behaving like such a fool, he spoke more forcefully. "But you are late again, Miss MacLaren, and our guests are waiting."

Gabrielle's pretty smile vanished when she realized that Jason couldn't wait to introduce her to another man, a whole roomful of men in fact. "Forgive me. I did not realize a few more minutes' time would make me appear so rude." She walked off and left him then, not content to let him escort her down the stairs when his purpose was such an obvious one. Attempting to smile as she entered the parlor, she found it a simple matter to recognize the bachelors from Jason's sketches, but when one man walked up to her she was taken aback by his enthusiastic greeting.

"Miss MacLaren? I am Michael Jenkins and I've been waiting months to make your acquaintance."

"How do you do, Mr. Jenkins?" Gabrielle felt a curious sense of detachment now that she stood face to face with one of the bachelors. Michael was an earnest young man, rather nice looking, tall with light brown hair and brown eyes. His smile very pleasant, but she felt not the slightest bit of excitement as his hand touched hers in a polite handshake. It was as though a chill wind had swept all emotion from her slender body, and although she returned his smile she knew her response was no more than a polite reaction she had been taught to affect. As he began to inquire about her trip, she scanned the room distractedly, mentally attaching names to the men's faces. There was no stranger present. Not one of the men appeared to be the Joshua Taylor she'd included so faithfully each night in her prayers.

Jason was so infuriated by Gabrielle's rebuff that he was tempted to leave before the party had even begun, but knowing that would be unfair to Clayton, he forced himself to remain. They had removed the furniture from the dining room so it could be used for dancing—the two musicians they had hired proved to be very accomplished—but Jason had no interest in dancing himself. He wandered through the first-floor rooms of the large house, making certain Clayton's housekeeper and the two maids they'd hired kept providing plentiful refreshments, and seeing that everyone was having a good time, but he had never enjoyed a gathering less. Far too often he found himself simply observing Gabrielle. Her dress was a vivid sapphire blue, the crisp taffeta the exact color of her eyes. In the prevailing style, the gown revealed a creamy expanse of fair skin at her shoulders, while the tight-fitting bodice showed off her tiny waist to every advantage. The deep ruffle of the full skirt swished musically with each of her steps, and he thought her such an attractive sight he found it difficult to appear interested in anyone else in the room. She had such a gracious manner. On more than one occasion when two men appeared at her side he had seen her gracefully guide them across the room to where a less popular young woman stood alone. Iris, on the other hand, seemed to enjoy drawing men to her as though she were pulling in fish with a net. She flirted openly with them all, alternating bright smiles with coy glances but clearly giving the greater portion of her attention to the men who were the most expensively dressed. What was obvious to Jason seemed to escape the men, however, so each time Iris became surrounded he walked over to quietly suggest his friends not neglect the other young women at the party.

While Jason tried to remain on the edge of the noisy gathering, he frequently saw Gabrielle glance about the room as though she were looking for someone. On those occasions, when their eyes met she would look away quickly, as if the mere sight of him were painful. When the musicians took a short break, he strolled outside with them, happy for an excuse to get some fresh air. Nothing was going as he'd expected. Gabrielle was having a wonderful time and he was miserable. He'd never been jealous, not in his entire life, and scarcely recognized the emotion, but he knew he didn't like seeing her in other men's arms. She was one of the best dancers. Displaying the elegance of a prima ballerina, she was so light on her feet that she seemed to dance on air regardless of how clumsy her partner might be. Most of the men were awkward, he realized. They'd had little opportunity to dance in recent years and couldn't be expected to know the latest steps. Indeed, he'd seen Iris leave more than one man in the middle of the dance floor rather than suffer through a musical number with a poor partner, but Gabrielle, he'd noticed had continued to smile no matter how often her partner stepped upon her feet. As usual her compassion seemed to extend to all men but him, and he looked up at the stars, thinking their cold brilliance far warmer than her heart.

By ten o'clock, Gabrielle's earlier detachment had turned to sheer terror. She had tried, truly she had, but with each man her reaction had been the same. She felt nothing for any of them, only a rapidly increasing sense of dread as each man appeared at her side. They were all polite, well mannered, and so eager to impress her she could not help but feel honored.

However, there was not one whom she cared to see again. When she saw Jason step through the door which led to the back yard, she followed him at her first opportunity.

"Jason!" she called in a hoarse whisper, hoping he would not send her back inside before she said what she had to tell him.

Jason spun around, shocked to see Gabrielle rushing toward him. "What are you doing out here? It's too cold for one thing and for another—"

"Please listen to me for just a minute, I won't need more." Gabrielle did not even wait to see if he'd agree to her request before she began. "Where is Joshua Taylor? Why hasn't he come to this party with all the others?"

Jason shrugged. "I really couldn't say. I told you I don't know the man. Why is it so important that he be here? It looked to me like you had plenty of other company."

Gabrielle looked back toward the house to be certain the musicians were engrossed in their own conversation before she attempted to explain. "I have said a prayer for him every night and have wanted to meet him, that's all. I am sure he will be no different from any of your other friends, Jason, but if he doesn't appear tomorrow night I'm not coming downstairs."

"What?" Jason could make no sense of her remark.

"I counted twenty men here, I am the extra woman and it's not fair for me to receive the attention which rightfully belongs to the others. I won't join in the parties if I am one too many. I simply can't."

Realizing how greatly upset Gabrielle was, Jason took her trembling hand to lead her over to a small bench. "Sit down here for a moment and tell me exactly what is wrong. I thought you were enjoying the party. Aren't you having a good time?" It truly had seemed to him that she was having a marvelous evening.

"No!" Gabrielle responded with an anguished cry; then seeing his startled expression, she attempted to explain. "I mean yes. The men couldn't be nicer, Jason. They are sweet and some even had tears in their eyes when they told me they did not expect such pretty young women to come so far to get married. I don't know what they expected, but clearly we have provided a most wonderful surprise. I should say you have, since you and Mr. Horne chose us."

Jason had seen Gabrielle throw screaming fits of temper all too often but never had he seen her so beside herself with anxiety. He did not really understand what was causing her discomfort. "Now let me see if I understand you before you go any further. You find the men's compliments flattering; is that at least true?"

"Yes, but I don't deserve such attention, Jason, nor do I want it. What I mean is, I can't accept it. It seems years ago that I spoke with you in Kansas City. I truly thought I could marry one of these men then, but now I know that's simply impossible. I have some money, I'll give you whatever the man paid and you can refund it to Joshua or to one of the others. But I am never going to be able to marry one of these men when I know I will never come to love him." She bit her lip savagely to force back her tears, for having to make this declaration only increased her distress.

"I seem to recall love wasn't all that important to you at one time. Are you saying that it now is?" Jason asked hopefully.

Gabrielle shook her head. "I can't love any of those men; that is important. I thought I could hide my feelings so my husband would never know I didn't love him, but I can't do that. I simply can't! I would make the worst of wives. My husband would be as miserable as I would. I can't do that to any man. I want to be released from the agreement I made with you and Mr. Horne, right now, tonight. I will leave. I won't stay here in Mr. Horne's house. It would cause comment if I were to remain when I'm no longer one of the brides."

Jason took a deep breath and then held it until he thought he could speak in a reasonable tone of voice. "I want you to listen to me because I'm going to say this only once. Beau is dead and

287

no amount of hysteria on your part is going to bring him back. That's what you're doing isn't it, comparing each of the bachelors with Beau and finding them woefully lacking? I don't care how good-looking the man was, or how smart or clever. Whatever it was you found so attractive about him no longer matters. I am going to take you right back into that party, and you are going to be every bit as charming as you have been for the first part of the evening. I have your signature on a contract which states you'll give these men every chance to impress you favorably, and I intend to see you honor that promise. Is that clear?"

Gabrielle was afraid she was going to faint, simply pass out right there across his lap rather than agree to such an unreasonable demand. Why he continually dredged up Beau's name she didn't know. It made her feel that a dagger had been thrust deep into her heart and then twisted. She had not even thought of Beau that evening. She had thought only of Jason, of how handsome he looked and of how cruel he had been to leave her to fend for herself when she wanted so badly to be with him.

"I have asked you before and I'll do so again, please do not mention Beau's name. It hurts me more than I can say. I know I signed one of your contracts, but you can't force me to marry against my will. You can't do that!"

"No one is going to force you to do anything, Gabrielle. I am merely insisting you keep your promise to give these men a fair chance. How can you make any decision when you've barely spoken with them? You told me yourself two weeks wasn't long enough to pick a mate and now you've decided one evening is enough time to dismiss twenty men after no more than a few brief words of conversation? I certainly hope none of the others is as fickle as you."

"I am not fickle!" Gabrielle protested sharply. "I simply did not know what a man would expect from his wife, the closeness that should exist between them, but now I do!"

"So this is all my fault, is that it?" Jason got to his feet and when she made no move to rise he reached down for her elbow and yanked her to hers. "It is your aunt's fault, if anyone's, that you were so ignorant. It did not even occur to me when you told me your views on marriage in Kansas City that you had no idea what you were talking about! I think you say exactly what suits your purpose at the moment without bothering to consider the consequences, but you will damn well learn to be more thoughtful in the future! For tonight you need only keep the bachelors amused. You dance so beautifully I doubt that any man recalls what you said while you were in his arms, so just keep dancing if making simple conversation is too difficult for you!"

With that piece of scathing advice, Jason escorted Gabrielle right back into the party and left her with the first man they encountered. He then walked out the front door, strode back to the hotel, and slammed the door of his room so soundly he nearly tore it from the hinges. His emotions were under no better control than Gabrielle's, but at least he didn't have to stand in a crowded room for the rest of the evening and watch her make polite conversation with men so eager to make her their bride it showed in their every expression and gesture.

Gabrielle smiled as if speaking with Michael Jenkins again had been exactly what she'd wanted to do. She felt it unfair to make him suffer for the impossibility of her situation. Encouraged by her warm attentiveness he now began talking about his farm and how good the harvest had been.

"Mr. Horne seems to have timed things perfectly. Now all of us have the whole winter to devote to making a wife feel welcome." He positively beamed as he mulled over that splendid thought in his mind.

"What is the weather like here in the winter, Mr. Jenkins?" Gabrielle managed to ask, although she was not in the least bit curious.

"We get a lot of rain, unfortunately. It turns the roads into

289

rivers of mud and most are impassable for several months. We're all more or less isolated until spring once the rains begin."

"You mean you can't get into town at all?" Gabrielle was appalled by the prospect of being alone for several months with a new husband about whom she cared nothing.

Michael laughed at her stricken expression and tried to reassure her. "No. But we all know what provisions we'll need to have on hand and I guess most of us are pretty self-sufficient. It isn't so bad, it just gets lonely is all."

"I'm sure it must." Again Gabrielle saw the eagerness in Michael's gaze, an almost tangible hunger for a bride to share his life, and she was ashamed she could offer no more than a word or two of sympathy. Feeling their conversation might swiftly take on too personal a tone, she glanced toward the musicians who had just begun a new tune.

"Would you care to dance?"

Michael wasn't certain if a lady was supposed to make that suggestion but having found Gabrielle's manners to be perfect, he assumed she would know what was correct.

"My dancing is nothing to brag about, Miss MacLaren, but if you'd like to, I'll try my best."

"Perhaps it is only that you need a bit of practice," Gabrielle offered. Her statement had been overly optimistic. Michael had no sense of rhythm and he simply could not move in time with the music. He held her in a firm embrace, however, smiling confidently as if he thought he were doing well, and she did not hurt his feelings by telling him the truth. Her next partner, a robust man whose grasp left her fingers bruised, was no more accomplished, and when the next gentleman suggested they have a cup of punch rather than share a dance, she was grateful for the chance to rest. Farming was also his consuming interest, but she tried to broaden their conversation as best she could.

"Do you raise horses by any chance, Mr. Schuler?"

"No, not really. I own a few, everybody does. Why do you ask?"

"I brought my horse with me, a stallion of considerable beauty, and I am thinking of raising horses as a pastime."

Matthew Schuler scoffed at that idea. "Why a pretty little lady like you could never handle a stallion, and as for a woman raising horses, I'd certainly never allow my wife to start such an enterprise."

Gabrielle did not respond. She simply excused herself and walked away, but before she'd taken more than three steps, another man appeared at her side. In the hope of finding at least one gentleman who shared her passion for horses, if nothing else, she began to ask each man she met if he had such an interest. None of the men admitted to having any special regard for the graceful animals. Several described the advantages of owning mules and oxen, but by the end of the evening she'd not encountered a single man who thought he might like to breed prize-winning horses. By the time Clayton ushered the last bachelor out the front door, she was exhausted and dreaded the thought that she would have to see the same group of men again the next evening. Her roommates, all in far better moods, nearly danced up the stairs as Gabrielle went to the bedroom they shared.

"Did you have an opportunity to speak with Lewis Bradley?" Erica wanted to know.

"Yes, I spoke at least a few words with every man here. Did you like him?"

"He is a few years older than I thought he'd be, not quite so tall, but I wasn't disappointed in him and he seemed to like me. Did you find someone you thought rather special?"

"I thought they were all very nice men," Gabrielle responded noncommittally.

When the conversation worked itself around to Iris she announced smugly, "I am going out to see John Randolph's farm tomorrow. I'll let you know my opinion of him when

I return."

Johanna thought Iris foolish and said so. "I don't think you should go alone, Iris. He may mistake your keen interest in his farm for an interest in him and then what will you do?"

"I can take care of him," the self-centered brunette responded sharply. "He will behave as a gentleman should or he'll be very sorry."

Erica leaned over to whisper to Gabrielle. "I think he'll be very sorry no matter how he behaves!"

Gabrielle agreed with a subtle nod. As she prepared for bed, she listened to her friends' comments but did not join in the discussion. Since Jason had been so emphatic in his refusal to listen to her reason for withdrawing from the brides' group, she had decided to speak with Clayton instead. However, when she went downstairs the next morning, she found the man had gone to the bank to conduct some business and wasn't expected back for an hour or two. In his absence, Jason was there to solve any problems which might arise, but she saw no point in going over the matter again with him.

Surprised to see Gabrielle downstairs so early, Jason inquired politely, "Did you sleep well, Miss MacLaren?"

Gabrielle stared up at the arrogant man, certain he knew she'd been far too restless to sleep comfortably. "Unfortunately no, Mr. Royal, but that fact should come as no surprise to you."

"Well, tonight's party will be less formal. Perhaps you will find it more amusing than last night's was." He thought her beauty undiminished by her reported lack of sleep. There was not the slightest trace of weariness in her bright blue eyes or upon her sweet features. She was wearing her hair in an upswept style and he found her elegant curls most distracting. He cleared his throat noisily, hoping she wouldn't notice how he'd been staring at her.

"The company will be exactly the same. I meant what I said. If Joshua doesn't appear tonight, neither will I." Not that it really matters whether the man comes to the party or not, she reminded herself. She knew her feelings for him would be no different than for the others.

"I think everyone will be more at ease tonight. You may be pleasantly surprised at how charming some of the men can be," Jason suggested sensibly. "All I ask is that you give them a chance. No one can even speak with you if you hide in your room."

Gabrielle looked away. It was impossible for her to talk with him about a matter of such importance when his nonchalance was so very painful.

"Is your home nearby?"

"What's that got to do with anything?" Jason asked critically.

"Nothing. I just wonder if your home is at all like this one. I am merely trying to make polite conversation rather than argue with you over an issue I already consider resolved."

Jason drew his fingers through his dark curls, exasperated by her defiant attitude. "My home is some miles out of town. That's why I've been staying at the hotel. I live in the simple log cabin my father built when we first arrived in Oregon. Compared to Clayton's house it's little more than a shack, but it is adequate for my needs since I am seldom there and require little in the way of material comforts when I am."

"Are you not required to farm the land in order to keep the title?" Gabrielle asked curiously.

"Yes," Jason agreed with a chuckle. "I always manage to toss some seed about in the spring so anyone who comes to check will see crops growing, but I haven't yet gotten around to harvesting whatever wheat grew this fall. Maybe later this week I'll have an opportunity to go out there and do some work." The idea was certainly appealing to him. Any distraction that would take him away from Gabrielle was worth pursuing in his opinion. "Maybe I'll go tomorrow if Clayton can spare me."

"Most of the men seemed very anxious to show off their homes. It is all right for us to go with them for a visit, isn't it?" Gabrielle asked breathlessly. She crossed her fingers behind her back, hoping he'd invite her to see his house no matter how small or plain it might prove to be.

Jason hesitated for several moments, considering her question fully. "After what you girls survived on the trail, a brief trip out to one of the bachelor's farms should not prove particularly hazardous. I left early last night. Did one of the men actually impress you sufficiently that you agreed to go see his farm today?"

"Would it please you if one had?"

"It would astonish me!" Jason responded with a teasing grin.

Gabrielle clenched her fists at her sides. She was tempted to wipe the smirk from his face with a well-placed smack, but she did no more than smile. "I attempted to discuss my problem with you last night, Mr. Royal. Since you had so little interest in it then, I won't bore you with my plans for today. Now if you'll excuse me, I want to have some breakfast before it is time to leave."

Jason watched her walk toward the kitchen, the slow undulating roll of her hips hypnotically attractive, and he was furious with himself for not demanding that she tell him exactly where she was going and with whom. "Damn!" he said under his breath, not about to let her see how much the company she kept truly did matter to him. He decided right then that he'd not wait until Clayton approved of his plans. The minute his partner returned home he'd go out to his farm and stay there until he could untangle the knots Gabrielle MacLaren had tied in the once-smooth thread of his life. Taking a seat out on the front porch, he propped his feet up on the rail and hoped Clayton would arrive before the auburn-haired beauty's date came up the walk. He feared he'd be sorely tempted to fight the man for the maddening privilege of having Gabrielle's perverse company for the day. He sat up straight, shocked at the thought. Then he began to laugh. With Clayton gone, he was in charge and he'd simply forbid any of the young women to leave the house. Pleased that he had found an ideal solution for keeping an eye on one woman without arousing the suspicions of the others, he decided perhaps he'd remain in town a few more days after all.

Chapter XV

Clayton called Jason into his study just minutes before the second party was scheduled to begin.

"I think your decision to keep the girls here today was a wise one. It will undoubtedly whet the men's appetites for their company tonight." He leaned back against his desk and crossed his arms over his chest, pleased with the splendid way things seemed to be progressing. "It occurred to me today that I am old enough to have a daughter the age of our brides and I'd certainly not allow her to visit a man's home without a chaperon."

"There're just the two of us, Clay, and twenty-one young women. I didn't see how we were going to adequately chaperon them all so I insisted none leave. The men didn't seem too disappointed to visit their favorites here," Jason explained nonchalantly as if his concern had truly been for the welfare of all their charges rather than for only one.

"It worked for today at least; tomorrow I can't say what the mood will be. Eventually we'll have to let the men have some time alone with our young ladies or they'll never have a chance to propose."

"That's true." Jason went to the window, more to hide his smile than to admire the view. Gabrielle had had several callers, but he'd been unable to ascertain which man had wanted to take her out to his farm for the day. It didn't matter really, since she would not have been permitted to leave with any of them.

"Now for the second reason I needed to see you. It's Miss MacLaren," Clayton confided in a more serious tone.

Jason turned back to face his partner. His serene expression displayed none of his apprehension. "Gabrielle? What about her?" he inquired softly.

"She came to see me about an hour ago. It seems she wants out of the contract she signed. If Mr. Taylor again fails to appear we'd still be all right if she left, but if he comes tonight then we'd be one bride short. That would be decidedly awkward. I spoke several times with the Robinson family on our way here. Their elder daughter is attractive, so perhaps I could invite her to join our enterprise since Gabrielle is no longer interested."

"No, not yet," Jason cautioned forcefully. "Don't allow Gabrielle to leave. She's clearly the leader of her own group, and is admired by many of the other young women as well. If she bolts, several more may follow her. You'll be courting disaster if you allow her to back out now. Don't do it."

"I hadn't thought of the influence she exerts upon the others, but you're right as usual." Clayton frowned, cross with himself for not seeing the obvious. "I told Gabrielle I'd consider her request on the condition that she attend tonight's party regardless of whether she wishes to remain or not. She won't expect my answer for a day or two at least."

"Good. She may change her mind by then anyway." Jason was relieved that Gabrielle had been put off so easily. He'd not thought she'd go to Clay, but since she had he was glad his partner had not given in to her demand immediately. "Perhaps when she's had an opportunity to become better acquainted with the bachelors, the prospect of marriage won't prove so frightening."

"You think that's it? She's just nervous?" Clayton inquired

incredulously since he considered Gabrielle to be one of the more poised as well as one of the most beautiful of the group.

Jason shrugged. "It seems the most obvious possibility. Let's just hope she keeps her anxieties to herself rather than spreading them."

Clayton pulled his gold watch from his vest pocket and flipped open the cover. "We have no more time to discuss Miss MacLaren's problems now; the men will be arriving shortly. I know these parties are not nearly lively enough for your taste, but try to stay a little later tonight, will you? I had the devil of a time getting the men out of here last night. To say they were reluctant to leave is a gross understatement."

Jason chuckled as he walked to the door. "I'll make no promises, Clay, but I'll do my best to be more helpful if you think you'll need me."

"I know I will!" Clayton exclaimed heartily.

Horne had planned to serve a light supper that evening so each man might spend more time with one young woman rather than talking for a few minutes with them all. His housekeeper and the two maids had worked all day to prepare a buffet which would have delighted anyone, but it was especially tempting to the young women who'd had such a restricted diet for so many months. There were honey-cured hams and succulent roast chickens, string beans with bacon, coleslaw, thick slices of hot bread, plenty of freshly churned butter, and delicious wild-blackberry pies for dessert. It was a veritable feast. Before it was served each bachelor had the opportunity to select the young woman with whom he wished to share the fine meal. When several asked Jason what was keeping Gabrielle, he had no choice but to go upstairs to find her since he didn't want to send a young woman who did not already have a partner for supper after her. He cursed to himself as he mounted the stairs two at a time, but to his dismay the door of the room Gabrielle shared with her friends was ajar. The striking young woman was seated by the window, obviously dressed and groomed for the party.

"There are several men anxiously awaiting your company. Your hair looks splendid as does your gown; now why aren't you downstairs where you belong?" he called from the doorway.

Gabrielle was again wearing blue, this dress a softly flowing muslin which clung to her figure seductively as she turned to face him. "I was waiting for Joshua to arrive. Since he has yet to appear, I'm not going to the party. I told you last night that I wouldn't go, so why are you pretending to be surprised?"

Exasperated, Jason shook his head. "I know for a fact Clay told you to attend. It isn't your choice to make, Gabrielle."

Turning back toward the window, the lively redhead disagreed. "Do you recall telling me once to trust my own emotions? I thought it extremely good advice at the time, and it's what I intend to do now."

Jason did, indeed, remember giving her that advice, he could recall each exquisite detail of that morning clearly. That was the first time they'd made love and she'd called him darling— but only once. Perplexed by the calmness of her mood, he crossed the room and sat down on the foot of the bed nearest the window. "I had no idea my comments ever had the slightest effect upon you, so you must forgive me if I appear shocked when you say that at least one remark did. Your emotions, however, have nothing to do with attending the party tonight. Clayton told you to be there, and if I have to carry you down the stairs, you will go. Now why don't you spare both of us that embarrassment and just come with me without any further argument?"

"No," Gabrielle responded firmly. "I am not going to marry one of those men, Jason. It is as simple as that, and I'll not distract them from the other girls who truly are looking for a husband."

Watching her gaze intently out the window as if she were fascinated by the brilliance of the sunset, Jason regretted he'd had no opportunity to draw Gabrielle's face in profile. No cameo ever had a more lovely subject carved in relief, but unfortunately she appeared to be as unmovable as such a sculpture. He could think of no way to convince her to come downstairs. She'd refused a request he thought he'd worded very reasonably so he changed the subject momentarily.

"Have you told any of your friends of your decision?"

"No," Gabrielle admitted hesitantly. "It is not one I can easily explain. They are all very pleased with the men they've met, and I don't want to inflict my pain upon them when they are so happy."

"Yet you were going to go with one of the bachelors to his farm today, weren't you?" Jason suddenly remembered the conversation they'd had before breakfast and he realized her comments had been very contradictory.

"No. You said that, I didn't," Gabrielle explained coolly. "Iris was infuriated by your refusal to let her go with John Randolph, by the way. She wants to see a man's home before she makes up her mind to marry him, and in her opinion, you simply wasted the whole day for her. What made you change your mind about allowing us to leave?" She turned to face him then, her inquisitive glance as unsettling as her query.

"We are talking about you, not Iris," Jason reminded her sternly, adroitly avoiding the necessity of answering her question. He did not wish to lie about his motives, but he knew he could not reveal them. "Now you must attend tonight's party. I meant what I said. I'll toss you over my shoulder like a sack of flour if I have to, but I'm taking you downstairs right now." He rose to his feet as he spoke, hoping his sheer size might convince her to come with him quietly.

"No. You mustn't do that!" Gabrielle sprang to her feet, obviously greatly alarmed by his threat. It was too soon for her to be certain she'd become pregnant the last time they were together, but if she had, she desperately wanted his baby. Life had taught her how fleeting happiness could be, and so she dearly wanted a child as a living reminder of the love they'd shared, no matter how brief or one-sided it had been. "You need not treat me as if I were a bag of produce. I can walk down the stairs on my own." She nearly flew to the door, not waiting for him in her haste to escape a rude embrace that she feared might do her great harm. "Well, aren't you coming to the party too?"

Jason tried to think of what he'd said that had made such a difference. The woman had flatly refused to attend the party, and now she was telling him to hurry! It made no sense at all, but he came forward to walk by her side.

"Tell everyone you couldn't find your shoes or something; don't say you were talking with me."

Gabrielle eyed him coldly, her bright blue gaze icy with hatred. "Heaven forbid that I would admit such a thing, Mr. Royal!" Her head held high she preceded him down the stairs and said good evening so graciously to Michael Jenkins that he thought she was truly pleased to find him waiting for her at the bottom of the steps.

Jason stared after her, still attempting to discern some meaning in her conflicting statements and actions. She was not crazy or stupid. On the contrary, she was exceptionally bright so she must have had valid reasons for each of her decisions, but he was damned if he could understand them. "Women!" he growled unhappily. Then, forcing himself to adopt a pleasant expression, he went into the parlor to make certain none of the girls was alone. Again he had to remind the bachelors who seemed so fond of Iris that they could not neglect the other young women. He found the brunette's continual stream of flattery tiresome, but clearly many of the men were captivated by her rather theatrical type of charm and were displeased when he insisted they focus their attention elsewhere. To his immense relief, now that Gabrielle had consented to attend the gathering, she maintained a warm smile and seemed to be listening attentively to each man with whom she spoke. Jason was positive none of her comments would be insincere ones.

After supper the brides performed the songs they'd been rehearsing for many months, their voices now blending so harmoniously Jason's applause was as enthusiastic as that of the rest of the men. He waited until Clayton signaled that it was time to encourage the men to leave; then with his usual good-natured charm he ushered the bachelors through the front door. He followed them out into the night without a backward glance, but he could not shut Gabrielle out of his thoughts as easily as he had solved Clayton's problems for the evening. Taking charge of a group of twenty men was a far easier task than influencing one lissome beauty. Unfortunately time was now on her side rather than his, and that realization was doubly disconcerting.

"Gabrielle?" Erica whispered insistently. "Are you asleep?"

"No," Gabrielle admitted softly. It had taken her hours to fall asleep the previous night, and she anticipated another long bout of restlessness. Her mind gave her no peace but kept racing, memories crashing against each other with such violence she could not relax for even an instant, let alone long enough for sleep to overtake her. She could tell from the gentle sounds of deep breathing which surrounded her that only she and Erica still remained awake. "What is it?" she asked sleepily.

"I'm going to sneak out of the house before dawn and meet Lewis. Will you cover for me with Mr. Horne? Tell him I'm sleeping late or taking a bath—anything—so he won't become suspicious and demand to see me?"

Since Lewis and Erica had spent most of the evening together, Gabrielle wasn't surprised they had made plans to meet secretly. Her first reaction was to say no. She never told lies of any sort, but her own life was now so far from exemplary

303

she did not see how she could refuse.

"I doubt he'll notice. We're very seldom all together and you'll be back by evening, won't you?"

"Yes. At least I think so. Lewis wants to show me around his farm. He seems very proud of it so naturally I'm anxious to see it." Erica was quiet for several minutes and then asked shyly, "What do you suppose it's like to make love?" Her mother had given her no advice whatsoever, and while she was terribly curious, she was more than a little bit frightened as well.

Gabrielle turned over on her stomach and pounded her pillow in an attempt to make herself more comfortable while they talked. She didn't dare tell Erica the truth, but she hated to appear as innocent as the pretty blonde when she no longer was. "I think it must be very nice, like kissing a man you like only much better."

"Do you really think so? Lewis is very gentle. When he holds me to dance or takes my arm as we move from one room to the next his touch is most pleasant. Some of the men are so clumsy they've crushed my fingers with the force of their grip or nearly broken my toes with their efforts to dance. While their conversation is not crude, I can't help but want to avoid them."

"I know exactly who you mean," Gabrielle agreed sympathetically. "Perhaps they simply lack experience with women and do not realize we are far more fragile than we appear."

"Experience?" Erica asked skeptically. "Would that make such a great difference in a man's behavior?"

"I really don't know. Perhaps." Not wishing to discuss the matter any further, Gabrielle turned away. "Shouldn't you try to sleep if you must be up so early tomorrow?"

"Yes," Erica agreed reluctantly. After yawning noisily, she closed her eyes, hoping to get some rest before the sun rose. However, she was so excited by the prospect of spending the day with Lewis that she doubted she'd be able to sleep a wink.

Gabrielle hugged her pillow more tightly, glad Erica had not

304

chosen to pursue the subject of making love since it was such a dangerous one. At least Jason had said being with her was far more pleasurable than being with any other woman he'd ever known. That compliment provided scant solace, however, when he'd not thought the enjoyment she gave him so willingly worthy of a marriage proposal. Hot tears of anger stung her eyes, but she dared not give in to such a weakness for fear Erica would hear her sobs and demand to know why she was so distraught. She felt like leaving the house by herself before dawn also, simply to go for a walk and have a few moments of privacy since that was a luxury she'd not had for almost five months' time and sorely missed. She made a greater effort to relax, to rid herself of the tension which filled her slender body as well as her thoughts, but the memory of Jason's taunting smile was impossible to erase. She lay wide awake while her friends slept peacefully, their dreams filled with romantic visions of the men they liked best and soon hoped to marry.

Despite Gabrielle's desire to have some time alone, she slept so late there was no hope of avoiding her roommates' lively chatter. They were too excited to keep still, and she again hid her own sorrow while she listened to their enthusiastic comments about the bachelors. Barbara had still not made up her mind about whom she liked best, while Marlene and Margaret had both found men whose attentions they had hoped to keep. Johanna had spent the previous evening with a rather shy young man who seemed to share her deep religious convictions, and she was looking forward to seeing him again that day. Iris had left their room early, certain she could influence Clayton to let her visit John Randolph's farm, but to her chagrin, he did not appear to invite her. She did have several callers that morning, but she was terribly disappointed when they were not the men she'd wanted most to see.

After her friends went downstairs to enjoy the fresh air in the garden or to speak with their visitors, Gabrielle remained in their bedroom. She pretended to be busy sorting through her

305

wardrobe for things which needed mending, but in reality she was hoping to think of some effective way to postpone the inevitable proposal she knew Michael Jenkins was sure to make. He was a very nice man, and had it not been for the confusion Jason had created in her life, Jenkins would have been precisely the type of man she would have thought herself fortunate to marry when she'd answered the ad to become a mail-order bride. He was sincere, personable. His appearance and manners were pleasing, and perhaps with skillful tutoring he could even learn to dance well. Now Gabrielle felt guilty that he liked her so much. But when he came to see her that afternoon, she again found herself listening to his polite attempts at conversation, and was unable to tell him how hopeless his attraction to her was. She knew what she was doing was dishonest and she didn't want to hurt him. Obviously the longer she delayed speaking the truth, the more betrayed he would feel. Gathering all her courage, she had just started to tell him her position when the front door of Clayton's impressive home flew open with a tremendous crash and both she and Michael turned to see who had caused such an uproar.

Since Erica had made not the slightest attempt to be discreet, nearly everyone in the house heard her entrance. She was screaming at Lewis Bradley, shrieking at the top of her voice that he was a scoundrel to whom she'd never speak again. Not one to take such a fiery insult quietly, Lewis had followed her through the front door and was about to run straight up the stairs after her when Jason tackled him and wrestled him into Clayton's study.

Alarmed by her good friend's unexpectedly emotional arrival, Gabrielle turned to Michael. "Will you please excuse me? If Erica has come to some harm she may need my assistance."

Michael had been as badly startled as Gabrielle by Erica's hysterical entrance, but he had no desire to lose his attractive

306

companion. He reached out to take her hand, hoping to make her stay. "She appeared to be in perfect health to me. It's probably no more than a lovers' quarrel and you'll simply be interfering where you're not wanted. Don't go."

Gabrielle pushed his hand away as she rose to her feet. "I must," she stated simply and then with a light running step she left the parlor and hurried up the stairs. She found Erica in a dreadful state, lying across a cot and sobbing pathetically as though her heart were broken. Gabrielle knew immediately she'd been right to come upstairs to be with her. She sat down beside her friend and patted her back gently as she tried to ascertain what was wrong.

"What happened between you and Lewis? It can't possibly be so terrible as this," she offered sympathetically.

"No. It was worse!" Erica insisted in a high-pitched wail, more distraught than ever now that she had someone to heed her outraged cries.

A curious crowd had gathered at the bedroom door and Gabrielle rose quickly to ask them to disperse so she and Erica might have some privacy. She closed the door softly and then returned to her friend's side. "Mr. Horne is sure to scold you for leaving the house without permission, and he'll want to know exactly what happened. If you will tell me now what went wrong, I can help you think of some way to explain it to him so you won't be in any greater trouble than you already are."

Erica shook her head vigorously and continued to weep, too despondent to worry over what Clayton Horne would think of her behavior. When she heard a soft knock at the door, she sat up suddenly, looking about the room with a frantic glance as though searching for a safe place to hide. "Send whoever it is away, please!"

"Of course," Gabrielle agreed, but when she opened the door she found Jason standing in the hall. "Can't it wait?" she whispered, "Erica is too upset to speak with anyone now."

"No. It can't wait. Lewis didn't rape her, but she's behaving as if he did her some grievous injury. I won't permit such a tantrum to continue! Now kindly step aside."

Gabrielle knew better than to argue with Jason when he was in so foul a mood, but as soon as she allowed him to enter his manner changed completely. He waited a moment for Erica to compose herself; then, drawing a chair close to her bed, he sat down and began to speak in a low, comforting tone. "I think you should be far more angry with Clayton and me than with Lewis, Erica. Apparently we should have discussed the arrangement a lot of the men have had with Indian women and we failed to do it. It did not occur to us that it would upset any of you as greatly as this." He looked over at Gabrielle as if he expected some help from her, and she came forward.

"I don't understand what Mr. Royal is talking about, Erica. What has an Indian woman to do with you and Lewis?"

Erica dried her eyes on the back of her hand, sniffing loudly as she did so. "We went out to his farm, and it is as pretty a place as he'd told me it was," she began slowly. "His house is rather small, but very neatly kept. When I noticed a small rag doll on the mantel I asked whose it was."

"Then he told you about Raven and the baby?" Jason asked softly.

Erica nodded sadly, but she was unable to continue because a fresh wave of tears flooded her eyes. She threw herself across the bed again, sobbing with loud desperate wails, but she gave no further clue as to what was troubling her so greatly.

Gabrielle sat down beside her best friend. Being far too curious to let the matter drop, she glanced over at Jason. "I'd like to hear about Raven and her baby. Since Erica can't tell me, will you?"

Jason leaned back in his chair. "There's not all that much to tell. Lewis, like many of the men who came here alone, had an Indian mistress. They had a son, but he sent the boy and his mother home to her tribe when you women arrived because he wants a white wife. He'd never married Raven."

"You don't mean it?" Gabrielle asked with a sharp gasp. "He simply sent this Indian woman away, their child too, as if Indians aren't people who have feelings and worth? I can't believe any man would be so low." Clearly she was as appalled as Erica by what Lewis had done.

Jason shrugged noncommittally. "I'll admit our customs are far different than what you've known. That's why I said Clayton and I probably should have discussed this issue with you all, even though it is a delicate one. Raven and her baby boy were well provided for, sent home with money and gifts. Most likely she will soon marry an Indian man who will raise Lewis' son as his own. The Indian tribes have far more liberal views of such matters than we do. They don't regard any man as a half-breed you see, only as a man. All in all, the child will be far better off with his mother's people than if he had stayed with his white father. Lewis obviously made a great mistake in telling Erica about his mistress and child, but since he's not the only one of our bachelors who had such an arrangement, other young women may soon be as heartbroken as she is and I'd like to avoid that."

Gabrielle reached out to give Erica a soothing pat upon the back before she asked the question which was foremost in her own mind. "Do you have an Indian mistress too?"

Jason opened his mouth to give a flippant response, meaning to state only that he was too seldom home to require such a companion, but Gabrielle's glance was so filled with pain he suddenly wanted her to know the truth. "I'm not the sort of man who could send his children away, Gabrielle, so I've kept no Indian mistress nor do I ever intend to have one. But I don't fault the men who do."

"To have a mistress is one thing, Jason, to father children quite another. How many of the bachelors who have been coming to see us have families they have conveniently disposed of so as not to offend us?"

Jason went through the list in his mind. "About half I'd say, but they're living alone now."

"Well, I don't want some man who has an Indian child for my husband!" Erica vowed tearfully, her unhappiness undiminished by the amount of tears she'd shed.

Recalling how much she'd liked Lewis, Gabrielle tried to make Erica see his point of view. "I imagine Lewis has been terribly lonely. That he would want an agreeable companion is not impossible to understand, nor is the fact he would want a wife of his own kind difficult to comprehend. We knew the men wanted wives most desperately when we answered that ad in Kansas City." When Erica didn't respond she hesitated to continue that approach. "Why don't you just rest for a while and we can talk about this later." She glanced at Jason then, sorry she'd been of so little help. "I don't know what you and Clayton could say to the others. Lewis appears to have been honest in describing the way he's lived, but perhaps having had a mistress and son is not something a man should reveal to his prospective bride."

"Definitely not," Jason agreed. He liked Erica very much. She and Lewis had seemed made for each other until she'd come home in such a hysterical state. "I'll talk with the men first. This is not a scene I want to see repeated." He rose to his feet and replaced the chair beside the dresser on his way to the door.

Following him, Gabrielle reached out to touch his sleeve lightly. "We are all very young, naïve in so many ways. Certainly no farmer we've ever known has kept a mistress, so it's understandable that Erica was deeply shocked."

"Would such an admission change your choice of husband?" Jason inquired curiously.

Gabrielle whispered so Erica would not overhear. "Why can't you remember that I'm not going to marry any of the bachelors? Their habits are, therefore, none of my concern."

Jason did not reply, but the dark glance he gave her spoke volumes, all things she had no wish to hear. As he turned away

310

she closed the door and leaned back against it, attempting unsuccessfully to shut out the sharp pain his indifference continued to cause her. She forced herself to think of Erica instead, for she could well imagine how devastated she was to learn that Lewis had conveniently sent away his Indian wife and child to make room for her. Such an act was despicable to Gabrielle. She didn't care if the other men excused it by saying half-Indian children would be better off with their mother's tribe. It was clear the Indian women had simply been used and then tossed aside at the men's first opportunity to marry white women. How could any woman accept a man with such a shocking lack of morals as a husband. Jason might see such an arrangement as unacceptable because he considered children too precious to be sent away, but how had he treated her? It was clear her happiness mattered so little to him that he wanted to see her married to someone else, and as soon as possible. When she became another man's bride, his conscience would be clear, for she'd be another man's responsibility, not his. She had failed in her purpose, she realized, for even when she'd tried to focus upon Erica's problem she had again returned to contemplation of her own.

She paced restlessly up and down beside the bed she and her friend shared, unable to provide Erica with any consoling thoughts when her own problems were so severe. Fortunately, exhausted by tears, Erica had fallen asleep so Gabrielle's lack of sympathy went unnoticed. When she moved to the window she was surprised to see it was nearly sundown. Where had the afternoon gone? She'd been talking with Michael, and then . . . "Oh no, Michael!" she exclaimed with deep remorse. What must the man think of her for leaving him so rudely and never returning to the parlor? She could not recall the plans for the evening, more dancing perhaps, or musical entertainment of another type. It didn't really matter. She'd stay with Erica regardless of what amusement Clayton presented. Perhaps, without her presence to distract him, Michael would

311

find another young woman who would respond to his warmth and kindness as she'd been unable to do. She sincerely hoped he would since he didn't deserve to be hurt because she'd been too cowardly to refuse his attentions.

Soon her other roommates tiptoed into the bedroom, wide-eyed and curious. They wanted to dress for the evening, but Gabrielle put a finger to her lips, warning them not to awaken Erica. There would be time enough for the truth later. More than enough time, she was certain, but Marlene could not wait to ask a question and she came close.

"Is it true Erica won't marry Lewis because he kept an Indian woman?" she whispered shyly.

"It is true he kept an Indian woman, but I'll not speak for Erica. She'll have to tell you what her plans are herself when she's able."

Marlene looked down at the sleeping woman, her expression a forlorn one. "He told her the truth about himself and lost her. That's what happened, isn't it?"

"I make no claim to be able to predict the future, Marlene. I can't say what will happen between Erica and Lewis now." She turned away, thinking their brief conversation over, but Marlene moved to block her path.

"Wait! I have been debating with myself whether or not to reveal my true age to Charles. Since I think he likes me as much as I like him, I feel he deserves such honesty, but I dare not speak the truth if I'll lose him for it!"

"None of the men has even thought to ask my age, Marlene. Why do you think Charles will care how old you are? It is so trivial a concern I wish you would cease to worry over it," Gabrielle remarked critically.

"That is easy for you to say because you have no secrets!" Marlene responded impatiently, annoyed that Gabrielle had been so unsympathetic to her plight when she'd always been the most understanding of friends.

"Secrets," Gabrielle thought, why that's all I have! Sud-

312

denly she had to get out of the crowded bedroom. Iris was in a belligerent mood, ordering Margaret out of the way so she could smooth out the full skirt of her gown, but Gabrielle brushed past them both on the way to the door, caring little that she shoved the young women in her haste. As she rushed down the stairs, determined to leave the accursed house where she was surrounded by so many insoluble problems, she heard male voices in the parlor and knew she'd not be able to sneak out the front door without being observed. She could go back upstairs and use the stairway at the other end of the hall. Then she could exit through the kitchen. But she would be seen by the help and her absence would be swiftly reported. Infuriated that she seemed to meet a dead end at every turn, she stood still, and when her temper began to cool, she realized it was Jason who was speaking. She moved stealthily to the doorway of the parlor so she could overhear what was being said.

"I've asked Lewis to go home and stay there for a few days, but I hope the rest of you will have learned something from this regrettable incident. The young ladies we've brought here to be your brides are just that, ladies, and they deserve to marry gentlemen. You do not need to apologize for the way you've lived your lives before you met them. That is your own business. I strongly suggest that one of the finest qualities any man can have is the ability to keep his own counsel. The young ladies are certain to gossip amongst themselves about this and I can't control that, but I will say it is most unfortunate that Erica was so badly hurt. It was a great shock for her to learn that the man she admired had not only kept an Indian mistress but had fathered a child he'd abandoned as well. You all know the scandal such actions would have caused in your hometowns, so you should be able to predict how the women who've come here to be your brides would perceive such behavior. They will clearly see it as most distressing and will probably consider it immoral as well. Now, is there still a doubt in any man's mind as to how he wants to represent himself to

313

our young ladies?"

There was some low mumbling, one man offering sympathy to another who had much to hide, but all thought Jason's advice was worth taking and no protests were offered. Finally, one man raised his hand and made a suggestion. "I think the sooner we marry the young ladies the better. Do either you or Mr. Horne have any objection if we ask the preacher to start performing the wedding ceremonies as soon as we can get them to say yes?"

Jason laughed, delighted that one man still had his sense of humor. "None at all, and I'll be proud to be the best man for any of you." His response was met with applause and laughter. The solemn mood of the gathering broken, the men began to tease each other about their choice of brides.

Having heard all she wished to, Gabrielle drew away. She was turning back toward the stairs as Jason walked out of the parlor. He saw her and called her name in a hoarse whisper.

"Gabrielle! You are not to breathe a word of what you just heard me say. Do you understand?" He had done his best to smooth over an incident which could have proven disastrous for a great many of the men, and he wasn't pleased to think she had overheard his remarks. "You must forget what I told you about how many of the men were involved with Indian women too. That was something I never should have admitted."

Gabrielle stood on the bottom step, watching Jason's expression closely as he continued to lecture her sternly. His striking good looks were such a distraction that she could scarcely focus her attention upon his words, but she understood his message plainly. When he finally paused to take a breath, she responded confidently. "To abandon an Indian woman and a child in favor of one of us is unforgivable in my view, Jason, but I think you are right in advising the men to keep such a secret to themselves. It would be far better for a man to carry such a sin to his grave than to inflict that burden upon his wife when she is entirely innocent of the deed. I will not spread the tale. You need have no worries that I will cause any of your bachelors, or should I say the men who have pretended to be bachelors, any more problems than they have created for themselves."

Jason was caught off guard by her ready cooperation and realized he'd been far too abrupt. "I'm sorry, none of this is your fault. Forgive me for being so rude."

"Why not?" Gabrielle replied flippantly. "I've forgiven you for everything else." She ran up the stairs then, and even without looking back she knew his eyes had changed from soft smoky gray to a black as deep as his shiny curls. He'd been that angered by her insult. But, by God, he had deserved it!

Chapter XVI

Sunday morning, Erica astonished her roommates by dressing for church and announcing her intention to attend the services with the rest of the brides. "I made the mistake of giving in to my emotions last night, but this morning I realize I was a fool to allow my disappointment in Lewis to cause me such unnecessary grief. He is not the only bachelor in Oregon City. I plan to use my time well today and find another man who will please me as I now know Lewis never will." She brushed her honey-colored curls with long easy strokes, clearly in complete control of herself that morning regardless of the unfortunate spectacle she'd created the previous afternoon.

Gabrielle thought her friend a bit too reserved and said so. "I don't think you should make any decisions without careful consideration, Erica. Lewis made no secret of his past, and apparently his situation is not unique. Since none of us can change the past, it is the future we'll live together which should be our primary concern."

Erica sat her brush aside but continued to appraise her reflection critically in the mirror above the dresser. The skin around her eyes was a bit puffy; still, for having cried herself to sleep she thought she looked remarkably good that morning. "No son of mine is going to have an Indian half brother, that's all there is to it. If none of the bachelors Clayton Horne has provided for us can swear his only children will be the ones he'll give me then I simply will not marry until I do meet such a man."

Gabrielle sat, silently remembering how fine a man Scream of Lightning had appeared to be. She'd certainly not be ashamed if he were her own half brother, or thus related to the sons she might one day have. "I know Indians frighten you far more than they do me, so I can understand why Lewis' past has affected you so greatly. If you can neither forgive him for it nor simply accept it as the way men have lived here, then you should refuse to see him again for you'll be happier with other mates."

"What if Michael Jenkins were to tell you he'd not only had an Indian woman keep his house and warm his bed, but that he'd fathered a half-breed brat as well? Are you saying you'd still consider him a fine prospect for a husband? Could you forgive such a disgrace, or merely overlook it?" She wheeled around to face Gabrielle, her anger bringing a bright blush to her cheeks and making her green eyes glow with a fierce light.

Gabrielle rose from the bed and walked to the dresser to use the mirror to put on her bonnet. She tied the ribbons securely beneath her chin in an attractive bow. She'd stopped curling her hair now that she'd decided not to continue the pretense that she was one of the brides. The flowing red tresses fell to her waist, their dark auburn hue glossy in the morning sunlight which filled the room. While she appeared to be engrossed in her own appearance, she was in fact concentrating on formulating some sensible reply. "That is merely borrowing trouble, Erica. He may not have such a story to tell, or if he does, he may choose to keep it to himself. That's not a question I'll answer."

Frustrated by that noncommittal reply, Erica turned a curious glance upon the other occupants of the room. "Well, what about the rest of you? Do you think I'm being unreasonable in not wanting to share my husband with a squaw?"

Iris smiled knowingly. "These are mature men, Erica, not the innocent teenage boys you may have known, and I have no interest in hearing of their exploits with other women. I will expect my husband to be faithful to me after we are married, but I'll make no judgments on the way he's lived before we met. I shall merely expect him to be discreet about his past, as a gentleman should be. I'll ask no more than that of him."

Barbara shrugged. "I can't imagine any of the men in whom I'm interested even wanting an Indian maiden, so I've no idea what I'd say if one made such a confession to me."

Margaret shook her head, having no opinion in the matter, while Marlene blushed deeply, too shocked by the possibility that Charles might have had an Indian mistress to make any comment. Johanna picked up her Bible as she went to the door. "I for one would do exactly what you have done, Erica. I'd not consider a man worthy of being my husband if he had not married the mother of his child, be she Indian or white. Now we really must hurry or we shall be late for church, and I'm certain the entire community will turn out to meet us."

Happy to leave a discussion in which she wished to take no further part, Gabrielle followed Johanna down the stairs while the other young women completed their preparations. Saturday night she had had plenty of time to think while Erica had slept and everyone else had been at the party downstairs. As soon as they returned from church she was going to tell Clayton Horne she was leaving, regardless of what his decision might be on the matter. There was at least one hotel in the town, she knew that for a fact. She'd take a room there and look for work the first thing Monday morning. She had been independent enough to choose to come to Oregon, so she was certain she could find a way to be self-supporting in order to stay.

When Gabrielle stepped out onto the front porch, Michael

319

Jenkins rushed up the steps to meet her. Like most of the men, he had brought his buggy to Clayton's home that morning. He wanted to escort Gabrielle to church and home again since it would be an opportunity for at least a few minutes of private conversation.

"I have my buggy, may I offer you a ride to church this morning, Miss MacLaren?" He gripped his hat nervously, hoping she would not refuse his politely worded request.

Gabrielle was so ashamed of the way she'd left Michael in the parlor on Saturday afternoon, never to return, that she dared not hurt his feelings again. "Why thank you, I didn't realize the church was too distant to walk."

"It is on the opposite side of town." Pleased by her ready acceptance, Michael took her arm to direct her to his vehicle, which he'd spent considerable time washing and polishing that morning. He helped her up onto the seat and then pretended to check his horse's harness for some flaw until everyone else had left for the church. He then climbed up into the seat and said with a hopeful smile, "We will have such a brief time to converse on the way to church and back, I was hoping you'd come home with me instead. There will be such a crowd at the service this morning I doubt our absence will be noted."

Michael was such a dear man, the light in his brown eyes so warm and caring, that Gabrielle knew she must tell him of her decision to leave before she told Clayton. "Yes, I would like very much to have some time to talk privately with you. Do we need to go all the way to your farm though? Isn't there some picturesque spot nearby? The scenery is so pretty here. Almost any place will do."

"I want to take you home," Michael answered promptly, his plans apparently already made. "The trip is not a long one and the road is quite good at this time of year."

"All right then," Gabrielle agreed. Knowing how greatly what she had to reveal would disappoint him, she thought he should at least have the comfort of hearing it in his own home. The beauty of the Willamette Valley was spectacular in the autumn, the day warm yet with a touch of crispness which promised winter was not far behind. The road was lined with tall firs, and Michael explained that fallen branches often blocked the way after a heavy rain storm. He kept up a steady stream of conversation, and away from the rather stilted atmosphere of the parties at Clayton's home, his personality was surprisingly charming.

"I always keep an ax with me, as I've had to chop up branches which were too heavy to move out of this road on more than one occasion. The firs were here first though, so I can't blame them for dropping their branches so carelessly," he confided with a teasing grin.

"You must have had to work very hard to clear your land if it is covered with trees as tall as these," Gabrielle remarked, her respect for the pleasant young man growing.

"Very hard doesn't begin to describe what is more torture than work, but I keep at it every chance I get. My land is nearly all cleared now, but I kept a few trees near the house. They provide much-needed shade in summer and block the winds in winter. I figured I needed them more than another quarter acre of wheat or oats."

"Yes, that sounds like a very sensible idea," Gabrielle agreed, and when at last they arrived at his home she thought the naturalness of the setting very appealing. While built of logs rather than the finished planks Iris insisted upon having, his house was well crafted, and Gabrielle thought it more than adequate for the needs of most young families. She strolled around the yard while he took care of his horse, then they went inside and she accepted his offer of tea. She sat down in the rocking chair near the fireplace and watched him prepare it, hoping as he brought sugar and cream that she would be able to think of some tactful way to tell him what she knew had to be said. He seemed to be so pleased to have her as his guest, and she was dreadfully sorry she would not be the bride she knew he wanted so badly.

Michael drew up a chair close to hers and, after taking a sip of his tea, set his cup down on the neatly swept floor by his side. "There's something I want to say to you and there's no sense in waiting."

"Please, Michael. There's something I think I should tell you first." Gabrielle took a deep breath, hoping to get it over with quickly.

"No. I insist you listen to me first," Michael ordered with surprising conviction. "You are very sweet, Gabrielle, far more beautiful than I had dreamed any of the women would be." He smiled shyly then, praying he was correct in his assumption. "I hope you like me too."

"Of course I do!" Gabrielle replied promptly, but she didn't want him to continue. "Now won't you give me an opportunity to say something too?"

"No, not yet. Let me finish. Whenever we talk you make all the correct replies, but I never feel that I have your full attention. Is there something about me which offends you? I know my dancing is poor but—"

Gabrielle set her cup aside too and reached out to take his hands tenderly in hers. "Michael, I think you are delightful company and I always enjoy being with you. I had no idea my inattentiveness was so obvious, but the fault is most certainly not yours. It is entirely mine."

"If it's one of the other men you want, you can just say so, Gabrielle. I won't like it, but I'll understand." Michael brought her trembling hands to his lips, kissing her fingertips lightly, no longer feeling in the least bit shy now that they were in his home.

"I wish that I did have so simple an explanation to offer," Gabrielle began slowly. "When I first spoke with Mr. Horne in Kansas City, I thought coming here to Oregon to marry one of you men would be the very best future I could ever hope to have. So much happened to us on the way, however—the trip was a long and strenuous one emotionally as well as physically—now that I am here, I know it would be wrong of me to marry. Please don't ask me to explain why, but it is

322

impossible for me to accept a proposal from any of the men. I have already spoken to Mr. Horne about leaving the group, but he was very reluctant to let me go. You must have realized there are twenty-one of us and only twenty men. Since I was the last woman accepted for this venture, I am the one who should leave, and I intend to move out of the house this afternoon. I shall stay at the hotel."

Shocked by such an unexpected response to his question, Michael simply stared at Gabrielle for several moments. "That excuse is a very noble one, but it makes no sense. There are plenty of men who'd pay three times what we did to meet you ladies. In fact, I heard there was another man, but for some reason he hasn't shown up at any of the parties. If it is just a question of numbers, I'm sure that can be straightened out. You needn't refuse a marriage proposal because of that."

"No, it is only one of the reasons I can't stay, Michael. Nothing you can say will make any difference to me. My decision is made and I'll not change it," Gabrielle insisted firmly.

A slow smile spread across Michael's lips as he asked a teasing question. "You came here with me though, didn't you?"

Gabrielle tried to pull her hands from his, but he held on more tightly, seemingly convinced that no matter what she said her presence in his home meant more than it did. "Yes, because I believed you to be a gentleman and I expect you to behave like one!"

Michael began to laugh, greatly amused by the proud light which burned so brightly in Gabrielle's lovely blue eyes. "I do believe, Miss MacLaren, that I have your full attention at long last, and that's not an opportunity I'll let go to waste."

Jason had walked from the hotel to the white frame church, knowing the preacher would probably be so shocked to see him attending the service he'd be unable to deliver his sermon, a risk he'd willingly take. He waited out front as Clayton arrived with the first of the brides. That men who attended church as seldom as he did had also chosen to come on this particular morning surprised him at first, but he soon realized they were seeking to make a good impression and ceased to think it odd. As the last of the young women arrived he began to worry about Gabrielle who was still missing. He made his way into the already crowded church and found Clayton.

"Why didn't Gabrielle come with the others?"

Frowning, Clayton looked back over his shoulder at those seated in the pews behind him. "Isn't she here yet? She was with Michael Jenkins. They should have been here by now."

"I'll see what's keeping them," Jason responded, with what he hoped would pass for a smile, but as soon as he had looked up the street and found it deserted, he knew Michael was probably well on the way to his farm with Gabrielle. He did not find that alternative to Sunday morning services acceptable, and he ran the whole way to Clayton's home, cutting corners and leaping over picket fences in his haste to get there since Duke and Sunny were stabled in his partner's barn. He saddled the two stallions with such a frantic economy of motion he had them galloping down the road in less than five minutes time. He and Michael Jenkins were acquaintances only, certainly not close friends. He scarcely knew the man, but he was positive he didn't want Gabrielle to spend even a minute alone with him. He urged Duke to his fastest pace, then realized he'd been stupid not to ride Sunny since he was the far swifter of the two mounts. The red horse did not enjoy being led and drew alongside Duke tossing his mane in the wind as a clear challenge, but Jason kept his own horse under firm control and shouted to Sunny in an effort to make him behave as well as he usually did with Gabrielle. When at last Duke began to tire, Jason reined him in and changed mounts. He then gave the roan his head while Duke loped along behind them and got his second wind.

Jason knew where Michael Jenkins lived, and he urged

Sunny to cover the remaining distance swiftly. Gabrielle was so contrary a young woman he never knew what to expect from her, but if she had gone to Michael's farm rather than coming to church, he knew there was a very real possibility she had decided to marry the man. How he could have been such a complete fool Jason didn't know, but it suddenly no longer mattered to him that she was still in love with a dead man. He wanted her for his wife; that choice was now the only one he'd consider. He whipped Sunny's flanks with the ends of his reins, terrified that he'd be too late to win Gabrielle for his own. Why had he not taken his own advice, trusted his own emotions, no matter how greatly making such a defiant young woman his bride would complicate his life? He didn't need a wife, but he needed Gabrielle too desperately to worry over that confusing contradiction. He had to have her, and if he had to fight Michael Jenkins, or all the other men combined, to win her it would be well worth the pain.

Sunny sensed his rider's growing sense of urgency and lengthened his stride, grateful for the freedom to run after spending several days in a cramped stall in Clayton's barn. He nearly flew down the road, the sound of his thundering hoofbeats muffled by the softness of the dirt and the whisper of the gentle wind in the tall firs. As fleet as the wind itself he could have run forever had Jason not sighted the narrow path which led to Michael's home and reined him to a far slower pace so they would not arrive at the man's doorstep in such an obvious state of uncontrolled panic.

Gabrielle did not want to believe Michael would attempt to keep her there against her will or that he would force himself upon her, but those possibilities were so real she wrenched her hands from his and ran toward the front door. She flung it open and dashed onto the porch, not certain how she'd return to town if Michael would not take her, and at that very instant Jason rode into view. That he'd again ridden Sunny so hard did

325

not please her, but she considered that a minor disappointment when he'd managed to arrive at precisely the moment she needed assistance so desperately. She waved to him and smiled, confident she'd now have a way home.

Michael had followed Gabrielle out onto the porch, and finding Jason Royal riding up the path startled him badly. "I didn't mean to frighten you," he whispered hoarsely, for were the pretty young woman to ask Jason for protection he had no doubt the man would give him a beating and a severe one. He wiped his suddenly perspiring palms on his suit coat and tried to think of something clever to say or do. He desperately wanted to prevent a painful confrontation. Jason Royal had once had a reputation for being hot tempered and Michael had no desire to provoke the man. He knew the result would be a bloody fight, and the blood split would be his own. He was so badly frightened that he began to shake and then despised himself for letting Gabrielle see what a coward he was.

Gabrielle glanced up at Michael, surprised by his obvious terror at Jason's appearance. Knowing a fight between the two men would be decidedly unequal, she had no intention of being the cause of such an unfortunate mismatch. She reached for his hand and gave his fingers a comforting squeeze. "Don't worry so, I won't say a thing if you will promise to take me back to town as soon as he leaves."

Michael nodded gratefully, having no time to reply in words as Jason leaped from Sunny's back and strode toward them. A bluff seemed the best greeting, so he came up with what he hoped would be an amusing one. "What's the problem, Jason? I didn't think you'd mind so much if we missed Sunday School." Gabrielle still held his hand and he hoped that intimate gesture would be enough to discourage Jason from making any fuss over her being with him instead of in church.

Jason frowned angrily. What he'd expected to find he didn't know, but clearly Gabrielle was enjoying herself and he did not intend her to stay. "I am responsible for Miss MacLaren, Michael. We had planned to begin giving permission this afternoon for the young ladies to go wherever an escort wished to take them. Had you had the simple courtesy to make such a request to either Clayton or me this morning, we would have told you what our new policy is. Since you didn't bother to inform us where Gabrielle would be, I had to make the trip out here myself to be certain she returns safely to town immediately." He focused his attention upon Gabrielle then. "I brought Sunny so you'd have your own mount to ride. Let's go."

"You knew damn well where Gabrielle was, Jason, and that I'd see her home at a reasonable hour too." Once Michael knew Gabrielle would not dispute his word, he had the confidence to challenge the stronger man, at least verbally. "You needn't take her with you now, it's my responsibility to see she returns home since I brought her here."

"I said Miss MacLaren is leaving now. There will be no argument about it." Jason took a step forward, not about to back down.

Not wanting this unfortunate situation to deteriorate any further, Gabrielle suggested what she thought was the most sensible solution. "I will be happy to return to town now if you insist upon it, Mr. Royal, but I would prefer to ride in Mr. Jenkins' buggy rather than on horseback since I am wearing such nice clothing." She gestured gracefully to the soft woolen skirt of the dove gray suit she wore. The outfit, trimmed with black velvet ribbon, was clearly not intended for use as a riding habit. "I am wearing slippers rather than shoes with a heel, and that would be dangerous. My foot might slip through the stirrup and cause me to fall."

Jason swore an emphatic oath under his breath, knowing she was correct about the unsuitability of her attire. "As you wish, Miss MacLaren. I will follow the buggy so there is no chance Mr. Jenkins again takes it upon himself to choose a destination other than the approved one." He walked back to where he'd left the two horses and this time swung himself up into Duke's saddle.

Considering himself extremely lucky to have escaped with no more than a sarcastic rebuke from Jason, Michael went immediately to bring his buggy to the front of the house. He helped Gabrielle up into the seat, then took his place beside her and clucked to his horse. When they had reached the main road, he turned quickly to be certain Jason was far enough behind not to overhear his remarks and then he began to apologize. "Truly I did not mean to frighten you so badly. I was only teasing you. I would not have expected even so much as a kiss, but that is no excuse for my lack of manners. That you did not tell Jason Royal how rude I was was very generous of you."

Gabrielle tried to smile, but her heart was still beating so rapidly she could scarcely draw a deep breath. "Rude is not a strong enough term, Michael. You must promise never to give any of the other girls such a fright or I will tell Jason what you did as soon as we get home."

"I will promise whatever you like, but please do not set Royal on me." Michael's fear was too deep to hide and he turned away, ashamed he couldn't give a better accounting of himself.

Gabrielle knew exactly why Michael was now so eager to please her. "As long as I have your word that your conduct will be that of a gentleman, I'll forget the incident. I have no wish to see you take a beating; I'd not enjoy that any more than you would. Jason can be as vicious as a mad dog and I'd not set him on anyone unless I had no other choice."

"You've seen him fight?" Michael asked curiously.

"Twice, in fact. That was more than enough." Gabrielle folded her hands primly in her lap and gave her full concentration to the enchanting view. "This is such a pretty road; I'm sorry to hear it becomes so difficult to traverse in the winter."

Puzzled by her abrupt change of subject, Michael nonetheless thought himself fortunate she'd accepted his apology so graciously. "It's damn near impossible to get through to town after the first rainstorm, but if you're determined to move into

328

the hotel and live there, then I will consider the journey well worth the effort no matter how difficult it proves to be. That is, if you would be willing to see me after today."

Gabrielle had tried to explain her feelings, but it was clear that Michael would not accept her withdrawal from the group of brides no matter where she chose to reside. "I am very flattered that you like me, despite the fact I am usually so preoccupied with my own thoughts that I can't give our conversations the attention they deserve. It would be far better, however, if you concentrated your attentions upon one of the other young women." Having a sudden inspiration, she suggested her best friend. "Perhaps Erica Nelson. She's spent most of her time with Lewis Bradley, but she'll not even speak to him now. I am certain she would be pleased to accept your calls."

Michael couldn't help but laugh. "After that scene she created yesterday afternoon, I'd say she'd be lucky to have any of us tip his hat were she walking down street, let alone call on her."

"Oh no. Is that true? Have you men agreed to snub her simply to get even for what she did to Lewis? That's cruel, Michael, terribly cruel. She can't help the way she feels any more than I can control my own emotions."

"But you expect me to control mine?" Michael asked bitterly. "Do you really think I can forget in one day that you are the woman I want and attempt to charm another simply for the practice?"

"I am sorry if that is the way my suggestion sounded." Gabrielle moved closer to his side, putting her arm in his. "Please forgive me, I have become so involved in my own dilemma I can't seem to consider the feelings of others as I should." She recalled how rude she'd been to Marlene the previous evening and regretted that too. "I should not have run off and left you sitting alone in the parlor yesterday, but Erica was so miserable I didn't want to leave her by herself."

"Well, if it is Indian women that worry you too, I've never

329

found a one I considered attractive enough to even speak with, let alone invite into my home." He shook his head, not knowing what more to say to impress her. "It's because I'm so tired of living such a solitary life that I leaped at the chance Clayton offered to have a bride."

Gabrielle laid her head upon his shoulder and closed her eyes. "I am sorry, Michael, dreadfully sorry, but I can't be the woman you want."

The young man smiled. It felt very nice to have her cuddled up against him so closely. As long as it was not another man but her own confusion he was battling, he decided patience might be the best weapon. He put his arm around her shoulders and gave her an affectionate hug. "It will all work out for the best, Gabrielle, it always does."

"That's a wonderful thought. I only wish it were true." Gabrielle sighed wistfully.

"Oh, believe me, it is true," Michael vowed confidently. It was still a long way into town and he planned to make the trip as slowly as possible, savoring each precious moment he had with the beautiful Gabrielle MacLaren. If she did actually move into the hotel she'd need help with her luggage, so he'd just stick around Clayton's and show her how helpful he could be. Lost in his own dreams of the future, he forgot all about Jason Royal and did not once look back to see if the man was still following them.

Jason actually had to draw Duke to a halt or he would have passed Michael's buggy in a walk the man was traveling so slowly. As he gave the horses a rest for a few minutes, Sunny eyed him suspiciously, clearly seeing no good reason for having raced down the road in one direction only to turn around and walk back the same way at a snail's pace. The stallion's glance was, as always, defiant; and Jason gave him a dirty look in return. "Think I'm crazy as usual, don't you, Sunrise? Well you are damn fortunate to be a horse rather than a man who has to put up with your mistress' tricks." He tapped his heels against Duke's sides then, starting off at a walk and cursing bitterly the entire way back to Clayton's house. When they at last arrived, he dismounted quickly and walked up to Gabrielle.

"I want to speak with you as soon as I have taken Duke and Sunny to the barn. Wait for me in Clayton's study." As he turned to leave, she called after him.

"I beg your pardon? I am certain I could not possibly have understood you since you are usually so polite. I don't believe I heard you say please." Gabrielle was tired, and in as ill-tempered a mood as Jason.

"You will please wait for me in Clayton's study! Now is that plain enough for you?" Jason repeated his directions in an angry snarl, and then, yanking the horses' reins with a fierce grip, he led them away without waiting for her to offer any further criticism.

Michael was stunned by that hostile exchange, because of what it revealed rather than the angry tone of the participants. "It's Royal, isn't it? He's the one you want. You said your feeings about getting married had changed during the trip out here. He's the reason why, isn't he?"

Since he seemed more astonished than provoked with her, Gabrielle saw no reason to deny the truth he had just discovered. "Yes, but I hope you will keep that secret to yourself since it would hurt all three of us badly if you were to reveal it."

Michael's dark eyes narrowed slightly, his confusion plain in his glance. "Of course I'll keep it to myself. It's easy to see why any woman would be impressed with Jason Royal, but surely you must know he's definitely not the marrying kind. You'll just be wasting your time if you wait for a proposal from him."

"Yes, I know that," Gabrielle admitted sadly. "It is my right to do so, however. But I'll not waste your time, Michael. If Erica doesn't appeal to you, find one of the others who does and soon!" She reached up to kiss his cheek sweetly, then left

331

him standing beside his buggy as she ran up the steps of the impressive home and hurried inside. She found the bedroom she shared empty now that the bachelors could invite her friends to go elsewhere. She removed her bonnet, washed her hands and face, and then brushed her hair before she went downstairs to Clayton's study. She had to wait only a minute or two before Jason came into the room and slammed the door soundly, but she'd had long enough to decide what she wanted to say.

"Must you be so dramatic? You have my attention; you needn't slam the door so loudly to get it." She lifted her hand to her forehead, not looking forward to another confrontation with Jason. Her head ached already just thinking what he'd say. "I find it difficult to believe it upset you so greatly to find I'd gone to Michael's farm rather than to church, especially if you'd planned to allow us to go where we pleased this very afternoon."

Jason walked around the desk and sat down in Clayton's chair. He leaned back to make himself comfortable, attempting to project a more relaxed mood now that he was finally alone with Gabrielle. Rather than reacting to her sarcastic comment, he began his own line of questioning. "Did Michael propose to you? He certainly had plenty of time to do it. I swear I could have walked here faster than he brought you home in his buggy."

"Whether or not he proposed and the speed with which he wishes to travel are none of your business, Jason." Gabrielle sat up straight then, preparing for the long and bitter scene she knew would be forthcoming.

"How he wishes to travel may not be one of my legitimate concerns, I'll grant you that, but whether or not he proposed to you certainly is. I brought you to Oregon to be a bride. Yesterday you told me you weren't going to marry any of the bachelors, but this morning you went out to Michael's farm. Even you must admit that seems a bit contradictory, or have you decided you do want to get married after all?"

"No," Gabrielle responded in a vain attempt to control her temper. "Michael has made no secret of his interest in me, and I thought he deserved to be told I'd decided not to marry before I moved out of this house. I didn't want him to come here especially to see me and find me gone."

"Hell, you could have told him that on the front porch. You didn't have to ride all the way out to his farm to do it," Jason scoffed rudely.

Gabrielle looked away, seeing no point in arguing over what she'd done. "If I have satisfied your curiosity, may I please be excused?"

"No. Not until I have satisfied yours," Jason answered calmly. "I've decided to tell you the truth about Joshua Taylor since you've taken such a personal interest in him."

"You mean he's come here? You've finally met him?" Gabrielle leaned forward, very curious indeed.

"Not exactly." Jason took a deep breath, attempting to compose his thoughts in some rational order before he continued. "I'm uncertain where to begin. Perhaps you remember the night we had dinner in Kansas City? I gave you my hotel room when there was none available for you."

"How could I possibly forget your generosity? What has it to do with Mr. Taylor though?" Gabrielle wanted him to stick to the point of his story.

"Quite a bit actually. I offered to find some way for you to come to Oregon, but you misunderstood my motives and said you'd come as one of the brides or not at all."

Gabrielle blushed deeply, recalling that scene all too well. She had sense enough not to point out her appraisal of his motives had been shockingly accurate however. She wasn't in the least bit ashamed of what had happened between them, but she regretted that it had meant so little to him. "Is there some point to your rambling narrative, Jason? If so, I fail to see what it has to do with Mr. Taylor."

Jason's gray eyes grew dark as he continued to explain, his glance as frightening as his words. "I wanted you to come with us very badly. Since we needed one more bachelor to accommodate one more bride I simply created one. I won quite a bit of money playing poker that night, and when I returned to the hotel I wrote the letter that supposedly came from Joshua Taylor. I included the fee plus a bit more than the other men had paid. The night clerk was sound asleep at his desk so it was a simple matter to slip the letter into Clayton's mailbox where he found it the next morning. He never doubted it was from a real man and neither did you."

Gabrielle didn't know whether to laugh or cry, she found Jason's tale so preposterous. She considered it for a moment then asked, "What did you expect to happen when we arrived here and there was no Mr. Taylor waiting to claim a bride? You must have had something clever planned in order to avoid having to reveal what you'd done. Since it's probably equally amusing, I'd like to hear it."

"No," Jason responded confidently. "I simply wanted you to meet all the men so you'd have a choice; then I planned for you to marry me."

Gabrielle's thick fringe of long lashes swept her brows as she leaped from her chair. "That is a damn lie and you know it!"

Jason rose slowly to his feet, towering above her. It was a lie of course, but the fact he'd considered marriage between them an impossibility until that very day was due to his own stupidity rather than to a lack of desire to make her his wife. He'd certainly never admit that to her. "I wanted you the minute you knocked upon our door, Gabrielle, and don't tell me now that fact wasn't obvious. I wouldn't have left Kansas City without you, but inventing Joshua Taylor seemed to be a far better method to win your confidence than tying you up and tossing you atop one of the brides' carriages like part of the luggage."

"You bastard," Gabrielle hissed menacingly. "You got

334

exactly what you wanted, how dare you tell me now that you had marriage in mind all those months you demanded I meet you in secret? You could have proposed to me at any time, and there were several places along the Oregon Trail where we could have been married. What's happened to you, Jason? Is your conscience finally troubling you? Have you begun to feel guilty because you continually used my affection for you without offering anything in return?"

Jason had little choice but to stand there and take whatever abuse she cared to hurl. The deep red of her hair seemed tinged with the flames of her anger, the blue of her eyes was so deep they appeared purple. He thought her the most desirable woman ever born. "I'd say I gave as much as I took," he replied, exhibiting far more pride than he actually felt. "You gave me little reason to believe you'd accept my proposal, Gabrielle. How can you fault me for not making one?"

"Oh!" Gabrielle shrieked in frustration. "You're lying! You know you are, but what I don't understand is why you'd bother." She turned away then, pacing up and down in front of him with the frantic stride of a wild beast on too short a leash. She looked ready to explode as she continued. "What you are describing is a deceit of monstrous proportion. To have lied to me from the moment we met merely to gratify your own insatiable lusts is so despicable it makes what Lewis Bradley did to his Indian mistress seem like a minor insult! How can you possibly think I'd believe you have always wanted me for your wife? That is simply ludicrous after the way you have behaved!"

Clayton knocked softly at the door before peering inside. "Is everything all right in here?"

"No!" Gabrielle shouted loudly, and the man was so startled by that response he offered no more than a brief apology for interrupting their conversation and closed the door at once.

"Perhaps you should keep your voice down, my dearest." Jason offered his advice with a sly grin. "Clayton is discreet, but I doubt many of the others in this house are."

"Of course, discretion has always meant more to you than my feelings, hasn't it? There's not a woman alive who deserves to have a snake like you for a husband, not one!"

"Does that mean you are refusing my proposal?" Jason asked nonchalantly, seeming to care little what her decision might be.

"What proposal?" Gabrielle cried indignantly. "I have not ever heard anything which sounded remotely like a proposal from you!"

Jason kept reminding himself that despite her astonishing beauty Gabrielle was no more than eighteen years old and could not be expected to react any differently to his confession than she had. "If you would be polite enough to be seated once again, I might be able to summon the courage to make an acceptable proposal. I hope you will forgive my inexperience with this subject, however, and not be too critical of my words since you know my feelings are sincere."

"That would be a miracle!" Gabrielle replied in a renewed burst of hostility, but she returned to her chair and sat down upon the edge, eager to hear whatever it was he wished to say.

Jason walked around to the front of the desk and sat down upon it, his pose a surprisingly informal one for so serious a discussion. "As I see it, I am responsible for your being here in Oregon. I brought you here to be my wife, and you've told me yourself you have no interest in marrying any of the other men you've met since your arrival here. I'll admit we have had more than our share of disagreements, but I think once we are married we can solve our problems far more easily. Since we are definitely compatible when it comes to the physical side of marriage, I am willing to overlook your uncontrollable temper. It would be only fair for you to overlook any faults I might have as well. You didn't want to rush into marriage with a man you didn't know well, and I doubt you'll ever come to know any other man as well as you already know me. We've been through several extremely trying situations together, probably the worst life has to offer, and I think we make a very good team. Call me all the vile names you want and distrust my motives if you must, but I still desire you for my wife. If you'll agree, there's plenty of time for us to get married this afternoon. It's up to you, Gabrielle; do you want to marry me or not?''

Gabrielle licked her lips slowly, unable to make any coherent reply for the moment. She had not even thought it possible for a man to make such an unemotional proposal, but clearly Jason was attempting to win her with logic, not with love. She looked down at her hands, twisting them nervously in her lap while she tried to think how best to respond. Their marriage would be sure to cause the most tantalizing of gossip, as would the fact their first child was very likely to arrive in less than nine months time. She did not want to wait until she was positive about the baby, not because of the trap Iris had laughed about but because she would feel as though she, not Jason, had been caught against her will.

Jason found Gabrielle a fascinating sight at any time, but now the conflicts which had made her decide to withdraw from the group of brides were so close to the surface he could readily see them in her troubled expression. He wanted her to say yes, but didn't know what else to do to convince her to marry him if she truly did not want to. He opened his mouth to insist she make up her mind quickly, then thought better of it and was still. He would just sit there until nightfall if it took her that long to make up her mind. She is well worth the wait, he reminded himself. Still, it was difficult to sit calmly when he wanted so badly to reach out and shake her until she'd say yes to whatever question he asked.

Finally Gabrielle looked up at him. "I wish that I could say the same thing to you that I said to Scream of Lightning, but I don't feel in the least bit honored since you've waited so dreadfully long to propose. You led me to believe marriage was not something you'd consider unless you had no choice, and that was terribly cruel. I can't help but think you were lying then or you are lying now, and neither of those possibilities pleases me. You may think I know you, but you're wrong for I can't predict what you'll do in the next five minutes, let alone imagine what sort of husband you'd prove to be."

"A simple yes or no will do, Gabrielle," Jason reminded her softly, not certain what her decision would be but impatient to hear it nonetheless.

"A marriage proposal is not a simple question, Jason. I can't give you a reply so easily." Gabrielle was overcome with sorrow, for she loved him dearly but his feelings for her were clearly of the most primitive kind. Would it be wrong of her to marry him and hope that one day his feelings for her would deepen as hers had for him? Would that be wrong, or merely incredibly foolish? She sat back in her chair and considered the other alternative. If she did not marry him but went on loving him, the resulting agony would be every bit as painful as losing Beau had been. She'd experienced far too much of the grief of lost love and not nearly enough of the bliss of its shared beauty. This time, the choice was hers rather than fate's and suddenly she knew exactly what she wanted to do. She rose gracefully to her feet, crossed the short distance between them, and placed her hands upon Jason's shoulders. She kissed his lips lightly and then smiled.

"Yes. I do want to marry you, this very afternoon if you cannot abide a longer engagement."

Jason made no further attempt to understand the curious thought patterns of the rare beauty in his arms. He drew her close and, winding his fingers in her long, flowing hair, kissed her again and again until he was certain by the depth of her response that she would not change her mind before he could get her to the church. He drew away then, laughing as he got to his feet and took her hand.

"I will allow you five minutes to gather the things you'll need tonight. We'll take whomever we can find to the church with us to serve as witnesses and then we'll spend the night at the hotel. I'll take you home with me in the morning." He swept her along beside him through the door and sent her up the stairs with a playful swat. "Don't keep me waiting, Miss MacLaren!" he called after her, and then, nearly bursting with happiness, he went to find Clayton to ask him to be his best man.

Chapter XVII

Erica sat up quickly, turning away to hide her tears as Gabrielle came running into their room. She was ashamed to be caught weeping again after having sounded so confident that morning. Her courage had now deserted her completely, and she was feeling so wretchedly alone she didn't think she'd ever get over her heartbreak at losing Lewis. Attempting to smile bravely as though she'd only been resting, she hoped Gabrielle would be too polite to ask why she'd been crying.

"I didn't know anyone was home." Gabrielle greeted her friend brightly, too considerate to remark upon the signs of tears still visible upon her flushed cheeks. "I was up here just a short while ago."

"I was probably out in the garden then. After church everyone sort of disappeared," Erica explained dejectedly. "I'm the only one here."

"I am so glad that you are, for I would not have wanted to get married without your being there." Gabrielle took Erica's hands firmly in hers to lift her from the bed. "I'm getting married this afternoon. Aren't you excited for me?"

"What?" Erica exclaimed in an enthusiastic screech, so astonished she instantly forgot her own sorrow. "You and Michael have already decided to get married? When you are such a cautious type it never occurred to me you might be the first of us to take a husband."

Gabrielle could not help but laugh at Erica's confusion. "Michael is a delightful man. However, he's not the one I'm going to marry so I would greatly appreciate it if you would give him some of your time and lift his spirits as he's sure to be very disappointed in me. Would you please do that? Perhaps you've not noticed that he's taller than Lewis Bradley and several years younger too." With that teasing remark, Gabrielle left her to begin gathering the things she'd need. "Jason only gave me five minutes so I'll have to talk as I pack."

"Jason?" Erica gasped in disbelief. "You don't mean Jason Royal, do you?"

"Of course, he's the only Jason I know," Gabrielle responded with another lilting laugh, too excited now to worry about what anyone thought of her choice of husband.

"But I saw you with Michael Jenkins only this morning!" Erica pointed out logically.

"Yes, you did. As I said he'll not be pleased I'm marrying Jason, but I'm certain you can distract him from his grief quite easily. You were so positive you wanted Lewis before we even arrived in Oregon City that I don't think you've really given any of the other men a fair chance to impress you. Michael can be very charming, truly he can. From what I saw of his farm I'd say he's very ambitious too."

Erica did not know which question to ask first, she was so confused. But as she thought back over the months they'd spent together she grew increasingly curious. "You and Jason aren't even friends. I thought you regarded him as being lower than a serpent!"

"A snake." Gabrielle corrected her friend, an impish smile on her face; then she went back to folding her nightgown. "I've called him a snake on more than one occasion and a lot worse to his face, but since he's to become my husband I hope you won't repeat that insult to anyone, most especially not to him."

"You needn't worry. So few people are speaking to me now, nobody would care to listen." Erica flopped back down on the bed, feeling very sorry for herself.

Gabrielle had no patience with her friend's self-pity. "If you have decided you want Lewis no matter how he's lived, then just say so. I'm sure Clayton can have him back here tonight. If, on the other hand, you truly are finished with the man, then you'll have to make more of an effort to meet someone new. You can't just mope around here and let all the other girls have their first choice of the men without any competition!" She tugged on Erica's hands to lift her from the bed and, with an emphatic push, propelled her to the mirror. "Just look at yourself for a minute, none of the others is as pretty as you. Now come to the church with us and tonight go downstairs and be sociable. I don't care how much it hurts. You owe these men a chance to impress you, and none will have the courage to come up here to your bedroom to do it!"

Despite the previous blackness of her mood, Erica began to smile, so amused was she by Gabrielle's teasing compliments. "I am definitely finished with Lewis, so I guess I'll have to take your advice about attending the rest of the parties no matter how I dread them. Now what can I do to help you? Why have you such a short time to prepare for the ceremony?"

"I have learned there are times when it is best to let Jason have his own way. This happens to be one of them. I'm taking only a few things now. We'll come back in the morning for the rest of my belongings."

Erica's green eyes lit up with a saucy sparkle. "Tomorrow you must tell me every single detail about tonight. I want to know exactly what Jason says and does every delicious minute!"

"Oh, no I won't!" Gabrielle argued. "You'll be a bride yourself in a week or two. You can wait until then to learn with your own husband what it is like to be married." She busied herself, wrapping in a silk scarf the clothing and personal items she wanted to take. Then she retied her bonnet under her chin and walked toward the door. "Let's go. I do not want Jason to leave for the church without me."

Erica stood, hands on her hips, her pretty features set in a fierce pout. "I wish just once you'd tell me one of your secrets. I swear you are the most private person ever born! Some wife you'll make!"

"I'll let Jason be the judge of that. Now let's go before the man changes his mind about wanting me!" Gabrielle stamped her foot for emphasis, ready to leave whether Erica was or not.

Clayton took the news of Jason's impending marriage with far less calm than Erica had shown. He simply stared at the young man for several seconds and then fell into a wild fit of coughing, after which he tried to talk his partner out of his hasty decision. Jason slapped him on the back and brought him a glass of water. Finally, Clayton summoned the breath to speak. "You of all men, Jason, I never expected you to take a wife and of all women Gabrielle MacLaren would be the last one I'd think you'd choose. I know I cautioned you about her on more than one occasion, but more often than not you two were in the midst of some heated argument or not speaking to each other at all. I haven't even seen you with her at our parties. Have you danced with her even once?"

"No. Now that you mention it, I don't believe I have. A mere oversight, I assure you." Jason rocked back on his heels, too pleased with himself for having won Gabrielle's consent to their marriage to care what advice Clayton had to give. "You will be my best man, won't you? You're the best friend I have."

"Of course I'll be your best man, but must the ceremony be today? Since Gabrielle is the first to marry I imagine all the girls will want to be there, and you know they're scattered all over the valley this afternoon. Couldn't this wait until the morning when we can invite everyone to attend?"

The prospect of waiting one additional hour, let alone an entire day was more than Jason could bear to consider. "No. Neither of us wants to wait." He turned to look up the stairs then as he heard the musical sound of Gabrielle's laughter. She and Erica were walking arm and arm, nearly skipping down the stairs, and he rushed to her side to take her hand. "Good. You found Erica. We each have a friend then. Shall we go?" He knew his smile was far too wide, but he could not seem to hide his happiness now that Gabrielle would at last be his wife. That she appeared to be as happy as he made him so proud he wanted to toss her into the air and shout for joy, but he restrained himself for the time being, intending to put his energy to a far better use later when they would be alone.

Clayton offered to go to the barn for his buggy, but knowing the four of them could not be seated in it comfortably, he tried to think of some alternative arrangement.

"I'll ride one of the horses; then the three of you can ride in the buggy," he said.

Meanwhile Erica had strolled over to the window, and seeing Michael still waiting outside, she offered another suggestion. "If Michael Jenkins has nothing to do perhaps he would give me a ride to the church, would that help?"

"Yes!" Gabrielle agreed at once. It sounds like a very good idea to me." She looked up at Jason then, hoping he'd not still be mad at Michael. "I'd like to invite him to our wedding if I may."

"You may invite anyone you choose; just hurry up about it," Jason replied with a teasing chuckle. "Go out and speak with him while Clay and I bring the buggy around to the front."

Gabrielle glanced over at Erica and, seeing her shy smile, walked quickly to the door. "We'll be ready as soon as you gentlemen are."

"We'll hurry." Jason called over his shoulder, and after giving Clayton a hearty slap on the back, he started toward the back of the house intent upon completing his errand rapidly.

Michael had been leaning back against his buggy, deep in thought. He was hoping to devise some compelling argument to influence Gabrielle in his favor when he heard her call his name. He stood up abruptly and smiled as she walked toward him. Seeing she was not alone, he included Erica in his greeting. "Good afternoon, Miss Nelson, Gabrielle."

Gabrielle gave the young man a warm hug and followed it with a light kiss upon his cheek when he began to blush. "Michael, I have a favor to ask. Jason and I are going to the church now to be married. Since all of us won't fit comfortably in one buggy, may Erica ride with you? I do so want you to be there. You will come with us, won't you?"

It was not as though he hadn't been warned, but Michael was dumfounded all the same. "It seems I badly underestimated Mr. Royal's desire to become a family man," he finally managed to mumble. "Of course I want to attend your wedding and I'd be honored to escort you, Miss Nelson."

"Why thank you, Mr. Jenkins." Erica had a bewitching smile and she used it to her best advantage now as she took Michael's hand and stepped up into his buggy. She thought him quite handsome and was sorry she had not paid more attention to him. If Gabrielle considered him charming, then she was certain she would as well. When he climbed up beside her, she slipped her arm through his as though they were the best of friends, then she gave Gabrielle a knowing wink to show her how pleased she was to have such a nice escort. She vowed to herself right then that by the end of the evening Michael Jenkins would have forgotten he'd ever met Gabrielle MacLaren.

Jason used the few minutes they had alone on the ride to the church to tell Gabrielle how delighted he was with her decision. He hugged her shoulders warmly and drew her close to his side. "I am certain we will be the happiest of couples, Gabrielle. We need no more than the chance to be by ourselves for a change instead of trying to elude a crowd."

Gabrielle smiled sweetly, trying not to grin as widely as he since to do so might be unseemly. She had no desire to appear as pleased as he obviously was. She was the bride and should not look as though she was bursting with pride for having caught so handsome a husband. She tried to strike the proper balance between the demure young lady she was supposed to be and the vixen she knew she truly was, but she was not certain she had succeeded.

"You seem enormously pleased with yourself, Jason." To my delight, she thought.

Jason laughed at her teasing. "That I am, but I have good reason to be." He kept urging the mare Clayton had hitched to the buggy to greater speed, not wanting to waste a moment of the afternoon in travel. "Clay went on ahead to see if the preacher has returned to the church. He usually receives at least one dinner invitation on Sunday, but I don't want to have to wait for him to come home."

"I will not change my mind, Jason. Will you?" Gabrielle asked playfully. "If he does not come home until supper time I will still be happy to become your wife."

"Let's hope we do not have to wait that long." Jason moaned in mock sorrow. "Were we Indians, I would have to do no more than announce my intention to make you my wife and then take you home. That is all there would be to it."

Gabrielle considered his words thoughtfully for a moment and then asked, "You mean we would already be husband and wife if we were Indians? All that is lacking is an announcement, for we have already done what an Indian brave and his bride would do when they reached his home, haven't we?"

"I'll thank you to keep that bit of information to yourself, my dear," Jason whispered softly, but he knew her comment was quite right and could not suppress a deep chuckle.

Since he was in so agreeable a mood, Gabrielle persisted in her questioning. "If the Indians consider a man and woman who live together married, then why did you say Lewis wasn't married to his mistress? Her people considered them married, didn't they?"

Jason's expression grew solemn as he turned to give Gabrielle a long glance, but seeing that her query was a serious one, he replied calmly, not angered by her inquisitiveness. "Yes, but a white man does not consider himself married as easily as an Indian brave does. It is a convenient way to think I'll grant you, certainly all in the man's favor rather than the

347

Indian woman's. I told you the truth. I'd not begin such an alliance since the advantage would all be mine and the arrangement a very poor one for the Indian maiden."

"To say nothing of the children," Gabrielle whispered softly, her gaze suddenly a very pensive one.

Jason grew silent too, not wanting to mention the subject of children to Gabrielle when it had always precipitated an argument between them. He hoped they would have a child and soon, but he'd not press her to discuss the issue until she brought it up herself. He gave her another affectionate squeeze as the church came into view. "It is a shame you did not attend the service this morning; then you would have met the preacher at least once."

"Do you know the man well?" Gabrielle inquired politely, thinking it unlikely that he did.

"No," Jason admitted. "But he'll do this favor for me, I'm certain of it."

Clayton had arrived first, having ridden on horseback, and since he was to be the best man he'd informed the minister of the reason for their call and then returned to the front of the church to greet Jason and Gabrielle when they arrived. "Reverend Murdock would like to speak with you both in his study," he warned them, frowning. "It seems our enterprise has caused considerable gossip, and he wants to be certain you two are serious about your desire to marry."

When Jason appeared ready to explode in anger at that unexpected announcement, Gabrielle reached out to take his hand. "It is not surprising that the man doesn't want to begin performing twenty-one marriage ceremonies when we've been here less than a week. I'm sure we can prove to him our situation is a different one since we have had half a year in which to become acquainted rather than only a few days."

Hoping she was correct in her assumption, Jason tried to smile. "I'll do my best not to insult the man. Let's hope we can be as persuasive as you seem to think we can." He escorted her around to the side of the neatly kept frame building to the entrance which led directly to the minister's study. With a ready smile, he introduced Gabrielle and hoped the man would be favorably impressed despite what he knew must appear to be an unreasonable haste to marry.

Patrick Murdock was a young man, thin and slightly balding. He'd been in Oregon City for less than one year and had no desire to outrage any members of his congregation by turning the church for which he was responsible into a wedding chapel. Not wishing to offend Jason Royal either, he welcomed the man and his lovely fiancée warmly. "I am pleased to make your acquaintance, Miss MacLaren, and to see you again, Mr. Royal." He had met Jason soon after coming to the town but could not recall ever seeing him at a Sunday morning service. He removed his gold-rimmed spectacles and began to polish them on his handkerchief as he attempted to explain his hesitation to perform a wedding ceremony on such short notice. "This is Oregon City as you are undoubtedly aware, Mr. Royal, not Gretna Green. Usually couples present themselves to me several weeks before they plan to marry. I know you and Mr. Horne have contracted to provide brides for respectable bachelors in our community, but I hope they will not all wish to be married on such short notice as this." He replaced his glasses then, adjusting them for a comfortable fit upon the bridge of his nose. But he found his alternatives no more clear now that the lenses were clean. "Why don't we sit down and discuss your request for a moment?"

Jason first showed Gabrielle to a chair and, when Reverend Murdock had taken his, sat down opposite him. "Perhaps Clayton and I should have discussed this question with you before we left for Missouri last spring, but it did not occur to either of us that you would hesitate to perform wedding ceremonies for adults in good standing in the community."

Gesturing nervously, Patrick tried to explain. "I am not hesitating, Mr. Royal, not at all. I am merely surprised that you would appear at my door this afternoon with such an urgent request. Can you honestly swear that you and Miss MacLaren

349

have given this most serious step the proper consideration it rightly deserves?" A bachelor himself, the minister hoped he did not sound too pompous since marital bliss was not a state he enjoyed.

"Yes," Jason replied promptly, not bothering to let Gabrielle respond for herself. "I have never given any question the consideration marriage has received. We might have married some weeks ago had I not been the wagon master and therefore too busy with my duties escorting a wagon train to Oregon to give Gabrielle the attention a new bride deserves. I have not had the advantage the other bachelors have had of being here all summer. We need to marry now so that we can have our farm properly prepared for the winter. As this is the optimum time for us to begin our lives together, I do not want to have to suffer any delay if it can be avoided."

As Jason explained the compelling reasons for them to be married that very afternoon Gabrielle again marveled at his detachment. He seemed to think the need to lay in provisions before the rains began the best reason he could possibly give. She waited in vain for some word of regard for her, but he spoke nothing of that in his effort to convince the young minister of his sincerity. When Reverend Murdock at last turned to her, she smiled as though she agreed with all Jason had said, though she would have preferred to have risen from her chair and given her handsome bridegroom a swift kick in the shins. "All the bachelors will have a similar concern, sir. They have already waited many months for us to arrive. I know I can speak for the brides when I say we all gave the matter of marriage very serious thought before we first spoke with Mr. Horne about coming to Oregon. None of this is as hasty as it seems. It is the result of many months of effort to bring together men and women who wish to share in the responsibilities of marriage. There are none among us who will not live up to our wedding vows. Your church is such a pretty one, I am certain you perform a beautiful wedding ceremony. Is there any need for you to delay ours any longer?"

Patrick Murdock shook his head, fascinated by the mellow tones of the lovely Miss MacLaren's voice as well as by her astonishing beauty. He thought her arguments not only intelligent but compelling and rose to his feet to see she was kept waiting no longer. "Have you brought a witness? I will be happy to begin the ceremony as soon as everyone is assembled."

"Thank you." Jason leaped to his feet, delighted that the man had agreed with their request. He gave Gabrielle his hand to help her rise, then dropped his arm to encircle her waist as they followed the minister into the church where they found their friends waiting. He winked slyly at Clayton, too happy that they had overcome Murdock's objections to hide his elation. "Our guests are all here. Where would you like us to stand?"

Patrick gave his directions quickly, placing Gabrielle on Jason's left with Erica by her side while Clayton stood at Jason's right. "I am sorry our organist is not here. Had I known there was to be a wedding I would have asked her to remain in town."

"Music is not necessary to make the marriage legal," Jason pointed out swiftly, wanting only to get the ceremony over with as rapidly as possible. He smiled at Gabrielle, hoping she would not object to the simple ceremony. To his delight she seemed not to mind and gave his hand a warm squeeze. Apparently she was as eager as he for the ceremony to begin.

"You have the ring?" Patrick asked Jason softly. "Give it to Mr. Horne to hold."

Jason had not even remembered a ring would be required. He turned to give Clayton a stricken glance before replying. "I'm sorry, I've had no opportunity to buy one for Gabrielle."

While the young minister tried to recall what to do in such a situation, Gabrielle fixed Jason with a steady stare. Had he truly been planning to marry her all along, he would most certainly have remembered so important a detail as purchasing a ring. She was deeply hurt, angry as well, to realize this was

351

further proof that he'd been lying to her when he'd proposed. She'd not challenge him with that fact now though, for it would only embarrass everyone present. Furthermore, she knew if he'd not tell her the truth when they were alone he'd not be likely to do it in front of witnesses. Despite the convincing presentations they'd given the minister, she knew their marriage was every bit as hasty as it had first appeared to be. She just prayed it was not ill advised as well.

Clayton had a small gold ring which he wore on his little finger. His initials were engraved upon it in graceful swirls, but he thought it would do for the time being and quickly removed it. "Use this one for now and buy your bride a ring in the morning. Now is there anything else you've forgotten?"

"I certainly hope not." Jason glanced down at Gabrielle, and by the proud set of her chin, he knew exactly what she was thinking. She was furious with him, but he could not blame her. They hardly appeared to be a couple who'd given marriage the careful consideration they'd described to Patrick Murdock when he'd not even bothered to buy a ring. Damn! Had it not been Sunday he would have left immediately to attend to that errand. Now he had no choice but to use Clayton's ring and thank him for it. He held his breath, hoping the minister would have the presence of mind to begin before Gabrielle ran screaming from the church. He had only himself to blame for disappointing her so badly, that he knew full well. Having finally made the decision to marry her that morning, he'd considered nothing else worthy of contemplation. The details of the ceremony had slipped his mind completely, but he'd not ask for a delay when he'd insisted upon an immediate wedding. The church was very warm, and he hoped the stagnant air would not cause Gabrielle to faint for he feared by the time they revived her she would have changed her mind about the wisdom of marrying him. He gripped her hand more tightly, hoping she'd stand by his side for just a few minutes longer.

When Patrick Murdock opened his book to begin reading the ceremony, Gabrielle found it difficult to believe she was

352

the bride. She felt completely detached from the others in the small gathering. Her mind wandered, filled with irrelevant thoughts which had no bearing upon the occasion. Her pearl gray suit was attractive, but was not a wedding gown, and that suddenly distressed her. She'd not even thought to gather a few flowers from Clayton's garden so she had a bouquet to carry. The very last thing she'd expected to do that day was marry Jason, but here she stood, calmly waiting for the pale, young minister to reach the part of the ceremony where she would have to repeat her vows. She tried to pay careful attention, but it was difficult. His voice was rather high, not one suited to the delivery of dynamic sermons, and she wondered if he were well regarded by his congregation. Forcing herself to stop daydreaming, she realized he was now looking toward her. She was relieved to find she'd not missed a response; he was merely glancing in her direction as he continued to read the service.

Jason held his breath, waiting for something else to go wrong as the ceremony continued. He had never wanted anything in his entire life as badly as he wanted Gabrielle to be his bride, but he was ashamed to think how he'd rushed her to the church. He should have been far more considerate. Clayton's comment that he'd not danced with her at their parties was only a reminder of the many things he'd neglected to do. He knew she'd never let him forget he'd failed to buy her a ring; that was so appalling an error he did not know how he'd ever make it up to her. He found it increasingly difficult to stand still and shuffled his feet nervously, now concerned that he might well be the one to faint before Patrick Murdock pronounced them husband and wife. His mouth had grown so dry he doubted he could speak the proper replies, and to make matters worse, he could feel Gabrielle's hand trembling in his. That she was not simply in tears over the lack of formality in their wedding ceremony amazed him. He'd known couples who recalled exchanging their vows with great fondness, but he knew he would want only to forget this day because Gabrielle deserved so much more than he'd had time to provide. He'd chosen to make her his wife before he lost her to another man who would court her with the courtesy and tenderness she deserved. He'd won. But that victory brought no feeling of pride, only remorse as he glanced down at the graceful beauty who would soon be his bride. When Patrick paused for him to repeat his portion of the vows, he was surprised by the calm he projected. He spoke as though he were in complete control of the situation. Gabrielle's voice held the husky tone which had first drawn him to her, but her promises were spoken as steadily as his, with no trace of tears. He slipped Clayton's gold ring upon her finger, then leaned down to give her a gentle kiss. He did not know how he had been so lucky, but by some miracle no mishap had occurred and the woman he adored was now his wife.

After they'd signed the necessary documents, Gabrielle took Jason's arm as he turned toward the double doors at the entrance of the church. He moved up the aisle with so long a stride she had to break into a run to keep up with him and implored him to use a more sedate pace. "Jason, please, this is not a race!" She could not understand why he was so anxious to leave. They were married, that was what he'd wanted. Why couldn't he wait a few moments to accept their friends' good wishes?

Once outside Jason took a deep breath then reached up to loosen his tie. "Another thirty seconds in there and I would have fainted from the heat!"

Gabrielle could not help but laugh at his stricken expression, for indeed he did seem to have been suffering terribly when she'd not thought the church overwarm. "It is the bride who is allowed to faint, not the groom!"

Clayton overtook them then, grabbing Jason's hand in a firm clasp. "Come back to the house with us. We've time to celebrate before dinner and I've plenty of champagne."

Gabrielle waited for Jason to respond. She would welcome a chance to relax at a party, for she was afraid they'd only find themselves arguing again if they went directly to his hotel. She twisted Clayton's ring nervously on her finger and held her tongue, hoping Jason would agree without her having to intervene, but he seemed most reluctant to accept his friend's invitation.

"No. Gabrielle and I have many plans to make. As you know I've not really lived on my parents' farm for several years and it will take considerable effort to make it a proper home. There are many things we'll need to buy once the stores open in the morning, and I don't want to waste time here in town when there's so much work to be done at the farm. May I borrow your wagon in the morning to transport everything?"

Clayton simply stared at his young friend, appalled that Jason was so preoccupied with the details of getting his farm in order when he should be concentrating on providing Gabrielle with a proper honeymoon. Gesturing toward her, he said pointedly, "Jason, this beautiful creature is now your bride. Have you no intention of celebrating that event in a suitable manner?"

Jason looked away, clearly embarrassed. All he'd wanted was to be alone with Gabrielle, to begin what he hoped would prove to be an endless honeymoon. The farm had only been an excuse, not his real interest. "You needn't tell me how to be a husband, Clay. I know what is required."

"The hell you do!" Clayton responded in a hoarse whisper. "Forgive me, Gabrielle, but Jason is maddeningly blind at times and this seems to be one of them."

Since Erica and Michael were standing nearby with Reverend Murdock, Gabrielle hoped to avoid an unfortunate argument. She spoke sweetly. "I think we can spare the time to share a glass of champagne to celebrate our marriage, Jason. There will be ample time later to make a comprehensive list so nothing is forgotten when we go shopping tomorrow."

She'd made her request so politely that Jason knew he could not refuse, but he was not a bit pleased. "If it will make you happy, then of course we will accept Clay's invitation," he replied tersely, and stopping to invite the minister as well as Michael and Erica to join them, he escorted Gabrielle to their buggy. He made little effort to hide his true feelings from his bride, however, and said not a word to her until they had returned to Clayton's home. "I thought I'd finally succeeded in getting you away from everyone. Let's plan to be gone within the hour. I don't want to stay for dinner and then have the party that is planned for this evening turn into a reception for us. We'd be lucky to get away before midnight if that happens."

Gabrielle made no hostile reply, but the coolness of her glance could not be misunderstood. "I'll leave my things here in the buggy then since we'll be here only a few minutes."

"Good." Jason escorted her inside the beautifully furnished home, and to his dismay he found several couples who had been out for the afternoon had already returned. Instead of having to accept the congratulations of only a few close friends, they were swiftly surrounded by pretty young women and by bachelors who hoped to join the ranks of married men themselves. What had begun as an invitation for one glass of champagne soon turned into a festive gathering. Jason despaired of ever being able to leave, but Gabrielle at last drew him to the edge of the crowd and whispered.

"They are having such a good time, no one will notice if we slip away now."

Delighted by her suggestion, he took her hand and began to edge slowly toward the door. Michael and Erica, realizing what they were doing, rushed over to say goodbye.

Michael stepped forward to shake Jason's hand, and after congratulating him once again, he kissed Gabrielle's cheek shyly. "I wish you both only the best life has to offer." He spoke politely as a gentleman should, for despite his own disappointment he was sincere in his hopes for Gabrielle.

Erica gave each of the newlyweds a warm hug then took Michael's arm again. "I know you're anxious to begin work on your own home, but you'll come into town for the rest of the weddings won't you?" She dared not look up at Michael as she asked that question, but truly she had found his company to be as entertaining as Gabrielle had described it to be and her mood was now a most optimistic one.

"Of course!" Jason agreed quickly. "We'll not miss a one." With a wide grin, he bid them goodbye and, slipping his arm around Gabrielle's waist, spirited her out the front door and down the walk to Clayton's buggy, knowing it would be a long while before any of the other couples so enthusiastically celebrating their marriage noted that they were gone.

Chapter XVIII

As he climbed up into his seat in the buggy, Jason found a bottle of champagne with a note attached. He read it hurriedly, then shoved the message into his coat pocket before handing Gabrielle the bottle of sparkling wine. "More advice from Clay," he explained with a frown, obviously reluctant to divulge the contents of the brief note more fully.

"I can imagine what he said." Gabrielle leaned close to whisper. "When I go back to the house to pick up the rest of my belongings, Erica wants me to give her a full report on what transpires between us tonight."

"She actually said that?" Jason inquired, incredulous, his expression as startled as his tone.

"Yes, but you needn't worry I'll give away our secrets. I told her she'd have to wait for her own wedding night to satisfy her curiosity." Perhaps it was the champagne Clayton had poured so generously, but Gabrielle was filled with excitment now and did not attempt to stifle the giggle which came readily to her lips.

Jason laughed heartily, for he thought his bride's sparkling smile charming regardless of its cause. "You are not sorry then, that your own curiosity has already been satisfied as to what occurs between a bride and groom on their wedding night?"

"No," Gabrielle confessed without hesitation. "I would not change anything that has happened between us."

Jason gave her a skeptical glance. If their many angry confrontations had slipped her mind, he'd not remind her of them now. When they reached the hotel he helped her down from the buggy, and seeing a young man he knew lounging nearby, Jason paid him a small sum to return the carriage to Clayton's barn. He then offered his arm to escort his bride into the hotel, which he suddenly realized lacked the elegance to which she was entitled. He made no excuses, however, but stopped briefly at the desk to tell the astonished clerk his wife would be sharing his room for the night and they'd like to have supper brought to them at seven. He carried the bottle of champagne as well as Gabrielle's bundle of clothing and led her upstairs to his room which occupied the right front corner on the second floor. It was neatly kept for the maid was a diligent worker who saw that everything was put in order each day. Actually Jason had spent little time there, and he was grateful they'd be leaving first thing in the morning.

Gabrielle surveyed Jason's lodgings with rapt interest, hoping to discover some clue which would provide an insight into his fascinating personality, but the Spartan décor gave no hint of the character of the present resident. The iron bed was covered with an attractive blue and white quilt, two straight-backed chairs were placed beside a small round table which stood in front of the windows, and along one wall was a five-drawer dresser with a mirror attached. Against the opposite wall stood a large wooden wardrobe. The three large windows were the most attractive feature of the room. They faced west and provided more than ample illumination since the afternoon was a bright one. The lace curtains rustled in the breeze. They had been freshly laundered and still held the perfumed scent of soap which gave the air a fragrance nearly as delightful as that of fresh flowers. The room was sunny and clean, but Gabrielle could think of no comment to make on it so she asked about her few possessions.

"May I put my things away in the dresser for the night?"

"Of course," Jason responded graciously. He carried the bottle of champagne over to the table and busied himself with trying to uncork it. "I think the bottom two drawers are empty."

Gabrielle untied the ends of the silk scarf, and after shaking out the garments she'd brought to wear the next day, she refolded them upon the bed before carrying them over to the dresser. When she opened the fourth drawer, she found Jason had used it to store his sketch book. Curious as to what he'd been drawing, she opened it and began to thumb through the pages. The first sketch was of a family who'd been part of the wagon train. They stood clustered around their wagon smiling broadly. The next three pages held careful studies of horses—he had caught the spirited animals in motion—but the final sketches in the book brought a sharp gasp to her lips. They were all beautifully drawn nudes, clearly recognizable to her. She turned slowly to stare at the man who was now her husband, her expression one of utter confusion and disbelief.

Jason had managed to open the champagne without mishap, and while the two glasses he had were not crystal, he thought the wine would taste every bit as delicious as it had at Clayton's. He poured them each a glass, then looked up to see what was keeping Gabrielle. When he saw his sketch book in her hands, he remembered tossing it into a drawer so the maid wouldn't find it. However, he would have much rather that woman had seen it than Gabrielle. "I'm sorry, I didn't mean for you to see those."

"Obviously not," Gabrielle replied angrily. "But I'd like to know just who has."

Jason walked over to her side as he answered truthfully. "No one has seen those sketches except you. That's hardly the kind of thing I'd want to share with other men since it makes the depth of our relationship so plain."

"Oh, I see. You drew these only for yourself to enjoy? I must say your memory is an extremely good one." Her cheeks flushed and she could not recall ever having been so dreadfully embarrassed in her life.

"Gabrielle . . ." Jason spoke her name softly, hoping to make her understand his purpose had been a most loving one. "You are a very beautiful woman and I like to draw. That I would wish to make sketches of you is not so remarkable."

"No, it's not remarkable, only shocking!" she responded bitterly. The sketches were a fine example of his extraordinary talent, for he'd selected the most graceful of classical poses to complement the perfection of her figure. She knew the drawings were pretty rather than obscene, but she hated them nonetheless and slammed the book shut. She would have thrown it at him had he not been standing so close. "Here! Since these please you then by all means keep them, but I don't want to see them ever again!" She was near tears, so outraged was she by what he'd done. She yanked Clayton's ring from her finger, flung it upon the dresser, and turned her back on him.

Jason opened the top drawer and slipped his sketch book inside before picking up the gold ring. "What's this supposed to mean?"

"When you have not forgotten the smallest detail of my figure, it is amazing you'd forget so important an item as buying me a ring!" Gabrielle was shaking with rage. She knew she shouldn't have said that to him, but she couldn't help herself when his oversight had hurt her so deeply.

Jason longed to put his arms around his bride, to draw her near and cover her sweet face with kisses, but discouraged by her continual refusal to accept any of his explanations as the truth, he turned away. He did not stop to consider the fact that most of his excuses bore little relationship to the truth since that struck him as unimportant. He wanted her to accept his words simply because he spoke them. He walked back to the small table, sat down in one of the chairs, and tossed down his champagne in one gulp. "You're right. I should have had a ring for you. It will be the first thing we'll buy in the morning. Now, come sit down and help me think as I don't want to forget anything else when we go shopping."

Gabrielle wheeled around to face him, furious still. "That's all I am? Just another item on your list of necessities for your farm. One wife. Where did you have my name written, somewhere between the butter churn and the new plow?"

"I had forgotten the churn since I don't own a cow," Jason remarked, his glance reflecting the fury in her deep blue gaze. "Now, come and sit down!" he poured himself another glass of champagne and finished it as quickly as the first, but the warmth with which the wine filled his muscular body did little to improve his mood.

"Oh!" Gabrielle screamed in frustation, but she crossed the room in three swift strides and sat down to face him. "Just what are you planning to do, Jason? You might have helped your father, but you've never been solely responsible for running a farm yourself. I've lived my whole life in town. I don't know the first thing about being a farmer's bride. I thought I'd marry a man who'd be able to teach me what I'd need to know, but since I didn't, what are we going to do?"

The many reasons Jason had recited to himself for not needing a bride swiftly flooded his mind, but he forced them away since they were no longer relevant. He had married Gabrielle, and now he had to make some kind of a home for her no matter how ill prepared he was to do it. He got up to get a sheet of paper, a pen, and ink to begin making their list. Sitting down again, he tried to reassure her things were not so dire as she seemed to believe. "I left home at fourteen, Gabrielle, so there is little I haven't done when it comes to the running of a farm. The hardest work is in the spring when the ground has to be prepared and the crops sewn. Our only challenge now will be to make my house livable and to take care of ourselves for the winter. I doubt either of those tasks will be beyond our capabilities."

As always, Jason radiated confidence and Gabrielle did not doubt he would surmount each obstacle in their path, but she had never felt so inadequate. "You plan to be a farmer now, is that it? You'll no longer guide wagon trains to Oregon?" That she'd not even thought to ask him that question when he'd proposed filled her with dismay.

Jason shrugged. "I'll do whatever I must to keep a roof over our heads, but let's worry about next spring when it comes, Gabrielle, not before. It is not essential that we buy everything tomorrow. We can come back into town several times if need be. I know you'll want to attend your friends' weddings so that will give us the opportunity to stock up on anything we've forgotten."

Gabrielle took a small sip of her champagne and then another. She doubted this was the way a wedding night was supposed to begin, but it was only late afternoon and she had hopes Jason's mood would become more romantic. "We'll need chickens to have eggs, and feed for them," she suggested absently, her interest clearly not in their task but in her new husband.

Jason began to print the items they decided they'd need. Finally, he felt they had a comprehensive list prepared. When their supper arrived at seven, he was amazed that they'd spent so much time talking about provisions. The waiter was even more surprised to find a honeymoon couple engaged in such a mundane activity. The young man produced a white linen cloth for their table and, after serving their plates, left promptly, deciding discretion was called for even though he could detect no evidence to justify the need for such diplomatic behavior.

Gabrielle found the poached salmon very tasty, but she had little appetite. She'd not thought being alone with Jason would prove to be so awkward. She felt every bit as self-conscious as she would have had she wed a total stranger. He had very fine manners, and as always, she found him so attractive he was a delight simply to observe. Still, she wanted so much more from him than he seemed to think it necessary to give that she had difficulty hiding her growing depression. She had known it wouldn't be easy to win his love when she'd accepted his proposal, but she'd not realized how much pain the aching emptiness of his promises would cause. She reminded herself she'd have to be patient, but that did not ease the hurt his indifference continued to cause. She wanted him to speak of love on their wedding night, but he seemed to have no interest in doing so. Instead, he spoke at length about the prosperity he knew it was possible to achieve from farming with conscientious effort.

Jason found Gabrielle's melancholy gaze increasingly discomforting. Clay's note had admonished him to respect her youth and innocence, but she'd never seemed naïve in her views, nor was she as innocent as his partner believed. He was sorry now that he'd not just taken her home, where they could have been completely alone. She'd always been so affectionate when they'd been together, but he knew the atmosphere of the small hotel room did little to create a romantic mood. He was as ill at ease as she, and that was no way to begin a marriage. However, he could think of nothing to do or say to lift her spirits. He was certain she was thinking of Beau. Surely he was the man she'd meant when she'd said she'd planned to marry a farmer who would be able to teach her what was required of his wife. Beau was the husband she'd hoped to have, but Jason dared not mention the man's name when he knew her response would be a most furious one. As time passed, she replied to all his attempts at conversation with no more than one-word replies, and finally he gave up his efforts to amuse her and became as silent as she.

After the red glow cast by the setting sun had faded away, Jason got up to light the two small lamps the hotel had provided, but rather than creating an intimate warmth while they dined, they merely threw eerie shadows upon the walls. He finished his supper as slowly as possible in an attempt to allow himself sufficient time to devise some clever means to charm Gabrielle. Unfortunately no idea of any merit occurred to him. She was still sitting opposite him, waiting for him to devour every morsel on his plate, her food all but untouched.

Her glance was rather curious now, but he remembered the soft glow passion lent to her bright blue eyes too fondly to be satisfied with anything less. When she spoke to him, he was startled by the sound of her voice, for she'd been unnaturally quiet all afternoon.

"This has been a remarkable day, Jason. It began with me trying to explain to Michael why marriage was out of the question for me and now I find myself dining with my husband. I am sorry I have been such poor company for you, but surely tomorrow will not prove to be so confusing."

No longer able to hide his own apprehension, Jason suddenly blurted out the truth. "I can make no promises about tomorrow when my mind is so preoccupied with tonight!"

Gabrielle tried not to laugh, but she could not help herself now that he'd admitted he was as nervous as she. She rose quickly from her chair and, seeing he'd not a scrap left on his plate, sat down upon his lap and put her arms around his neck, hugging him warmly. "I think you're right, we've spent far too little time together. All we need for a successful marriage is the chance to grow comfortable in each other's company."

Jason put his arms around Gabrielle's tiny waist to hold her captive upon his knee as he began to nuzzle the silken skin of her throat with affectionate nibbles. "You already know all a farmer's wife truly must, my pet. Don't worry that you'll ever fail to please me."

Gabrielle closed her eyes as she snuggled against him. She wound her fingers in his dark curls and ceased to concern herself with her lack of housekeeping skills, so delighted was she to be in his arms. She found his kiss delicious and was sorry she'd become so angry over his sketches because the disagreement had depressed them both deeply. Perhaps they would have spent the late afternoon in a far more interesting fashion if she'd kept still about what she'd found. He'd offered to forgive her for having a terrible temper, but could she forgive herself for having that fault when it caused them both such needless pain?

Jason had saved the last of the champagne and when he poured them each a glass Gabrielle drank hers, toasting his health with a lilting laugh. Then he lifted her into his arms to carry her the short distance to the bed. When he could not seem to unfasten the small pearl buttons on her blouse, she pushed his hands away and did it herself. "Since this outfit constitutes my wedding dress, I'd like to preserve it if I may."

Jason leaned back to watch her disrobe, his pleasure undiminished for he'd never known a woman who could remove her clothes with the slow, sensuous grace Gabrielle always displayed. She rose from the bed to lay her garments aside, seemingly unaware of the beauty in her fluid motions, but he savored it with a wide smile he made no effort to suppress. Thinking that she'd be his forever was a delightful prospect. He'd spent many years relishing the pleasures of life whenever he could, but Gabrielle would share his bed until his last night on earth and he now felt having a wife was the only sensible way for a man to live.

Gabrielle turned and, finding Jason doing no more than observing her with a satisfied grin, asked pointedly, "Do you plan to sleep in that suit? If not, may I suggest you hang it in the wardrobe where it will not become wrinkled because if I must undress you myself I'll simply toss your clothing upon the floor. And if you object to the way it looks in the morning, you'll have to press it yourself."

"That's hardly fair," Jason observed slyly.

"It's your choice." Gabrielle was still clad in her chemise. She saw no reason to don her nightgown when she knew how quickly Jason would remove it.

"I don't care how these clothes look in the morning. Come here." Jason held out his hand and when Gabrielle put her fingertips in his he drew her back upon the bed, his lips too hungry for hers to debate the state of his attire another second. She returned his ardent kiss, but then began to tickle his ribs as she reached for the buttons on his shirt. Her touch was light, teasing, and he soon had to give up the pretense that he could

367

ignore her enticing charms. He pushed her away with a playful shove and, standing up, removed his apparel with such haste she had time to draw no more than one breath before he rejoined her upon the comfortable bed.

Gabrielle whispered softly as she drew him near, "I am so sorry for becoming angry with you. I do not mean to yell when I'd much rather do this." Her tongue traced the shape of his lips with a tantalizing caress before she deepened her kiss. She adored her husband and needed little in the way of encouragement to show him the extent of her affection. Her fingertips moved lightly down his spine and over his slender hips as she pressed his body closer to her own. His skin was so warm, his sleek form superb. She let the touch of her hands convey the same erotic message which filled her kiss. She wanted him, badly, her need too compelling to be construed as anything other than a deep hunger for his love.

Jason was captivated by the lissome beauty in his embrace. Again she was the irresistible vixen whose fiery passions he longed to ignite. He gave no verbal response to her apology but wound his fingers in her deep red tresses to hold her still so he could enjoy her teasing kiss before responding with a demanding intensity. Sensing his urgency, Gabrielle slipped off her chemise and lay back in his arms, nearly purring with pleasure as his lips strayed lower to caress the flushed peak of her breast. As always he treated her most tenderly, cherishing the gift of her affection, but he did not trust himself to pay her any coherent compliments. So he spoke none of the pretty phrases which would have pleased her as greatly as his tantalizing touch. He wanted only to lift her heart to the rapture they knew so well, but she moved against him, the soft curves of her body luring him past the bounds of reason with a magical spell woven in so subtle a fashion he was entranced before he realized how easily she'd again conquered his will.

Enveloped in the lamps' soft glow, the room took on an air of mystery which Gabrielle found far more exciting than the clear blue sky under which they'd last made love. Unable to passively accept Jason's generous kisses, she slipped from his embrace, the flowing strands of her auburn hair brushing his chest with a silken caress as she leaned down to kiss him. His mouth clung to hers, but she pulled away, not content with such innocent play when she knew how to please him in another far more intimate way. She trailed light kisses down his throat and across his broad chest, then slowly over the taut bronze skin of his flat stomach. Finally, he could take no more of her seductive affection, and with a deep laugh, he caught her in a close embrace and pushed her down upon the feather pillows.

"This is our wedding night. Will you not even pretend to be an innocent bride?" he asked with an amused chuckle, for what she'd been about to do was not something the innocent girl Clayton thought her would not even know was possible, let alone perform so expertly.

"Would that please you more?" Gabrielle replied in a husky voice which sounded as sweet as music to his ears.

"No," Jason responded truthfully, "I can't complain since all you know you have learned from me." And you have taught me far more, he thought suddenly. But he hadn't time to admit that when his need for her was so very great. He moved his hand slowly down the velvet smoothness of her hip, his fingertips playful as they reached her thigh and then strayed toward his real goal. His caress now grew teasing, arousing her desire until her breath came in hoarse gasps as she moaned his name and he knew his pleasure would be shared in full measure. He gave up the effort to exercise restraint then and eagerly sought the ecstasy she was so willing to share. As he shifted his position, her body welcomed him with a rush of warmth which seared his very soul and he lost himself in the beauty of her loving, not caring in the least that she had not come to adore him as she had Beau. He had a liftime to win her love. If he had to devote each night to filling her body with pleasure before he touched her heart, he would consider his time well spent. He surrendered that thought to his own needs, passionate desire flooding his powerful body. His sudden intense pleasure was close to pain, so powerful it was stunning. Again he was shaken to the very marrow by the depth of the joy she had given him. With Gabrielle, making love had always been perfection, each experience uniquely rapturous. But he knew no words to express how greatly she had pleased him. A part of Jason even feared it had been a fantasy of Gabrielle's making, that to her he was Beau in her waking dreams.

Late the next morning, when the enticing aroma of crisply fried bacon and steaming cocoa teased her senses with a fragrance too delicious to ignore, Gabrielle opened her long-lashed eyes slowly and began to smile, delighted with the surprise. "Why, Jason, you've brought my breakfast to me? How very considerate of you." She raised the pretty blue and white quilt for modesty's sake as she sat up, and he placed the white wicker tray he'd brought from the hotel's dining room across her lap. In addition to slices of bacon and hot cocoa, the tray held a plate of freshly baked muffins drenched in butter and a small crystal vase containing a single pink rose.

"I've already eaten and this will take less time than eating downstairs," he explained logically, but his engaging grin let her know he appreciated her compliment.

"Oh, of course," Gabrielle responded happily, knowing even if he refused to admit it, he'd brought her breakfast solely to please her. "Nevertheless, this is a rare treat and I appreciate your thoughtfulness." She took a sip of cocoa and then began to eat one of the feather-light muffins. She'd eaten so little for supper she was ravenously hungry, but she tried to take dainty bites so as not to appear lacking in manners. "Everything is delicious, but if you continue to pamper me like this I shall become dreadfully spoiled," she teased, giving him an impish smile between bites.

"You're already so damn spoiled this small gesture won't harm you!" Jason replied with a hearty chuckle.

"I am not spoiled!" Gabrielle argued, but she, too, broke into laughter. When Jason drew a chair up next to the bed and produced a handful of gold rings, she was so astonished she nearly upset her tray and had to grab the cup of hot cocoa to keep it from spilling all over the attractive quilt. "Where did you get those?"

"From the jeweler." Jason took her left hand and slipped one of the gleaming wedding bands upon her third finger. "I wasn't certain of the size but if one of these doesn't fit properly I'll go and get some more."

Gabrielle thought the plain band very tasteful, but it was a bit too large. "Is there one slightly smaller?"

Jason sorted through the rings to select another. "Give this one a try," he suggested agreeably, seemingly in no hurry.

The second ring was more delicate than the first, its design a spray of ivy leaves entwined to form a graceful circle. Gabrielle loved it instantly and was delighted when the ring fit perfectly. "This is the one I want. I've never seen another ring as lovely as this. May I keep it please?"

Jason could scarcely respond, he was so touched by the sweetness of her question. She seemed so young that morning, and her pretty blue eyes were filled with such an enthusiastic sparkle it was difficult for him to believe she was the same exotic beauty with whom he'd spent the most erotic of nights. He took her hand tenderly in his and brought it to his lips.

"This ring was my favorite too," he finally admitted.

"Why didn't you say so?" Gabrielle asked curiously.

Embarrassed by her question Jason released her hand with a gentle squeeze and rose to his feet. "Because I wanted the choice to be yours, not mine. Now, finish your breakfast. The maid will draw a bath when you're ready. I'll just return these other rings to my friend, and then I'll borrow Clayton's wagon so we can go shopping."

"I'll be ready when you get back," Gabrielle promised sincerely. She wanted to please him, and if time were of the essence then she'd not keep him waiting.

* * *

Jason was glad he'd thought to borrow the wagon as it was soon filled with the useful items he and Gabrielle had spent the previous afternoon discussing. He'd not even been out to his home yet, but he was certain their needs were many. He knew no matter how thorough they'd attempted to be, they'd surely overlooked something. "Why don't you buy some fabric for gowns? You know how to sew, don't you?"

"I'd rather buy material to make curtains as I imagine we'll need new ones. Perhaps I should wait until we can take the measurements though; I want to be certain I purchase enough."

Gabrielle looked over the bolts of fabric stacked upon the shelves behind the counter in the dry goods store. "They have several bright prints, but I'd like to see the house first before I make my decision."

"You don't want to make any new dresses?" Jason asked skeptically. "All your clothes are lovely, but surely you must want some new ones."

Gabrielle shook her head. She'd need new dresses all right, with each passing day she was more certain of it, but she'd not begin fashioning loose-fitting gowns until she absolutely had to. "First let me sort out my wardrobe. I'll buy some yardage later if I find there's something I need."

Jason lifted a well-shaped brow quizzically. "There is a fine seamstress here in town. You needn't make your own clothes if you don't know how."

"I do know how!" Gabrielle responded heatedly. Then she forced herself to be calm. "Please let's not argue about so foolish a question as the extent of my wardrobe. I'm anxious to see your house, can't we go out there now and worry about new dresses for me later?"

Jason leaned close to whisper. "Money is no problem, perhaps you did not realize that, but you needn't be so damn thrifty when there is no reason to be."

Gabrielle blushed deeply for she'd not given the extent of Jason's resources the slightest thought. "I am certain you will

372

be able to provide for my welfare, but from what you say there will be so much to do I'll scarcely have time to sit down and sew for several weeks. Fabric is the last thing I need to buy today. Now, may we please go?"

"As you wish." Jason shrugged, uncertain why Gabrielle had suddenly grown so contrary.

He paid for the last of their purchases and then drove the heavily laden wagon over to Clayton's so they could pick up her belongings. He had not even considered the reception they'd receive, but all the young women seemed to be at home that morning and each glance which met his was an openly curious one. Why women were taught so little by their mothers he did not know, but he decided to act as though he and Gabrielle had lived their entire lives together. After all, the fact that they'd spent the night in the same bed was not at all remarkable.

"Run on up to your room and pack; then call me when you want everything brought downstairs. I'll talk with Clay while I'm waiting," he said.

"I won't be a minute," Gabrielle called over her shoulder, but she'd misjudged her roommates' fascination with her marriage. They soon huddled closely about her, their curiosity undisguised.

"It seems Jason Royal was interested in more than that stallion of yours after all," Iris remarked caustically.

"Apparently he was," Gabrielle responded pleasantly for she did not intend to allow Iris' spitefulness to irritate her.

"Personally, I think such haste to wed is unseemly. I plan to announce my engagement at least a week before I marry." The haughty brunette continued to make the insulting comments she considered conversation with women she thought her rivals.

Folding her clothing neatly to stack it in her bag, Gabrielle asked, "Have you already accepted a proposal then, Iris?"

"No, of course not. I plan to wait until I'm certain I've found a man who suits me. I'll not marry the first one to propose." She tossed her dark curls as if she'd received so many offers of marriage she'd lost count.

"I'm sure that's wise of you," Erica agreed. "Have you noticed how interested in Christina John Randolph has become? You were wise not to give him all of your attention when he's proven to be so fickle."

Iris' dark eyes narrowed to vicious slits. "You don't think I care about how he spends his time do you? Why he means nothing to me, he can marry Christine for all I care!"

"He just might," Erica predicted with exaggerated sweetness. "You are fortunate to have so many other suitors the loss of one will not matter."

Too outraged by that taunt to reply, Iris stormed out of the room, slamming the door with a loud bang. There were still plenty of men who were interested in her. She didn't intend to take such teasing from Erica, and she vowed not to speak to the young woman for the rest of the day.

Erica broke into a high-pitched giggle, delighted that she'd upset Iris so greatly. "Well, it's true. Iris does seem to attract a lot of attention, but I noticed last night that the crowd around her has grown smaller. Even those who still seem to admire her are spending more of their time with others. John Randolph is only the first to stray, but I'll wager the rest will follow his lead."

"I only hope Iris marries a man who deserves her," Gabrielle commented agreeably, and that remark sent her companions into peals of gleeful laughter. "You shall have to keep us informed as Jason and I want to attend your weddings," Gabrielle continued when at last her friends again grew still.

Erica sat down on the edge of the bed they'd shared to relate her own happiness. "Michael Jenkins is quite the nicest man I've ever met. It was lucky for me he was waiting outside just when I needed a ride to your wedding." Her sly smile let everyone know she'd taken every advantage of that coincidence. "He seemed to like me too, but I'll not get my hopes up until he comes to call."

Gabrielle made it a point to ask about Marlene's friend, hoping to make up for the rudeness she'd shown her. "How are things going between you and Charles?" she inquired, hoping the young woman had forgotten her worries about her age.

"Very well," Marlene revealed proudly. "It seems the matter I mentioned to you was of no importance to him, he likes me exactly the way I am."

"Really?" Gabrielle was amazed that the shy girl had had the courage to confide in the young man when she'd been so unsure of the outcome. "I told you it would not matter, but I see you believe Charles more than you did me." She took the time to ask Barbara and Margaret about their beaus too, and then turned to Johanna. "How are things going for you?"

"Not so well, I'm afraid. It seems Frank only pretended an interest in religion to impress me. When we went to church on Sunday, the preacher did not even know him."

Johanna had continued to wear her pretty curls loose, and while her manner was serious, her appearance was so cute she seemed unconcerned over the man's ruse.

"Perhaps he has been too busy to attend services, but that does not necessarily mean he has no interest in religion," Gabrielle suggested sympathetically.

"That was exactly what he said," Johanna explained. "But I do not believe him."

"Well, do not be so hasty in your judgment," Erica cautioned. "I know from bitter experience how much trouble that can get you into."

Johanna shook her head. "I plan to allow enough time for him to show me whether his beliefs are sincere or not, but I'll not marry him if he is only trying to please me now and will prove to be a poor husband once we are wed."

"A wise decision," Gabrielle assured her. She gave Johanna a warm hug and then quickly escaped before anyone had an opportunity to inquire as to what sort of husband Jason had proved to be. Hurrying downstairs, she called Jason. He came quickly to carry her one bag and her books which were still wrapped in the oilcloth he'd given her. It took a moment for him to find space for her belongings; then he drove the sturdy wagon around to the barn to get Duke and Sunny. He'd not even considered hitching them to the wooden vehicle as they were far too suspicious of each other to function as a compatible team. He merely tied their reins to the tailgate, then tossed the saddles upon their heap of goods. He waved goodbye to Clayton and the young women who stood at the windows of the man's well-built house before climbing up into his seat and turning to give Gabrielle a sly wink. She took his arm and moved close, clearly as delighted as he to be on their way. He whistled a happy tune as he started the wagon rolling down the road toward their home, hoping with all his heart fortune would smile upon them and he could make the future a happy one for the woman he loved.

Chapter XIX

As they rode along arm in arm, Jason could not help but chuckle. "Clay was remarkably discreet this morning. Were your friends able to contain their curiosity too?"

Gabrielle smiled prettily as she described the scene in the girls' bedroom. "Their reactions were easily predictable. Iris was spiteful as always, but Erica amused us by teasing her. Then I asked the others to tell me about the men in whom they are interested, and none remembered to ask me about you."

"That's just as well, I suppose." After a moment's pause, Jason became curious. "What would you have said about me had they not become so easily distracted?"

Gabrielle's perceptive glance swept her husband's deeply bronzed features fondly. The clear gray of his eyes was unusual, but combined with his dark complexion and black curls, they made him all the more handsome. It was difficult for her to formulate a coherent reply when his attractiveness stirred the memory of the deep pleasure they'd shared on their wedding night. However, knowing he would soon grow impatient with her silence, she forced herself to state the first thought that occurred to her. "I had no remarks prepared as I prefer to keep my opinions to myself in such personal matters."

Disappointed in her evasive response, Jason persisted.

"You'll not keep your opinion from me, I hope."

Gabrielle laid her right hand upon his sleeve. He was again dressed in buckskins and the softness of the suede was delightful to touch, almost as alive and warm as his own skin. "Are you simply fishing for compliments this morning, sir, or has my delight in becoming your bride escaped your notice?"

Patting her hand affectionately, Jason responded truthfully. "I enjoy hearing compliments as much as you do. That should come as no surprise."

"You wish me to continue?" Gabrielle queried playfully. "I shall have little time to help you with your house if I must spend the whole day flattering you."

"Our house," Jason corrected. "Compared to Clayton's it is quite primitive. I hope you'll not be too badly disappointed in it."

"Since it is your home, I shall not be disappointed," she reassured him emphatically.

When they reached the house his father had built she was amazed that his description had been so inadequate. Like Michael Jenkins' home it was constructed of logs, but it was more than twice the size of his. The front door opened upon a large living room with an enormous stone fireplace at one end, while the kitchen occupied the far corner. A wide loft ran the length of the room. It had obviously been built to provide ample space for the beds of the brothers and sisters Jason's parents had hoped he'd have, and Gabrielle was saddened to think that their other offspring had survived only briefly. Jason's father had built a separate master bedroom. It was spacious and had its own fireplace. A magnificent brass bed, an ornately carved wardrobe, and a handsome dresser served as furnishings.

Unable to believe Jason would not be proud of such a lovely house, Gabrielle asked him pointedly, "Why would anyone be disappointed in your home, Jason? I think it is an extremely nice one."

Jason shrugged noncommittally. "I grew up here. Perhaps

that's why it seems so ordinary to me."

"Well it is far from ordinary!" Gabrielle drew close to examine the decorative carving on the wardrobe. Fashioned from local pine, the piece was superb in both construction and style. "Did your father build furniture too? This piece is quite beautiful, better than anything I ever saw in Liberty."

"Yes. He made all the furniture in the house." Since Gabrielle's compliment was obviously sincere, he told her something about his father. "He and my mother were very young when they married. They had little money to pay for things they needed so he was forced to make everything himself. By the time we came to Oregon, he had become quite proficient."

"Then it is obviously from him that you inherited your artistic talent, for not only is his craftsmanship excellent, his designs are as well." She went over to look more closely at the dresser, marveling at the companion piece to the wardrobe before she turned to look at the bed. "He bought the bed though, didn't he?"

"I believe he traded something for it, but that was so long ago I've forgotten just exactly what the bargain entailed." As Jason focused his attention upon the bed, he suddenly recalled how comfortable it was and turned to his bride with a sly grin. "It is an exceptionally fine bed, but you needn't take my word for it. We can try it out right now if you'd like."

Gabrielle came close to slip her arms around his waist, intending to decline his invitation gracefully. "That would not be wise when we've left all our worldly goods and four tired and thirsty horses out in the front yard. Let's see to the chores to be done before we lose ourselves in each other."

"I had no idea you were so practical, Gabrielle, but this is a poor time for you to display that trait because since you are right I'll have to agree." He turned her around then and with a playful swat sent her toward the door. "I'll unload the wagon and see to the horses; then I'll help you clean up in here so we can put everything away."

"Whatever you wish, sir," Gabrielle replied with a saucy smile, but she hurried out of his way.

"You know damn well what I wish, and I'll not let you escape me so easily later!" He laughed happily as he went out the front door, certain his bride was such a passionate creature she would not object to the amusement he had in mind for the first spare moment they found.

While Jason was busy unloading the wagon, Gabrielle strolled through the house once again, taking her time to admire the furnishings more closely. While every item the house contained was beautifully crafted, a thick layer of dust covered them all. She went to the door to call to her husband.

"Have you found the mop and broom?"

"Not yet." Jason kept sorting through their purchases until he found the implements she wanted. He carried them to the door and leaned down to give her a light kiss. "The house has been vacant for months. It's in a sorry state, so you can't expect to clean it thoroughly in one afternoon."

"Perhaps not, but I can try," Gabrielle vowed seriously, for she knew they both deserved to live in a tidy home. Suddenly puzzled by his remark, she inquired, "You haven't come out here at all, have you?"

"No," Jason admitted grudgingly. He looked away, his mood darkening at the realization that any man seriously contemplating marriage as he'd sworn he was would have taken the time to clean his house before he brought his bride home. "Another of my many oversights. I shouldn't have brought you here to do all this work. I should have had the house presentable before you arrived."

"Jason!" Gabrielle reached out to catch his arm as he turned away. "That wasn't what I meant! I know how busy you've been. I'm not overly concerned about a little dust. Since this is to be my home, I do not mind putting everything in order."

"It should have been my job, not yours." Jason scowled as he left the porch, unconvinced by her reassurance. He went back to the wagon to finish stacking their provisions by the front door. When he'd completed that chore, he led the team into the barn before unhitching them from the wagon. He then put Clayton's horses in the small corral behind the barn and gave them plenty of hay and water before turning his attention to Sunny's and Duke's needs. Duke would be content in the corral, but the red stallion had gazed so longingly at the open fields he hesitated to confine him to a stall in the barn. Certain the spirited horse would not leave his mistress, he turned him loose to graze. What they needed, he realized, was a fenced pasture of sufficient size to provide the handsome animal with room to exercise. However, knowing that project would have to wait until spring, he returned to the house, uncertain as to what sort of reception Gabrielle would give him after he'd been so rude to her. He didn't want her to lie and he knew he'd been most remiss in not seeing that his house was properly cleaned before her arrival, but he felt anger would have been a far more logical response than her calm determination to set everything right. She'd wanted to be a farmer's bride, and he'd supplied the farm as well as a somewhat reluctant farmer; but he could not really believe she would be content with either of them for very long.

When Gabrielle saw Jason at the door, she pointed to the three braided rugs she'd placed beside it. "Would you please take these rugs outside and shake them a bit?"

"Yes, ma'am," Jason drawled, and glad for the excuse to work elsewhere, he lugged the rugs outdoors and went to find the rug beater that he kept in the barn. Beating the rugs was a good outlet for his frustration but they'd not been on the farm more than an hour and he already felt as though he were suffocating. He had hated the endless chores that had filled his days as a boy. To have come back willingly to lead the farming existence he had once fled was an act to which he could still not quite reconcile himself. He'd wanted Gabrielle, and he'd been willing to pay the price, though being tied to the land again was an extremely high one. She'd asked if he intended to give up leading wagon trains, but he already knew the freedom that job allowed was not worth the agony he'd suffer if he left her home alone for months at a time. Everything in life has its price, he thought. But he did not need to remind himself that having Gabrielle as his wife was worth the sacrifice.

He slung the first rug over a rope stretched between two trees. Then he hit the defenseless carpet with a barrage of savage blows as if somehow the tightly braided woolen rug were to blame for his dilemma although he knew it was as innocent as Gabrielle. Finally, satisfied it was clean, he carried it back into the house before giving his attention to the other two. Once that job was finished he decided to wash the windows. They certainly needed cleaning, and doing so gave him a valid excuse to remain outside while Gabrielle struggled to restore neatness to the interior of their home.

By late afternoon, Gabrielle was yawning frequently for she'd had no time to stop and rest. When she heard Jason chopping wood by the back door, she went out on the porch to watch for a moment. He'd tossed his shirt aside, and while she'd meant to stay outdoors only briefly, she found herself so fascinated by the perfection of his powerful build that she could not turn away. The well-developed muscles of his arms and shoulders grew tense and then relaxed as he swung the ax with a slow, steady rhythm. His dark skin shone with a light coating of sweat, giving his body the gleaming appearance of a heroic figure cast in bronze. She stood quietly, watching him work, her gaze openly adoring, until he turned slightly and saw her observing him.

"Yes?" Jason responded, thinking he'd not heard her call to him. "Was there something you needed?" He held the ax loosely in his grip as he awaited her reply.

Gabrielle's cheeks filled with a bright blush as she answered, "I was just wishing that I knew how to draw as well as you do. You would make a very fine subject."

Jason lay the ax aside and walked toward his bride, wondering if she now understood why he'd enjoyed drawing the luscious curves of her figure in such fine detail. "If you'd like to learn I will teach you. Since you needn't teach me how to read, we'll need some useful pursuit to keep us occupied this winter."

When he reached the porch upon which she stood, his eyes were level with hers and so full of mischief she could not help but smile. "I would enjoy lessons of any sort if you were my teacher," she confided in a throaty whisper, her voice as seductive as his expression.

Jason rested his hand upon her shoulder, his thumb moving to cover the pulse which throbbed steadily in her throat as he drew her lips to his. He meant only to kiss her lightly, his gesture a promise of the pleasures yet to come, but she entered his arms with a grace which made any further delay in sampling her affection seem a deprivation. Blood began to rush through his ears with a fearful intensity, blocking out all awareness of the warm fall afternoon. Her mouth opened so eagerly to accept his deepening kiss it was plain that her hunger for love was as desperate as his own. The tension between them continued to mount until it was a tangible force which compelled Jason's immediate response. He swept Gabrielle up into his arms and carried her swiftly into the house, straight to the brass bed whose comfort he'd invited her to share. She offered no more than a lilting laugh in objection to his haste, so he began to peel away the layers of her clothing, tossing her garments carelessly over his shoulder until her superb figure was completely revealed to his view. His glance raked over her slowly, then returned to lock upon the blue of her eyes as he removed what remained of his own attire.

Gabrielle curled up gracefully, propping her elbow upon the feather pillows as she waited for her husband to join her. Her pretty mouth curved invitingly, her delight in him as obvious as a spoken compliment would have been. He hesitated a moment, knowing the advantage was his, but he dared not tease her when he longed to arouse the fire of her passions rather than the fury of her anger. He moved across the high bed and pulled her into his arms, dismissing all thought of games, his desire insistent. There was a smudge of dirt upon her left cheek and he brushed it away with his fingertips before covering her face with a flurry of hungry kisses.

Gabrielle was in no mood for playful affection either. She wrapped her arms tightly around her husband's neck, holding him captive in her embrace as she moved slowly to lure him toward a far more exotic type of pleasure. She was thrilled to be his bride, to be sharing his home, and her joy was as infectious as her intoxicating kiss. She saw no reason to be coy or flirtatious when sincerity brought such delight to them both. She knew he enjoyed being with her even though he seldom admitted any fondness for her, and feeling shivers of anticipation course down his spine, she was pleased to know she was the cause. The muscular bands which crisscrossed his back flexed with dynamic rhythm as he tightened his embrace, but his touch, as always, remained gentle. His fingertips strayed lightly over the soft swells of her lovely figure, tracing the creamy smoothness of her skin with an adoring caress, and she ceased to let her mind interfere with the rapturous warmth which flooded her senses. She basked in Jason's delicious affection, and knew she'd never tire of being his bride.

Jason found his wife in so obliging a mood he hoped it would continue until dawn. Her light touch, her soft sighs of surrender, her graceful pose as she wound herself around him, all her charming ways inspired him to seek more novel ways to express the love which filled his heart. His mouth lingered at her breast, the full curves of her slender figure delighting him anew, but soon he wanted much more. While his lips strayed lower still, his fingertips moved slowly up the inside of her thigh until he could feel her skin tingle. Her whole being welcomed his caresses with a joy she made no effort to hide. Thinking her the loveliest of creatures, he moved swiftly to show her the depth of his appreciation for her beauty. Lost in his own pleasure, he hoped the tenderness of his kisses would make his feelings clear since he could never seem to express the poetry of his thoughts in words.

When Jason's lips returned to hers, Gabrielle pressed her lithe body along the length of his. Her warmth was slight compared to the heat of his lean physique so she wanted to absorb his fire and then share it. Enjoying his closeness, she let her fingertips slide down his muscular arms, her hands remaining over his until their fingers entwined. He was the most daring of lovers, his kiss an endless delight, his touch teasing. Suddenly her whole body shuddered with the pain of unquenched desire. She could neither beg him to stop, nor plead with him to continue. As she whispered his name her voice, no longer filled with desire, was a hoarse passionate sob.

Jason dared not leave his bride's emotions in such turmoil. He drew her slender hips to his, pulling her so near their bodies at last merged into one vibrant being. Their hearts beat rapidly in unison, their breathing so shallow neither could whisper the sweet endearments the other longed to hear. Passion swept them through time, their need for each other intense, their shared pleasure so glorious the minutes flowed into hours. Indeed, the afternoon passed so swiftly it seemed to have been no more than a wonderful dream which took place in the wink of an eye. Still, neither could bear to leave the other, so their bodies entwined, the gentle peace of sleep overtook them.

The room was veiled in deep shadows by the time Jason woke and forced himself to leave the comfortable bed.

"Please don't go." Gabrielle reached out to catch his hand and whispered an enticing invitation, but she knew he'd not grant her plea even as she spoke it.

"I must," Jason responded sensibly. He gathered up his buckskin breeches as he explained, "If I do not chop more wood we'll be unable to cook our supper or build a sufficient fire to warm the house tonight."

Gabrielle hugged her pillow as she turned away. She wanted him to stay with her—now—as he'd never done before, but he'd refused her request as if it were no more than a distraction from his routine. The bond which existed between them was a tenuous one, and in her opinion, seeking to strengthen that tie was surely every bit as important as chopping wood.

Gabrielle's cool disdain was quickly transmitted to a man as perceptive as Jason, and seeing that he'd disappointed her he leaned down to kiss the elegant curve of her bare shoulder sweetly. "We'll have the rest of our lives to be lovers, Gabrielle. Don't be so greedy."

It wasn't greed which had motivated her to ask for more of her husband's company, Gabrielle knew that full well. She closed her eyes in an attempt to recapture in her mind the closeness they'd shared. It escaped them so frequently in reality.

Jason put his hands on his hips, frustrated by the auburn-haired beauty's sudden aloofness. "Gabrielle!" he scolded sternly.

"Um?" she replied, exhibiting no real curiosity as to what he might have to say.

"This blasted farm requires backbreaking toil from dawn to dusk every damn day in order to turn even a modest profit. I'd much rather stay in bed with you, but since that's impossible there's no reason for you to pout like a spoiled child who's just lost her favorite toy!"

Deeply hurt by that scathing insult, Gabrielle responded testily. "I am not pouting!" She turned to face him then, eager to learn the truth. "You don't really want to live here, do you?"

Shocked by the depth of her insight, Jason dismissed her question as nonsense. "Of course I want to live here. Neither of us would be here if I didn't! Stay in bed if you like, but I've got work to do!" Knowing his bride had seen far more than he'd meant to reveal, Jason left their bedroom quickly, intending to complete his chores before he got himself into even deeper trouble.

Gabrielle thought her husband's attitude extremely odd, especially the derogatory way he'd described the work required to maintain their new home. She was doing her part, but apparently that wasn't enough. She rose from bed to see if she'd neglected any chores before he pointed them out to her in a fit of temper.

As they ate supper, Jason could not avoid Gabrielle's curious gaze, but he attempted to keep her lively mind from focusing upon his careless remark about the farm. "Clay has made an arrangement with Patrick Murdock to perform wedding ceremonies each Saturday until all the girls are married. That's best for the reverend, and it will work to our advantage too. I know you want to attend all the weddings, but traipsing back and forth between here and town can get very tedious after a while."

The young minister had impressed her as a sincere man and Gabrielle wondered if he had a family. "Is the Reverend Murdock married?"

"No," Jason admitted with a sly chuckle since he could see where their conversation was leading. "Unfortunately, we did not think to offer to bring him a bride."

Another of Jason's many oversights, Gabrielle thought to herself, but she did not want to upset him by offering that opinion aloud. "Johanna is very religious. She likes Frank Fischer, but she thinks he might be professing a devotion to God merely to impress her."

Jason reached out to take Gabrielle's hand as he replied. "Johanna is a pretty little thing, especially so now that she has taken to wearing her hair in curls. I imagine Frank would say whatever he thought necessary to impress her."

"But that's dishonest! How could any man lie about so important a matter as religion?"

"We don't know that he is, Gabrielle," Jason offered logically. "I'll not question his motives but if Johanna is hesitant to accept Frank's proposal perhaps she should discuss her doubts with Reverend Murdock rather than her friends."

Gabrielle saw the teasing glimmer in her husband's eyes and shook her head. "You devil! You know exactly what will happen if she begins to see him, don't you?"

"I can't predict the future with any accuracy, but if Johanna

387

truly wants a man devoted to religion then Patrick Murdock seems like the perfect choice."

Gabrielle gave her husband a skeptical glance. "I plan to stay out of the matchmaking business and I'd advise you to do the same."

"A man would be a fool to disregard the advice of his wife when it is as sensible as that," Jason agreed amicably.

"I know precisely how little my advice is worth to you, Jason Royal, so you needn't pretend otherwise." Gabrielle left the table to begin clearing away their supper dishes, changing the subject as she moved away from him. "What chores do you find especially disagreeable? Perhaps I could do more to help you if you'd only teach me what has to be done. I know there is far more to making this farm run smoothly than is apparent at first glance, and I want to do my share."

Jason sat quietly, admiring his wife's graceful beauty as she cleared the table with an economy of motion. It was his own fault he'd let her know how tedious he found the work on the farm, and he did not intend to ask for her help. "You are far too pretty to be doing housework, Gabrielle, let alone any of the more strenuous tasks here. I should be the one to help you, not the other way around."

"What does prettiness have to do with anything? Someone must keep our house neat and cook our meals, and I am more than willing to help with whatever else needs to be done," Gabrielle replied flippantly. She wanted to ask Jason about raising horses, but since he already seemed to feel overburdened she decided to wait for a more opportune time to discuss that enterprise.

Jason scowled as he got to his feet. He had tried to think of a gracious way to refuse her offer of assistance, but she'd obviously not been pleased by his response. "Let's just see that our work is done quickly each day so we'll have plenty of time for each other."

"Why, Jason, is that an apology for this afternoon? If so, I will be happy to accept it, and I promise always to have time for you." Gabrielle gave him a charming smile, hoping she had not pushed him too far with that comment.

Jason could not bring himself to admit to her what a fool he'd been to leave her alone in their bed. Changing the subject abruptly, he gestured toward the wood-burning stove. "Heat some water. I'll put my mother's copper bathtub in front of the fire and we can bathe before we go to bed."

Gabrielle's expression grew puzzled. Each time she made an attempt to encourage Jason to respond truthfully about his feelings, he quickly changed the subject. He was a pleasant companion, his mood often a teasing one, but why was he so unwilling to share the best part of himself with her? Although thick lashes veiled his glance, she could feel his tension if not understand its cause. If he would not confide in her, she realized that she had no choice but to wait until she won his confidence. She knew exactly what would happen if they were to take turns bathing, and if it were her body he wanted rather than her understanding she'd be a fool to object. Smiling once again, she put the kettle on the back of the stove. "How do we decide who will bathe first?" she asked coyly.

"Ladies should always be first," Jason responded slyly, and he went to fetch the tub from the back porch. He'd dusted out the copper tub that afternoon knowing Gabrielle would want to bathe and now he congratulated himself on that clever bit of foresight.

"Do you usually bathe in front of the fire?" Gabrielle added the last of the hot water and then bent down to judge the bath water's temperature. "Not that it isn't a good idea, but modesty will compel me to seek a more private place in the future."

"You are not in the least bit modest, my pet, but I consider that a favorable trait rather than a fault." Jason stepped up behind his bride, brushing her long hair aside as he nibbled the tender skin of her throat.

"Do you want me to smack you with this kettle?" Gabrielle asked, laughing softly.

To avoid such a ridiculous possibility, Jason took the kettle from her hand and returned it to the stove. "Forgive me, what is it that you wish me to say? That you are the most demure and modest of women?" He could not keep his face straight as he spoke and broke into laughter as he drew her into his arms. His fingers moved swiftly down the buttons on her bodice, undressing her with the same haste he'd shown that afternoon. The ribbon bows on her lingerie came loose with a few gentle tugs, and in a moment, he had undressed the lovely young woman who was now his wife. He held her hand as she stepped into the tub and then knelt down beside her, handing her one of the bars of perfumed soap he'd purchased that morning. The exotic fragrance of gardenias had seemed perfect for her translucent skin.

Gabrielle sank down into the warm water, letting the blissful peace of the bath soothe the muscles of her back and arms which still ached from her efforts to clean the house. She closed her eyes only briefly, then feeling guilty for enjoying such an indulgence, sat up straight and made a rich lather with the soap to begin washing herself clean. With Jason hovering so near it was impossible to give much attention to her task, but she tried to ignore his appreciative glance and bathed hurriedly. When she finished and stood up, he handed her the towel he had ready. "If I were to spend another minute in this tub, I'm afraid I'd fall asleep. The water's still warm. Do you wish to use it or shall we heat some more?"

Jason was in too great a hurry to take her to bed to bother heating fresh water, and only after he'd stepped into the tub did he realize the heady scent of gardenias was inappropriate for him. He had other soap, but decided an additional scent would only make matters worse. "I did not realize I would end up smelling like a . . ." He almost said French whore, but caught himself at the last second for that was not what he'd had in mind when he'd purchased the fragrant soap for her.

Gabrielle knelt down beside him and, taking the soap from his hand, began to lather the dark curls which covered his broad chest. "Like what? Like the most modest of brides?" she teased playfully, and as if her words were not enough her fingertips strayed down his sleek body, her expert touch making the thought of cleanliness a totally irrelevant one.

Jason grabbed Gabrielle's hand, pulling her close to give her a savage kiss, his tongue ravaging her mouth without mercy. When at last he released her, he could scarcely draw breath to speak. "Unless you want to get in this tub with me, I suggest you let me bathe myself."

Responding as if his kiss had been sweet rather than brutally demanding, Gabrielle gave him a bewitching smile. "What an intriguing idea." She rose to her feet, untucked the end of the towel which had secured it over her breasts, and tossing it aside stepped into the tub with him.

Jason threw back his head and howled with laughter as the slippery beauty knelt between his knees. They were soon covered with perfumed bubbles, playing like children, but the tub was far too small for the more adult entertainment Jason had in mind. Taking a firm hold on the sides of the copper tub, he stood up, and with the greatest of care, he helped Gabrielle step out of the water onto one of the braided rugs he'd cleaned. Joining her upon the rug, he reached down for the towel she'd discarded, and after patting her fair skin lightly until she was dry, he scooped her up in his arms. "I swear that is the only way to bathe, but I'll have to buy a larger tub."

Gabrielle lifted her arms to encircle his neck as he carried her to the bed. "That tub is perfect," she whispered against his ear. "Perfect."

Jason was in no mood to offer her an argument on any subject. They'd survived one day on his farm without many differences; now he meant to enjoy the night. His lips caressed the lightly perfumed skin of his bride's breast. She was warm and so loving he could not wait another instant to make her his own once again. He wound his fingers in her long, damp hair, holding her lips captive beneath his own as he hastened to bring her teasing play to its natural conclusion. No woman excited him as Gabrielle did and he could not hold back the wave of ecstasy that crested within him and then flooded her slender body with a fiery shudder. He tightened his loving embrace, unwilling to let her go. When, much later, she fell asleep in his arms, he whispered softly. "I will stay with you forever, Gabrielle . . . forever." But she was already lost in a beautiful dream and did not hear the sweet promise that would have pleased her as deeply as the wildness of his passion.

Chapter XX

By Saturday morning, Jason had found no trace of insincerity in Gabrielle's enthusiasm for the farming life they'd begun. Everywhere he looked there was evidence of her handiwork. Their house was more than neat, it sparkled with cleanliness, and the meals she prepared were superb although she'd admitted to having little skill in cooking until she'd helped Paul Slaughter prepare the meals for the women who'd shared her wagon on the long journey west. She took great pride in each task she began, completing it promptly and efficiently. However, seeing her smile as their paths crossed during the day, Jason could not help but feel that her happiness was due to the fruition of her dream to live in Oregon rather than to his efforts to make her feel welcome in his home. He had known almost from the moment they'd met that all he could ever hope to be was a surrogate for Beau. He knew it, but he could not truly accept it. While he now enjoyed her affection he knew that would soon be too little for both of them. Fate had cheated her of the man she loved, but it had also robbed him of any chance to win her heart. Gabrielle would never mention Beau's name to him again, he was certain of that, but he didn't have to hear the man's name to remember the light of love which had shone so brightly in her deep blue eyes the night she'd related the tragic tale of his death.

To escape the depression he felt when he dwelt on that thought, Jason threw himself into becoming a farmer with almost fanatic zeal. He bought a dozen young hens and a rooster from a neighbor, as well as a cow, so they had a ready supply of eggs and milk to supplement their diet. He spent a considerable amount of time hunting, with sufficient success to assure himself he'd be able to provide fresh meat for their table all winter. He made repairs to the barn roof, then cleaned out the sturdy structure so it would provide a comfortable home for Sunny, Duke, and the cow during the winter. In short, he was as busy as Gabrielle, occupying himself with such useful work that he had no time to brood over his wife's lost love. Still, he did not believe she would ever forget the man who had claimed her heart when she'd been no more than a child.

Now Gabrielle tied the ribbons on her bonnet securely beneath her chin and made a few last-minute additions to their shopping list. Once in their home, they'd soon discovered they'd forgotten several of the most common necessities, so in addition to purchasing material to make new curtains, they needed to do some other shopping. "I have looked everywhere, Jason. I know your mother must have had at least one iron, but I simply can't find it."

Jason looked around the large living room, trying to recall where everything had been kept. "The expense is slight, buy a dozen if you wish."

"Two would be sufficient—one to use while the other is heating. I'll not need more than two." Gabrielle had found her husband to be an extremely generous man. Whenever she happened to think of an item she needed he told her to add it to the list regardless of the expense, but she had not taken advantage of his openhandedness. "I'm ready if you are, shall we go?"

Jason smiled agreeably. "Yes, I'll have to think of some way to return Clay's wagon before too much longer. We also have his team of horses, but Sunny and Duke would never work together so I'm not certain how I can get my own wagon into town and back. My father had a pair of mules, but I'm not fond of those beasts since they can be so contrary."

As Gabrielle walked by her husband's side to the front door, she seized the opportunity to discuss buying additional horses. "Why don't we pair our stallions with Clay's horses today? That way they wouldn't have to be together."

Jason shook his head. "That's a good idea, but how do we get our own wagon back here after we return Clayton's horses? We'll have only the two stallions and they won't work as a team."

"Well," Gabrielle began, as if she'd not given the matter a great deal of consideration beforehand, "I just thought maybe we could purchase a mare or two from him. You know how fond I am of horses, and since Sunny is such a fine stallion, it would be a shame not to use him to breed a fine herd of our own."

After slamming the front door closed, Jason remained standing on the porch. He was astonished by Gabrielle's suggestion because it was so completely unexpected. He stared down at her with a troubled gaze. "You want to raise horses?" he asked incredulously.

His puzzled expression was enough to warn her to be cautious, but Gabrielle thought her idea a sensible one and wouldn't back down on it. "Well, yes. I spoke with almost all of the men who came to the parties at Clayton's and not one had any interest in raising horses. With so little competition, the opportunity to earn a profit seems assured. Everybody needs a horse or two for transportation even those who use oxen or mules for the heavy labor on their farms."

Jason took his bride's arm to lead her to the wagon. He helped her climb up and then walked around to the other side and slid onto the seat beside her. He could think of no good reason to refuse her request, but he was loath to grant it. He wanted to be the recipient of her affection and he was afraid she'd lavish much of it upon her horses. "The only horses

Clayton owns now are those your friends rode on the way here. They do not include the prize brood mares you'd need to produce the best colts."

"That's certainly true." Gabrielle sighed unhappily. "Well, do you know where we might buy a few mares from better stock?"

"Not offhand I don't, but this mild weather won't last much longer. If we wait until spring, I can build a fence to create a proper pasture, and after that's ready, I can go shopping for mares."

"Oh, Jason, could we do that?" Gabrielle asked with unabashed glee. "It's not that I'm not content here, farming is worthwhile work, I know it is, but I prefer raising animals to growing crops."

Jason found his bride's adoring gaze difficult to return since his motivation for putting off buying the horses had been a purely selfish one. But if she truly wanted a few mares, he knew he'd be foolish not to buy them without argument. He wanted her to be happy, and if all it cost him to make her so was the expense of brood mares, he'd consider himself lucky. "Now is there anything else you'd like? Perhaps a few goats so we could make cheese, or some geese so we'd have feathers for our pillows? Sheep are quite useful too. Do you know how to weave?"

Gabrielle gave her husband's arm a playful squeeze. "Shame on you for teasing me! I want only a few brood mares, not a whole zoo!"

"How about pigs?" Jason asked, winking slyly. "Fresh pork is delicious to say nothing of the money we'd save if we cured our own hams and bacon."

"Jason!" The pretty young woman punched his arm this time, but he kept right on teasing her.

"We ought to have a dog, and a cat too, don't you think?"

Gabrielle gave up then. The man was having too much fun for her to be angry with him so she sighed resignedly. "By all means we must have a dog and cat. My aunt had a canary once, but we spent more time keeping his cage clean than we did enjoying the sweetness of his melodies so I'll not insist upon owning a bird."

"Good," Jason replied. "The cat would probably just eat the little fellow anyway." Pleased that she'd responded to his playful jests with amusement rather than anger, he did his best to keep their conversation lively all the way into town. He knew Gabrielle might never come to love him, but at the very least, he'd see she never grew bored with his company.

They first stopped at Clayton's house to see if any weddings had been scheduled for that day. While three were to take place, the brides were not among Gabrielle's closest friends.

"I'd like to stay and attend anyway," she said. "Is that all right with you?"

"Of course," Jason replied. "Why don't you stay here and visit with Erica while I do some of the shopping. We can buy material for the curtains this afternoon."

After agreeing to meet her husband later at the church, Gabrielle ran up the stairs; she was so anxious to see her friends. The house was filled with laughter that morning. The women were all busy dressing for the weddings and chattering happily as they did so. Gabrielle knocked lightly on the bedroom door before she peeked inside.

"May I come in?"

"Gabrielle!"

Erica ran to embrace her friend, drawing her into the center of the crowded room. Marlene stood in front of the dresser, brushing out her hair, while Margaret and Barbara were both helping Iris dress. Johanna sat on a bed, her Bible in her lap, trying to concentrate on her reading despite the flurry of activity which surrounded her, but she looked up to smile at Gabrielle.

"I was hoping you'd come into town today. Will Jason bring you every Saturday?" Erica asked excitedly.

"Yes, I think so." Gabrielle greeted each of her former roommates warmly but was happy to see they were so involved in their own preparations for the upcoming weddings they paid little attention to her. "I thought perhaps one of you would be getting married today. Has none of you any good news to tell me?" When that question met with a deathly silence, she turned to Erica with a bewildered gaze. "What's happened to you all? Out with it. Just because I'm not living here with you doesn't mean I'm not interested in what's happening anymore."

"John Randolph is marrying Christina this morning," Erica whispered nervously.

"You needn't pretend I'm deaf, Erica," Iris remarked spitefully. "If he wants that little fortune hunter for a wife, then he can have her."

"Fortune hunter? Isn't that a rather ridiculous accusation for you to make?" Gabrielle replied instantly. "You've made no secret that financial success is your main criteria for selecting a mate."

Iris tossed her raven-hued curls as she turned away. "A woman would be a fool to marry for any other reason, but John Randolph is not the only successful man I've met so his choice of wife does not upset me."

Erica gave Gabrielle a skeptical glance but kept still until the obnoxious Iris had left the room. "She's absolutely livid over losing John. None of us is fooled by her pretense to the contrary. One by one, the men who used to stand in line for a minute of her time have found more attentive young women to court, and last night I doubt she danced with more than three partners all evening."

"You don't mean it!" Gabrielle gasped in dismay. "I can't really say I'm surprised, except that it took the men so long to see through her flirtatious manner."

"Enough of Iris, we've missed you!" Barbara squealed with delight as she came forward to give Gabrielle a warm hug. "I must say you look even more beautiful than ever. Is Jason good to you?"

"Very," Gabrielle admitted, smiling enchantingly before

she changed the subject to a less dangerous one. "Have you not decided to accept a proposal yet?"

Barbara's shake of the head sent her bright curls flying. "I have narrowed it down to two men, Mark Bowman and Roger Delaney, but I simply can't make up my mind between them."

"Well, when you do, perhaps I should just take whichever man you don't want," Margaret offered sweetly, for she liked all the men equally well and could not make up her mind either.

"That's just the trouble!" Barbara explained to Gabrielle. "I know as soon as I choose one man, all the girls will pounce on the other and I'll regret my decision no matter which it is!"

Amid much teasing and laughter, the young women finished making their toilet and one by one left the room to go downstairs. When only Johanna and Erica remained, Gabrielle inquired curiously, "What has happened with Frank Fischer in the last week, Johanna? Has he been able to impress you more favorably or not?"

Johanna marked her place carefully and then closed her Bible before getting up from her comfortable perch in the middle of her bed. "I asked him to recite his favorite verse of scripture, and when he could not recall even one, I knew he had been lying to me about his interest in religion. He seemed to be such a serious young man, but apparently he just pretended to be religious to impress me. I suggested he spend his time with one of the others, and he did not object too strenuously."

"Is there someone else in whom you're interested now?" Gabrielle asked hopefully, for Johanna's disappointment in Frank was revealed in her downcast expression.

"You'll laugh if I tell you who he is," Johanna admitted shyly, her pale cheeks filling with color.

"Never!" Erica promised, too anxious to know the man's name to worry over the possibility that his identity would send her into peals of laughter. "You can trust us to keep your secret forever."

Johanna looked at the rapt glance of each young woman and was certain her secret would be safe with them. "Well, I was impressed by the Reverend Murdock's sermon last Sunday, and when I learned he had a group which met on Wednesday morning for Bible study I decided to attend."

Erica frowned, not understanding where Johanna's story was leading. "Does one of the bachelors attend those meetings?" she asked curiously.

"The Reverend Murdock is the only man in the group," Johanna said softly, her brown eyes filling with mischief as she waited for Erica to guess the truth.

"The preacher? He is the man you're interested in now?" Erica finally realized what Johanna had revealed.

"You'll have to forgive Erica, Johanna, she seems a bit slow this morning." Gabrielle gave Johanna a fond hug as she continued. "We'll not breathe a word of this to the others. Perhaps the reverend will come back to the house after the weddings and you can speak with him again."

"Yes, I would like that," Johanna agreed with a bright smile.

"Now why didn't I think of him?" Erica shook her head in dismay. "The preacher would be perfect for you, the best match possible."

"Well, what's happened between you and Michael? You two seemed to be having a very good time together after our wedding," Gabrielle commented sincerely.

Erica took a deep breath and then rushed through an explanation she'd obviously rehearsed. "He is being very cautious, Gabrielle. I know he likes me, but perhaps that just isn't enough to inspire him to offer marriage. I don't know whether it's because of my reaction to Lewis that he's so reticent to speak about his feelings, or because he hasn't gotten over losing you. Either way, he's been very careful not to make any promises. He's not even invited me to go out to his home."

"Has he taken any of the others out there?" Gabrielle asked sympathetically.

"No. So while I know he's not fallen madly in love with me,

he hasn't fallen for anyone else either."

"I think you both need a little more time. You needn't rush into marriage."

As the three young women walked toward the door, Erica said mischievously, "I can't believe you'd give such advice. After all, your marriage was certainly a sudden one."

Gabrielle responded with no more than a slight smile. She'd not admit that her relationship with Jason had been established during the months they'd shared on the Oregon trail. If her marriage appeared to be a hasty one it mattered little, for she'd already made up her mind before Jason had proposed that she'd never marry any man but him. "Husband," she whispered softly to herself as they moved down the stairs. Erica had once thought that the best of words, and now she had to agree.

Jason was standing in front of the white frame church. He'd intended to offer encouragement to the three bachelors about to join the ranks of married men, but each was so eager to take a bride further inspiration was scarcely needed. They'd all been smart enough to purchase rings for their brides, and as soon as Jason learned that, he assured them they'd all make the best of husbands. His enthusiastic recommendation of marriage provoked several coarsely worded jests, but he turned the jokes aside with good humor and was still in a jovial mood when Gabrielle arrived.

The church had been decorated with great care that morning. The altar was trimmed with yellow and orange chrysanthemums entwined in fresh boughs of pine which scented the air with a tangy fragrance. When Jason escorted her into one of the front pews Gabrielle moved close to his side as she whispered, "I forgot flowers. We'll want to buy some bulbs so we'll have flowers in the spring."

Jason nodded slightly as they took their seats. The last of his mother's flowers had died off years ago, and he should have realized Gabrielle would want to plant some near the house. There seemed to be no end to the things she wanted to do to add beauty to their home, but he gave her a reassuring smile so she'd know he thought flowers a fine idea too. He took her hand and patted it tenderly as they waited for the weddings to begin. As he'd thought, the Reverend Murdock read the marriage ceremony only once, but he had each couple repeat their vows separately. He'd not really heard the words when they'd been said to him, but now he pondered them seriously. He prayed Gabrielle would be thinking of their own wedding as he was rather than of Beau, but as he looked down at her the tears upon her long lashes were unmistakable and he knew the sorrow of her memories had caused her present pain. He tightened his grip upon her slender fingers and hoped the small comfort he could give would be enough.

Gabrielle smiled as she turned to look up at her husband. It was foolish to cry at weddings, she knew that, and yet there was something about the seriousness of the ceremony that compelled her to weep. Her life seemed to be rushing past her with such haste when she longed to savor each minute for an eternity. All her life she'd attended weddings, christenings, confirmations, and all too frequently funerals at which beloved friends were laid to rest. There was a rhythm to the life of man just as there was in nature but it was rapid, far too rapid. She clung to her husband's hand, wanting the sweet closeness they shared in that precious moment to last forever. Despite her hopes, however, the ceremony was soon over and the congregation filed outside. Everyone seemed to be in a joyful mood, eager to begin the celebration which would doubtless lead to more engagements and subsequent weddings the next weekend.

As they stood outside the church making preparations to return to Clayton's home for the reception, Gabrielle gazed about the crowd with undisguised curiosity. A week's time had brought several changes among the couples, and she noted some pairings with surprise while others seemed so perfect a match she was astonished to think the men and women had not found each other sooner. Despite Erica's misgivings, Michael was at her side, smiling warmly as though pleased to be her escort. She saw Johanna approach the young minister when he was left standing alone and could not help but smile to herself at the ease with which the young woman had managed to speak with him again. Iris' brittle laughter rang out above the more polite level of conversation, but the brunette was at Clayton's side, teasing him about the price of champagne, rather than being with one of the bachelors she'd considered a good prospect. All in all, things seemed to be going very well and Gabrielle thought Clayton's hope that each bachelor and each young woman would live happily with a chosen spouse might become reality.

The morning was warm, the sky clear, and Gabrielle breathed deeply, happy to be alive on such a perfect day. When a commotion in the street caught her attention, she turned away from her husband's side to watch a noisy group of men ride by. They were easily recognizable as trappers, by their buckskin clothing and their raucous behavior. They were laughing uproariously, perhaps still slightly drunk from the previous evening's revelry. The youngest of the men caught her eye. He had turned away and was calling over his shoulder to a man who lagged behind. In the noonday sun, his curly blond hair shone with golden highlights, and his size, coloring, and muscular build reminded her instantly of Beau. Fascinated, she could not look away as he rode by in a single file with his companions. His message completed, the blond man again sat straight in his saddle. Before moving on, he glanced toward the crowd standing in front of the church, and in that brief second, when she saw his face clearly, Gabrielle had no doubt as to the young man's identity. As if she'd been struck by a bolt of lightning, her heart ceased to beat and lay frozen in her chest. Her face turned a deathly pale. She reached for Jason's arm for support, but there was no strength in her fingers and had he not caught her she would have slipped to the grass at his feet as she fainted. She tried to run through the blackness which enveloped her. She called Beau's name, for if she were dead they could be together. A deafening silence was the only reply.

A long while later Gabrielle awoke to the sound of hushed whispers. She was lying upon a small sofa in the room she recognized as Reverend Murdock's study. Jason was by her side, and Erica was peering anxiously over his shoulder while a man she did not know held her right wrist between his fingers. She blinked her eyes twice to clear her vision, but she did not understand how she'd come to be the center of such unnecessary attention. She tried to sit up.

"Just a moment, Mrs. Royal. I think it would be wise for you to rest awhile longer. I'm Dr. Patterson. Your husband sent for me when you fainted."

Gabrielle looked up at Jason. He appeared ready to weep, he was so worried; and she tried to smile reassuringly at him. It all came back to her then, with a flash of pain so intense she could not suppress a shudder. She had seen Beau riding down the main street of Oregon City, but that was impossible because Beau had been dead for more than a year. It must have been some ghastly trick of her imagination, not Beau at all but a stranger who resembled him slightly.

"I am all right. Perhaps it was only the warmth of the day," she lied, in what she hoped would be a convincing tone.

Jason's frown deepened for he saw far more in his bride's expression than mere discomfort from the heat. Her fair skin had lost its healthy golden sheen and was as white as the satin pillow upon which they'd laid her head. She appeared to have received some dreadful shock, but what it might have been he could not begin to imagine. The physician, confident that Gabrielle's pulse was returning to normal, released her hand, and Jason took it in his.

"It was not the sun but something more. As you fainted your expression revealed such pure terror you frightened me as well. What did you overhear, or see, that upset you so badly?"

Gabrielle took a deep breath and held it a moment before replying with what she felt was a plausible explanation, if not the true one. "The church was crowded, the day warm. You

404

said that you nearly fainted when we were married last Sunday, so you should understand what happened to me." There was no way she could tell him the truth, but she felt an overwhelming sense of loss, as if the news of Beau's death had just reached her. Grief as deep as hers causes real physical pain so she did not try to sit up again.

Dr. Patterson put away the small vial of smelling salts he'd used to revive Gabrielle and offered an opinion of his own. "Since you've just been married a week I won't make my usual comment, but I've found very few healthy young women faint unless they are pregnant." He closed his black leather bag with a confident snap and turned to smile at Jason. "I think you may take your wife home now, Jason. Just see that she does nothing more strenuous than rest in bed for a few days, however, until we can be certain it was no more than the warmth of the sun which caused her to faint today. Then perhaps in a month or so, you'll bring her in to see me." He nodded slightly, knowing Jason would understand what he meant. He'd delivered more than one baby who had arrived sooner than nine months after his parents' wedding day, and he didn't doubt that his suspicions were true in this case.

A bright blush brought some color back to Gabrielle's cheeks, but she could see from Erica's shocked glance that her friend didn't believe there could be any truth to Patterson's supposition. Jason looked startled too, but he recovered quickly, and after giving Gabrielle a knowing glance, he shook the doctor's hand and bid him a good day.

"Why don't you go on to the party with Michael, Erica? I'm certain Gabrielle will be fine and you needn't wait for us." As soon as the doctor had left, Jason ushered the astonished young woman out of the study and closed the door without giving her an opportunity to offer any argument. Turning back to Gabrielle, he asked softly, "How long have you known?"

She could at least reply to this question truthfully, for she was still not entirely certain. "I don't know, Jason. What the doctor suggested might be true, or it might not; but I beg you not to share his opinion with your friends for it would embarrass me greatly no matter what the truth proves to be."

Angered that she'd accuse him of being so thoughtless, Jason replied heatedly, "If you think I'd tell anyone who would listen that my bride of one week is pregnant, you're wrong!"

Gabrielle raised her hand to cover her eyes. "I'm sorry, I didn't mean to sound so critical of you. Forgive me, for I still don't feel well. Would you please just take me home?" It was all she could do to hold back her tears, but how could she cry over Beau in front of him?

Jason was easily convinced of his bride's discomfort; he'd never seen her so pale and drawn. If she were pregnant, then perhaps a miscarriage was imminent, and wanting to take every precaution to avoid that possibility, he readily agreed to her request. "Let's wait just a bit longer until everyone has left for Clayton's. Erica will tell him you're all right so we needn't stop by his house to reassure him." He began to pace anxiously up and down beside the small couch, uncertain what would be the best way to transport his bride home. "Perhaps I should borrow some blankets and pillows from him so you could lie down in the back of the wagon. Would that be more comfortable for you?"

Gabrielle didn't feel dizzy or sick to her stomach, only unbearably sad. "No. I'd rather just sit beside you if I may."

Jason was not convinced she could make it home yet without fainting again so he waited awhile before he brought the borrowed wagon around to the side door. Since everyone had gone to the reception at Clayton's, he was spared the ordeal of having to offer an explanation for Gabrielle's sudden fainting spell—a bit of good fortune for which he was very grateful. He carried the pretty young woman out to the wagon and apologized that he had no more comfortable conveyance to offer.

"When we begin to raise horses next spring I will have to purchase a fine buggy to show them off. I don't mean to make you ride in a farm wagon forever."

Gabrielle took her husband's arm and rested her head against his shoulder, snuggling close to him on the high seat. She held her bonnet on her lap and let her long hair fly, unrestrained, in the breeze as they started for home. "I'm sorry we won't be able to buy the material for the curtains today, perhaps next week—"

"The curtains can wait, Gabrielle. Don't give them another thought." Jason rejected her apology swiftly. "I mean to see you follow Dr. Patterson's orders and do not get out of bed for a week."

Although she tried to make a teasing reply, to say that would be agreeable if he shared the bed with her, Gabrielle could not bring herself to speak the words. She just wanted to go home, to go into the bedroom, shut the door, and cry until she felt better. She bit her lip to force back her tears, but they soon began to trickle down her pale cheeks in a salty profusion. She missed Beau so terribly, and nothing but tears would take away her pain, not even the warm embrace of the handsome man by her side.

Beau Ramsey visited Oregon City only rarely. That morning he had bought little more than powder for his rifle and lead to be melted down into bullets. His partners, however, fascinated by the contents of the dry goods store, were taking far too long to make their selections so he left them. He walked along the sidewalk, looking in the shop windows as he made his way toward the saloon. The day was a pleasant one and he had little on his mind as he traversed the length of the thriving town. He was standing in front of the office where the local newspaper was printed, reading the headlines on the latest edition posted in the window when a wagon went by. Even in the reflection in the glass the rich sheen of Gabrielle's distinctive shade of red hair was unmistakable. Astonished by the unexpected sight of her, Beau wheeled around so rapidly he collided with an old man who'd been passing by, knocking the poor soul into the dirt of the street. He hurriedly picked the gentleman up, set him on his feet, and brushed the dust from his clothes as he offered a sincere apology. Then when he turned to see the direction in which the wagon had gone, there was no sight of it.

"Pay more attention to where you're going, son!" the disheveled man ordered, and with a disgusted snarl, he shuffled off down the walk.

Beau grabbed his victim's arm, hoping for some help. "Did you see the couple who just rode by in the wagon? Do you know who they are?" He told himself it was ridiculous to hope that Gabrielle was in Oregon City, but if she were, he wanted to waste no time in finding her. "Well, do you know them?"

The elderly gentleman shook his head, "You might say I do but then again I don't," he replied mysteriously. Then, seeing the young man was in no mood for riddles, he explained. "The man was Jason Royal, but I've yet to meet his new bride so I can't say I know her yet. Now was that so important you had to knock me into the street?"

"His bride? Did you say his bride?" Beau looked up and down the deserted street with an anxious glance. If Gabrielle had somehow made her way to Oregon City, she'd not be another man's wife; still, he had to find out who the woman with the red hair had been. Suddenly remembering he was standing in front of the newspaper office, he again offered his apologies to the old man and then rushed through the open door in search of the answers he needed. Finding a man seated behind the counter, he called to him in a loud voice, his anxiety plain. "Do you keep a record of marriages here?"

The editor of the paper looked up from his desk. He'd meant to go home for lunch at noon, but he hadn't yet resolved a problem in his bookkeeping. "This isn't the courthouse," he replied testily and went back to trying to balance his ledger.

"Damn it all, I need only one name. Do you know a man named Jason Royal?"

The weary editor turned again. "There are few in town who don't, but why don't you just find the man yourself if you're so eager to talk with him?"

"All I need to know is his wife's name. I caught no more than a glimpse of her red hair as they rode by just now, but she reminded me of someone I know. Do you know her name?"

The paper frequently published notices of marriages since they were often short of more significant news, and the editor recalled the wedding in question had taken place no more than a week earlier. Getting up from his desk, he opened his files and in a few minutes found the information required.

"Jason Royal married a young lady by the name of Gabrielle MacLaren last Sunday afternoon. Now are you satisfied?"

But when the editor turned toward the counter he found the shop empty, his visitor had fled with such haste he'd not even heard him depart. "Damn fool," he muttered to himself. Taking his place at his desk, he again attempted to concentrate on the totals in the newspaper's various accounts, but his problem was still the same: no matter where he put the money, there just wasn't enough to go around.

Chapter XXI

On the journey home, Jason could feel Gabrielle tremble. She was clinging to his arm so tightly he could scarcely keep a grip on the team's reins. The longer he thought about it, the more improbable her story became. He knew, no matter what fantasy she'd spun for the doctor's benefit, she'd not been affected by the heat. There had been not the slightest hint of distress in her manner earlier in the day. She'd seemed in remarkably good humor, in fact. They'd been surrounded by her friends when suddenly she'd simply gone to pieces, and he'd be damned if he'd accept the pathetic excuse she'd given for fainting.

When they arrived home he lifted her gently into his arms and carried her inside, but rather than placing her upon the bed as he'd promised, he took her to the rocking chair in front of the main fireplace. He brought the quilt from their bed and told her to make herself comfortable for a moment while he changed his clothes and unhitched the team. Once he'd put his suit in the wardrobe and donned his comfortable buckskins, he saw to his chores quickly and returned to the house to brew a pot of tea. After he'd watched Gabrielle sip two cups of the soothing beverage, he felt certain she'd be up to answering a few questions. "Would you like more tea?" he asked solicitously, his manner too open and friendly to put her on guard.

"No, thank you. You've been so thoughtful, but I'd really just like to lie down for an hour or two. I'm certain I was just overtired, I'll be fine by supper time." Her hands were still shaking so badly she had come dangerously close to drenching herself with hot tea on more than one occasion, but her voice was unnaturally calm as she spoke.

Before she could rise from her chair, Jason stepped in front of her to block the way. "You may sleep until dawn if you like, but first I've something to say. You're the bravest woman I've ever known, Gabrielle. In fact, I've seen you coolly face challenges which would make grown men weep. No matter in what sort of difficulty I found myself, I'd want you on my side."

"Well, thank you," Gabrielle responded, not understanding just what he was trying to say.

"You're welcome." That courtesy out of the way, Jason tackled the issue at hand squarely. "We both know you were lying to the doctor about what happened outside the church today. Rather than the heat, was it something I said or did?" He was fairly certain the incident had had nothing to do with him, but he was leading her as best he could, hoping she'd confide in him now that they were alone.

Gabrielle set her cup and saucer down on the floor at her side, afraid she still might drop them since her grip was so unsteady. "You have been wonderful to me, Jason," she managed to mumble, again on the verge of tears. Her hands now free, she twisted the edge of the quilt nervously in her fingers, hoping he'd accept the feeble excuse she'd offered and let her be. She dared not look up at him and focused all her attention on the tiny stitches with which his mother had sewn the quilt. The pattern was that of an ornate star repeated again and again. It was a popular motif and was beautifully carried out. The bright reds and blues had faded to soft pastels over the years, but the colors were no less attractive.

"That's gratifying to hear, but beside the point. I want the truth and right now, Gabrielle. You know I can make you tell me, don't you?" Jason promised in a voice too inviting to be mistaken for a threat. Clearly he meant to get the truth out of her with pleasure, not pain.

Gabrielle risked a hesitant glance at her husband's face. She'd seen his determined frown too often to doubt him, but she dared not reveal the source of her pain when he would suffer as well. "I've nothing more to say," she finally answered, but before he could respond their conversation was interrupted by a fierce pounding upon the front door. Gabrielle's eyes widened as Jason turned toward the door. She was certain she knew who'd come to call, and she was terrified of what her husband's reaction would be.

"No, wait!"

Jason again saw terror on his bride's face, and he reached for the loaded rifle he kept above the mantel before going to the door. When he found only an earnest-looking young man on his doorstep, he kept the weapon pointed toward the floor. "You need not pound on my door so frantically, for I turn no one in need away." That Gabrielle could dread seeing this man puzzled him, for he saw no reason for her fear in their visitor's inquisitive gaze.

Beau tried to see past Jason into the house, but the tall man's broad shoulders blocked his view. "If you're Jason Royal I wish to speak with your wife."

"Unfortunately, she is not receiving callers this afternoon," Jason announced forcefully, determined to spare her the bother.

"She'll see me," the handsome young man replied confidently. "Just tell her Beau Ramsey is here."

If Gabrielle had ever mentioned Beau's last name Jason had forgotten it, but since the first name was not a common one he had no doubt who the young man was. That Beau was so good-looking and obviously fit was something of a shock, but he let none of his surprise show in his glance. Reluctantly, he had to admit the caller was right. "Yes, I'm certain she will and I'd like to hear your story too. Won't you please come in?" he asked with exaggerated courtesy. It was now plain what had happened to Gabrielle. She must have seen Beau and the sight of her beloved, appearing as if risen from the dead, had completely unnerved her. He stepped aside to permit Beau to enter and found that Gabrielle had folded the quilt he'd draped over her lap and had placed it over the back of the rocker by which she now stood. She appeared to be in the best of health, the pallor of her skin replaced with a radiant blush as she faced their visitor.

Gabrielle stared intently at the two men she loved so dearly. Side by side they were so similar in size and appearance she was shocked. She'd not realized how closely Jason resembled Beau until that very instant. Their coloring was different, her husband's black curls and smoky gray eyes a sharp contrast to Beau's fair curls and deep brown eyes, but their attractive features were nearly identical. They could have been brothers rather than complete strangers whom she knew would soon be bitter enemies. Both of them, however, were returning her astonished gaze with angry glances. "I thought you were dead," she finally managed to whisper hoarsely. "Your uncle sent word to your parents that you'd drowned while saving your cousins from the waters of the Platte."

"Do I look dead to you?" Beau responded angrily. He quickly crossed the large room to face Gabrielle as he rushed through a hurried explanation. "I was swept so far down that damn river I was lost for days. Had it not been for the kindness of an old trapper by the name of Sam Willis, I most certainly would have died of exposure and hunger, but obviously I didn't!"

"But your uncle thought—" Gabrielle tried to speak, but Beau interrupted her with an impatient oath.

"Blast my uncle! I've not seen the man since the day I plucked his children from the river! Even with Joe's help I couldn't catch up to the wagon train, and there's no trace of my relatives here in the Willamette Valley so he must have taken the cutoff to California. But I care little about them, what are you doing here and how did you become that man's wife?" He gestured accusingly toward Jason as though he were some sort of hideous troll whom she could not possibly have wed willingly.

Having heard enough to satisfy his initial curiosity, Jason excused himself from their reunion scene, knowing they'd much rather have some privacy. "Stay and chat as long as you like, Mr. Ramsey. I know my wife is delighted to discover the report of your death was in error." With that bitter farewell, he walked out the door, saddled Duke, and hurriedly rode away from the farm, hoping they'd think he'd gone hunting. He wiped away the hot tears which stung his eyes, ashamed to display such weakness even in the solitude of the fields, but he loved his wife dearly and could not bear to think that after only one week of marriage he'd already lost her.

"Well?" Beau demanded. "How did you get here and why did you marry him?" He was nearly shaking with rage and if she did not reply quickly, he meant to shake the truth out of her. He took another step forward, his intention clear in the fierceness of his dark gaze.

Gabrielle was exasperated because Jason had left her to deal with such a terrible misunderstanding all by herself. She needed his calm as well as his strength, but having no choice but to handle the matter alone, she straightened her shoulders proudly and gave the only response she could. "A year passed before I left Liberty. Had I received even one brief letter from you in that time I would have been overjoyed to learn you were alive and I would have waited forever for you to come back for me."

"Forever?" Beau snarled. "It looks to me like you got yourself a husband with remarkable speed if you were so heartbroken by the news of my supposed death!"

"You're not being fair, Beau. I was heartbroken, so thoroughly wretched I didn't even want to go on living without you. What saved me were my memories and my dream of making a home in Oregon as we'd planned to do."

The fire in his eyes did not subside as she spoke, and she recalled that he lost his temper as easily and as often as she lost hers. She'd never criticized him for that fault, but now it frightened her to recall how uncontrollable his anger had often been. The home from which he'd come had not been a happy one. Perpetually short of money, his parents had had frequent and bitter arguments which had, on more than one occasion, led to an exchange of blows. She'd never thought Beau would ever strike her though, but she'd never done anything to provoke great anger in him either. She backed away, moving closer to the fireplace until the poker was within easy reach. She didn't want to hurt him, but if he dared to lift his hand to her she meant to hit him right back. She knew she'd need a weapon to convince him of her sincerity.

"One year is considered a respectable length of time for a widow to wait to remarry. I was not even a widow and it was closer to a year and a half after I'd been misinformed of your death before I married Jason."

"Was it no more than one week ago?" Beau cried out, his pain at that thought causing his voice to break.

"Yes, we were married last Sunday afternoon." That fact revealed little of their story Gabrielle realized, but it was all she cared to admit to Beau.

"You can have the marriage annulled—a divorce is difficult for a woman to get—but you're coming with me now. Get your things and we'll go," Beau commanded firmly.

Taken aback by his demand, Gabrielle attempted to stall for time. She hoped to be able to reason with him. "Where is your farm? Is it far?"

It was Beau's turn to search for a lucid reply this time. Suddenly put on the defensive, he hesitated a moment too long before beginning his reply. "I've been trapping. There's still money to be made in furs, if not a fortune like Astor's. I've been too busy to claim land, let alone do any farming as yet. I've been trying to earn enough money to provide for our future before I settle down. If this winter is a cold one, the beaver will have thick pelts and I'll have all the cash I need come spring."

"I see." Gabrielle swallowed the angry retort which filled her throat and asked calmly, "When did you plan to return to Liberty to marry me? In another year, perhaps, or two? In all the time you've been here, you did not think I deserved such a slight consideration as one letter from you to let me know I was still in your thoughts?"

"Damn it, Gabrielle, I knew you'd wait for me! At least I thought you would," he added hastily. "How was I to know you'd think me dead and marry somebody else?"

Too hurt to argue that question any further, Gabrielle turned away. "That I believed you dead is one tragedy, that you did nothing yourself to prove otherwise is another. I'll not apologize for marrying Jason and I've no intention of leaving him either."

Beau reached out to grab her shoulders, spinning her around to face him. "You can't mean that! You love me, you always have, and you always will!" He lowered his head to kiss her, but she turned away, avoiding his lips deftly as she struggled to break free.

Gabrielle could scarcely believe the distraught young man who held her in such a painful grasp could be the boy she'd loved. Apparently he'd not thought she'd fight him, and when she did he released her with a forceful shove that sent her stumbling back against the mantel. Recovering her balance, she tried to make him see her side of the situation. "I know finding me here today has been as great a shock for you as seeing you riding down the street was for me but—"

"What? You saw me and did not call my name? You did not wave or give me any sign you were nearby?" Beau shouted his accusation, furious with her for disregarding his feelings so completely.

Things were getting worse, not better, and Gabrielle silently cursed Jason for leaving her in such a difficult situation.

Where had the man gone? Since he wasn't present, she unleashed her anger on Beau. "Stop yelling at me. That won't help anything." She clenched her fists at her sides and waited a moment to make certain he'd not interrupt her. "When I caught sight of you riding by I was so shocked I fainted. When I awakened I thought I must surely have been mistaken, that I'd seen a stranger who resembled you. It did not even occur to me that it really had been you."

"Well, now you know, don't you?" Beau answered sarcastically. "This is a fine mess you've created, but I'll forgive you for marrying Royal if you truly thought me dead. Now let's quit arguing about it and go. Your husband recognized my name so you must have told him something about me. He'll understand why you've left him."

"I am not leaving him!" Gabrielle insisted, stamping her foot defiantly. "Have you heard nothing I've said? You should have written to me, a dozen times at least in the months you've been here. Now you say you thought I'd simply wait in Liberty, for years perhaps, until you finally got around to going back. You've done nothing about starting a farm as you promised, not even claimed land let alone built a home for us. Just where would you take me? To live with that rowdy group of trappers with whom I saw you today? Well, do you have any type of a home for me to share?"

Beau's cheeks burned with an angry blush as he tried to think of some way to refute Gabrielle's barrage of accusations, but he just stood there and took the abuse he knew he deserved. He'd justified his actions to himself, but he'd been so confident of Gabrielle's love he'd never even considered he might lose her. "If it's a home you want, I'll go and buy one!" he finally shouted. "I'll be back and then I won't take no for an answer, Gabrielle. I may not have been your first husband, but by God, I'll be your last!" He pulled her into a rude embrace, his mouth crushing hers with an assault so brutal he tasted blood before he drew away. He left her then as swiftly as he'd come, riding away at a furious pace as if he meant to fulfill his promise within the hour.

Shaken to the marrow by the fury of his farewell, Gabrielle gripped the back of the rocking chair tightly and willed herself not to faint for a second time that day. Finally she gathered enough strength to cross the room and rinse out her mouth with cold water, but she knew her lips were badly bruised and she feared Jason would think Beau had struck her. His kiss certainly had had the force of a punishing blow; the inside of her lower lip had been cut. Needing fresh air to clear her mind she left the close confines of the house and sat down upon the back porch, hugging her knees tightly to keep from shaking. She felt as though she were suffering from an acute attack of chills. She tried to breathe deeply, to begin counting backward from one hundred, to concentrate upon the movement of the leaves in the trees as the wind caressed them gently. She tried to distract herself from the searing pain she felt. Her aunt's dire predictions thundered in her ears. Over and over the woman had called Beau no more than a handsome dreamer who'd never give her anything but grief. She'd been a fool not to heed that warning! He was no closer to owning the farm they'd planned to have than he'd been the day he'd left Liberty. She doubted he had twenty dollars to his name, let alone a sufficient sum to purchase a farm and provide for a wife. She raised her hand to her eyes and wept silently. She'd adored him, but in well over a year he'd not even taken time to sit down and write one letter to her. He seemed so terribly young now. Actually he was only twenty, just out of his teens. Had the confidence she'd always admired been no more than the arrogance of a selfish boy? She wept bitter tears for her own folly, wept until darkness fell, and then, not wanting Jason to find her in such a sorry state, she hurried inside to prepare his supper. She lit the fire in the fireplace and stirred up the coals in the stove, but she was too distracted to cook. She paced up and down in front of the fire as she waited for her husband to come home. When he did not soon appear, she ran out to the barn to see if he'd taken Duke, and finding the animal gone, she returned quickly to the warmth of the house. He might have gone hunting and had an accident. He could have been thrown. That was an unlikely possibility but it could have happened. His rifle might have discharged and he could be severely injured. She couldn't search for him until dawn and he might have bled to death by then. She was terrified that he'd suffered some dreadful mishap, yet she was unable to do more than agonize over the horror of that possibility. She continued to pace distractedly until she was so exhausted she fell into the rocking chair. Covering herself with the soft quilt, she finally fell into a troubled sleep, tormented by dreams of Beau's hostile farewell and of her husband's maddening disappearance.

Jason spent the afternoon seated beneath the oak tree which marked the southern corner of his property. Leaning back against the gnarled trunk, he had no plan to hunt unless a stag happened to wander by, which was an unlikely eventuality. It would have been interesting to see the harvest his fields would produce, but he'd completely lost interest in being a farmer now. He brushed away a small beetle which had strayed up his pants leg and tried to force himself to face the obvious consequence of Beau's sudden appearance. Gabrielle would want to leave him, he had no doubt of that. But what would she do if he refused to divorce her? No. That idea was absurd. She'd despise him for that and just run away with Beau the first time he left her alone. She was not the type of woman to be intimidated, but he'd not offer her her freedom. He'd bide his time and wait for her to ask for it; she owed him that much.

Only that morning he'd given a most favorable opinion of marriage to John Randolph. Now his optimistic words came back to haunt him. Apparently one short week of wedded bliss was all he would have. He rose wearily as the sun began to set and rode into town. It was Saturday night. The atmosphere in his favorite saloon was a lively one, and he proceeded to get quite drunk in the company of some men with whom he'd once been very friendly. When one of them made the mistake of asking him why he was there rather than home in bed with his beautiful bride, Jason dragged him to his feet and knocked him unconscious with one blow. The proprietor of the bawdy establishment didn't object to an argument or two, but he drew the line at fist fights. Fearing Jason would start a brawl, he ordered him out of the place.

The chill night air helped to clear Jason's mind, but he could not readily decide where to go. Home was out of the question. There were several attractive women who would welcome him if he appeared on their doorsteps, but spending the night in another woman's bed would only compound his torment not end it. Clayton would take him in, but then he'd have to explain what had happened. He didn't want to reveal the depth of his anguish, even to such a close friend. Finally, deciding it was the best alternative, he made his way to the hotel and took a room for the night. He left Duke in the stable, went straight to bed, and slept until late the next morning.

The rooster's incessant crowing awakened Gabrielle before the first glimmer of dawn had begun to fill the sky. He was a feisty bird, intent upon declaring himself master of the territory in the most vocal manner possible, but she could not fault him for that. He obviously considered it his duty to greet the new day and took his obligation very seriously. "Damn bird," she moaned softly. Then, realizing she'd spent the night alone in front of the fireplace rather than in bed with Jason, she came fully awake in an instant. The house was too still, deathly quiet, but she laid logs and kindling upon the ashes in the fireplace and built a fire to disperse the night's chill. Next she built up the fire in the stove and brewed coffee. She had routine chores to do, but first she fortified herself with several hot cups of strong coffee. The cut on the inside of her lip had barely begun to heal. It caused considerable pain when she placed the cup to her mouth, but she was pleased that her lip was not as swollen as she'd expected. After a little practice, she was able to sip the steaming liquid without letting it dribble down her chin.

She took care of the horses, gathered the eggs, and milked the cow, a task in which she was not yet entirely proficient, and then she returned to the house. She considered searching for Jason. In the clear light of day, it seemed doubtful he'd been the victim of an accident. It was far more likely that he'd spent the night elsewhere. That thought infuriated her all the more. First he'd left her alone to face an angry confrontation with Beau as best she could, and then he'd not even bothered to come home. Needing a distraction, she dragged the copper tub inside, heated plenty of water to fill it, and climbed in. She washed her hair; then she leaned back to soak away the cramps in her tired muscles. She'd not recommend sleeping in a rocking chair to anyone—it had left her sore all over—but by the time the water began to lose its warmth she felt somewhat better. She didn't know what to do then. It was Sunday morning, but she had no desire to ride Sunny into town to attend church alone. That would only provoke questions to which she had no answers. Gossip must already be circulating about her since she'd fainted so dramatically the previous day. At last, she decided to put on a good dress and prepare Sunday dinner as she would if she had a husband who had the courtesy to come home for meals.

It was close to noon when Jason arrived home, and he was amazed by the savory aroma which greeted him when he opened the front door. Gabrielle was seated in the rocking chair, reading from one of her treasured books while the food she had placed in the oven was baking. It was such an unexpectedly pleasant scene he was astonished and did no more than stare at the pretty young woman, waiting for her to be the first to speak. He'd bathed at the hotel and borrowed a razor so his appearance gave no clue as to how he'd spent the night. His head ached painfully, but he knew he deserved that after the amount of whiskey he'd consumed.

Gabrielle leaped to her feet, tossing her book upon the chair cushion as she approached him. "Where have you been?" she demanded. It was plain he'd not been lying somewhere injured and too weak to drag himself home. She was furious because he'd treated her so meanly.

Jason opened his mouth, at first meaning to say that was none of her business, but he realized suddenly he was no longer a bachelor who could call his time his own. As a married man he owed his wife some explanation of his whereabouts. First he walked past her to replace his rifle upon the pegs above the mantel. "I thought you'd prefer to entertain Beau without my presence last night," he finally said as he turned back to face her.

"What?" Gabrielle's long lashes vividly fringed her bright blue eyes as she shrieked at her husband. "You thought I'd ask him to spend the night here, alone, with me? Is that what you're saying? That you actually thought I'd invite Beau to share your bed with me?" Clearly she was appalled by his comment and could barely contain the fury of her anger.

"I'm pleased to see you're feeling like your old self again," Jason remarked slyly. "I thought you'd be glad not to have me around. I knew how far you and Beau would want to take your delight at seeing each other again, and I was discreet enough to stay away. Not every husband would be so understanding, but you needn't thank me."

"I won't!" Gabrielle screamed as she slapped Jason's face with the back of her hand. He'd not seen the blow coming and it caught him full upon the right cheek, leaving a bright red mark which was visible even upon his deep tan.

Jason was more startled than angry. He stared at his bride, confused by her outrage, since they both knew damn well what had happened between her and Beau. "I think we'd both better leave what happened last night unsaid. Neither of us needs to give an accounting of our companion last night." He hoped she'd think he'd not slept alone either.

423

"How dare you!" Gabrielle clenched her fists at her sides to restrain herself from slapping him again. "Beau was here for no more than ten minutes. I didn't appreciate your leaving me here alone with him any more than I appreciated your not coming home! I won't stand for that, Jason. I simply won't. If you plan to sleep with other women, then just say so and I'll file for a divorce. I won't put up with you if you have no intention of being faithful to me."

In an instant, Jason realized the depth of his folly. He'd just given Gabrielle the ammunition to blast him right out of her life, and that had been the farthest thing from his mind when he'd come through the door. How in the world had this woman managed to turn the tide of their argument in her favor when she was the one who'd spent the night in the arms of her lover? Unless, of course, preposterous as it might sound, Beau truly had stayed no more than a few minutes before departing. Taking a deep breath, Jason tried to sort things out in his mind before speaking aloud. "I spent the night at the hotel, alone. I didn't want to embarrass you by walking in on any tender reunion scene so I stayed away all night. If what I did was unnecessary or if it unintentionally hurt you, then I apologize."

"Jason!" Gabrielle cried out in exasperation. "I am your wife! Do you think that means nothing to me?"

"No," Jason replied honestly. "I think you are a woman who'd respect her wedding vows but I also know how dearly you love Beau. Have you forgotten that?"

That Jason had no idea she loved him more broke Gabrielle's heart, but she knew this would be a poor time to make such a declaration. He'd think she was lying, merely trying to fool him while she continued to see Beau in secret. What a wretched mess she'd made of everything. It was too late now to try and make him understand that she'd loved him for a very long time and had never had the courage or the sense to say so because she'd feared he'd only be embarrassed and would not say he loved her too. She turned away, picking up the book she'd tossed so carelessly aside and smoothing out the pages before she replaced it in the bookcase.

"I was very worried about you. I thought perhaps something dreadful had happened to you, and I didn't even know where to look, how to try to find you. You've not taken me out riding to show me how far your property extends and—"

"Gabrielle," Jason called softly. "I said I was sorry. Let's have something to eat, and then I'll take you out riding all afternoon if you like. I'll show you the farm and where I go to hunt as well—whatever you'd like to see. Would you like that?"

Gabrielle smiled slightly. "Yes, I really would. I don't know what supper will taste like. I was so preoccupied I'm not even certain what I put in the oven." She hurried to look and was pleased to find several slices of ham baked to perfection, some yams, and a pan of corn bread. She tried not to cry as she set the table and served her husband, but she felt that everything had gone wrong and in spite of his encouragement she didn't know how to put it right.

Chapter XXII

Jason kept a close eye on Gabrielle as he escorted her around the boundaries of his property. The wheat he'd planted in the spring before departing for Missouri had simply withered in the fields, leaving nothing to harvest. He'd been trying to justify the fact that he'd not put the acreage he owned to good use without explaining why he'd had so little interest in farming to Gabrielle. That seemed like a ridiculous way to spend the afternoon if she planned to leave him, but despite his pledge to himself to make her be the one to request a divorce, he finally had to ask her a question about Beau. He reined Duke in and turned to confront her. "Where is Beau's farm?"

Startled by that question since her husband had been discussing his land and that of his immediate neighbors, Gabrielle stuttered nervously as she searched for a lucid response. "He . . . well, he doesn't have one." She brushed a wisp of hair away from her eyes and hoped he'd return to the commentary he'd been providing on his own holdings.

Finding her announcement absurd, Jason leaned forward. "But I thought that's why he made the decision to come to Oregon first, so he'd already have land and a house built when you—"

"Oh, stop it, Jason!" Gabrielle snapped angrily. Unwilling to reveal any more of the brief conversation she'd had with Beau, she jabbed her heels into Sunny's sides and left her husband where he sat. Blinded by tears, she let the stallion run across the barren fields until he slowed of his own accord. Jason overtook her then and yanked the reins from her hands with a vicious grab.

"Have you gone mad? Or have you merely chosen to ignore the danger in riding Sunrise like that?" he demanded, his handsome features set in a furious scowl.

Gabrielle didn't reply. She wound her fingers in Sunny's long flowing mane and let Jason lead her back home at the sedate walk they'd maintained all afternoon. The wild ride had been worth it though. For a few brief moments she'd enjoyed the same freedom the magnificent horse had known and she doubted there had really been any great risk. Sunny was sure footed, and she knew the burrow of a field mouse wasn't large enough to catch his hoof and trip him.

By the time they reached the barn, Jason's temper had cooled sufficiently to allow him to speak in a more reasonable tone. He helped Gabrielle down from her saddle with great care, placed her gently upon her feet, and then stepped back with a mock bow.

"You mustn't risk your life so foolishly. If you have something you want to tell me then just say it."

Gabrielle's expression grew puzzled, for she'd not understood his remark. His voice was soft, his manner inviting, but she didn't know what he expected her to confess. "The ground looked safe enough to me, surely there's no danger of quicksand or of prairie-dog burrows here."

Jason shook his head, surprised by the innocence of her response. "I was referring to the danger to you, not to Sunny." When she still appeared confused, he simply raised an eyebrow quizzically as his gaze swept the slender lines of her figure and lingered at her waist.

Gabrielle turned away quickly to hide her deep blush. She'd wanted to win his love by being a devoted wife, not by being the mother of his child. That was the same ploy she'd been unwilling to use to trap him into marriage, and she'd not use it now to keep him. She hurried into the house.

Jason did not pursue her but saw to the stallions' needs before joining his wife. She was never going to tell him a damn thing, he realized, and he was so frustrated by her silence he couldn't bear it. "This is going to be the worst winter of our lives if you continue to be so secretive, Gabrielle. What do you plan to do, just ignore me every time I ask a question to which you'd rather not respond? That won't make me any the less curious you know."

Gabrielle picked up the poker and proceeded to give the coals smoldering on the hearth a few vicious jabs to vent her anger. "Jason, please!" She cried out, her frustration equal to his.

"Please what?" he inquired politely.

"Please just leave me alone to sort out everything for myself."

Jason laughed ruefully. "The last thing I will ever do is leave you alone, my pet. As long as we are man and wife, our relationship will be exactly the same as it has been."

"That's not what I meant!" Gabrielle sank down into the rocking chair, her expression a mask of sorrow as she lifted a hand to her eyes. Was he trying to fool her or himself? Nothing was the same now that they knew Beau was alive. Gathering all her courage, she looked up at her husband. "I didn't tell you the truth at the church because I didn't even know what it was. When I awakened in Reverend Murdock's study I thought my imagination had played a horribly gruesome trick on me. I didn't really believe I'd seen Beau, I thought I'd seen a man who merely resembled him. I haven't kept secrets from you, nor do I plan to do so," she explained calmly, knowing all the while that not revealing the love she felt for him was the greatest secret possible.

Jason busied himself with laying a new fire, not wanting to hear any more about Beau but unwilling to tell her to be quiet now that she'd begun to speak of her own accord. "I understand," he finally managed to mumble, but truly he didn't and his words sounded unconvincing even in his own ears.

Mistaking his response for sarcasm, Gabrielle lost her temper completely. "Both of you are furious with me, but none of this mess was my doing!"

Jason straightened up slowly, then turned to face her. "Is it our marriage you're calling a mess?" he asked through clenched teeth.

"No!" Gabrielle shouted emphatically. She was at a loss, able only to blame the fates for causing their argument and for ruining what little hope she'd had to make Jason happy.

Knowing he was dangerously close to forcing Gabrielle into saying the last thing he wanted to hear, Jason decided instead to seize the initiative himself. "I've no doubt Beau must have made some sort of promise to return to see you. I won't allow that, Gabrielle. The three of us are not going to pretend we're the best of friends. That's simply impossible for a reason too obvious to explain. I don't want him anywhere near you. From what I heard him say, he has no excuse for not writing to you or his parents. He was just too damn busy to bother, doing what I can't imagine if he wasn't working to make the home he'd promised you. He's no more than a boy, a tall and well built one, but also a very selfish one to have been so foolish as to have lost you." A mistake I very nearly made myself, Jason thought.

That is precisely the problem, Gabrielle thought sadly to herself. Beau hasn't lost me.

He'd been taken from her by a ghastly mistake; that was what hurt most of all. During the long painful months when she'd done little but grieve for him, he'd been alive and well and so involved in his own pursuits he'd given no thought to her. Her devotion had been repaid with willful neglect and that was too bitter a fact to accept.

"I don't even want to see him. You needn't forbid me his company; I'll do it gladly."

As her voice trailed off in a whisper, Jason's frown did not lift. There seemed to be no way he could turn this regrettable situation to his own advantage. Clearly she was simply angry with Beau for neglecting her. She was not refusing to see the man because she was a married woman. As usual, this was a matter between her and Beau and he was to be excluded. Turning away, he excused himself as he moved toward the door. "There's still light enough for me to see to some of the things I'd meant to do today. I'm not hungry so you needn't prepare any supper. Just go on to bed if you're tired. I'll not wake you when I come in."

Gabrielle did not even look up as he left her. What chores were so urgent she couldn't imagine, but she thought perhaps he just wanted to be alone with his thoughts too. The fire's warmth was comforting, and recalling the playful bath they'd taken together, she wished he'd suggested she wait up for him. He'd contradicted himself, she realized, for he'd said he wanted their relationship to remain a close one, then he'd told her not to wait up for him. "Oh, Jason, you're as confused as I am aren't you, my darling?"

Jason took a long walk, and he tried to devise some clever plan to rid himself of the aggravation of Beau Ramsey. He threw stones, kicked dirt clods, pulled weeds up by their roots, but none of that frantic activity served to ease his mind. Finally only one solution seemed practical: he'd find Beau and their fists would decide to whom Gabrielle belonged. She was so angry with the young man now, if he never returned she'd not complain. They could get on with the life they'd been leading before that scoundrel had had the audacity to return from the grave to haunt them. Laughing at his own grisly sense of humor, Jason returned home, determined to keep Gabrielle from becoming suspicious. If Beau simply disappeared from the Willamette Valley, he planned to take neither the credit nor the blame.

Hearing Jason come in, Gabrielle moved over to allow him plenty of room in their bed, but she didn't plan to leave him alone. She doubted she could have even had she wanted to pretend to be aloof. Deciding it would be better if she gave him an opportunity to approach her, she fluffed up her pillow and curled up in a comfortable pose, pretending to be asleep. She could hear him moving about the living room. Perhaps he'd decided he was hungry after all and was making himself something to eat. She forced herself to wait patiently for what seemed like an eternity before he joined her.

Actually Jason had been plotting the best way to lure Beau off by himself. He wanted any fight they had to be a private one so the story would never get back to Gabrielle. Preoccupied, he sat up a long while; then he went into the bedroom and undressed quietly so as not to disturb his bride. When he lifted the covers and slipped into bed, he listened a moment until the easy rhythm of her breathing assured him she was asleep. He stretched out to get comfortable then, trying to recall whether he'd ever occupied a woman's bed and done no more than sleep. Surprisingly it was rather a pleasant thought to just sleep with Gabrielle. He could tell by the sweet fragrance of gardenias she'd bathed before going to bed, and while that could be construed as an invitation, he decided to ignore it. She was always beautifully groomed, her flowing red hair sparklingly clean. Even on the trail she'd been a delectable sight. Jason smiled slowly to himself as he thought how easy it would be to remove Beau from her life forever. He'd not kill him—he'd no intention of doing anything so dire as that—but he'd give him a good thrashing and see that he moved on without telling Gabrielle goodbye. By the time she got over her anger and decided she wanted to see him, Beau would not be found.

Exasperated by her husband's indifference, Gabrielle decided she'd waited long enough for him to reach out for her. Stealthily she slid her fingertips toward him, finally raising her hand to draw her nails slowly across the taut muscles of his stomach. When he let out a loud shriek, she sat up and laughed until tears ran down her cheeks. She'd never expected to frighten him and was greatly amused to have done so.

Jason could not believe his bride had such an outrageous

sense of humor, but obviously she did. He began to laugh too, seeing no reason to be angry with her when she'd meant to be enticing. But she'd startled him badly with a touch he'd mistaken for an instant as the wicked claws of a mountain lion. Deciding to beat her at her own game he let his fingertips wander up the inside of her thigh. "You could have tried this," he teased. "Or this." He moved his hands with tantalizing smoothness until she came into his arms, all thought of laughter gone from her mind. "That is better, my little cat. You've no need to use your claws on me," he whispered in her ear, letting his lips trail tender kisses down the warm skin of her throat until she could no longer stand such play. Weaving her fingers in his curls, she kept his mouth poised above her own as her tongue caressed his with a slow, easy passion, savoring his taste until he was drunk with hers. Her demand was too intense to be misinterpreted, and Jason responded, with a powerful thrust beginning the loving she so obviously craved. He understood the perplexing young woman who was his wife no better than he had before, but when she wanted him, he knew he'd never say no. He felt her pleasure spread as he moved within her, the fiery warmth of her graceful body flooding his senses until her shudder of ecstasy became his. Whatever he had to do to keep Gabrielle for his own, he would gladly do and soon.

The next morning was chilly and by the time they had completed the first of their chores a light mist had dampened their clothes. Jason built up the fire to make certain the house would be warm while he was away. "I've got to return Clay's wagon," he announced, confident Gabrielle would not suspect the real reason he was going to town.

"Can't it wait? What if this mist turns to rain?" She moved to the window, her expression an anxious one as she surveyed the darkening clouds.

"It most certainly will, which is why I've got to be on my way. I'll take Duke and ride him home. I won't be gone all day."

433

Just long enough to return the wagon and locate Beau Ramsey's whereabouts, he thought to himself. Since Beau had mentioned Sam Willis, he'd start with him and his cronies. Trappers were a close-knit group and he doubted Beau would be difficult to find. He buttoned up his winter coat and pulled his gloves from the pocket. They were made from the hide of an unborn lamb; the outside a smooth suede, the inside snow-white fleece. He slipped them on quickly as he meant to leave immediately.

"You'll be all right here alone for a few hours, won't you?" His smile was a teasing one, the true purpose of his errand completely masked behind his good-natured charm.

"Of course," Gabrielle reassured him, but she still wasn't pleased by the change in the weather. "Just hurry back. I don't want you to risk catching pneumonia."

Jason chuckled as he bent down to kiss her goodbye. "I've never been sick a day in my life and this winter will be no different."

He left her then, with the jaunty salute she'd seen so often when he was leading the wagon train. That made her smile and she went to the window near the front door to wave goodbye to him as he drove away in the wagon. The sky had grown darker still, and she shivered as she approached the fire. The house was so well built there were no drafts. The heat created by the large fireplace warmed the whole room, and she needed no more than a shawl to be comfortable once she'd recovered from the chill of being outdoors.

A slow smile spread across her lips as she thought how good Jason's mood had been that morning. Perhaps she'd discovered a way to make him so gloriously happy his heart would be filled with love. He'd responded to her approach with the most delightful enthusiasm and she'd learned not to wait for him to make the first move when he'd so eagerly make the second. Sitting down for a moment, she considered the possibility that she'd become as manipulative as Iris, but she refused to accept that verdict since her affection was sincere whereas Iris' most

434

definitely wasn't. She could not help but wonder what would happen to Iris now that John Randolph had married Christina. Judging by Erica's comments, Iris had few suitors left.

"That is Iris' problem," she said suddenly.

That matter settled, she decided it was time to get busy. She'd found a pair of silver candlesticks that needed polishing, and she decided to tackle that chore first, scrubbing them diligently until the silver shone with a warm glow. They'd purchased dozens of candles since Jason didn't want her to have the bother of making her own, and she placed one in each silver candlestick. Then she set the pair upon the mantel. The house was coming along nicely in her estimation, and she was pleased to think Jason thought so too. Preoccupied as she was with plans for their home, the morning passed quickly for Gabrielle. When Jason returned, she ran to the door to greet him, but her pretty smile vanished instantly when she saw the seriousness of his expression. He'd apparently encountered something dreadful in Oregon City, and she feared it might concern one of her friends. "What's happened? What's wrong?" she asked impatiently.

Jason removed his hat and coat, and hung them on the peg beside the door before he began to explain. "The Cayuse attacked the Whitman Mission. Marcus and Narcissa are dead, so are ten others, many of them children who attended their school."

"Dear God, no!" Gabrielle put her arms around her husband's waist, pressing so close she could feel the steady beat of his heart as she tried to comprehend the full horror of his words. "They were such a dear couple. They gave us such an enthusiastic welcome. What could have prompted the Indians to murder them?"

Jason put his arms around his bride, kissing her soft shiny hair and hugging her tightly as he reported what he'd heard. "A measles epidemic wiped out half their tribe. The survivors blamed Marcus because he provided a stopping place for settlers, and it seems likely that's how the disease was spread."

Gabrielle stepped back slightly to look up at her husband's strained expression as she asked, "Measles? I don't recall anyone in our wagon train coming down with measles."

Jason sighed sadly. "The Cayuse, like every other tribe that's come into contact with the white man, have suffered terribly because they have no resistance to the diseases which have plagued us for centuries. There's no use trying to assess who's really to blame. The Indians trade freely with whomever they can. An Indian might have caught the disease at the Whitman Mission or in a dozen other places. In their grief they forgot the eleven years Marcus had tended their ills and they blamed him for bringing the sickness to their tribe. He provided an easy target for their revenge and they took it."

Gabrielle closed her eyes as she shuddered. "But they were so wrong, Jason, so terribly wrong to have killed the Whitmans. I'm certain they showed the Cayuse the same kindness they showed to us. That they slaughtered children as well is too horrible to even imagine. How many children did the Whitmans have?"

"Their only daughter drowned when she was four. Three years ago they adopted seven children who'd been orphaned when their parents died along the trail. They seemed to fill Narcissa's need for a family. She was a wonderful mother to them all."

"I don't understand how any man could kill a child," Gabrielle said sadly.

"Unfortunately, it is difficult for an Indian brave who's seen his family die of a white man's disease to think in such a reasonable manner." Jason put his hands around Gabrielle's waist as he stepped back. "An army of volunteers is being formed by men who knew and admired the Whitmans as greatly as I did. They've asked me to lead them and I've agreed."

"What?" Gabrielle's pretty blue eyes clouded with fear. "They mean to retaliate, to seek revenge for the murders, and you plan to lead them?"

"Yes," Jason replied calmly. "Can you understand why?"

"Well, yes, the Whitmans were your friends but—"

Jason took her hand, leading her over to the fire to enjoy its warmth as he tried to explain why he'd joined such an enterprise. "I'm a scout by profession, Gabrielle. These men are sincere, earnest in their purpose, but they're farmers who'd soon become so lost I'd have to be sent out to find them if they went alone. If I'm their leader there will be no bloodbath either. We can chase the Cayuse farther north without killing any more of the pathetic few who've survived." He paused a moment and then continued in a softer tone. "I'd meant to write to Marcus last week to tell him I'd married you. I'd told him about you when we were at the mission and he'd offered the encouragement I really needed. It's too late now to send him the news of our marriage, but I know he and Narcissa would have been very pleased."

The film of tears in her husband's eyes gave their gray color the glow of silver. She gave his hand a fond squeeze, hoping to ease his pain. She'd not believed he'd given their marriage a moment's thought until the afternoon he'd issued his completely unromantic proposal, but she knew he'd not lie about a conversation he'd had with a dead man. Perhaps he had pondered the decision to marry her more thoughtfully than she'd considered possible.

"You know I don't want you to go," she said hesitantly, "but if you feel you must I won't try to stop you."

"I am going." Jason stared into the flames, their crimson glow turning to the deep red of blood in his imagination. He'd known she'd not beg him to stay home, but if she had he'd not have remained with her. "The Cayuse were wrong, but killing off more of them won't bring the Whitmans back to life. White men can be every bit as brutal as any savage and I want to see there's as little bloodshed as possible. Marcus gave the last years of his life to caring for these people and he'd not want their deaths as a monument."

Looking up at her husband, Gabrielle thought his attitude a

most remarkably forgiving one since he and Marcus had been close friends. He'd frequently commented about Indians as they'd journeyed along the Oregon Trail, and she realized he'd studied the various tribes in some depth. As the warm glow of the fire made the bronze of his skin shine handsomely, she thought back over the many times they'd made love under the warmth and light of the sun. His body had a rich even color which simply deepened when he went without a shirt or hat, but his skin was naturally dark and she'd never stopped to consider why. "Which of your parents was the Indian, Jason, your mother or your father?"

Jason's eyes narrowed as though she'd slapped him; he was so shocked by her question. She was regarding him with open curiosity, however. Her question had been a sincere one, not an insult, so he answered her truthfully. "My father's mother was a Cherokee. While others flocked to Oregon for the opportunity to own land, his motivation for moving here was to escape being called a half-breed and it worked. He resembled his father, not his mother. Without gossip to give away the truth of his ancestry it wasn't discovered. If he were alive he'd be mortified to think you'd seen in me something he'd struggled half his life to keep hidden."

Gabrielle was too perceptive not to understand instantly what had happened between them. "He was ashamed of his Indian blood and you aren't, but in spite of his fears you've never told anyone, have you?"

"Only you," Jason replied softly. "And you have such a romantic view of Indians I knew you'd not care that my grandmother had been one."

"Of course I don't care! But what if I did?" she wanted to know.

Jason's eyes swept her figure knowingly. "Now it is too late for such an objection to matter."

It was the arrogance of his tone that was so unnerving. He was proud of himself, rather than guilty for not trusting her with such an important piece of information about his background.

"What else is there I really ought to know? If you have not bothered to tell me of your heritage what else have you neglected to mention? Do you plan to simply surprise me with things like this when they can no longer be kept secret?"

Jason turned away. "I have no time to argue. I have to gather my things and get back into town. There's no way I can give you any accurate idea of how long I'll be gone, but I want this job over and done as swiftly as possible."

Gabrielle's expression turned to one of amazement as her husband moved about the house collecting the items he wanted to take with him. That he liked to travel light was plain, for other than food and weapons he took little. In less than fifteen minutes, he was ready to leave and she had no idea how to tell him goodbye. "I've just realized I don't even know you," she whispered as he approached her. "I think I can guess now why you left home, but so much about your life is a mystery to me. It isn't fair that you must leave now when we've only been married one week and—"

"Gabrielle." Jason drew her into his arms, stilling her complaints with a slow, deep kiss which left her resting languidly in his embrace. "I will be back in a few weeks, but I don't want you to stay here alone. I'll tell Clay to come and get you. He's still got a houseful of women and can't go with us."

"But I want to stay here. This is my home now, and I've just begun to get everything the way I want it. I can't move back into Clay's house; I'd be completely out of place. What about the cow and the chickens? I can't go off and leave them alone!"

Jason shook his head. "The chickens can take care of themselves. Take the cow with you and leave her in Clay's barn. I'll not listen to any more arguments. I want you under Clay's roof while I'm gone and that's final."

Gabrielle backed away, shocked by the intensity of his gaze. Her heart fell as she realized why he wanted her to stay with his friend. "It's because of Beau, isn't it? Don't you trust me out of your sight?"

439

There was no point in denying her accusation since it was an accurate one. "I don't want you living here alone, Gabrielle. It's not a matter of trust, but a matter of avoiding a situation I know you couldn't handle."

"I think you'd better leave before you say another word, Jason."

Gabrielle turned her back on him, too furious to discuss the issue any further. This was no way to send him off on a mission she knew would be dangerous, but why had he been thinking only of Beau and not of her? She chewed her lip nervously, knowing if there were some way to ease his mind she'd use it. He might not respond as she wanted him to, but she wanted him to know she'd never betray his trust because she loved him. She spoke those words as she turned to face him, but the room was empty. He'd left so silently she'd not even heard him don his hat and coat and close the door.

Chapter XXIII

Gabrielle stamped her foot impatiently. "Husband," she muttered under her breath. There was no point in her going after Jason. If he'd walked out on her, surely he wouldn't care to hear the declaration of love she wished to make. She felt so cheated that she wanted to scream. She'd done her best to please a man who could not be pleased—except in bed, it seemed. She placed her hands upon her slender hips and continued to tap her toe. She'd be damned if she'd go to Clayton's like a little child who couldn't manage on her own. If she had no one with whom to converse other than the stock, then so be it. Sunny had been her trusted confidant for years and he'd not fail her now.

Not until the evening, when she put on her nightgown and sat down upon the edge of the brass bed to brush out her hair, did she realize how alone she was. Only the sound of the wind moaning through the trees near the house broke the eerie quiet, and in spite of her earlier confidence she grew frightened. She sat for a long while before laying her brush aside and getting under the covers. She wondered where Jason might be staying that night and if he were thinking of her, but somehow she knew he'd be far too busy for that. He'd set out to lead an army formed to avenge the massacre of his friends and he'd not be diverted from that purpose. He was an extremely responsible man. That was what had inspired her trust when they'd first met, but she'd not realized there were so many others who needed his strength as much or more than she did. Was this to be the pattern of their lives? He was a scout he'd said, not a man who'd retired from blazing trails through the wilds to build a home and raise a family with his wife. A single tear slipped down her cheek and she lifted her hand to wipe it away. Apparently she'd spend a lot of time by herself, but she knew she'd never grow to like it.

The next afternoon Beau Ramsey knocked at her door. He wore a sheepish grin and held out a small tan box tied with a red bow. "I found some maple sugar candy, and I remembered how much you liked it. I know Jason isn't home so won't you please invite me to come inside for a visit?"

"What makes you think Jason isn't here?" Gabrielle asked suspiciously, making no move to ask him to enter her home or to accept his gift.

"I saw him leave Oregon City this morning. He and his friends rode out of town in full view of anyone who cared to look," the young man replied, thinking the matter an unimportant one. "I came to apologize for the way I acted last Saturday. I was more mad at myself than you, but that's not the way it sounded. Now may I please come in? It's getting cold out here."

Gabrielle had known Beau all her life, and despite Jason's edict forbidding her to see him, she considered their house her home too. She'd not turn away her best friend. Looking up at the cloud-filled sky, she gestured toward his horse. "Would you like to leave your mount in the barn before you come in? He might as well be comfortable too."

"Thanks, I would." Beau led the horse across the yard and into the well-built structure. Rather than tethering the animal, he took him into a stall containing a good supply of hay, removed his saddle and bridle, and slapped him on the rump. "Make yourself comfortable. If I'm lucky, you'll have a warm home for a while." Chuckling to himself, he returned to where

Gabrielle stood waiting for him on her front porch.

"Please come in," she invited graciously. "I'll make some tea, or would you prefer coffee? If Jason has anything stronger, I don't know where he keeps it."

"Quite the proper housewife, aren't you?" Beau replied with a grin. "I'd rather have tea if that's what you'd like too." He looked around the large room, impressed by its size and well-crafted furnishings. "This looks more like a fur trader's lodge than a farmhouse. Are you sure your husband's a farmer?"

"No," Gabrielle replied honestly. "This was his parents' home, however. Apparently they'd anticipated having a large family but they did not." She put the kettle on to heat water for tea, then came back to sit down in the rocker. "Won't you sit down? Pull one of the chairs closer to the fire if you'd like." She watched him closely as he sat down beside her, leaving no more than a few inches of space between them. He was again dressed in buckskins, apparently favoring that mode of dress as Jason did. Since the day was overcast and cold, his fair complexion was flushed by the chill, but he had changed little in the year and a half they'd been apart. His muscular body was as sleek, his hair as blond, his eyes the same warm brown. They filled with a merry sparkle as he returned her inquisitive glance. When he held out the box of candy she took it this time.

"Thank you."

"Go ahead and open it. It's very good." His grin was a charming one as he waited for her to untie the ribbon and remove the lid. "Do you remember the time your aunt bought a pound of that for her church guild meeting and we ate it all before she could offer it to her guests?"

"Yes." Gabrielle had to laugh with him, for in addition to being punished for eating all the candy, they'd gotten very sick. It had been several years before she'd wanted to taste the sugary sweet again. "We did so many truly awful things to her, poor dear. I don't think she ever understood us though, or even made an attempt to try."

"How did you convince her to let you come out here?" Beau wanted to know.

"Of course, you wouldn't have heard." Gabrielle spoke her thought aloud. "She passed away last spring. She'd not been well for several weeks; the doctor said it was her heart. I left Liberty the day she was buried."

Beau regarded Gabrielle thoughtfully for a moment; then he nodded. "I heard you were one of Clayton Horne's brides." He looked toward the fire then, the muscles along his jaw tensing as he tried to control his anger. "If only—"

"Don't, Beau. Please don't." She reached out to touch his sleeve, fingering the long fringe lightly. "It's pointless to think how things might have been when there is no way to change the way they are now."

"Everything can be changed if you want to change it, Gabrielle. Your husband will be away a long while. He'd never find us if we left now. Let's just go." Beau held his breath, praying she'd agree to his plan.

His gaze was so filled with love that Gabrielle had to look away. "No. I told you I won't leave him and I won't."

"You've only been married a little over a week," Beau pointed out angrily. "You were my girl for years!"

Gabrielle sat back in her chair. Taking one of the leaf-shaped candies from the box, she took a small bite and let it melt in her mouth. "That's just the point, Beau. I'm no longer a girl; I'm a woman now." Jason Royal's woman, she thought proudly, even though her husband had left her without the courtesy of a formal goodbye.

Beau blushed deeply at that remark. "I don't care if you've been with him. You thought I was dead or it wouldn't have happened. You know that as well as I do, so don't try to deny it."

Gabrielle shook her head. "I won't deny it, but there's no point in going over this another time, Beau. I am Jason Royal's wife and I intend to remain married to him."

Beau's stare was intense, but he could detect no wavering in Gabrielle's resolve. Knowing he would only enrage her if he continued to argue he slumped back in his chair and stared into the fire. "I'm just no good without you, honey. We had so many plans, but without you here to help me I couldn't even get started. I haven't had much success as a trapper, and this winter will probably be no different if I stay here. I could claim the land for a farm, but then I'd not have the money to raise a house or buy what I'd need. If only you'd come with me, everything would have been different. We'd have our own farm by now. You always brought me luck, Gabrielle. Without you, I'm nothing."

Shocked by his somber mood and depressing words, Gabrielle hastened to argue. "That's not true, Beau, you know it isn't. You can be successful at whatever you attempt."

Beau shook his head. "I've had a year and a half to prove you wrong. Why I'd never even have learned anything in school if you hadn't helped me with my homework every afternoon. You were two years younger and a girl, but I loved you so much I just swallowed my pride and asked for your help whenever I needed it, which was damn often."

Gabrielle was shocked to think he'd felt badly all the years she'd been his tutor. She had learned her addition and subtraction facts quickly, and had known the times tables soon after. It had seemed like a game to her to help him, but he had never been able to understand new lessons until she'd explained them every day for at least a week. Then he had quickly forgotten everything she'd taught him when they went on to something new. He knew how to read haltingly, but when she read along with him he'd done better. He could write interesting compositions too, and as long as she corrected his spelling errors before he turned them in, he got good grades. As she sifted through her memories she realized he was right, without her help he had trouble learning. But she had wanted to help him and had never thought him unintelligent, merely untalented in schoolwork. That she had so keen a mind was not something she'd ever questioned, nor had she taunted him for being slow.

"Beau, you've got to stop brooding over the past. You learned everything you were supposed to and you would have done it without me. Perhaps I made things a little easier for you, but you would have done it on your own." At least she hoped he would have.

The young man wasn't convinced. "I doubt it." He jammed his hands in his pockets, stretched out his legs, and crossed his ankles, getting comfortable while they talked. "Other than a strong back, I've few assets, Gabrielle."

"I'm not going to sit here all afternoon and pay you compliments, Beau Ramsey. If that's all you came to hear, then you might as well leave now. You're a grown man and it's high time you start acting like one."

His smile was charming as he glanced toward her but despite his sly chuckle, he didn't seem convinced she was right. He had a very pleasant manner, handsome features, endless charm. She couldn't bear to think those assets masked deficits of character so serious he would never become a success. She jumped then, as a bolt of lightning flashed through the sky lighting the large room with the brilliance of its glow seconds before the deafening roar of thunder shook the windows.

"That was close." She leaped to her feet and ran to the window, afraid she'd see trees aflame, but through the steady rain she could see no damage.

"It's begun to rain," she commented absently.

"May I stay awhile longer then?" Beau asked politely. "I've a long way to go and maybe it will let up."

"Of course you may stay." The teakettle began to whistle then, reminding her she'd not served the refreshments she'd promised, and she hurried to the kitchen to prepare them.

As they sat in front of the fire, sipping tea and enjoying the maple sugar candy, Gabrielle turned their conversation to the memories she had of him, hoping to lift his spirits. "I did not teach you half the things you taught me, Beau. You had so much practical knowledge, so many useful skills, and I had none. I might have been successful in the schoolhouse but you were years ahead of me in everything that truly mattered."

Beau laughed at her praise; then he agreed that her estimation of herself had been correct. "I guess you were pretty helpless if you didn't have a book in your hands."

"I was pathetic, so shy I jumped at my own shadow."

"It was a very cute shadow as I recall."

Gabrielle blushed as he winked at her, and her blue eyes grew bright with the same mischief which had enchanted him when they were children.

"Come with me, Gabrielle," Beau said excitedly. "I want to go to California. We can go on down the Columbia River to Astoria and get a ship there for San Francisco. Together we can have any life we choose. We can make our dreams come true. There's millions to be made and together—"

Gabrielle shook her head slowly. "Our dream was a modest one, and had you truly believed in it as I did you would have claimed land here, built a small house, planted wheat, and come back to marry me. None of those tasks were impossible to accomplish. Plenty of other men have done them alone, including the twenty bachelors who asked Clayton Horne to bring them brides." She carried her empty teacup over to the sink, surprised by the calm with which she'd recounted his failure to live up to the promise he'd made her when they'd parted. "Go to California if that's what you want to do. Just start believing in yourself and that will be the first step to making any dream you have come true."

"There's no dream worth living if I don't have you." Beau rose to his feet and came toward her. "I've learned plenty about Jason Royal in the last few days and he's a rogue by any standard. Look what he's done to you. You've not been married two weeks and he's gone off chasing Indians. No husband worth his keep would have done that to his bride. He thrives on adventure. He couldn't live the peaceful life of a farmer for even two weeks, could he? He's gone, Gabrielle.

Lord knows when he'll bother to come back."

Gabrielle's stare grew as frosty as the chill rain which continued to fall outside. "I meant what I said, Beau. I won't leave Jason, not ever." She had little hope that what Beau said wasn't true, but she planned to make a home for Jason and his child no matter how infrequently he cared to occupy it. "I grew up loving you. You were the very best part of my childhood, and I shudder to think what sort of a person I'd be today if I hadn't had your love. Now I can offer you nothing but friendship. Jason means the world to me, and I'll be his wife for as long as he wants me."

"Which will be forever!" Beau responded hoarsely.

"I certainly hope so." Gabrielle went to the back door and opened it a crack to peer outside. "The storm's gotten worse. I'll not ask you to leave, but if you want to stay you must promise to treat me with the same respect you've always shown."

Beau clenched his fists at his sides, infuriated by that insult. "I'll not rape you if that's what you mean. I love you far too much to take by force what you no longer want to give."

Gabrielle closed the door and leaned back against it as she turned to face him. His defiant stare was difficult to return when she knew exactly what he was thinking. There had always been something magical about their relationship, something precious to them both. They had been far too cautious to make love. She'd been too young, and if she were to become pregnant they knew her aunt would have called it rape and sent Beau to prison. Neither of them had been willing to take that risk when they'd thought there would be plenty of time to express the depth of their love in every way possible once they were married. "I am trying to be glad for what we had, Beau, not to grieve any longer for what we've lost. I can't bear to see you bitter when our love was so very beautiful. Isn't there some way you can accept what must be and let me go?"

His eyes filling with angry tears, Beau responded swiftly. "No! Not when the woman I love insists she wants to stay married to a man who's deserted her on their honeymoon!"

Gabrielle thought honeymoon an odd way to describe the beginning of her marriage, for truly she and Jason had been working from dawn to dusk with only a few brief hours to enjoy the marvelous attraction which existed between them. "That's enough, Beau. Think me simply fickle, or a fool if you must, but stop insulting Jason or I'll insist you leave no matter how foul the weather has become."

Beau swore under his breath and turned away, deciding he'd be wise to simply bide his time. He added wood to the fire and, taking a book he recognized from the bookshelf, sat down and began to read.

Pleased that he'd decided to be so reasonable, Gabrielle turned her attention to preparing supper. She'd planned to make a pot of soup so there would be plenty of that for her unexpected guest. Once the rich stock was simmering, she added the vegetables which took the longest to cook and put a pan of cornbread in the oven. Returning to her place by the fire, she made herself comfortable and waited for Beau to speak. They'd read all of Shakespeare's plays, acting out the parts in order to understand the complexities of the plots, but to see Beau contentedly read such difficult material on his own impressed her.

Sensing her curiosity, Beau gave her a sly grin. "Remember Romeo and Juliet? Would you like to act it out again?"

Gabrielle shook her head emphatically. "Oh no. I think we came too close to living that tragedy to be amused by reading it."

Beau realized his mistake instantly and closed the heavy book. "I'm sorry you thought I was dead. I know that doesn't ease what you must have suffered, but I'd never knowingly hurt you, honey, you must know that."

As Gabrielle's gaze swept his well-shaped features, she wondered why he didn't realize that that was exactly what he had done by not even attempting to live up to the promises he'd made to her before he'd left for Oregon. She had grown up while he'd been gone, but obviously he hadn't. Perhaps he never would. Rather than respond to his question truthfully and begin another argument she went back to the stove to check the progress of their supper.

"I'm still not much of a cook, I'm afraid, but this soup is always good."

"I'm sure it will be delicious." Beau waited a moment, and when she did not reply but began to set the table, he again opened the book and continued to read.

As she served the simple meal, Gabrielle could not deny that she still enjoyed Beau's company. He smiled often and his love was so obvious in each gesture and glance that she could not help but be flattered. However, she had not the slightest desire to display the affection she still felt for him with more than words. Her emotions confused her. She knew she loved Beau, but she felt none of the deep longing she experienced when Jason was near. Jason's appeal was magnetic, an attraction she'd never been able to deny, while Beau's was like the gentle warmth of a summer day. She did not feel guilty for going against her husband's wishes and entertaining him when their relationship had become an innocent one.

When they'd finished eating and had washed the supper dishes, Beau walked to the door to assess the progress of the storm. "This downpour isn't going to let up all night, and since I know you don't want me in here, do you mind if I borrow a blanket or two and sleep in the barn?"

Gabrielle thought his request absurd. "There are extra beds in the loft. I'll give you bedding and you may sleep up there. I'll not ask the best friend I've ever had to sleep in the barn. That's good enough for the animals but not for you."

Beau closed the door and walked toward her. "Are you sure you want me in here tonight?"

The warmth of his smile was very inviting, but Gabrielle simply ignored it. "Yes, I trust you to behave well."

Beau's expression did not change. He'd known she'd not make him sleep in the barn before he'd suggested it, but he wanted to make her think his being inside had been her own idea. The storm was making a fearful racket, and he hoped as soon as she got into bed alone she'd become frightened. Then it would be most natural for her to seek comfort in his arms; she'd done it all her life. Only that night he meant to take things further than he ever had before, with her consent of course. They sat by the fire awhile longer; then she gave him the bedding she'd promised and he bid her good night without asking for so much as a kiss upon the cheek. Once he'd made one of the beds in the loft, he didn't bother to get in. He just pulled off his shirt and boots and stretched out on top of the covers, waiting for Gabrielle to call for him.

Gabrielle got ready for bed. Although she'd told Beau she trusted him, she was no fool. She bolted her bedroom door securely. What she'd told Beau about Jason was a brave front. She did feel deserted and she had little hope that her husband's return would be a rapid one, but she'd not use Beau's generous affection as a substitute for Jason's. She could scarcely sleep with the young man and then send him on his way the next morning as if she'd merely owed him her favors for the many years they'd loved each other but had been unable to express their affection with more than fevered kisses and caresses. Their exchanges, she recalled, had been as intimate as any lover's could be. In one way she could justify making love as something they should have done long ago, but since they hadn't, she knew it would betray the memory of their love to sleep together now and then part. She got into bed and said a quiet prayer for Jason's safety and then a prayer for Beau. It was a long while before she fell asleep.

Beau became increasingly impatient as lightning continued to flash through the heavens and thunder shook the sturdy house with the fury of its power. Finally he could wait no longer for Gabrielle to summon him. He climbed back down the ladder and went to her bedroom door. He laid his ear upon the wood and strained for the sound of weeping but heard none. Apparently Gabrielle was sound asleep while the thunderstorm

451

buffeted the house with a torrent of rain. Careful to make no sound, he tried the door handle. Finding it locked, he raised his hand and pounded upon her door. "Gabrielle! Wake up!" he called loudly.

Startled from her dreams by the sound of his voice, Gabrielle sat up to reply. "What is it, Beau?"

Having no ready response, Beau simply made up one. "There's water seeping in under the windows. I've cleaned it up, but perhaps you should come look at the problem before it gets any worse."

"I'll be right there." Not even suspecting his ruse, Gabrielle leaped out of bed, threw back the bolt, and opened her door. "Which windows are they?" she asked anxiously, surprised the rain had not seeped in before then.

Beau did not reply, but swept her into his arms, his mouth covering hers with an urgent kiss he had no intention of ending until she began to respond. She struggled against him, but he had her arms pinned to her sides and knew she could do him no harm.

Cursing herself for being such an incredible fool, Gabrielle tore her mouth away from Beau's and screamed at him to release her.

"How dare you!"

Undaunted, Beau grabbed a handful of her hair and drew her closer still as he whispered. "How dare you tell me no!" He shoved her backward into the bedroom, ready to toss her upon the bed. But he wanted her to admit she still wanted him so he kissed her again, hoping to revive the love he knew she'd once felt for him.

Imprisoned in Beau's passionate embrace, Gabrielle could scarcely breathe. His kisses were suffocating her while his hands moved over her breasts with a knowing touch she couldn't escape. If she gave in to his demands, she knew he'd treat her sweetly. If she didn't his uncontrollable temper would soon flare up and the force of his confining grasp might swiftly turn to savage blows which could cost the life of her

452

unborn child. She was no more than a few weeks pregnant, the new life within her doubtless a tenuous one, but she'd not risk the babe for any reason. Having to surrender to Beau's unbridled lust rather than risk a beating which could have tragic results seemed a terrible alternative, but as a bolt of lightning lit the room she had a sudden inspiration. She went limp in his arms, hoping he'd think she'd fainted, and he caught her as she ceased to struggle.

"Gabrielle!" Beau was the one who was terrified now. He'd not meant to harm the beautiful young woman he loved, only to make her admit she was rightfully his. Overcome with remorse he placed her gently upon the bed and quickly lit the lamp upon the dresser so he might see her face. He rubbed her hands and gave a sigh of relief when he saw her eyelids begin to flutter. "I didn't mean to hurt you, I swear I didn't!" He brought her hands to his lips as he begged her to forgive him.

Perhaps if he hadn't reminded her of how greatly they'd enjoyed acting out plays together, Gabrielle might not have tried such a dangerous ploy. However, she seized the advantage which was now hers and lifted her hand to cover her eyes as she whispered sadly, "Just leave me now, Beau, and in the morning neither of us need speak of this unfortunate encounter. I will forgive you if you will but leave me now of your own accord."

Ashamed to think how badly he'd treated the only woman he'd ever loved, Beau leaned down to kiss her cheek lightly and then left her room, closing the door. He climbed the ladder to the loft, threw himself across the bed he'd made up, and furious with his own folly, wept like a child for having been so mean to Gabrielle. He had failed her in every way possible, and it had cost him the greatest wealth he could ever hope to own, the treasure of her love. When he awakened the next morning with a splitting headache, he was too embarrassed to climb down the ladder and face her.

Gabrielle had awakened early. Delighted by the clear blue sky, she had dressed hurriedly and started to do her chores. When she found Beau's horse occupying a stall in the barn, she knew what his plan had been from the beginning. She scolded herself for trusting him when he'd proven himself to be totally irresponsible. The cow eyed her warily, not pleased by her new owner's clumsy efforts to milk her, but Gabrielle paid no attention to the animal's sullen stare. She completed her work quickly and, with a hearty slap to the rump, turned the docile beast out to graze as if they were the best of friends. She gave Sunny a hug and turned him loose too, hoping he'd not mistake any mud he encountered for quicksand and be frightened. When she returned to the house after she'd gathered the eggs, she put some bacon on to cook and called to Beau. "I'll not allow you to sleep all day, Mr. Ramsey, if you want to have breakfast before you're on your way you'd better get up right now."

Beau got up then and quickly made up the bed. He pulled on his shirt and boots, and scrambled down the ladder as if he were truly afraid she'd not feed him if he were a minute late. Once he saw her standing by the stove, dressed prettily, a slight smile gracing her delicate features, he looked down, unable to return her direct gaze.

"There's warm water if you'd like to wash. Jason has more than one razor so you're welcome to use his spare. Breakfast won't be ready for a while yet."

Her voice held a comforting warmth Beau found most encouraging, and accepting her generous offer, he made himself presentable before she called him to the table. As she set his plate in front of him, he reached for her hand but his touch was gentle, not confining. "Gabrielle, I—"

"Please forget it, Beau. I have." She slid into the chair opposite his and took a bite of her scrambled eggs. "The day is clear. Wherever you're bound your ride will be a pleasant one. Your horse enjoyed his stay, by the way."

That she was feeling well enough to tease him was hardly encouraging, but Beau wasn't offended by her jest. "I'm not ashamed for you to know I hoped to stay the night, only about what happened."

Gabrielle's glance was direct as she looked up. "Two good friends had dinner together and then said good night. That's all that happened, Beau, nothing more. If you continue to look so guilty I'll begin to think you're imagining things."

"Are we still friends then?" he asked hopefully, not really daring to believe she had forgiven him.

"The very best," Gabrielle reassured him. He looked so young and vulnerable that she reminded herself he was only twenty. He was a handsome boy, but a boy still rather than the man she'd thought him to be at eighteen. She reached for his hand then, to give his fingers a fond clasp. "Will you please let me know where you are if you do go to California? If you can send no more than one line at Christmas each year I will be grateful to receive it."

"And you'll be here?" Beau asked, already knowing what her answer would be.

"Right here." Gabrielle gave his fingers another affection-ate squeeze and then returned her hand to her lap. "I'll have to go out and see if there is any damage to the roof from the storm. There are branches strewn all over the yard and cleaning them up will keep me busy all day."

"No. I'll do it before I go," Beau insisted. "If you've lost any shingles I'll replace those too."

Gabrielle was about to argue with him, but since he seemed so sincere she accepted his help graciously. "Thank you. I knew it rained a great deal here, but I did not realize the storms were so severe."

"They usually aren't. Last night's was a fluke." By the time Beau finished his breakfast Gabrielle's easy conversation had restored his mood to its usually good-natured state, and he went out to begin work while she washed the dishes. He spent the rest of the morning gathering up fallen branches. Then when he found the roof intact, he volunteered to chop some wood so she'd not run low before Jason returned. He had just carried an armload inside to stack beside the fireplace when he heard a buggy roll into the yard.

Gabrielle went to the door, and seeing Clayton Horne with Iris, she quickly removed her apron and tossed it aside. "Do you know Clayton Horne?" she called over her shoulder to Beau.

"Never had the pleasure," he replied. He brushed off his hands and stood ready to meet the guests as Gabrielle showed them inside.

Iris' brown eyes filled with an amused sparkle when she saw Beau and she purred sweetly, "Well, Clay, perhaps Gabrielle is not nearly so lonely as we'd imagined." When Gabrielle introduced the handsome young man as a friend from Liberty, Iris thought if she'd had such a good-looking friend at home she'd never have left. He seemed ill-at-ease, every muscle of his powerful body tense as if he expected a fight and she couldn't help but wonder why.

"Do you live nearby, Mr. Ramsey?" Clayton sat down beside Iris, hoping that what appeared obvious at first glance wasn't true.

"No, but a journey of any distance is worth making to see Gabrielle." Beau perched on the edge of his chair, wondering why Gabrielle's two well-dressed visitors were staring at him so rudely. His parents had had few callers so he was not accustomed to entertaining guests, but these people made him uneasy just by the curiosity in their glance.

"Why, yes of course. She is a most charming woman," Clayton cleared his throat nervously, hoping only to complete the business which had brought him there without letting his imagination run wild. Because the boy was handsome and fond of Gabrielle, that didn't mean she returned his affection. "Jason asked me to come and get you, my dear. He was emphatic in his directions, in fact. He said you'd be far happier living in my house while he's away than you'd be here all alone. Why I imagine you must have been terrified by last night's storm."

Gabrielle glanced over at Beau, hoping he'd have the sense not to volunteer the information that she'd not been alone and

456

he kept still. "Thank you, Mr. Horne. I know Jason was worried about me, but he left so hurriedly we really had no time to discuss what I wanted to do. As you can see, I'm just fine. I'm fully capable of caring for myself here and I intend to do just that until Jason returns home."

Clayton attempted once more to reason with the attractive young woman. "That's admirable, of course, Gabrielle, but Jason trusted me to see to your welfare in his absence. I cannot shirk that duty. I must insist that you pack your belongings and come with us now."

Beau saw Gabrielle's determined frown, and having heard her refuse the man's invitation, he entered the conversation on her behalf. "Since Mrs. Royal says she wants to stay here, you must accept her decision. If her husband were really so worried about her welfare, he'd not have entrusted her care to others. He'd have remained here to look after her himself."

Clayton was astonished by that interruption. He had seen the glance that passed between the young man and Gabrielle at the mention of the storm, and if what that look implied were true, he'd not permit it to continue. "Forgive me if I sound rude, Mr. Ramsey, but you are merely a casual visitor who will soon be gone and—"

Beau smiled with undisguised delight. "I'll stay as long as Gabrielle needs me," he offered generously.

Not wishing to see the conversation deteriorate any further, Gabrielle rose to her feet. "There's really no need to argue over what I'm to do, gentlemen. I've made up my mind to stay here since this is my home, and while I thank you for your hospitality, Mr. Horne, I can't accept it. Now may I offer you some tea?"

When Clayton was too flustered to respond, Iris replied for him. "Why yes, I'd love some. Why don't you just bring a tray? I'm certain we can convince the gentlemen to join us." Her words dripped with sweetness as she eyed Beau. In his manner and dress, he looked like no gentleman she'd ever seen, but she was enormously intrigued by the young man all the same. When Gabrielle excused herself to prepare the tea, Iris inquired with a teasing smile, "Since you are dressed like a trapper, Mr. Ramsey, may I assume that you are one?"

"Yes," Beau replied. He thought of several names to describe what she obviously was, but he was too courteous to question her in return.

"That must be very exciting work," Iris continued in an effort to draw him into further conversation.

"No. It isn't. The fur trade is no longer as profitable as it once was, while the work is every bit as hard." He gave her a stare so cold he was certain she'd understand the subject was closed, and the three of them sat in an uneasy silence until Gabrielle returned to pour tea.

"I hope to come into town on Saturday. Have any other wedding plans been announced?" Gabrielle tried to behave as a gracious hostess should, but she was afraid she wasn't succeeding.

"Why yes," Iris replied with a satisfied grin. "Marlene is marrying Charles, three girls from the other wagons are getting married as well—and one other engagement has just been announced." She linked her arm in Clayton's then and waited for him to speak.

"Ah, yes. Iris has done me the honor of agreeing to become my wife," Clayton announced with obvious pride.

While Beau simply stared, Gabrielle's smile was genuine.

"How marvelous. Truly I do believe you are perfect for each other." Iris had wanted a mature and wealthy gentleman, and Clayton certainly fit that description. He'd not regained any of the weight he'd lost during their arduous journey, and he'd continued to keep his blond curls trimmed so they flattered his features. While he still had a fatherly manner, she knew that was precisely what Iris had hoped to find. She recalled how often she'd seen them together recently and realized if she had not been so preoccupied with her own concerns she might have seen their engagement as a real possibility rather than a surprise. "Have you set a date for the wedding?"

"No," Clayton responded regretfully. "I want to wait for Jason's return so he can be my best man. I asked him before he left and he agreed."

"I'm certain he'll be proud to do it." With conscientious effort, Gabrielle kept the conversation flowing, questioning her visitors about other romances which might be moving toward marriage. Then she encouraged Clayton to talk about Oregon City so Beau would not feel left out of the discussion. When they had all finished their tea, Clayton thanked her politely for the refreshments and escorted Iris to the door.

"We will see you on Saturday then." He knew better than to ask Gabrielle to reconsider her decision to remain at home, especially while Beau stood by her side, but he meant to do it again when he saw her later in the week at his home.

Beau waited until Clayton's buggy had reached the main road before he spoke. "I will stay if you want me to, Gabrielle, as a friend, I mean."

Gabrielle shook her head. "I appreciated your help today, Beau, but you can't stay here. It wouldn't be good for either of us. I can't depend on you and you mustn't depend on me. We have separate lives to live now, and we each must go our own way."

Beau nodded, not pleased with her decision but understanding it. "I'll finish with the wood and then I'll go, but if I may I'll come by to say goodbye before I go to California."

"Please do, I would like that."

Later Gabrielle gave Beau an early supper, then waved goodbye as he rode away. Suddenly the thought that she would see him only one more time was a surprisingly painful one.

When she arrived at Clayton's home on Saturday, Gabrielle found herself the object of such suspicious stares she could not imagine what was afoot until Erica drew her aside.

"It's Iris again, as always. She's told everyone you've taken up with some good-looking young trapper and he's keeping you company until Jason comes home. I know that's absurd, but she'll not keep still about it. She says she saw the man with

459

her own eyes. I swear if the bitch had no gossip she'd make up some, but the others seem to believe her about this."

Gabrielle took a deep breath and held it, attempting to stifle her temper before it erupted and caused an unfortunate scene. "I'd like nothing better than to rip out her tongue, but she and Clayton came out to visit me the day after the storm and met a friend of mine from Liberty. He's not living with me—that is absurd—but you and I both know Iris' imagination is a lurid one."

"Well, what are you going to do?" Erica wanted to know.

"Nothing. I'll just ignore that lie and let it die a natural death. Now hadn't we better leave for the church?"

Erica reached out to take Gabrielle's arm as they walked outside to the buggies for the ride to the church. "Michael went with Jason. It seems he knew the Whitmans well and felt he should go."

"Did he say anything to you before he left?"

"Only goodbye. I guess that's it, isn't it? If he'd wanted me to wait for him, he would have asked me to marry him," Erica mused sadly.

"Perhaps not. Jason was in an awful state when he left our house, and I said none of the things I wanted to. Maybe all Michael needs is some time away to realize how fond of you he's become."

"If he is in fact fond of me." Erica climbed into the first buggy and made herself comfortable for the brief ride. "Aren't you frightened to stay alone in Jason's house? Or if not, aren't you terribly lonely? I know I'm bored to distraction without Michael's company."

The two friends looked at each other, both having the same idea, but Gabrielle spoke first. "Why don't you come stay with me? It won't be a vacation—there's plenty of work—but it would be fun if you were there. At least neither of us would be bored while the men are away."

Erica hugged Gabrielle and then gave a delighted squeal, but when they told Clayton of their plan, he wasn't at all certain he shouldn't simply forbid it. "I want you to come here, Gabrielle. I don't want Erica to go all the way out there! Why is it you young ladies can't see what's best when it is so obvious to me?"

"Oh, please, Mr. Horne. We'll come into town every Saturday to shop and to see you." Erica smiled coquettishly, hoping to charm him in the same manner Iris did, and to her delight, it worked.

"Well, all right. But I'll only agree to one week at a time. You must come to report any problems you've had, and if I say you must come back, Erica, you must do so without argument. As for you Gabrielle—"

"I will see that Erica comes each week to receive your permission, Mr. Horne, but I am a married woman and need no permission from you to live in my own house." She smiled sweetly too, knowing he could not argue with her logic no matter what Jason had insisted he do.

Clayton's brow furrowed in a deep frown as he looked at the vibrantly beautiful redhead. At least if Erica were in residence he would be reasonably certain Beau Ramsey wouldn't be. That thought settled the issue. "Until next week then, ladies."

"Until next week."

After thanking him again, the young women packed up Erica's belongings and then, Erica astride the black mare and Gabrielle upon Sunny's back, they were swiftly on their way.

Chapter XXIV

Jason sat down wearily, leaned back against a tree trunk and rested his arms across his knees. Going up the Columbia River was a far more difficult task than floating downstream and he was exhausted. With strenuous paddling they had traversed a fair distance, but they'd also had to carry their canoes past long stretches of rapids. There was never a time when the going wasn't hard. He knew he'd pushed himself as far as he possibly could that day and there was not a man among them who could go farther. "We'll make camp here!" he shouted when he'd finally caught his breath.

Michael Jenkins sprawled across a heap of leaves by Jason's side, gasping like a fish out of water as he tried to speak. "Do you plan to keep up such a brutal pace the whole way?"

"No," Jason assured him with a wicked grin. "Tomorrow we'll go faster."

"Dear God." Michael put his face in the damp leaves and waited for death to overtake him. When the Grim Reaper failed to appear he looked up again. "Your name will become a legend after this, Royal. If any of us survive to tell the tale that is."

"You'll survive. I'm asking none of you to do what I haven't done myself," Jason pointed out matter-of-factly.

"That may be true, but few of us have your stamina, or is it simply rage?" Michael inquired curiously.

Jason shot him an evil glance as he replied honestly, "It is both."

Turning over on his back, Michael gazed up through the branches which filtered the last rays of the setting sun. "How far are you willing to take this, Royal?"

That he wanted to drive the Indians farther north without slaughtering every last one of them was a secret Jason planned to keep. The men who'd volunteered to go after the Cayuse were out for blood, but he was certain he would have their respect by the time they came within sight of the Indians' camp. He planned to use that respect then. It was pointless to reveal his plan to Michael Jenkins now, however. "I intend to teach the Cayuse a lesson they'll never forget. They'll not dare to butcher another settler because they'll know it'll mean a war in which their own families will be at risk. Is that clear enough for you?"

"Very."

Michael rested only a minute longer and then got to his feet to join the men who were setting up the camp. He was no killer, but it was clear to him that Jason Royal certainly was. He shuddered to think how the man must treat Gabrielle, but since she'd had her heart set on marrying him he'd waste no sympathy on her. His thoughts strayed swiftly to Erica then, and he wondered if he'd find the charming young woman married to someone else by the time he returned home. He was the only one of the bachelors who'd volunteered for this mission so there were plenty of men left in Oregon City to keep her entertained.

"Blast it all!" he swore loudly as he tripped over a gnarled root and nearly landed on his face in the dirt. He'd been so tired he'd not noticed the obstacle in his path. He looked around quickly, hoping no one had seen him since he didn't want to be the butt of any jokes, but fortunately the men were all occupied and paying no attention to him. He knew the others' names though he could call few among them friends, and he relaxed, relieved that his clumsiness hadn't been noted. He'd volunteered to join the group, not only because he'd thought he owed it to the Whitmans but because he'd needed to get out of Oregon City for a while. He'd felt that he couldn't sort out his feelings for Erica when he saw her every day. Clayton Horne had returned Lewis Bradley's money, and he'd heard the man had gone after his Indian woman to bring her and their son back home. Erica had never mentioned Lewis' name to him so he guessed she was over her infatuation with the man, but he didn't like being her second choice. Hell, he didn't even know if he was that high on her list since most of the other men simply ignored her. He couldn't understand their rudeness either, for she was a delightful creature with such pretty green eyes. With a sudden flash of insight, he realized he'd been an idiot to be so sensitive about being her second choice when she certainly had to know his first choice had been Gabrielle. He was mortified by that thought. It was obvious, yet it had escaped him during the many hours he'd agonized over the problem of taking a wife. As he helped to raise a tent, his mind was preoccupied with thoughts of how foolish he'd been, and he hoped by some miracle Erica might still be single by the time he returned home.

Jason remained seated for a while as he watched the others move about to make camp and gather wood for cooking fires. There was no reason for him to supervise this phase of the group's activities so he enjoyed the brief rest, feeling that he had earned it. He knew they'd get used to the pace he'd set in a day or two and the journey home would be a far easier one. His only worry was the possibility that the Cayuse would come looking for them as they made their way up the river. It was unlikely, but were he the Cayuse chief he'd be waiting for the white men who would be certain to come to avenge the Whitman massacre. He'd post sentries to watch the river so as not to be caught by surprise as those at the mission had been. A slow smile moved across Jason's lips as he realized the best plan would be to leave the river before they were sighted and to circle around the Indian's camp and attack it from the east. By keeping the men moving, they'd appear to be a larger force than they were, and the Cayuse would be sure to flee to the north. Satisfied with that plan, he got up and stretched, then went to see what was being prepared for supper since he was very hungry.

While Jason and the volunteer army moved stealthily toward a confrontation with the Cayuse, Gabrielle and Erica established a far more pleasant routine. The redhead could handle horses with ease, but she was happy to let Erica assume the responsibility for milking the cow. Erica named the bovine Tulip and insisted the animal had a very pleasant disposition regardless of Gabrielle's opinion of her. They divided the rest of the chores equally and then cooked the meals together, often giggling uproariously when the new recipes they tried to devise failed to meet their expectations. On Saturday they went into town and attended two more weddings. Gabrielle simply ignored the curious stares and rude whispers that her appearance provoked, and since neither she nor Erica wished to attend the reception, they went to the dry goods store to purchase material for curtains before reporting to Clayton. He was exasperated with them for being so confident, but it seemed obvious that they were managing well on their own so he gave them permission to continue their arrangement for another week. On the way home, however, Erica had only to glance at Gabrielle's expression to know something was wrong.

"I'd ask what's the matter, but I think I already know. Iris hasn't let the story of that trapper she met at your house slip anyone's mind. I was hoping you didn't hear any of the whispers when we entered the church, but you did, didn't you?"

"Yes. But I can hardly confront Iris as if she is telling an outright lie. Beau was there with me when she and Clayton came to call, but you'd think they'd caught us in bed together from the way everyone looks at me. I suppose such a delicious scandal will always be far more exciting than the truth. Still, I don't want Jason to suffer as a result of this gossip."

466

"Surely he'll not even hear it, and if he does he won't pay any attention to it," Erica insisted firmly. "Jason's hardly the type of man to listen to malicious gossip as you must know."

Gabrielle agreed—she did not want to explain that her husband had forbidden her to see Beau—but she knew Jason would be dreadfully disappointed in her and would say she'd brought this needless disgrace upon herself by disregarding his command.

"I just hope Jason will be home soon," she said. "Everything will be better then." At least she prayed it would.

Erica nodded enthusiastically. "Of course it will. Do you realize half the girls are married now? Even though you were the first bride, our wagon has not kept up with the other two when it comes to marriages."

Gabrielle was amused by that thought. "Was there some kind of a contest?"

"Not really, but as I sat there in the church this morning I realized we have fallen behind. Johanna seems to be making some progress with the preacher, and of course Iris is engaged; but Barbara and Margaret don't seem any closer to accepting proposals and the only man I'd accept hasn't bothered to ask me. So, our wagon is not doing well at all. Do you remember Jason telling us we'd all be married within two weeks? Looks like he was wrong."

"Well, I suppose Clayton and Iris could adopt any of you who don't wed. Would you like that?" Gabrielle offered brightly.

"Good heavens no! What a horrid idea!" Erica was convulsed with laughter at the lunacy of that prospect. "Not that Mr. Horne wouldn't make an understanding father, but Iris would be the worst mother possible. Why, the very thought makes my stomach lurch!"

The two young women passed the time on the rest of the way home by making up possible combinations of the bachelors and the young women who were still single. The next morning when they attended church, they could not help but recall the

467

silliest of the pairings as they gazed around. Being so amused, Gabrielle did not let the dark glances she received phase her, but when the young women returned home at noon to find Beau seated upon the front porch, it was difficult to maintain her composure. When she introduced him to her friend, he smiled warmly, but clearly he was anxious to speak with her alone. Seeing that, Erica excused herself discreetly to begin preparing the midday meal.

"Come for a walk with me. I want to talk with you." Beau reached for Gabrielle's hand the minute they were alone. "Just for a little way, not far."

"All right," Gabrielle agreed. "Just let me unsaddle the horses first." She led Sunny and the black mare to the barn, wondering what Beau could have to say other than goodbye. Unable to wait for him to begin, she asked impatiently, "Have you come to tell me goodbye?"

Beau took the mare's reins and led her into her stall for unsaddling. "Not exactly," he called over his shoulder. "But that's what I want to discuss."

Gabrielle made a silly face at him. "Don't tease me! Either it is or it isn't."

"How does Sunrise like it here?" Beau asked with a sly grin, not about to satisfy her curiosity until the time was right.

"He loves it!" Gabrielle called back. She removed Sunny's saddle and bridle with exceptional speed, then had to stand and wait for her caller to finish his share of the work. Finally he joined her, and taking her hand, he guided her down the path which led from the barn to the surrounding fields.

They strolled a considerable distance before he spoke. "I've decided to go to California, but I want to wait until Jason comes home before I leave." His glance was fond as he looked down at her, but his expression was reserved, as if there were more to his decision than he'd admit.

"I certainly hope you don't plan to come and tell him goodbye because that would be foolhardy in the extreme," Gabrielle suggested, not understanding why Beau had decided to wait for Jason's return. He seemed to be in a relaxed mood that day, confident as she'd remembered him, so she did not hesitate to question his motive.

"No, I'm not that great a fool," Beau replied with a chuckle, but after a moment's pause he grew more serious. "I want to make certain you are a married woman rather than a widow before I leave."

Gabrielle swiftly pulled her hand from his and drew away. "What a horrid thing to say! Even if you do wish Jason dead, how dare you admit such a dreadful thing to me?"

Beau gestured helplessly, raising his hands to the heavens. "I am not wishing the man dead! All I am saying is that someone is sure to be killed any time there's a battle with Indians, and if it's Jason, I'll not go off and leave you alone again."

Gabrielle shuddered, horrified. "The possibility I'll be a widow, ever, is too ghastly even to contemplate. I think we should just say our goodbyes now, and wish each other the best. I'll not encourage you to cling to the hope we'll be able to marry someday. It's just not going to happen, Beau, and if you let yourself think it will then you'll miss whatever chance you'll have to be happy with someone else. Please just make your plans and go as soon as it's convenient for you. My welfare should be your very last consideration."

Beau scuffed the toe of his boot in the moist soil before responding to her advice with a sarcastic question. "How would you feel if I insisted you were to stop loving Jason?"

"I couldn't do it." Gabrielle admitted frankly.

"Well then don't tell me I can't still love you." He looked up then, his dark eyes filled with a pain so deep it was close to hatred.

"I think we'd better go back to the house," Gabrielle replied breathlessly.

She turned to hurry up the path. She didn't want to prolong the sorrow of their goodbye, and she knew if she stayed there with him a minute longer, she'd be in tears since he'd communicated the sharpness of his anguish so well.

Beau followed along silently, thinking he'd made as bad a job of saying goodbye as he had of everything else. When they reached the front porch of her home, he went straight to his horse without having to be told to be on his way.

"I'll send that letter every Christmas, if you promise to send a reply."

Gabrielle walked to the young man's side, attempting to smile bravely. "I promise."

Beau looked down at her, his heartbreak compounding as he thought how unlikely it would be they'd ever meet again. His eyes filled with tears he made no move to brush away, and when he tried to say goodbye he could not even speak the words.

Drawn to him by the memory of the love they'd shared for so many years, Gabrielle rested her hands lightly upon Beau's chest and stood on her tiptoes to kiss him goodbye. Her lips were soft, her mouth inviting, and he hesitated only an instant before hugging her to him, pressing her so close she could feel the wild pounding of his heart rather than the gentle beat of her own. The warmth of his affection enveloped her with the same sweet longing which tore at his soul as they kissed for the last time. She was as stunned as he by the depth of her response, for it was as though they had never been apart and her love were still as strong as his. He kissed her then as he had the night of the storm, with a passion so intense she grew weak in his embrace. When he finally released her she stepped back quickly, preferring to wave from the safety of the front porch as he rode away. She waited until he was lost from view before wiping away the last traces of tears from her cheeks, but whether they had been Beau's or her own she could not really tell. As she turned to go inside, she found Erica standing at the open door, a look of such disbelief upon her sweet features she knew her friend had seen all there was to see.

"It's true isn't it? Iris isn't telling lies about you at all, but the truth!" She gasped sharply as she stared at the young

470

woman whose word she'd never once doubted. "My God, I'd just come to the door to see if Beau wouldn't like to stay for something to eat and there you were in his arms kissing him as though the world were coming to an end!"

"For him it has," Gabrielle responded softly.

"How can you do this to Jason? You two have only just gotten married and you've already taken a lover?"

Gabrielle shook her head. "No. Beau is not my lover but my best friend. He's going to California and as we'll never see each other again he came to say goodbye. That's all you saw, Erica. Don't think there is any more to it because there isn't."

"Even if there were you wouldn't tell me about it would you?" Erica asked pointedly, her green eyes aflame with anger.

"No." Gabrielle saw no reason to apologize for being the type of person she was. "If you want to go back to Clayton's, I'll understand. I'll miss you terribly, but if you think the worst of me too, then perhaps you should leave before your reputation is ruined simply by association."

Erica shrieked with frustration. "Oh no, I want to stay. Just because one of the handsomest men I've ever seen kisses you goodbye as though he had no intention of leaving is no reason for me to desert you." She marched toward the kitchen then, so confused she was no longer certain just what she really had seen.

Neither of them had much appetite for the meal, and finally Gabrielle gave up the effort to eat and laid her fork across her plate. "Forgive me. I know my secretive nature offends you, and since we've become so close, I don't want to do anything which will jeopardize our friendship. But I can't explain anything to you until Jason comes home because so much depends on him. I don't expect you to be content to wait, but I must beg you to try."

Erica had been pushing her food around her plate without eating a bite either. Now she lay her fork aside. She tried to read some deeper meaning in Gabrielle's troubled glance than she found in her words, but couldn't.

"Do you expect me to forget what I saw today?" she finally asked.

"No. I can't ask that, but please keep it to yourself."

Drumming her fingers nervously upon the table, Erica shook her head in wonder. "I've never seen anything like that, Gabrielle. I thought Beau was going to devour you and it certainly looked as though you were enjoying it."

"I was," Gabrielle admitted readily.

"But don't you love Jason?"

This time, Gabrielle made a greater effort to share her feelings with her friend. "I love my husband dearly, but I love Beau too. I love them both but in entirely different ways and for different reasons. I know it's confusing, but I must insist the subject of Beau is closed." Looking toward the embers glowing upon the hearth, she shivered suddenly, "Don't you think it's gotten chilly in here?"

She got up from the table to add wood to the fire, her decision to change the topic of conversation a firm one. Shivering still, she rubbed her arms to get warm, but she could not suppress the memory of Beau's lavish goodbye as easily as she'd asked Erica to disregard it. Their conversation had been far too unsettling. What if Jason were to die? What if the endlessly exciting man who was her husband were to perish before she could tell him she loved him? It would be futile to have the words carved on his tombstone since he'd never read them.

"I should have gone after him," she told herself angrily.

"What?" Erica had been carrying their dishes to the sink but she set them down quickly and rushed to her friend's side when she saw her pained expression. "I beg your pardon, what did you say?"

As Gabrielle looked up, she didn't see her friend's worried glance, only the memory of her husband's angry stare. "Oh, Erica, I am terrified. I'm afraid I've lost Jason. I don't think he's coming back."

"Of course he is!" Erica reassured her quickly. "Why

wouldn't he?"

Gabrielle turned back to the fire, watching the flames dance with the same fascination Jason had shown when they'd last talked together. "He might not be able to, Erica. In fact, he might already be dead and I won't even know it until the men return to tell us what happened."

Erica was so horrified by Gabrielle's gloomy words that she did not know what to do. She slipped an arm around her friend's waist and hugged her tightly. "Oh no, nothing's going to happen to Jason. He's far too clever to fall victim to a savage."

Gabrielle shook her head sadly as she whispered, "He may already have."

Jason wiped the sweat from his eyes and peered through the dense underbrush toward the sound of rifle fire as he knelt to reload his own weapon. The raid had begun with the first light of dawn. It was now close to noon and after hours of fighting the battle had dwindled to scattered fire in no more than a dozen places. They'd struck a decisive blow, of that he was certain. The majority of the Cayuse were retreating rapidly, leaving only a few warriors behind in this part of the forest to hinder their enemy's pursuit. Jason planned to deal with those braves, then regroup and treat the casualties before pushing farther north, sweeping the fleeing Indians before them. He'd given the men a final warning that morning: only mad dogs killed women and children. He knew they believed he'd come after any man who selected a woman or child as a target. Now he was going back over the terrain they'd crossed, searching for stragglers. Women and children, he feared, might have fled into the woods and been left behind during the first stages of the attack. He could be called a traitor to the cause he was leading, but no army worthy of the name killed civilians. He'd do his best to protect the Indians he knew to be innocent of the responsibility for the Whitmans' deaths.

Warned by the ominous snap of a dry twig, Jason lunged to the right, scrambling to his feet, hoping to provide a moving target and thus escape injury but the Cayuse warrior had crept up right behind him. The brave snarled a filthy curse as his knife pierced the taut muscles of Jason's upper arm for he'd aimed for the middle of his back and was disgusted he'd not moved with sufficient stealth to surprise the white man and kill him. He raised his knife again, ready to strike another vicious blow, but his prey was now on his feet and facing him.

Although his left arm was nearly useless, Jason had no intention of attempting to run away. He tossed his rifle aside since he'd not finished reloading it and drew his knife. Circling the Indian he now saw was a brawny brute, he returned the man's curse with an even stronger one. He knew how to fight very effectively with knives and relished the prospect since his adversary seemed so eager for hand-to-hand combat.

"Come and get me, you bastard, come on!" he shouted at the brave in his own tongue, knowing an enraged foe was a careless one.

Through the red haze of his anger, the Indian saw little except that he'd not killed the tall white man as he'd intended. He wanted to hack his foe's body into tiny bits so his comrades would find what was left of him and fear their own fate at the hands of the Cayuse. That he'd failed in his initial attempt didn't deter the brave and he lunged again, but missed. The injured man had managed to dodge his blow. He continued to swing his weapon in wide arcs, using brute force rather than cunning. He slashed the air but inflicted no further injury, for despite Jason's height and size he leaped from one spot to another with the agility of a young stag.

Jason knew he was bleeding too badly to make the fight a long one. He'd swiftly tire and then his death would be certain. In a surprising change of strategy he lunged, not away from his opponent but toward him, using his right shoulder to hit the man hard in the stomach and send him sprawling on his back in the leaves. He jumped astride the brave then, wrenching the

474

knife from his hand before his opponent regained the breath knocked out of him by that savage blow to the midsection. Dazed, the Indian's eyes filled with terror as he looked up at what he knew was the face of his own doom.

Jason tossed the brave's knife away and then went to work with his own. Holding it to the man's throat, he threatened him with every vile act which came to his mind should the Cayuse dare to return to their former home. He wanted to send what was left of their number so far north they'd never see another white settler let alone harm one. To emphasize his point, he drew the blade of his weapon slowly down to the man's navel, exerting just enough pressure to leave a long bloody trail without actually disemboweling him. He leaped to his feet then and gestured for the brave to rise. "Now go! I let you live to carry my message so don't delay in relaying it!"

The warrior scrambled to his feet, astonished, for what manner of man would be satisfied with making threats when he could have just killed him? Hoping this was not a trick of some sort, he nodded in agreement. Willing to carry any message if doing so would save his life, he dashed off into the woods, vanishing from sight.

For some moments Jason stood still, listening to the echoes of nearby gunfire as he watched blood drip from the ends of his fingers. His mind was far from clear, but he knew the excruciating pain in his left arm was cause for alarm. The Indian's blade had gone clear through his bicep, leaving a jagged wound as deep as the bone. If he ignored it much longer, he'd simply bleed to death. He sank to his knees, and after wrapping his neckerchief around the deep wound, he tied the ends as best he could using only his right hand and his teeth. When he tried to rise, he found his legs had become too weak to support him. He crawled over to where he'd left his rifle and, with deliberate care, finished loading it. Praying one of his friends would soon come along rather than another Cayuse, he propped himself up against the stump of a tree and waited for whomever fortune might send his way.

Chapter XXV

Michael Jenkins raced up the walk and took the steps in front of Clayton Horne's home two at a time. He rang the bell with frantic haste, pacing anxiously as he waited for the door to be opened. When he was told Erica Nelson was a guest at Gabrielle Royal's home, he thanked the maid politely but swore bitterly as he returned to his buggy. This was a circumstance he'd not foreseen, and it was a damned awkward one. He couldn't propose to Erica in Gabrielle's presence, but perhaps he could offer to bring her back into town and thereby have an opportunity to speak with her alone.

Up to their elbows in flour, the two young women exchanged an exasperated glance when they heard a knock upon the front door. Neither could imagine who had come to call.

"Do you want me to get that?" Erica asked as she wiped her hands upon a dish towel.

If Iris had decided to pay another visit, she didn't want Gabrielle to have to face her. Sick with worry over Jason, she simply hadn't been herself of late, and Erica hoped to spare her whatever unnecessary aggravation she could.

"Yes, would you please?"

Gabrielle turned the bread dough out upon a floured tea towel to begin kneading it. They were making several loaves and she wanted to get her baking finished early in the day.

When she found Michael Jenkins standing upon the front porch and smiling shyly, Erica turned back to call to Gabrielle before she greeted the young man. "It's Michael!" she exclaimed happily.

"Well, ask him to come in this instant!" Gabrielle replied excitedly, and abandoning her baking, she quickly wiped her hands and ran to welcome their guest. Since he was dressed neatly in a suit, she knew he'd had time to go home and change his clothes after returning to Oregon City so what was keeping Jason? "It is good to see you, Michael, but have all the men come home? Won't Jason be here soon? He's all right, isn't he?"

Realizing by that barrage of questions that he'd frightened Gabrielle needlessly, Michael tried to reassure her of her husband's safety. "I came on ahead, but Jason and the rest of the men should reach Oregon City shortly, he'll probably be home before tonight." To his amazement, rather than appearing happy, Gabrielle's eyes filled with a torrent of tears which spilled over her thick lashes faster than she could wipe them away. Not understanding how he could have caused such unhappiness he turned to Erica.

"I did not mean to upset her. Is something wrong here?"

"No, of course not," Erica replied with a smile. "Gabrielle is simply thrilled to hear Jason will be home so shortly, that's all." Giving her friend a warm hug, Erica guided her over to the rocking chair and insisted she sit down while she and Michael prepared tea. "Come and help me a minute, Michael, will you please?"

"Of course," the young man agreed, not knowing how he could politely refuse.

Erica put the kettle on the stove. Then she whispered to Michael as she began to knead the waiting mounds of bread dough. "Are you certain Jason is all right? Gabrielle has been absolutely terrified he'd come to some harm."

Turning his back toward the pretty redhead, Michael replied softly. "He was wounded, but not badly. He insisted the others

478

who'd suffered injuries stop by Dr. Patterson's office before going home, so I'm fairly certain he'll go there too."

Her gaze filling with alarm, Erica motioned for him to come closer. "Please don't tell Gabrielle. She'll only worry all the more, and I'm sure Jason wouldn't want that to happen. Are you certain he's all right?"

Michael took off his coat and rolled up his sleeves. "He is doing fine. Now let me help you with this mess and then I'll take you back to Clayton Horne's. Unless you'd like to be here when Jason arrives."

"Oh, you're right. That might be very awkward." Erica bit her lip, knowing Michael was assuming one kind of awkwardness while she was worried about another. "Would it be out of your way to take me back into town? I would really appreciate the ride."

Michael pressed the bread dough into a rectangle; then he folded it over and pressed it out again. He felt very foolish working in the kitchen when he'd worn his best suit in order to be properly dressed to propose. Fortunately he knew flour would just brush off his clothing when they were finished, and he did want to help Erica so they could leave promptly. "I came here to see you, Erica. Did you really think I'd come to visit Gabrielle?"

"Well, I'd hoped not," Erica responded with a deep blush. "I have missed you," she finally admitted shyly, not daring to look up as she spoke.

The shrill whistle of the teakettle interrupted them before Michael could respond, and wiping off her hands, Erica poured the boiling water into the teapot. She added tea leaves and let them steep for a moment before pouring a cup of the flavorful beverage for Gabrielle.

"Here. Just drink this and try to relax."

"As if I could!" Gabrielle responded hoarsely. Her hands were shaking so badly she couldn't hold the cup steady as she tried to take a sip of the steaming tea. "Aren't you and Michael going to join me?"

"In just a moment, as soon as we get the bread in the oven," Erica promised with a pretty smile.

Gabrielle turned around then, and seeing Michael had taken her place, she blushed with embarrassment. "I am sorry, Michael. You needn't do that, you can finish in a moment or two."

"I don't mind," Michael insisted with a good-natured grin. "I have to bake my own bread at home, I know how to do this so you needn't look so stricken."

"You really don't mind?" Gabrielle wondered what Iris would say were she to see this. She could well imagine what gossip asking a man to help in the kitchen would cause.

"Not at all."

Michael placed the first loaf in the waiting pan and began to knead the next ball of dough. He would gladly have cleaned the whole house or done the ironing for the chance to take Erica back into town. Working together, they soon had four loaves of bread baking. He then accepted a cup of tea and went to sit down near the fire while Erica packed her belongings.

Noticing that the fear had not left Gabrielle's eyes, Michael decided to distract her, but then he recalled how impossible that had always been for him. Nonetheless, he made an attempt by choosing a safe subject.

"It must have worked out well for you to have Erica here while Jason was away. It didn't occur to me she'd not want to stay in Oregon City with the others. I thought she'd want to attend Clayton's parties."

That he could be so mistaken made Gabrielle smile for the first time since he'd arrived. "She seemed to have no interest in attending parties when you weren't going to be there, but don't you dare tell her I told you that."

Michael shook his head. "I never thought I'd be discussing another woman with you." He chuckled at the thought, glad that Gabrielle seemed to regard him as a friend now, and he hoped she'd offer him some advice. "Do you think I might still have a chance with Erica? I mean, if she's not seeing any of the others maybe she does care for me a little."

"Oh, Michael." Gabrielle reached out to pat his hand lightly. "Of course she does, but you've given her little hope you care for her."

Michael was dumfounded by that news. "But I, well that is I—"

"Exactly." Gabrielle nodded as she leaned forward to whisper. "I assume you do know how to kiss a woman as though you love her with all the passion it is possible for a man to feel?"

Erica came out of the bedroom in time to see Michael blush a deep red, and not knowing what they had been discussing, she feared the worst. "I'm ready to go now, if you're still willing to take me."

Michael gave Gabrielle one last frantic glance before rising from his chair. He thought he knew what she was suggesting, but he wasn't at all sure that would please Erica.

"Yes, I'm ready."

They bid Gabrielle goodbye, certain they'd pass Jason on the road, and climbed up into the buggy in which Michael had arrived, waving as they rode away. Once they were alone, Michael found it impossible to speak. He'd been so anxious to see Erica again he'd not prepared any pretty phrases to express what he wanted to say and he now realized that had been a grave error. He was so nervous he didn't even know how to begin, let alone plead his cause effectively, and to make matters worse, Erica was directing all her attention toward the scenery as though the trees provided a more interesting view than he did. Gabrielle was obviously mistaken. The young woman by his side couldn't care anything for him. All she'd wanted was a ride into town.

Erica attempted to wait patiently for Michael to speak, but when he did not she didn't know what to do. She'd thought since he'd gone to the trouble of coming all the way out to Gabrielle's house to see her he had something important to say. However, his silence was telling the whole story.

"I guess it really was Gabrielle you went to see," she finally mumbled, unable to keep her thoughts to herself a moment longer.

Shocked by the ridiculousness of that notion, Michael pulled his horse to an abrupt halt. "I wanted to see you. Of course I like Gabrielle, but I wouldn't have gone out to her home if you hadn't been there."

Erica didn't reply. She hadn't really meant to speak her complaint aloud and was sorry she'd done so. She was embarrassed by his response, feeling he was only being polite, and she again looked away since it was far easier than returning his inquisitive glance.

Michael knotted the reins over the brake to leave his hands free and, hoping Gabrielle had known what she was talking about, slipped an arm around Erica's shoulders. "I have had very little experience with women. I don't know what it is I'm supposed to do or say to please you, but I would like to try. I like to think my dancing has improved since you came to Oregon City, so I know I can still learn whatever else I must if you'll just help me."

Erica frowned. Then she replied in a serious tone. "But if I have to tell you—I mean, if it is not something you wish to do spontaneously—then it's just no good, Michael. I shouldn't have to beg you to speak to me while we ride into town; you should simply want to tell me about your adventures." She was becoming angry now, she'd waited as patiently as she could for him to express some affection for her but clearly he was loath to do it.

Watching the color rise in Erica's cheeks, Michael knew he'd made a mistake by being so frank with her. He'd hoped to win her sympathy by being honest and was disappointed to have failed. "You want to hear about adventures? I wouldn't describe what I've just been through as an adventure. It was far closer to a glimpse of hell! I went because I thought I should, because I didn't want any more of my friends to be killed. I didn't want the Cayuse to think they could murder whomever

482

they pleased without fear of retaliation. I won't make up stories so you'll think me very brave because I have never been so scared. The only comfort I have is that I wasn't the only one who was terrified. Still, none of us let the others down. I'm glad it's over, and I hope I never have to do anything like that again. I'm not cut out to be a soldier. I just haven't got the guts for it. I enjoy being a farmer but that's pretty tame; it involves no adventure at all."

"I didn't mean to insult you!" Erica clenched her fists in her lap, mortified that she'd hurt him when she had not meant to give offense. "I just wanted you to talk to me!"

"That's all I've been thinking about the whole time I was away, just how good it would be to see you again and what I hoped to say. But I can't even have a simple conversation with you, let alone ask what I wanted to." Michael was thoroughly disgusted with himself and his downcast expression clearly showed it.

Puzzled by his remarks, Erica hoped to end his reticence. "You can ask me whatever you wish and I'll try to answer you."

"Erica!" Michael simply gave up then, frustrated because she appeared to have no idea what he wanted to ask. He yanked the reins from around the brake handle and slapped them soundly upon his horse's back. "I'll take you home as I promised, but I don't think I should ever come back."

Stricken by that announcement, Erica begged him to reconsider. "Oh please, Michael, please don't say that. I know I'm not Gabrielle, but I've tried, really I have, and—"

Completely exasperated now, Michael again pulled his horse to a stop. "You mean you do want me to continue to call upon you?"

"Yes, of course I do," Erica responded with an engaging smile.

"Well then, why can't you understand that it's you I want and not Gabrielle?"

Her concern that she might not see him again lessening at

that question, Erica began to hope that perhaps he did care for her. "Really?"

Since he thought he'd already blurted out the truth, Michael saw no reason not to continue. "I have been waiting as patiently as I could for you to want me because it would be senseless for us to marry if you're still in love with Lewis. There. I finally said it. Was that plain enough for you?"

"You are not still in love with Gabrielle?" Erica inquired softly.

"No, of course not. I barely knew her. She is pretty, but I always found her so distracted I was never truly comfortable with her."

Hoping she might construe that as a compliment, Erica persisted. "Are you saying that you are comfortable with me?"

"Well, I would like to be." Michael's expression grew stern, for he knew this was no way to propose. Still, while he felt Erica deserved better, he could only ask her in the blunt method he'd used.

Erica leaned forward, her lips slightly parted as she whispered, "Do you know how to kiss a woman like this?"

She hoped to experience only a tiny portion of the emotion she'd seen pass between Beau and Gabrielle, but Michael drew her into a ready embrace, proving that he did indeed know how to kiss a woman. When finally he released her she could not suppress her joy.

"I thought you were never going to kiss me."

"I did not even think you wanted me to," Michael replied with an astonished grin, for she had returned his kiss with a delight which had pleased him greatly.

"I have wanted you to kiss me for a very long time."

"While I mistakenly believed you really wanted Lewis," Michael mused sadly.

"And I was hopelessly confused about you," Erica replied with equal remorse. "What are we going to do now so we don't have such a dreadful misunderstanding again?" The lively sparkle in her pretty green eyes let him know she had a very good idea.

Putting his arms around her once more, Michael drew her close. "I would like very much for you to marry me. Will you at least consider it?"

"Kiss me again and then I will," Erica promised, but after he'd kissed her she found it nearly impossible to consider anything except how pleasant his affection was and how quickly she'd come to love him. She'd once thought adventure was what she craved, but now she knew the thrill she felt in Michael's arms would be excitement enough.

Gabrielle hurriedly heated water, hoping to bathe and dress before Jason arrived. However, she was soon ready and had more than enough time to grow frantic with worry. She recalled the bread in the oven only when the aroma became so enticing she realized she was hungry. She was glad she'd not allowed the loaves to burn. Bread and butter were a poor substitute for her husband's company, however, and she took only a few bites before going out to pace anxiously upon the front porch. Unfortunately, it wasn't until sunset, long after she'd returned to the warmth of the house, that she heard Jason ride by. He went straight to the barn rather than stopping first to speak with her. Certain that gesture foretold his mood, she did not dare go out to meet him.

When Jason finally walked through the front door, he slammed it soundly and did not bother with the courtesy of a greeting. "I have only two questions and I want honest answers," he said through clenched teeth. Without waiting for her to agree, he continued. "Clay said he asked you to come stay with him, that he told you I insisted you reside with him while I was away, but that you refused to move back into his house. Is that the truth?"

Gabrielle could not believe that after such a long absence Jason would wish to continue their argument right where they'd left off. However, not wanting to provoke him when he was in so belligerent a mood, she replied calmly, "I told you I'd be fine here and I was."

"Just answer my question, Gabrielle! You knew what I wanted you to do and you just didn't bother to do it. That's the truth, isn't it?"

Gabrielle saw no point in responding to that taunt. "Perhaps you should ask your second question since you won't accept my answer to your first."

"I'll be glad to. I told you I didn't want Beau here, but I know he was here on at least one occasion. Did he just move in here for the whole time I was gone? Isn't that why you wouldn't stay at Clay's house, because then you couldn't see Beau!" Clay had told him he'd met the young man. His friend had tried to make the incident sound as innocent as possible, but Jason knew it certainly wasn't.

This was not at all the homecoming she'd wanted, but Gabrielle did her best to stifle her temper in the hope that Jason would soon regain control of his. "Since this is now my home as well as yours, I saw no reason not to invite the best friend I've ever had to come in when he came to call. He was here twice, no more."

"You did not consider the fact that your husband forbid it reason enough? What sort of a stupid fool do you think I am?" Jason snarled. "Why can't you simply be honest with me and say you want to end this marriage? I certainly do!"

"What?" Gabrielle was stunned by that revelation. Jason was angry with her, but he understood so little. She knew he was hurt when there was no cause. She could explain nothing, however, when he was in such a jealous rage.

"You heard me. This marriage was a mistake for both of us. Joe Meek, one of the men who lost a daughter in the massacre at the Whitman Mission, has left for Washington to present a demand to Congress that Oregon be made a territory of the United States. Then the Army will send troops here so a tragedy like the one we just avenged won't occur again. However, there's no way the Army can be effective until they

486

become familiar with the terrain. They'll need scouts, and I am a good one. I'm no farmer. It was stupid of me to think I could be. Since neither of us is happy, let's just end our marriage as swiftly as possible."

Gabrielle stared at her husband. Devastated by the cruelty of his remarks, she had no idea how to reply and said nothing until he began to remove his coat. Noting the great difficulty with which he moved, she cried, "Oh Jason, you've been hurt! Why didn't you tell me?" She rushed forward to help him, but he pushed her away with an emphatic shove.

"I don't need any help from the likes of you!" In truth, he was so dizzy he could scarcely stand. Dr. Patterson had insisted upon stitching up his arm, and the pain he'd inflicted with a needle and thread was nearly as great as the initial stab wound had been. He was still weak from the loss of blood and wanted only to lie down on his bed before he fainted.

"Michael should have told me you'd been hurt." Gabrielle didn't understand why he'd not bothered to give her such a vital piece of information. "I would have come into town to meet you. You shouldn't have ridden out here alone."

"Your devotion is a bit late, lady. If I meant anything at all to you, if my feelings merited even the slightest bit of consideration, I'd have found you at Clayton's house where I fully expected you to be!" Jason pushed by her and went into the bedroom. He sat down upon the edge of the bed and tried to remove his moccasins with one hand, but just leaning over made him so ill that he had to give up the effort. When Gabrielle knelt by his feet to do it, he tried to push her away again but found he lacked the strength to do it.

"Since I am the only one here, you will have to accept my help whether or not you want it." She removed his well-worn moccasins quickly, then rose to her feet. "Now, shall I help you with the rest of your clothes?"

Jason glared at her through eyes dulled with pain, his expression one of undisguised hatred. "I can do it alone."

Gabrielle put her hands on her hips, her exasperation clear

in her voice. "Of course, you pride yourself on being self-sufficient, don't you? But you want to punish me for exerting the same independence. That is totally unfair, Jason. I won't accept it, but we can have that argument another time. Now your problem is your clothing. You'll be able to rest much more comfortably if you remove it. You really have no choice about accepting my help, no matter how revolting you may find my touch."

The problem was Jason did not find her touch revolting in the least. She was every bit as lovely as he'd remembered, her soft shiny hair providing a vibrant frame for her delicate features which expressed a solicitous concern he found impossible to accept as genuine. She could not really care for him when she disregarded every request he made. She was, for the moment, still his wife, however, and she was right about being the sole source of assistance available.

"I just want to go to sleep," he mumbled softly, and stretching out upon the quilt, he considered the matter closed.

"I know you're tired. You're obviously in pain too, and everything Clayton said paints a miserable portrait of my character; but please believe I'd never do anything which would destroy our marriage."

She was trying to understand his mood but that did not ease the hurt he'd inflicted on her by saying he had no desire to remain married to her. Unlacing his buckskin shirt, she worked quickly to remove it. When her fingertips brushed his chest, he opened his eyes to watch her as if he suspected some foul trick, but she forced herself to smile in response. He then pulled his arm out of the right sleeve, and she helped him to ease the left off carefully.

"How did this happen? Were you shot?" The doctor had bandaged the wound so she could not tell how severe it might be.

Jason sighed impatiently, disgusted with himself for having let it happen. "I was careless. A brave came up behind me with a knife."

"You mean you were stabbed?" Gabrielle felt her heart lurch. She'd assumed he'd been shot, perhaps only grazed by a stray bullet, but that he'd been stabbed horrified her. "Oh, Jason." Her glance filled with alarm for she could easily imagine how desperate his situation had been if an Indian had been that close when he'd attempted to kill him.

"It was my own fault," Jason admitted sheepishly. He pushed her hands away when she reached for his belt. "I can do that myself." He sat up slowly then and swung his legs off the bed to stand. When he swayed precariously, she came forward quickly to offer some support.

"How did you manage to make it home in such dreadful condition?" Gabrielle removed his pants with a swift tug and then helped him to get under the covers. "I'll have Michael's hide for this. He was here this afternoon, and from what he told me you were perfectly fine. I'll never believe another word he says!"

Jason stared at his bride, not knowing which was the more astonishing, that she'd admit Michael had come to see her or that she'd pretend to care what had happened to him. "You mustn't blame Michael. I didn't feel nearly this bad until Dr. Patterson insisted upon cleaning out the wound in my arm and sewing it up. Now please just go away and leave me alone."

When he'd closed his eyes, Gabrielle remained beside the bed for some time, not wanting to leave him. He'd given her little hope she could ever regain his confidence, but she vowed she'd not give up on their marriage as easily as he had. She leaned down to kiss him lightly upon the cheek then tiptoed out of the room to let him sleep.

That Jason had returned home safely, even though wounded, was reason enough for Gabrielle to feel her prayers had been answered, but she knew his attitude would have to improve dramatically for them to reach any sort of accord. Since she could solve none of their problems by herself, she prepared aa light supper and then attempted to read for an hour. She chose poetry, knowing with so much on her mind she'd be unable to follow the plot of a novel or play. When at last she grew sleepy, she knew the only place she would ever want to rest was beside her husband. She returned to their room then to prepare for bed, exercising great care to be quiet so as not to disturb him.

Jason appeared to be resting comfortably, and after donning her nightgown, she slipped into bed beside him. Snuggling up close, she laid an arm across his stomach and closed her eyes. Even if he did not know she was there, she enjoyed the comfort of his warmth. Elated with the hope for their future his presence brought, her night was filled with the sweetest of dreams.

Chapter XXVI

A hushed silence filled the house when Jason awakened the next morning. He yawned sleepily, trying to think of some compelling reason for getting out of bed. Then he recalled that he and Gabrielle hadn't settled a damned thing the previous night. He glanced over at her side of the bed and was surprised to see her nightgown laying where she'd left it that morning. He'd slept so soundly he'd not even realized she'd been lying next to him. That she had done so shocked him. There were other beds in the house, and he'd expected her to use one. As there was no sound coming from the rest of the house, he knew she must be outdoors. Feeling guilty because she'd had to do all the chores by herself, he sat up cautiously. His arm still hurt, but it was more of a dull ache now, not the racking pain he'd suffered the previous evening. "Looks like you'll live, Royal." He laughed to himself as he recalled Dr. Patterson's attempt at humor, but when the man had been stitching away on his arm it hadn't sounded a bit funny. He got up carefully, hoping he'd feel like his usual self. Although his legs were still a bit shaky, he was able to wash and shave on his own. By the time Gabrielle came back into the house with the milk and eggs, he was dressed and waiting for her.

"Why, Jason, I thought you'd probably sleep until past noon." She greeted him with a warm smile. "Would you like

491

me to fix you some breakfast?"

"I can make my own," Jason replied. "Had I known you planned to occupy that bed last night, I would have taken one of the others."

"Oh really?" Gabrielle scoffed at that idea. "You would never have made it up the ladder, Jason."

"Probably not, but I thought you could." There was not the slightest trace of a smile on Jason's face. He was handsome still, but his expression was more menacing than pleasant. His gray eyes were cold. They raked over Gabrielle with a taunting leer as if the mere sight of her disgusted him.

"Jason, you said you no longer wished to be my husband; I did not say I didn't want to be your wife." She approached him slowly, her heart aching with the loneliness his homecoming had done nothing to ease. "I had hoped, when you returned yesterday, that we could resolve our differences. If you're feeling well enough this morning, wouldn't you at least like to try?"

"Differences? Don't you think that's a rather ridiculous way to describe what's happening here? As I see it, I'll be away too often to have any need of a wife, and you're in love with another man. A divorce is the perfect solution for both of us. There's nothing more to discuss."

Gabrielle came closer still. "It will be awhile before the Army can send any troops here, probably not until spring. You'll need some place to live until they arrive and I would like to have you stay here with me."

"How very gracious of you. I would have sworn this was my house." Jason shook his head in disbelief, "What will Beau have to say about that?"

"Why nothing. I imagine he's already left for California, and what I do is no concern of his anyway," Gabrielle explained matter-of-factly. She had spent the early hours of the morning rehearsing possible dialogs with Tulip and Sunny, and had decided that no matter how Jason insulted her, she was not going to lose her temper. She'd told herself repeatedly that if she could make him listen to her she'd at least have a chance to make him change his mind about ending their marriage. If she became as hysterical as he was then all was lost.

Staring at his bride, Jason marveled at the way lies dripped from her tongue with the sweetness of honey. "I'll just bet he's gone to California. Why would he leave when you two have just been reunited after such a tragic separation? That makes no sense at all."

Gabrielle twisted her wedding ring nervously, unaware of the significance of her gesture. "My aunt always criticized Beau for being no more than a handsome dreamer, and it seems from the little he's accomplished in the time he's been here that she may have been right. He thinks there are more opportunities in California than there are here, but of course, he used to say there were far more opportunities here than there were in Liberty. Maybe that's just an excuse, a way to avoid responsibility, always thinking things will be better somewhere else."

Jason was amazed by that statement, "Did I just hear you say something nice about your aunt?"

"She wasn't an evil person, Jason, just a woman who didn't want the task of raising a small child thrust upon her. Unfortunately, she had no choice but to take me in when my parents died. She did the best she could, but she never gave me the love my parents would have provided."

Jason could not recall the last time he'd found Gabrielle in such a reasonable mood and that confused him all the more. "Well, surely your childhood couldn't have been all that lonely. Beau was your constant companion," he put in sarcastically.

Gabrielle moved toward the kitchen, hoping he would follow her, and when he did she placed the slices of bacon she'd cut in a pan. She put the pan on the stove to prepare his breakfast. Knowing it would be far easier to converse if her hands were occupied so she could avoid his defiant stare, she began to transfer the eggs she'd gathered from her basket into a bowl.

493

"Yes. He was a wonderful companion for a child, but I'm a woman now, Jason." She glanced up at him then, hoping he'd return her smile, but his gaze was no less suspicious.

Jason shifted his weight. Leaning back against a chair to rest, he considered the remarkable transformation that had come over his bride. As always, the uniqueness of her coloring made her beauty vividly bewitching, but he meant to get past her pretty façade to the treacherous heart it hid.

"Do you really expect me to believe Beau came here no more than twice while I was away?"

"It was only twice." Gabrielle gathered all her courage and began her explanation in a breathless rush. "He came the day you left. He wanted me to go away with him, but I refused. It started to rain, and I told him he could stay for the night but—"

"I don't want to hear anymore!" Jason stood up abruptly. "I can imagine what happened. You needn't confess it because I'm not going to be your husband for a minute longer than I have to!" He turned and left the house with the long sure stride which had carried him wherever he'd wanted to go for a good many years, but once outside, he could not think of a single place worth visiting that day. That did not deter him, however, from saddling Duke and riding away. The thought of going into town to consult an attorney finally occurred to him, but despite Gabrielle's open infidelity, he meant to do the gentlemanly thing. When he grew tired, he stopped to let Duke graze while he dozed in the shade. Then, in no great hurry, he waited until the sun had set before he returned home.

As he entered the house, Jason's eyes widened in amazement, for Gabrielle was wearing the attractive blue muslin gown she'd worn to Clayton's parties. She'd coiled her hair atop her head in the sophisticated sweep which displayed the elegant line of her creamy white throat and shoulders to every advantage, and his mind was swiftly filled with the most erotic of images. Cursing his own weakness he directed his attention to the rest of the room. It was readily apparent from

494

the tantalizing aroma wafting from the stove that she'd gone to considerable trouble to prepare a nice dinner. She'd covered the table with a starched white cloth and had set it with his mother's best china. He hadn't noticed the new curtains until then, but their snowy whiteness brightened the dark wood of the room. He was pained to think how many years it had been since his home had looked so inviting. But why would any woman go to such lengths when she knew her husband was leaving her?

Gabrielle did not look up from her book, for she felt very foolish now. She'd almost stopped hoping Jason would come home, but now that he had she waited for him to be the first to speak.

"Whatever you've got cooking smells delicious. I haven't eaten all day, will it be ready soon?" Jason said the first thing that came to him, knowing whatever occurred that night would be better faced on a full stomach.

"It was ready some time ago." Gabrielle closed her book carefully and replaced it in the bookcase before going into the kitchen to serve their supper. She knew the savory stew would be more flavorful for having baked awhile longer, but her voice clearly revealed her disappointment in him for not having arrived sooner.

Jason washed his hands and sat down at his place. "I was busy, I'm sorry to be so late."

As Gabrielle placed his plate before him, she stopped to remove several sprigs of dry grass from his dark curls. "Obviously," she remarked slyly.

Feeling like a complete fool now, Jason decided simply to ignore the evidence that he'd been doing nothing more strenuous than sleeping in the forest all day. When Gabrielle took her place opposite him, he waited for her to begin eating and then asked in the most reasonable tone he could manage, "Will you please tell me what it is you are trying to do here?" When she gave him an inquisitive glance, clearly not comprehending his question he explained more fully. "Why

495

would you dress so prettily, or go to such trouble with dinner? There's no point in it, so why did you bother?"

"I am glad you are home even if you are not happy to be here. I thought the occasion deserved some sort of celebration so I have done my best to provide it," Gabrielle replied softly.

Why he should suddenly feel so guilty Jason didn't know, but the lovely creature before him seemed so sincere he felt he was the one who'd done something wrong. But, damn it, she was the one who'd betrayed his trust not the other way around.

"It sounds as though you couldn't wait for me to get out of town to see Beau. Perhaps I might have understood if you'd said you'd been lonely, but good Lord, Gabrielle, how could you invite him to share your bed the first night I was gone?"

Although she was sorely tempted to scream every vile curse she knew, Gabrielle reacted coolly. "He did not share our bed. He slept in the loft. In the morning he chopped some wood for me and left a short while after Clayton did. I did not see him again until he came to tell me he was leaving for California. Erica was here then, and if you must have a witness, she can tell you he was here only briefly and did not come inside the house."

Jason watched her take another bite of supper, the elegance of her beauty, the grace of her gestures, the quiet dignity of her manner reminded him of the meal they'd shared in the hotel in Kansas City. He found himself merely watching her as she ate, his own hunger forgotten for the moment. Her story seemed preposterous. Jason could not imagine why she had not gone with Beau when he'd come for her. He forced himself to begin eating again, knowing if he didn't consume some nourishment he'd soon grow as weak as he'd been the previous evening. He was aware that he'd need all his strength to keep up with Gabrielle. When they'd finished eating and she'd served coffee, he cleared his throat and told her what he'd decided to do. "I want you to be the one to file for the divorce. As I said, I hope to work for the Army. It may be difficult to reach me, but you can always leave messages with Clay and I'll check with him when I'm in town. That way we needn't see each other. Now what is it you plan to do? If you're going to California with Beau just say so."

Gabrielle took a sip of her coffee, then set her cup and saucer aside. She was enormously pleased that her strategy had worked, for Jason was talking to her in so intelligent a manner she knew he'd listen to what she had to say. "We discussed what I'd like to do only briefly once, but I'd rather raise horses than anything else. I know I can do that alone here, but I do not want a divorce, Jason. The fact that you want to continue working as a scout seems very reasonable to me. I did not ask you to become a farmer when we married. That was your decision, and if you are unhappy with it, of course you should reconsider it now. As far as I am concerned, I will be happy to have you here whenever you can come home. I don't want this farm to seem like a prison to you. I know you enjoy your freedom and I'll make no demands upon you that restrict it."

Jason's expression turned slowly from confusion to shock. "You expect me to stay married to you? To let you live here, just come and go as I please when I know exactly who will be here when I'm gone? Oh no, that idea is absurd, Gabrielle, and I'll not even consider it."

Gabrielle rose slowly then carried her cup and saucer to the sink. "I told you Beau has gone to California so he'll have no part in this. I think I've suggested the perfect arrangement for us, and I insist you give it more serious thought. Now if you'll excuse me, I'm going to bed." She walked into the bedroom then and closed the door before lifting her hands to her mouth to keep from screaming. She'd made the most generous offer she could, but she'd not weep and throw herself at his feet. Love seemed to matter not at all to him, and she'd not use an unborn child to convince him to remain with her. All she'd truly be if he accepted her terms was a mistress, but that seemed to be the only hope she had and she'd seized it eagerly.

497

Jason remained at the table, thumping his spoon upon the tablecloth as he tried to make some sense of Gabrielle's last remarks. It appeared she was going to steadfastly deny anything had happened between her and Beau. Could that possibly be the truth? Even if it were, she was still willful and defiant, causing him an equal amount of grief for every moment of pleasure they shared. He got up and walked over to the fireplace to toss another log on the blaze. Taking a deep breath to clear his mind, he tried to recall what it was he'd wanted before he'd left to go after the Cayuse. Most of all he'd hoped to drive Beau out of their lives. Now Gabrielle had said repeatedly that the young man was gone. He'd rebelled at the restricted life the farm required, never intending to let her suspect his true feelings until he'd thought a divorce was inevitable. Now she'd set him free to live as he chose. By some strange quirk of fate he'd managed to have all his wishes granted so why did he feel as though he'd lost everything that made life worthwhile? Had any of what Gabrielle told him that night been the truth? Could she want him as a husband so badly she'd settle for his attentions on a part-time basis? That would present problems of another sort, he realized. She was far too desirable a young woman to leave alone for long periods of time. Apparently Michael Jenkins had come to see her that very afternoon. Would he come back the moment he knew she was alone?

"This is lunacy!" Jason knew he was simply borrowing trouble, something he always advised others not to do. He paced the large room for several minutes, then looked over at the bedroom door, wondering if Gabrielle had locked it. He couldn't deny how greatly he'd missed her, for despite the bitterness of their arguments she ignited his passions as no other woman ever had or ever would. Would she have made herself so attractive that night if she had not wanted to invite his attentions? Since she had offered terms for a marriage that were so favorable to him, why should he hesitate to accept

498

them? If he did, he would have this maddening creature for his own.

Gabrielle was seated in the middle of the bed, brushing out her hair, when Jason came through the door. "Did you want something?" she inquired innocently.

"Only you." Jason flashed a sly grin as he turned down the wick on the oil lamp, leaving only a soft circle of light which barely reached the bed. "Since we shared the same bed last night, you should have no objection to my joining you now."

As Gabrielle got up to replace her hairbrush upon the dresser, Jason caught her wrist and pulled her close. "If you do have some objection I suggest you voice it immediately or it is going to be too late."

If he'd expected her to try to escape his grasp, he was disappointed for Gabrielle laid her head upon his chest, the soft swells of her body melting against him as she whispered, "I've no objection whatsoever."

Jason gave her a warm hug, then stepped back. "Climb into bed." He waited for her to move away before removing his shirt carefully so as not to cause his arm any more pain. He laughed as Gabrielle carelessly tossed her nightgown aside before getting under the covers, and in a moment, he was nude and had joined her. He drew her into his arms, the confusion which had filled his heart vanishing as their lips met. She was simply the beautiful young woman he adored. He held her cradled tenderly in his embrace as he gazed down into her eyes. In the darkness her sultry glance was so enticing he let his fingertips wander slowly down the silken skin of her lithe body until he knew his touch would bring the madness only her total surrender would end. She moved against him, but he held his own emotions in check, seeking to satisfy his curiosity before sating the desires his powerful body had been denied for so many days. His lips brushed hers only lightly, creating a need for deeper kisses he withheld. He felt shivers of anticipation course down her spine as her breathing quickened, but he did not replace the slow gentle caress of his fingertips with the deeper pleasure his muscular body could provide. His smooth, sweet touch lured her to the brink of rapture and held her there, suspended, as he whispered. "When I am the worst of husbands, why do you want me so badly?"

Gabrielle heard his question only faintly, as though he were miles away rather than in her arms. What he was doing was the most exquisite torture for he'd created a desperate longing in her just to use her weakness to his own advantage. He'd aroused her emotions to a peak only to ask a question she felt her desire to preserve their marriage had already answered. Flames of anger leaped at the edges of her newly found composure, but she forced them away, not letting her temper overcome her reason. Seeking the only way he offered to end the torment of desire he'd created, she clung to him as she whispered softly in his ear, "I love you."

Jason was as shocked by that confession as he had been to discover her a virgin when they'd first made love. The emotion in her husky voice washed over him, creating a sea of wonder so deep he could not control the fury of his own response. His mouth captured hers in a shattering kiss, and he moved swiftly to conquer her vibrant body as well as her defiant heart, finally giving expression to the torrent of emotion raging within him. Her love was a prize he'd never dared dream would be his, and the thrill of her words inspired a passion so intense he was lost in its beauty. Only later, when reason had returned, did he relax his embrace and draw back, afraid that he might have hurt her in his quest to give her pleasure. But one glance at her radiant smile was all he needed to reassure him that his fears were groundless.

"I would have said that long ago had I known how desperate you were to hear it," Gabrielle purred softly.

Jason kissed her again, his mood now a far more tender one. "I swear I fell in love with you when you knocked upon our door in Kansas City, and it has been agony to think you would never love anyone but Beau."

"He is a charming boy, Jason, but you are the man I want for my husband." Gabrielle drew his mouth back to hers, sealing her words with an unspoken vow of devotion. "I have loved you for a very long time too. Please forgive me for lacking the courage to admit my feelings to you, but I had no idea they would be returned so sweetly."

"Oh, Gabrielle." Jason tightened his embrace, nearly crushing her with an enthusiastic hug. "I love you more with each new day, or should I say night?"

Gabrielle laughed throatily as she put her hands upon his chest in a playful attempt to push him away. "I love you too, my darling, but I must ask you not to be so forceful with your affection or I shall be so bruised I'll not be able to get out of bed in the morning."

Jason laughed at that possibility and then lowered his voice to a seductive whisper. "If you can't leave our bed, then neither will I."

"Your company would be very nice, but I'm afraid it would get rather crowded in here after a while," Gabrielle advised.

"Crowded?" Jason leaned back to observe his bride's teasing smile and suddenly knew exactly what she meant. "You mean you're certain now? We are going to have a child?"

"Yes, now I'm certain." Confident of his love, Gabrielle no longer had a reason to keep such a secret from him.

"When did it happen, do you know?"

"Do you remember when we were at Fort Walla Walla and you came to meet me? I asked you to kiss me goodbye, but you took our farewell much further."

Even with Gabrielle snuggled so warmly against him, Jason could not help but shiver as the cold wind of fear swept over him, leaving him as confused as he'd been only an hour earlier. "Tell me the truth, Gabrielle, is this the real reason Beau left you? Because you're carrying my child?"

His tension was so easy to feel that Gabrielle wasn't angry.

"I did not tell Beau, or anybody else, Jason. This is our baby and I wanted you to know first." She covered his face with light kisses. "I love you; that's why I refused to go with Beau, not because of the baby."

"I'm sorry, I did not mean to insult you again."

"Do I seem insulted?" Gabrielle slipped from his arms, her tantalizing touch and teasing kisses supplying the answer to her own question. She adored him and wanted to show it, but he quickly caught her in an easy grasp and tossed her upon the pillows.

"Did you really mean what you said tonight? That you won't mind living here while I ply my trade as a scout?"

"Of course. I know that is what you truly want to do."

"Then I'm afraid I'm going to disappoint you," Jason admitted slyly.

"Disappoint me? In what way?"

"I'm not ever going to leave you, Gabrielle. The whole damn Army can get lost on the plains for all I care, I'll not go out looking for them."

"Why, Jason, do you truly think you'll be content here?" Gabrielle reached up to push his curls off his forehead with her fingertips, the same gesture she'd often seen him make. He caught her hand in his then and brought it to his lips.

"Duke is a fine stallion; there's no sense in Sunny getting all the mares you want to buy. I rather like the idea of raising horses because it will be a damn sight more exciting than raising crops ever was."

Now Gabrielle knew Sunny was the far superior of the two stallions. His conformation was perfect, his color handsome, and his greater speed easily proven; but she held her tongue. She knew the difference in the quality of colts their horses sired would soon prove her point effectively without her ever having to utter a word of argument against her husband's plan. My aunt would be proud of me for finally conquering my temper, she thought, recalling the dear lady with a wistful smile. "I wish my aunt could have met you, Jason."

"I think I'm damn lucky she didn't," Jason mused thoughtfully. But the mention of her aunt made him curious. "As I recall, it was your temper to which she objected most strenuously, but I've seen no evidence of your usual fiery disposition in the last two days. Is it motherhood which has made such a difference in your temperament?"

Gabrielle hesitated to confess the truth to him, but after several of his enticing kisses she spoke. "I was afraid I'd lose you if I became as angry with you as you were with me. It's not motherhood which has made me so cautious, simply desperation."

Jason gave her another hug, this time being far more gentle. "I love you, Gabrielle. Do you understand that now? You needn't change the way you are to please me. If I upset you, scream at me as you always have, for I will love you still."

"Is that a promise?" she asked hopefully.

"Yes. Now isn't that enough conversation for one night?" Jason hoped his bride would not take offense at his teasing hint.

"I'm sorry if I've been too talkative but it is simply that I enjoy being with you again. When I left Liberty I never expected to meet a man as wonderful as you. I've really missed you, Jason. Welcome home."

Jason thought Gabrielle was sometimes delightfully innocent for such a complex young woman. While she had the manners of a perfect lady, she was a wanton seductress in his bed. She was the most fascinating of female creatures and he wished to hear all she wanted to say, but morning would be soon enough to listen.

"Good night, my love."

He pulled her into an affectionate embrace, giving her a good-night kiss so passionate she quickly realized that although he had ended their discussion he was clearly not ready to go to sleep. Nibbling his ear playfully, she let him know she wasn't the least bit sleepy either.

When Saturday arrived, Gabrielle dressed in the stunning gray suit she'd worn for her wedding; then she helped Jason put on his suit. His arm still caused him considerable discomfort and she knew he could use her assistance. He was in a festive humor for he was to be the best man for Clayton and for Michael as well. Her own mood was not nearly so ebullient, however. Recalling her last visit to church, she tried to think of some way to warn him of what her reception would be.

"Jason, did Clayton tell you Iris was with him the day he came here and met Beau?"

Jason handed his tie to her and stood still while she tied it for him. "No. Is that important for some reason?"

"Well, yes." Gabrielle did her best, then stood back to admire his appearance. "You look splendid," she finally offered with a shy smile.

Jason readily saw that Gabrielle was preoccupied about something and he wanted to know what was troubling her. "I know you and Iris have never been friends, but Clay adores her and she seems to be delighted with him, judging by the times I've seen them together. Since Erica and Michael are getting married too, why don't you simply forget Iris and concentrate on celebrating with them."

"I have done my best to ignore Iris for several weeks, Jason, but she's told anyone who will listen that I had a lover living here with me while you were away. You'll see the way people react to my presence in church, and I don't want you to be hurt by it."

Jason's expression darkened to a menacing scowl as he considered the pain such malicious gossip had obviously caused her. "Why didn't you tell me about this before today? I would have gone into town and insisted Iris retract her lies. You may be gracious enough to ignore her slander, but I'm certainly not."

"I had hoped the story would have ceased to circulate by the time you returned home, but I am afraid it hasn't. I don't want to cause any bad feeling between you and your best friend. Please don't say anything to Iris. In time the people of Oregon City will learn which of us deserves their respect."

Jason saw no point in arguing the issue. "Let us simply go into town and see what happens, Gabrielle. Perhaps the fact that we are together will silence whatever gossip there may have been." That sounded reasonable to him, but the moment they stepped through Clayton's front door the stares they received changed his mind. Losing Clay's friendship seemed like a small sacrifice compared to the damage to his wife's reputation, and when she went upstairs to see if Erica needed any assistance, he took the man aside.

"I'm going to speak with Reverend Murdock. I don't think he'll want to perform a ceremony for you and Iris when she is so lacking in Christian spirit."

"What?" Clayton was aghast at that threat. "What are you talking about?"

"I'm talking about the scandalous lies she spread about Gabrielle. I expect her to retract them immediately." Jason smiled knowingly. "I don't envy you your task, Clay, but perhaps, in time, you can make a lady out of Iris."

Clayton grew flustered, "If Iris has been indiscreet, I can assure you it will not be repeated, but—"

Jason was nearly a head taller than the older man and he now straightened up to his full height to emphasize the seriousness of his words. "I mean it, Clay. You must speak with Iris immediately. First she must apologize to Gabrielle, and then I want her to admit to each of those she entertained with her imaginative gossip that her tales were complete fabrications. She mistook my wife's childhood friend for her paramour, a ridiculous error which has embarrassed Gabrielle needlessly and infuriated me."

Clayton gestured helplessly. "Damn it all, Jason, had you been there you would have assumed the same thing!"

505

"Assuming a beautiful woman is not also a virtuous one is a grave error, Clay. Had I been there this ugly rumor would never have gotten started! Iris is going to put a stop to it before your wedding or there will be none. Either she apologizes to Gabrielle or I am going to Murdock. The choice is yours."

Clayton knew Jason too well not to know his threats weren't idle. He left his study and in a few minutes' time returned with Iris. When she saw Jason she smiled coquettishly until she realized his expression was far from civil. As he stated his terms, she grew pale and then turned to Clayton, "I'll not take any of it back!" she shrieked. "How dare you let him treat me this way?"

Clayton grew stern as he addressed the volatile young woman, "Perhaps I am responsible for this regrettable situation, for I overheard the vicious innuendos concerning Gabrielle and should have realized they could have had only one source. Now cease your complaining. March up those stairs and apologize to Gabrielle and whomever else you can find before it gets any later or it won't be Jason who calls off our wedding but I!" The fury in his expression convinced her immediately that he meant precisely what he said.

Iris' dark eyes widened and then filled with a new glow of respect. She had not even suspected her future husband could be so masterful. "Well, if it will please you, Clayton, then I will be happy to do it," she purred sweetly, and hoping to extricate herself from an impossible situation, she swiftly left the room.

Clayton shook his head. "Manipulating little bitch, isn't she?"

Jason laughed aloud at that remark since it was so unexpected. He was greatly amused to learn that Clayton knew exactly what kind of woman he was marrying. "As long as you know it, Clay, I will cease to worry."

Iris had moved to another bedroom once the household had grown less crowded. Now, wanting to get her humiliation over quickly, she went straight to Erica's room where she knew she'd be certain to find Gabrielle.

"I am dreadfully sorry if I embarrassed you, Gabrielle. Whom you wish to entertain in your home is your own business, and I should never have mentioned that I met Beau there to anybody. Will you please forgive me?" Her large eyes filled with tears as her voice trailed off to a whisper, her sorrow almost convincing.

Gabrielle was surprised for only an instant, then she knew exactly what had prompted Iris' suddenly contrite attitude. "Only if you promise that each person who heard your lies will know you have apologized to me."

Since Iris knew neither Jason nor Clayton would be satisfied if her apology were not a sincere one, she agreed at once. "I will see to it today."

"Thank you, Iris. Since Jason and Clay are such good friends it would be a shame for us to be enemies when there is no cause," Gabrielle said graciously.

Iris nodded, too embarrassed to respond, and excusing herself to complete the preparations for her wedding, she returned to her own room.

"What do you make of that?" Erica asked, her voice filled with wonder.

"I think my husband is trying to undo the mischief Iris has caused. If you require no further assistance in dressing, I'd like to go and thank him."

Erica placed the last pin in her golden hair and stepped back to admire her reflection. "Just don't be too grateful. I don't want you to miss our wedding."

With a bright smile, Gabrielle assured her good friend that would be an impossibility and then she nearly skipped down the stairs in her haste to speak with her husband. Finding him with Clayton, she hesitated to interrupt but he came forward to usher her into the room.

"Are you ready to leave for the church?" Jason asked with an innocent smile as soon as Clay had left to summon the buggies.

"Yes, but first I'd like a word with you." Gabrielle put her hands on his shoulders and gave him a light kiss before turning to close the study door. "We've had several most interesting conversations in this room, haven't we?"

"Yes, that's certainly true. Is this to be another of them?" Jason asked, grinning slyly.

"Perhaps. I just had a remarkable, if brief, conversation with Iris. She seems to be filled with remorse at having linked my name with Beau's to create a sensational scandal. Do you suppose she has developed a conscience at this late date, or do you suppose someone could be behind her wish to apologize to me?" She laid her palms on Jason's chest and batted her eyelashes coyly the way Iris loved to do.

Since Gabrielle's playful attitude made it obvious she was not angry with him, Jason put his arms around her waist to draw her close. "You are very precious to me, and since I've waited so long to display my devotion, I hope you will forgive my enthusiasm and accept it as further evidence of my love."

"Why, Jason, I don't believe I've ever heard you say anything quite so"—*saccharine* was the word, but she'd no wish to insult him—"sweet."

Jason chuckled at her tact. "I know that sounded rather foolish, but you do understand what I am trying to say, don't you?"

"I'd rather you say you love me like this, darling." Gabrielle lifted her arms to encircle his neck as she stood on tiptoe to kiss him. He was a wonderfully affectionate man, and at last she understood his tenderness. All the love he'd ever given her had been sincere. She was ashamed that she'd not realized it from the very beginning.

Delighted by the intensity of her kiss, Jason was quick to take Gabrielle's hand and draw her to his side as they walked to the door. "I think we'd better wait until we return home to take this particular conversation any further. Anyone who is the least bit rude to you today will be instantly sorry."

Her blue eyes filling with mischief, Gabrielle whispered softly, "You may have put an end to this scandal, Jason, but everyone who can count to nine is going to be suspicious when our baby is born. What do you plan to do then when there is gossip about us?"

"My love, I will only be proud," Jason answered, and with a sly wink, he escorted his ravishing bride out into the sunshine.